Felicity couldn't pull her gaze away from the allure of Conrad's clear blue eyes.

He passed her the black foil box of candy, gold bow glinting in the bright hall light. Their fingers brushed, and the air crackled with awareness.

She skimmed a finger along the intricate bow without taking the box. "I'm not sure what to make of this."

"Romance," he said, his voice husky. "Will you accept the gift?"

She laughed, clutching the box to her chest. "Try to pry it out of my hands."

He grinned back at her. "Tally told me you had a weakness for chocolate."

Felicity placed the candy on the half-moon table next to a succulent plant. "It's no fair how you keep getting the inside scoop. What's your weakness?"

His eyes flamed. "You."

Her breath hitched in her chest as his head dipped. His mouth slanted over hers, warm, firm. Tingles spread through her at the first touch. She clenched her fingers in his jacket, anchoring herself in the wash of sensation, the fine fabric of his lapels and the sweep of his tongue over hers.

The deeper she sank into the kiss, the more he brought her body alive again, the more she realized she was right in thinking this connection couldn't be ignored.

* * *

The Billionaire Renegade is part of the Alaskan Oil Barons series from *USA TODAY* bestselling author Catherine Mann!

Dear Reader,

I'm a longtime fan of a hero in a Stetson or on a horse! Writing *The Billionaire Renegade* provided me with the perfect opportunity to put a fun new spin on the theme. Alaskan cowboy Conrad Steele shows up in his Stetson and on his horse at the most unexpected times and unexpected places to romance wary hospital social worker Felicity Hunt!

Thank you for checking out my latest Alaskan Oil Barons novel. Each one can be read as a stand-alone story, but there are also plenty more for you to enjoy if you like connected books. Details on each of the eight stories can be found on my website, catherinemann.com, along with info about monthly contests and newsletters.

Happy reading!

Cathy

CATHERINE MANN

THE BILLIONAIRE RENEGADE

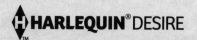

To Barbara Collins Rosenberg—an amazing agent and a dear friend.

ISBN-13: 978-1-335-60340-1

The Billionaire Renegade

Copyright © 2018 by Catherine Mann

Recycling programs for this product may not exist in your area.

Printed in U.S.A.

HARLEQUIN®
www.Harlequin.com

USA TODAY bestselling author **Catherine Mann** has won numerous awards for her novels, including both a prestigious RITA® Award and an *RT Book Reviews* Reviewers' Choice Award. After years of moving around the country bringing up four children, Catherine has settled in her home state of South Carolina, where she's active in animal rescue. For more information, visit her website, catherinemann.com.

Books by Catherine Mann

Harlequin Desire

Alaskan Oil Barons

The Baby Claim
The Double Deal
The Love Child
The Twin Birthright
The Second Chance
The Rancher's Seduction
The Billionaire Renegade

Visit her Author Profile page at Harlequin.com, or catherinemann.com, for more titles.

ALASKAN OIL BARONS - STEELE MIKKELSON FAMILY TREE

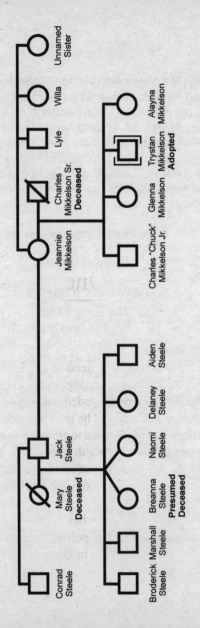

One

He was back.

Felicity Hunt didn't need to see more than the buff-colored Stetson resting on his knee to know Conrad Steele hadn't heeded her request that they stop seeing each other. The man threatened the balance she'd worked so hard to create in regaining her professional life after her divorce.

But the Alaskan oil magnate had a reputation for determination. The smooth-talking kind that persisted until he won.

Well, he wouldn't win her.

Although he was sure pulling out all the stops to gain her attention today in the hospital's enclosed memory garden.

Conrad was currently leading story time, pint-size patients gathered around him in a heart-tugging cluster.

On her way back from supervising a critically ill three-year-old who'd just entered the foster system, Felicity steeled her resolve to keep this man at arm's length. Easier said than done. As a social worker at Anchorage General Hospital, she had a soft spot for her young clients.

Children sat in wheelchairs and on floor mats, wide-eyed with rapt attention focused on the cowboy spinning a tale about a magical horse. His deep voice rumbled over the words, the book all but dwarfed by his large hands. He kept it open for his audience to see, the current page containing a watercolor image of the horse with a blanket and saddle over its back.

A little girl raised her hand with a question. "What's hanging off the saddle?"

"Those are stirrups, for the rider's feet," Conrad answered, tapping his boots on the floor. He then expanded the explanation with ease, his knowledge of all things equine shining through.

His gaze rose from the children, colliding with Felicity's as she leaned against a pillar. The air crackled between them with a connection she should have been used to by now, but the potency still caught her unaware. Just a look not more than three heartbeats long left her shaken long after he returned his attention to the book.

God, he was handsome in a rugged, movie star way with a strong jaw and cheekbones. His dark hair was trimmed neatly, hints of silver at his temples tempting her fingers to stroke. And those eyes, pale blue like the hottest of flames.

He had broad shoulders that filled out his crisp white shirt just so, his suit coat draped over the back of the rolling chair. His red silk tie drew her attention to the strong column of his neck.

This was a man others leaned on.

She forced even breaths in and out, willing her heart rate to slow. The scent of plants and flowers mingled with the antiseptic smell of the highly sterilized space.

Fidgeting with the badge on her silver lanyard, Felicity knew she should walk right out of the memory garden, and she would, before he finished the story.

Meanwhile, she couldn't stop thoughts of how she'd met Conrad, of how he'd pursued her with such flattering intensity. Her work as a county social worker had brought her to this hospital often, and his nephew had been dating a friend of Felicity's who volunteered in the NICU. Felicity had finally caved and dated Conrad briefly, against her better judgment, but she'd broken things off just before Christmas and taking on a new job.

It was a dream come true being hired on as a hospital social worker for underage patients. The recent change offered all the more reason she needed to stay focused on her career, and not on romance. Her broken marriage had left her full of crushing heartbreak. The grief had taken its toll on her at the office, crippling her concentration. She'd labored long and hard to rebuild her résumé. She refused to endure another setback in her professional—or personal—life.

After Conrad closed the last page of the book, he turned over story time to a volunteer with puppets. Felicity let go of her lanyard, her fingers numb. She'd gripped it so hard the ridges bit into her skin.

She'd waited too long, lost in thoughts of this man. If she moved quickly, she could still make an escape...

But wouldn't that delay the inevitable?

She couldn't just walk away today without confronting Conrad about his refusal to give her space. Her heart sped.

Conrad slid on his suit jacket, then scooped up his Stetson and overcoat. He wove his way through the audience, past geraniums spilling over the side of terra-cotta planters, massive urns with trees and a babbling stone fountain. While the puppeteer set up her portable stage, children stretched and wriggled, mats rustling and IV poles clinking. Conrad paused, leaning to answer a question from a young girl with a bandanna covering her bald head, then continued his journey across the indoor garden.

And his eyes were locked on Felicity.

Felicity exhaled hard, her heart double-timing against her will. He didn't miss a beat in his beeline to her, his long legs eating up the space between them, boots thudding on the tile floor.

"Hello," he said simply, his head dipping low enough his breath caressed her cheek. "It's good to see you."

She bit her lip and struggled to keep her gaze off his mouth and on his eyes, memories of their brief time together bombarding her. "We should step out. I wouldn't want to disrupt the performance."

Taped flute music started as the puppeteer slid into place behind the stage. The children stilled for the rest of the entertainment.

Conrad opened the door leading out of the memory garden and into the busy hallway, winter coat draped over his arm. Staff in scrubs mixed with visitors in street clothes, and the flow of human traffic streamed both ways, the opposing currents somehow weaving around each other fluidly. The wide corridor sported a wall of windows showcasing a snowplow making its way through the lot beside a towering parking garage.

Conrad clasped her elbow and guided her to a nook lined with vending machines. The simple touch set her body on fire. His equally hot gaze made her feel like a siren in spite of her businesslike pin-striped skirt and ruffled white blouse.

He planted a hand on the wall, his shoulders blocking out the corridor, making a public space suddenly intimate. "Congratulations on your new job."

So he did know, probably from her friend Tally Benson, who was dating Marshall Steele—Conrad's nephew. Felicity had the confirmation. His time here wasn't coincidental. He was looking for her.

Frustration—and an unwanted tingle of pleasure—filled her. "Tally told you?"

"Marshall did," Conrad acknowledged. "I didn't know you were looking to make a change at work."

She struggled to focus on his words, difficult to do with the spicy scent of him filling her every breath.

"I wasn't unhappy at my other position, but this is a dream job of mine." All the more reason she needed to keep her focus narrowed.

"They're lucky to have you." His hand was close enough to stroke her hair, but he didn't move.

The phantom touch, the promise, was just as potent.

Enough polite chitchat. "Why are you here? I'm not buying this sudden interest of yours for story time with sick children."

"You didn't want our date from the bachelor auction last month, so I'm fulfilling the time purchased here."

She'd been irate when he'd paid the money in her name for his time at the charity bachelor auction. She didn't like being manipulated. Another reason she was irritated to see him here today, despite the way his nearness made her temperature spike.

Still, she couldn't deny he was doing a good thing

for the patients, many of them here long term in the pediatric oncology ward. "That's very altruistic of you. What made you think of reading books instead of something like volunteering in the gift shop?"

"I like kids, even though I don't have any of my own. I've always been a proud and involved uncle. And my family's charity foundation is initiating a number of projects here at Anchorage General."

Could that be true and she just hadn't heard about it yet? Or was he making another excuse to pursue her because she'd had the nerve to say no to a Steele?

"What kinds of projects?"

"We're starting with a program donating books to patients." He answered without hesitation.

She believed him. About that much at least. "That's a wonderful thing to do, but I need to make sure you know, my interest is not for sale."

His easy smile faded. "Neither is my honor. My family has always supported this hospital out of gratitude for their top-notch care. My nieces and nephews were born here. My niece Naomi underwent cancer treatment here—and then went on to deliver her twins here. The book donation is a part of the new pilot program."

"New pilot program?" she couldn't resist asking, the professional in her intrigued. So much for playing it as cool and formidable as the Alaskan tundra.

"The Steele and Mikkelson families' new charity foundation is looking for more ways to make a difference at the hospital. One of those ways is to provide children with new books, volumes they can keep so there's no risk of germ cross-contamination with shared materials."

How could she find fault with that plan? She couldn't. "That's really thoughtful. I'm sure the children and parents will be very grateful."

Finances could become strained with long-term hospitalizations, so much so that even buying books was a luxury.

"Today's package for each child included a copy of the story they just heard." A half smile tugged on his mouth, those signature Steele eyes full of promise.

It had been a riveting tale, no question, especially when read by a larger-than-life cowboy. "You said *ways*—plural—of helping here. What else is the foundation doing?"

She was curious, yes. But she also needed to know where to avoid him so she didn't keep testing her resolve where he was concerned.

"The vote was taken yesterday, so technically, it's okay for me to share now even though the press release won't go out until tomorrow." His smile widened and her stringent resolve waned.

"Okay, I'll admit it. You've got my interest—on a professional basis only."

His brows shot up almost imperceptibly. "Of course." His smile was confident—and sexy. "We're making a donation to the oncology ward in honor of my niece. They'll be renaming it, to be made official at a dinner for the hospital board of directors and the charity foundation board."

His words sunk in. This wasn't a simple book drop-off or some quickly concocted plan to bump into her in passing. He and his family's charitable foundation had a genuine, vested interest in being a part of this hospital's financial landscape.

Realization filled her with the inescapable truth—and she couldn't deny a shiver of excitement. "You're not going anywhere, are you?"

Stetson in hand, Conrad watched Felicity walk away in a huff down the hospital corridor.

He was definitely getting under her skin, and that was a good thing. Damn straight, he wasn't going anywhere. He had wanted her since the first time he'd seen her. He'd worked to win her over since then, not an easy task as she was still stinging from her divorce. But then, he wasn't one to shy away from a battle.

Letting his gaze linger on her, he stepped away from the vending machines and back into the flow of foot traffic in the wide corridor, winter coat over his arm. Felicity's sleek brown hair was pulled back into a neat French twist, midday sunlight through the window reflecting off honey-colored streaks.

Her pin-striped skirt was both professional yet

also appealing in an understated way as it hugged her curves, sweeping down to touch the top of her knee-length leather boots. The ruffles on her blouse drew his eyes to her neck and wrists. Not that it took much to bring his attention to her.

He was selective, dating professional women who weren't interested in a walk down the aisle. He'd had a brief marriage and a near miss, having been left at the altar by his fiancée. His attempts at happily-ever-after had left him gun-shy.

Then when his older brother had lost his wife and child in a plane crash, seeing his brother's unrelenting grief had cemented Conrad's resolution to stay single. He'd devoted himself to helping bring up his nieces and nephews. He loved kids. It hadn't been a hardship to lend a hand to his overburdened big brother, Jack. Conrad was fifteen years younger and had energy and time to spare. He couldn't help wondering, though, if the fact that his brother's kids were grown now attributed to some restlessness on Conrad's part.

His gaze zoned back in on Felicity as she stepped into an elevator. She certainly had his attention and he imagined she would have at any time in his life. He'd hoped things would go a little more smoothly today, but he also enjoyed a good challenge.

He started toward the elevators just as the double set of electric doors opened, a blast of cold air gusting inside. A familiar face stopped him short. Marshall.

His nephew. The middle child in Jack Steele's brood, Marshall was a bit of a recluse, preferring to oversee the original homestead ranch. He'd never voiced an interest in the day-to-day operations of the family's oil business.

They'd all had to step up, though, when Jack Steele had become engaged to the widowed matriarch of their corporate rival, the Mikkelson family. Shortly after that, Jack had suffered a fall from a horse that could have killed him, but didn't. Still, it had left him with a recovery from spinal surgery that had lasted months.

Even though Jack had married Jeannie Mikkelson, the family had still been in turmoil at a critical juncture in the merger into the combined companies that became Alaska Oil Barons Inc., with stock prices fluctuating as a result. They needed to provide a unified, stable front. Hopefully the charity foundation—with both the Steeles and Mikkelsons at the helm—would help blend the families while also reassuring investors.

Marshall closed the last few feet between them, shaking snow off the brim of his hat. "What are you doing here? Is something wrong?"

"Everything's fine." They were all still a little jumpy after Jack's accident, and then Shana Mikkelson's aneurysm. A larger family meant more cause for concern as well as happiness. "I was delivering the books to the children's ward, am just finishing up reading one."

"Seriously? I suspect a different agenda here." Marshall's brown eyes narrowed, the quiet perception in the depths so like the gaze of Marshall's mother, who'd died in a plane crash. "Felicity's working here full-time now, isn't she?"

"I recall reading to you when you were a kid," Conrad dodged neatly.

"As *I* recall, you were doing it then for extra credit for your high school English class."

He waved dismissively. "Two birds with one stone. I'm a multitasker."

"Ah, like today." Marshall held up a hand. "No worries if you don't want to talk about Felicity. I'm here to pick up Tally and take her to lunch. Are you still coming by tomorrow with Nanuq and Shila?"

He'd been housing a couple of horses for Marshall since one of his two barns had burned and he needed some flex space for his animals while the rebuilding was under way. The aesthetics weren't complete, but the stalls were secure and warm. Nanuq and Shila, which meant white bear and flame, were ready for transport.

"Absolutely. See you then."

In fact, he could use a ride to work out the tension he would no doubt feel after the impending confrontation with Felicity. Before the day was out, she would learn just how closely they would be working together.

* * *

Striding down the hospital corridor toward her office, Felicity wished it was as easy to haul her thoughts away from the first-floor lobby and one big sexy distraction in a Stetson.

But then her nerves had been a mess since she'd bumped into Conrad. She needed to get herself together before the meeting with her new boss. Felicity wove by a nurse with a vitals cart and a cluster of visitors lost in their conversation.

Her new supervisor had been cryptic about the reason for the meeting other than to say it was about a way for Felicity to make a mark in her job. Her interest was piqued. She couldn't get there fast enough. Looking down to pull her notes from her portfolio bag, she nearly slammed into someone—

Tally Benson, waving at her.

"Hello there," her friend exclaimed in surprise. "I'm just finishing up volunteering. I thought I wasn't going to see you today. How's the new job?"

"I'm excited about the opportunity." The words sounded hollow in Felicity's mouth, making her wonder why she bothered faking emotions with her friends. Back in high school, she'd briefly tried out for a school production of *King Lear* because her foster mom loved Shakespeare. During the course of her tryouts, Felicity had realized masking her feelings required a lot more work than actors onstage and on-screen made it out to be.

Strangely, during her work, she'd never had to fake an emotion she didn't feel. Her deep well of empathy supplied her strength as she moved through the difficult spaces of social work.

Today, she felt like that high schooler reading lines. The words didn't match her body's articulation of apprehension, intrigue.

"Then why are you frowning?" Tally scrunched her nose.

Felicity adjusted her lanyard, unable to resist asking, "Did you know that Conrad is reading to the kids in pediatrics?"

She opted to dodge the question that had too much of a matchmaking vibe. "I've heard the family's charitable foundation has big plans for the hospital."

And that level of donation couldn't be a simple romantic ploy. Renaming a wing involved a significant amount of money. She felt small for having accused him of reading to the kids for show.

Felicity forced a smile. "The hospital is lucky to have such a generous benefactor."

"To be honest, I'm a little overwhelmed by the family. There are so many of them." And the redhead would certainly know that since not too long ago she'd been hired to help Marshall around the house while he recovered from a broken arm. Now they were a couple. "But the charity foundation has been a rewarding way to get to know them."

When the Steele patriarch had married his rival's

widow, the business world had been full of reports about the merger of their two companies and there had been fluctuations in the market with concerns about who would take the helm. There still hadn't been an official announcement of who would be the CEO for the newly formed Alaska Oil Barons Inc., but she'd heard rumblings they were closing in on a choice.

"Oh," Felicity remembered, reaching into her portfolio bag, "I have your letter of recommendation ready." She had convinced Tally to apply for a scholarship to pursue a degree in social work. The woman was a natural.

Tally's smile beamed, her eyes watering. "Thank you." She took the envelope, sliding it carefully into her purse. "Your support and encouragement means the world to me. I'm afraid to get my hopes up that I'll get in, much less receive the scholarship."

Hope was a scary thing, no question. Felicity remembered too well how difficult it had been to trust in a positive future after her divorce. "I'm rooting for you. Let me know the minute you hear."

"I will," Tally promised, giving her a quick hug. "I should let you go. Let's do lunch soon and catch up. My treat."

"Sounds great. Let's keep in touch…" Felicity backed away with a smile and a wave before spinning toward her new office. She lifted her key card and swiped her way into the space—all hers with a window of her own. She could see the snowy mountains and make the most of what little daylight there was during an Alaska winter. She still had boxes stacked in the corner, but had started unpacking the most important items first. Starting with a bulletin board of thank-you notes from parents and newly adopted clients, along with a few childishly drawn pictures she'd framed. These meant more to her than any accolades, seeing how her work made life better for children who were helpless.

She understood the feeling too well.

Swallowing back a wad of emotion, she searched through the stack of files on her desk until she found the one she was looking for under a brass paperweight, a Texas buffalo. She glanced at the clock and gasped. She needed to get moving.

She locked her door, then raced down the hall toward the elevator bank, her leather boots scuffing against the tile floor in her speed. Just ahead, an elevator door began to slide close.

"Wait," she called. "Please hold that elevator."

A hand shot out and the doors bumped back open. Sighing in relief, she angled through sideways.

"Thank you," she said breathlessly. "I'm running late for a meeting."

A masculine voice chuckled from the other side of the packed elevator.

A familiar masculine voice.

She closed her eyes. "Hello, Conrad."

What were the odds?

Gathering her composure, she opened her eyes to find him standing next to a young nurse who was making no effort to hide checking him out. And he gave no acknowledgment to the flirtatious behavior, which Felicity had to admit moved her. He dated widely, but she'd never heard a negative word about him from other women.

Damn it. She didn't need these thoughts. "Fifth floor, please."

She made a point of reviewing the proposal she wanted to give her boss about a new playlist of music and movies for the children in oncology during treatment time.

The elevator slid open again and the cluster of occupants departed, leaving Felicity alone with Conrad. It must have been too much to hope for that he would leave too and make this easier on her. Another part of her whispered that his presence shouldn't bother her this much.

He stepped up alongside her. "Would you like to go out to dinner?"

She tucked her papers away. "You're persistent. I'll give you that."

"Don't you want to know more about the foundation's plans for the hospital?"

She looked up sharply, her gaze colliding with his. A shiver rippled through her as the spicy scent of his aftershave filled her breaths in the small confines of the elevator. Quite simply put, he was yummy, and also offering information she craved.

"I'm intrigued. But I have to say no thank you to dinner."

He chuckled softly.

"Laughing at me certainly isn't going to win me over."

"Trust me, I'm not laughing at you. You do amuse me, but it's your wit, which I admire and find sexy as hell." He grinned at her. "Am I doing better?"

Sighing, she searched his face, his too-damn-handsome face. "I don't understand why you're still pursuing me."

"You're just that amazing." His eyes held hers again, stirring more of those tingles up and down her spine, making her imagine what it would be like to lean into him, just a hint.

The elevator doors slid open, the movement and people on the other side jarring her out of her daze. Securing her bag, she stepped forward. There was no denying the attraction between them. That had never been in question.

Even now, she could swear she felt the warmth of him just behind her. Because she did.

He'd followed her out of the elevator, on the very floor of her meeting with her boss about an exciting new opportunity. On the very day Conrad had mentioned his family's charity foundation beginning new endeavors at Anchorage General. With the children. Foreboding swelled through her.

Gesturing forward, Conrad smiled. "It's going to be a pleasure working together."

Two

Conrad knew better than to push his luck.

He held the door open for Felicity on their way back out of her boss's office an hour later. Follow-up meetings had been scheduled for brainstorming potential initiatives for the Steele-Mikkelson charity foundation, to best utilize their donations. They just needed to coordinate with Isabeau Mikkelson for times that worked for her as well, since she was the foundation's official PR person.

Their primary goal? To have a prospectus in place to unveil at the banquet for the board next month. The next four weeks would offer the perfect opportunities to win over Felicity.

And if she still said no after that? He didn't want

to believe that would happen. But he also wasn't a jerk. It wasn't like the two of them had fallen in love at first sight.

Still, he was certain they could have one hell of an affair.

He stopped at the elevator, the set of her shoulders telling him he'd pushed his luck far enough for one day. He pulled out his phone and stepped away from the sliding doors. She shot a surprised look his way and he stifled a smile, surfing his emails by the window to check for updates before heading back to the office.

An hour later, he strode down the corridors of the Alaska Oil Barons Inc.'s corporate offices. He served on the board of directors for his brother's company, while maintaining an investment business of his own.

Windows along the length of the corridor overlooked the frozen harbor. The other wall was lined with framed artistic photographs of the Alaskan countryside. This building had been the Steele offices, and since the merger, it was the primary headquarters. The Mikkelson tower was still open and filled to capacity, and the styles of the two offices had begun to merge. The chrome decor of the Steele building now sported some metal-tipped teak pieces.

Conrad opened the conference room door. The lengthy table was already more than halfway full. At the head, his brother, Jack sat, beside his new wife,

Jeannie Mikkelson-Steele, whose influence extended well beyond changes to the furniture.

Jack leaned back in his seat, waving his brother into the room. "We're just waiting for Naomi to arrive. How did things go at the hospital?"

Conrad rolled a chair away from the table and placed his briefcase on the sleek, polished wood. "The kids were grateful for the books and the story time."

Jack smiled slowly. "I was talking about the meeting with Felicity Hunt, her boss and the hospital's PR director."

Taking his seat, Conrad used the excuse of pulling out paperwork to delay answering the question. The last thing he needed was an overeager family spooking Felicity.

From his briefcase, he pulled an extra copy of the children's book he'd read at the hospital. He passed the paperback to Glenna Mikkelson-Steele—Jeannie's oldest daughter. "I brought this for Fleur."

To everyone's surprise, Glenna had married Jack's oldest son, who many had thought would assume the family helm. But Broderick had held firm to his position of splitting the CFO duties with his wife so they could focus on their growing family. Everyone in the family was stretched thin, and the acting CEO had moved to North Dakota for a less taxing position so he could spend more time with his wife and start a family.

The board was in final talks trying to lure Ward Benally from the competition. Landing him would be a coup. He worked for a rival company and was a respected—and feared—leader in the oil industry. Benally was also a tough negotiator—which made hammering out a contract a challenge, but it would be a boon if they pulled it off.

Conrad was doing his best to help his family through the transition of the merger. He slid another copy to the far end of the table where Trystan Mikkelson—black sheep of the family—sat with his very pregnant wife. The company's PR consultant, Isabeau Mikkelson, rested one hand on her very pregnant stomach and her other hand on her service dog's head. The Labrador retriever assisted in alerting to Isabeau's diabetes, especially important with a baby on the way.

Jack snagged an extra copy from his brother's briefcase, fanning through the pages. "And your meeting?"

"I'm not sure what you mean," Conrad evaded while pulling his tablet from his briefcase. "I attended. We discussed data and look forward to having Isabeau at the next meeting."

"And Felicity was okay with being the point person with you when Isabeau's unavailable?" Jack pressed.

Couldn't his brother have brought this up away

from all these prying eyes? "She's professional. And this is business."

Jack grinned. "Would you have volunteered for the charity board if she wasn't involved?"

Conrad snapped his case shut. "I've always been loyal to the family." That went without saying. Although it was best to go ahead and address the elephant in the room. "I'm not denying I want to spend more time with her. It's nice how life lines up sometimes."

Saving him from further questions, Naomi Steele-Miller pushed open the door. His niece had faced death as a teen and many had thought she wouldn't survive cancer. Conrad hadn't been sure how his brother would make it through losing another child after Breanna. Thank God, that hadn't happened.

And as it turned out, he hadn't lost Breanna either.

Standing, Conrad pulled out a chair for his niece. Brea and Naomi had looked so much alike as children. How was it that they'd all missed any resemblance when Breanna, posing as Milla Jones, had taken a job as a receptionist? Of course, her hair had been bleached blond. Could they have all been thrown off by something that simple?

Although Brea and Naomi were fraternal twins, not identical.

Naomi pulled her chair into place. "Thank you for being patient. Sorry I'm late. It took longer to settle the girls than I expected."

Conrad snagged another copy of the children's book and passed it to his niece. An attorney for Alaska Oil Barons Inc., she had only just started coming to work without her twin daughters in a double stroller. She and her husband worked from home as much as possible. Her husband, Royce, was a research scientist for the corporation.

Jack took a swallow from his water glass before starting. "No need to apologize, Naomi. Everyone else only just arrived."

Everyone?

Strangely, there were no other board members there—or rather, no one who wasn't a family member. Could this meeting have a different agenda?

Jack cupped the glass, his jaw tight. "Shana called with an update into the investigation."

Conrad straightened in his seat. Shana and Chuck Mikkelson were taking a train ride to North Dakota to house hunt for their upcoming move. Chuck was taking a job heading up offices at that end of the pipeline. For her to call, it must have been important. All eyes were trained on Jack.

"Milla Jones—Brea—has made contact through an attorney. She's willing to talk as long as there's legal representation present."

Conrad couldn't miss the toll this was taking on his older brother. Stark lines fanned from his eyes, dark circles underneath.

Jack shook his head, scraping his hand through his

hair. "She's our Brea, but she wants lawyers to be involved in the reunion? It's so surreal."

Jeannie rested a hand on her husband's arm. "She's been gone a long time. There's no telling what she's been through. Let's focus on the fact she's reached out."

Broderick snorted in disgust. "Because she got word we were closing in on her."

"That's rather cynical," Jack said.

"I'm just setting realistic expectations, Dad. No matter who she is, we can't forget she was leaking corporate secrets before she ran away without a word to any of us."

Jack pushed his water glass away. "No matter what happened when she came here as Milla Jones, she *is* our Breanna. Nothing is more important than that."

Nods made their way around the table, some more reluctant than others.

Jeannie rolled her chair back. "Let's break for a few, get our heads in the game again, then reconvene to discuss the latest round of contract negotiations with Ward Benally."

A wise suggestion to take a breather, given the tension pulsing from both the Steeles and the Mikkelsons. There'd been recent allegations made that someone in the Mikkelson family could have been involved in Brea's disappearance. It seemed inconceivable, but then so did the possibility that Brea could truly be alive.

These days, anything was possible.

Conrad tossed his tablet into his briefcase. Since he'd weighed in with his written feedback, Conrad took the opportunity to step out of this portion of the meeting.

Once back in the corridor, he turned on his cell and it immediately buzzed with missed calls and texts.

And right at the top of the list of those who'd phoned?

Felicity Hunt.

Felicity tried not to stare at her phone on her kitchen counter.

Calling Conrad had been an impulsive move, which was surprising in and of itself since she wasn't the impulsive type. But when a friend from work had texted her with questions about a rumor regarding Breanna Steele… Felicity had found herself remembering a discussion with Conrad about how devastating his niece's disappearance had been for him.

Felicity punched in Conrad's number before she could think.

Property in Alaska was costly and social workers didn't bring in large paychecks. Since she lived alone and spent most of her free time at work, it made sense to rent a one-bedroom apartment. She hadn't brought anything from Texas with her anyway, preferring to leave all her furniture and the bad memories associated with it behind her.

Her living area was tight, but comfy, with a generic tan sofa alongside a space-saver rattan chair, and her one indulgence—a fat, raspberry-colored reading chair perched by the window and under a skylight. She missed her Texas sun but couldn't deny the magnificence of the views here were unrivaled.

She'd wanted a place far from memories of her painful past, and she'd found a haven here.

Turning back to her coffeepot, she tapped the "water only" feature to make tea. She pulled a mug from the cabinet, a stoneware piece she'd bought at a local festival. Leaving her belongings behind had offered the opportunity to explore new styles and reinvent herself.

She'd kept the most important things in her life, letters from people who cared about her. Foster siblings. Her final foster parents. A social worker who'd made a world of difference in her life.

Her work meant everything to her. She still couldn't ever turn her back on the career that gave her purpose. Her life's calling was to make the same difference for helpless children.

A mantra she repeated to herself daily.

More than once daily lately, since Conrad Steele had entered her world.

She blew in her tea before taking a sip. The warmth soothed her nerves.

Her phone chimed, and she reached for the cell while lifting her mug for another drink. The name on the screen stilled her hand.

Conrad Steele.

Her heart leaped at the incoming call, too much. But she wasn't going to play games by making it ring longer. She was an adult.

She thumbed the speakerphone. "Hello, Conrad."

"I see I missed a call from you."

In spite of insisting to herself this was no big deal, she found herself tongue-tied. "I don't want to be presumptuous. I just wanted to make sure everything's okay."

"Things are still on track for the hospital donations. No need to be concerned."

She hated that he thought her reason for calling could be only self-serving. "I heard there's news about your niece. I don't want to pry and invade your family's privacy, but I thought of you—"

"You're not prying. You're being thoughtful. Thank you. I know you have ties to the family through your friendship with Tally. You care."

"I do."

His heavy exhale filled the phone. "Brea has reached out. We don't know the full story as to where she's been and why she came back the way she did, pretending to be someone else. But at least we're going to have answers."

"This has to be so difficult for you."

"My brother is tied in knots," he said tightly.

She knew him well enough to realize how deeply this would affect him, too. He was close to his family. One of the things that drew her to him. "And you're taking a backseat to your own feelings since you're an uncle."

"Are you using those counselor skills on me?"

"It's second nature, I guess." She just hadn't thought she was quite so transparent. Or maybe he was that perceptive. Either way, she needed to choose her words more carefully.

"I'll be fine. Thank you again for the concern," he said softly before continuing. "Was there another reason for your call?"

She needed to work with him, but also needed him to understand her position. "I got a text from a coworker with information I thought I should pass along."

"What kind of information?"

"The rumors are already churning about Milla Jones possibly being your missing niece. Photos of Milla—Brea—have been circulating."

"Yes, we had those released when we first started our investigation."

"Everyone in the break room has been talking about the volunteer who filed a report about the same woman delivering flowers to patients one night." She toyed with her lanyard. "The volunteer said she plans to notify your family, but I wanted to make sure you knew."

"Delivering flowers? That's strange."

"My friend said a volunteer came to her and explained she was approached by Milla and paid a large sum of money to loan her volunteer smock. Unethical on so many levels, which is why she didn't come forward sooner."

"How long ago did this happen?"

"Last fall. I'm sure the Steele family will be notified through official channels soon."

"Last fall? That's around the time when Naomi's twins were born."

A chill went through her to think of Breanna Steele stalking the halls incognito to see her twin's newborn babies. Hospital security was paramount, especially in the maternity ward. The babies all wore bracelets that would set off alarms if they were taken from the floor. But still. This was more than a little unsettling.

What had happened to Breanna that caused her to distrust her own family so deeply? A sense of foreboding rolled over Felicity, born of too many years on the job, telling her that finding the woman wasn't going to bring an easy, happy reunion.

Conrad cleared his throat. "Thank you for sharing that information. I'll pass it along."

"I hope it helps in some way."

"Every piece of this crazy puzzle is helpful." He paused for a moment. "Was there something else?"

"Actually, yes. I want us to start fresh for the good of the hospital project."

"What do you mean by starting fresh?"

"A working friendship, on neutral ground." She couldn't be any more succinct than that.

"I've made it clear I want more. Is that going to be a problem for you?"

"And it's clear we have to work together. I can be professional." She hoped. If only he wasn't so damn hot.

Except she knew it was more than that. There were plenty of attractive men in the workplace and she didn't find herself tempted by them, not in the way this man seemed to seep into her thoughts no matter how hard she tried to put him out of her mind.

"Okay, then," he continued, "do you ride?"

She couldn't hold back her laugh. "Do I know how to ride? I'm a Texan."

His chuckle sent a thrill up her spine.

"Alright, then, Felicity. I'm helping exercise my nephew's horses while his second barn is rebuilt. Bundle up and join me."

It was just horseback riding. Not like a romantic dinner out.

And still, she found herself far too excited at the

prospect of spending more time with a tempting man she'd vowed never to see again.

Conrad had spent the last twenty-four hours trying to get Felicity's voice out of his head. Attraction was one thing. Total loss of focus? That was unacceptable.

He'd worn himself out in his home gym in preparation for her arrival in hopes of giving himself a much-needed edge.

Warmth from the shower still clung to his skin as he made his way across his in-home basketball court. Stretching his arms overhead, he exhaled hard as he closed the distance to the door. He combed his fingers through his damp hair, anticipation zinging through him over this outing with Felicity.

Opening the door, he left the harsh fluorescent lights of his gym behind. As his eyes adjusted to the gentler light in his wood-paneled living room, his boots thudded on the pine flooring as he picked his way around the large area rug and black-and-tan sectional. Light filtered in from the large windows, filling the oversize tray ceiling.

Yanking his heavy coat off the rack and snagging his black Stetson, he opened his door and shrugged into the wool coat, which still had the lingering scent of antiseptic and hand sanitizer from all his time at the hospital. Even a pine-scented gust of wind that caused snow to stir slightly didn't completely dissipate the hospital smell.

It wasn't altogether unpleasant, though. The smell reminded him of Felicity. The sexy social worker who'd agreed to meet him today at the small barn that loomed slightly to the north. To call it small felt like a misnomer. More like, small as far as his family's standards went. There was room for only ten horses and one tack room. But large, relatively speaking. He lived a good life.

Snow covered the tiered roof, icicles spiking from the eaves. Three horses trotted around the front paddock. Literally frolicking in the snow. Sally, the oldest mare he owned, played with an oversize ball. Careening around it like a little filly. The old chestnut mare still so full of life and wonder.

His brother had a larger barn with more rides, but then, he had children. Conrad had his horse and mounts for his nieces and nephews to ride when they came over. But he led a bachelor's existence, more scaled back than his brother's.

That wasn't to say Conrad hadn't once envisioned a life for himself with kids and a spread like his brother. But that wasn't in the cards for him. He'd seen that clearly after the breakup of two significant relationships. He'd given it his best shot, only to get his heart stomped and the betrayal stung him still.

So he'd thrown himself into helping his brother. He'd watched Jack's kids grow up, had helped with them as much as his brother would allow. Conrad led a full life.

His boots crunched in the snow as he moved toward the barn. Conrad opened the latch to the climate-controlled stable. Warmth brushed against his cheeks as he grabbed the necessary tack for today's ride. He placed the saddles one by one on the built-in saddle racks on the walls of the barn. Hung the bridles next to them. He returned to the tack room for grooming supplies. Settled into his routine.

A whinny emerged from down the barn. Jackson, his palomino stallion, poked his golden head out. Ears flicking in anticipation, matching Conrad's own pent-up energy. Setting the grooming supplies down, he moved toward his horse. Gave the stallion a scratch behind the ears as he slipped the leather halter over Jackson's head.

Leading the palomino to the first crossties, he clipped the golden horse. Jackson adjusted his weight, popping his front right hoof on an angle, and let out a sigh that seemed almost bored. Of all the horses Conrad had ever worked with, he'd never come across one with so much personality. And a personality that matched his so well.

Giving the horse another scratch, Conrad determined which ride he would choose for Felicity. Glancing around the barn, he settled on Patches. A quiet, steady pinto gelding, well mannered.

Conrad retrieved Felicity's mount and began

grooming Patches first. As he finished grooming the pinto, he heard the distinct sound of a car engine approach and then fall silent.

A few moments later, Felicity walked into the barn. He was half-surprised she'd shown. For a moment, the world seemed to tilt as he was struck by her natural beauty, the curves visible even through her snow gear.

Her brown hair was swept into a thick braid draped over one shoulder. Her deep purple parka matched her snow pants. Her scarf was loose around her neck, but long enough to cover her face if the wind picked up.

She tugged the ends of the fringed scarf tighter as she approached him. "Well, hello, Conrad. I have to confess, I didn't expect this."

Her eyes flitted to the open door behind her, gaze lingering on his one-story home, which overlooked a mountain range.

"What *did* you expect?" He finished currycombing Jackson, who stretched his neck out far, releasing a shuddering shake from ears to tailbone. Conrad bent over, hoof pick in hand, watching her out of the corner of his eyes.

"I envisioned you living in a penthouse condo. Not a…well, a home."

"Technically, this—" he motioned around the space "—is a barn."

She laughed, the wind through the open door carrying a whiff of her citrus scent, mixing with the familiar smell of leather and hay. "You're right. It is. But I was referring to your house, as well."

Interesting how she saw space when he thought of his estate as scaled back. Releasing Jackson's hoof, Conrad made his way to the door. Shut it to keep out the cold. No use freezing before they started riding.

"It's not the size of my brother's, but I don't need as much room."

"It's still very spacious, especially by Alaska standards with property being so expensive." She winced, setting her leather bag on the recessed shelving near where the saddles hung. She positioned the bag near the helmets he'd always made children wear. "That was crass of me to mention money."

"Not at all. High real estate prices here are a fact." Hefting Patches's saddle and saddle pad off the rack, he slung the bridle over his shoulder.

A glance at Felicity's wind-pinkened face filled his mind with thoughts of skimming kisses over her before claiming her mouth. The memory of her was powerful, so much so, it could tempt him to move too fast and risk the progress he'd made with her. Drawing in a steadying breath, he focused on the task of readying the horses.

As he moved toward the pinto, Patches's ears flicked as if interested in the conversation at hand as the saddle settled on his back. Conrad was a hard worker, but plenty of people worked hard and didn't have this kind of luxury. He knew luck had played in as well and he didn't lose sight of that. After adjusting the girth, he slid the bit into the horse's mouth, fiddling with the chin strap. He placed the reins on Patches's neck. The well-trained horse didn't move, but stood at attention as Conrad tacked up Jackson.

"Even in Texas, I grew up in smaller places, my parents' apartment, then foster homes. This is incredible."

He warmed at how she expressed appreciation for the life he'd built, rather than comparing it with Jack Steele's sprawling compound. Conrad passed her the reins to Patches, the wind blowing the loose strands of her hair forward. His hands itched with the urge to stroke her hair back.

Too easily, he could lose himself in looking at her. But if he made a move, she would likely bolt.

Patience.

He offered her a leg up out of courtesy but also to determine her skill. He would be able to tell if she was as good a rider as she claimed by the way she sat in the saddle. How she positioned her body and weight.

Felicity seemed to be a natural.

Now confident she could hold her own, he led his horse out by the reins. The sun was high and bright, reflecting off the snow in a nearly blinding light. Closing the barn door behind him, he led Jackson a few steps away from the steel-reinforced door. Conrad pulled himself into the saddle, hands adjusting the reins by muscle memory.

Pressing his calves into Jackson's sensitive side, he urged the horse toward an open gate. He figured this enclosed area would be safer—just in case Felicity lost her seat. Much easier to contain than potentially chasing Patches through the wilderness.

Felicity skillfully picked up the reins, bringing Patches to attention as she set her horse beside his. "Have you heard anything more about your niece?"

"We've locked down a time for Brea's arrival. We'll be meeting with her attorney present—at her request." The hair on the back of his neck bristled at all the ways things could go badly.

"This can't be easy for any of you."

He pushed his weight in the saddle, grounding down. Nothing about Brea's return had been something he could have imagined. At least not like this.

"We never dreamed we could have her back at all. We're staying focused on the fact she's alive." Truthful, but it didn't negate the hell of wondering what led her to infiltrate the company, to resent and mistrust them all to this degree.

"I hope it's not awkward if I ask, but is there a chance her mother is alive, too?" An eagle soaring overhead cast a wide-wingspan shadow along the snow ahead of Felicity.

"No, none," he said without hesitation. "Mary's body was thrown from the plane. They were able to make a positive ID. With Brea, they only located teeth in the charred wreckage."

It never got easier discussing that part of the aftermath.

She shivered. "Your family has been through so much."

"Nothing guarantees life will be easy." The glare of the sun along the icy pasture was so bright he shielded his eyes with his hand. "We're just lucky to have each other for support along the way."

"That's a healthy outlook."

Her words made him realize she was listening with a professional ear. "I recall you saying you became a social worker because of growing up in foster care. What made you decide to switch to the hospital position?"

Her posture grew surer as she answered him, guiding Patches around snow-covered bushes. "As a child, I saw what a difference a caring professional could make, in my life and in others'. There are so many components, from the caseworker, to the courts, and yes, too often, hospitals. This gave me another avenue to make a difference."

"You're certainly doing that." He respected her devotion to her job, one of the many things that had attracted him to her. He'd thought her career focus would also make them a great pair. He'd thought wrong and needed to figure out another way around to win her.

"I'm grateful to your family for what they're doing for the hospital." Wind blew flurries around her horse's hooves. "The children in oncology... I don't need to spell out their needs for you. You saw it with your niece Naomi."

"I did. What kinds of needs do you see for the children in the hospital?" he asked, to make the most of working together. And because he found he was genuinely curious in her input.

"That's such a broad question."

He tilted his head, looking forward on the trail in the pasture and checking for uneven ground that could be masked by the snow. "Say the first thing that pops into your head."

"I have a list in my office on staffing and structural needs," she said, still not answering his question.

But he understood how her professional instincts might be in play, not wanting to commit to an item when there was a more important need.

"Send me the list. I feel certain we can address those issues. What else?" he pressed. "Something you didn't even imagine could go on your wish list." He pushed Jackson into a slow trot, the palomino's stride putting slight distance between them. Glancing over his shoulder, Conrad saw a determined smile settle on Felicity's face.

Keeping her hands low on Patches's neck, she clicked her tongue, coaxing the horse into a smooth jog. Though the horse's pace increased, Felicity's seat stayed steady. Flawless execution.

"Well, the children in behavioral health could use more pet therapy teams."

Felicity's roots might be Texan, but she held her own with the horse and the cold like she'd lived here her whole life. He was surprised and impressed. "We're on it. Isabeau Mikkelson is on the committee for PR and she brought up that very subject in an earlier meeting."

"She and her husband live on a ranch outside Juneau, right?"

"Yes, she just arrived in town today. They're staying with the family during her last trimester of pregnancy. She's high risk because of her diabetes, and they want to use the same doctor Naomi had for the delivery."

"I'm glad they have the support of so many relatives. Are you sure she's up to the task of helping with this?"

Even with Isabeau being high risk, he hadn't considered something could go wrong. "She checked with her doctors first and got the okay. She's been going stir-crazy taking off work and this was a good compromise. She's been helping pick up slack, too, that would have been covered by Jeannie's former assistant, Sage Hammond."

"What happened to Sage?"

"She took a sudden sabbatical to Europe. Really

left the family in a lurch, kind of surprising since she's related to Jeannie." He shrugged. "Anyway, Isabeau raised the idea of pet therapy since she has a service dog for her diabetes. Even though a service dog is different from a therapy dog, Isabeau's a great resource on the topic. She's familiar with the various roles a pet can play in health care."

Felicity nodded. "A service dog performs a task for one person for life, and a therapy dog provides comfort in groups or for a number of different people individually."

"Exactly. We're looking into therapy dog programs for individual room visits as well as group settings. Having a couple of dogs present during reading time would be a great place to start."

"That sounds wonderful. You've clearly put a lot of thought into this." She glanced at him. "Your family, too. It's not just a…"

"Not just a promotional tool? No. That's not to say we aren't happy for the good press, because our success gives us more charitable options."

"I'll do my best to be sure the money's spent wisely so the foundation can do even more."

"I'm sure you will." Applying slight pressure with his reins, Conrad looped his horse back toward the barn. Created somewhat of a bad circle in the snow.

Felicity maneuvered Patches to follow him. "How are you so certain?"

"You were willing to come riding with me today

in spite of pushing me away with both hands," he said with a cocky grin.

Silence fell between them. The only sounds echoing in the air were the crunch of horse hooves against fresh snow.

She shook her head, her smile half amused. "I don't dislike you."

He laughed, appreciating how she didn't dish out flattery just because he had money to donate. "Watch it, or my ego will overinflate with the lavish compliments."

"I don't mean to be rude. I just want to be sure we're clear that this is business."

He needed to make sure she understood. "I would never make a move without your consent."

"But that's not the same as continuing to pursue me," she said with a wry smile, her cheeks turning red from the wind.

"You're too perceptive for me to even try to deny that."

"As long as you're clear on where I stand."

"Yes, ma'am." He tapped the brim of his Stetson, tipping it slightly in salute. "We should get back before your Texas roots freeze out here."

They'd reached the gate again. Conrad guided Jackson through the opening. Though if he was being honest the horse knew it was time to return home. A renewed pep in his step, Jackson moved toward the barn. Patches let out a low nicker as they drew closer to the structure.

He'd made progress with Felicity and his quest. He'd meant it when he said he wouldn't leverage the attraction between them until she gave him the green light. But he was a patient man. He could still spend time with her. Get to know her better. Persuade her that they could have something special.

In fact, he welcomed the challenge—as well as the distraction from the stress of his niece's complicated return.

Three

Breanna Steele still struggled with thinking of herself by her birth name. She'd been Milla Jones for over fifteen years. It felt like longer, in fact, since the Brea days were distant, muddied by so many factors since the plane crash.

Pushing away her in-flight meal, she pressed her fingertips against the cool glass of the airplane window. Since the plane crash all those years ago, flying sent her stomach into knots. Particularly when the private jet was so small, just like that aircraft all those years ago. But the transportation had been chartered by the Steeles. Snow-covered mountains sent her nerves into overdrive so she returned her focus to the main cabin.

Her lawyer accompanied her, a young attorney who'd taken her case pro bono, looking to make a name for himself. He was cutthroat. All the more reason to trust him with a future so scary and unsure.

Taking the flight offered by the Steeles had made her nervous, but ultimately it was the logical thing to do. She'd also been very clear in her acceptance that she'd left safeguards in place if anything happened to her. The world would know exactly where she'd been.

People thought she was acting paranoid. She didn't care.

She tore apart the roll, tossing the pieces into her bowl of uneaten salad. Stress had taken a toll on her appetite. Since the death of her "adoptive" parents last year, she'd been unable to resist searching for answers about her past. Her mind was a jumble. She'd been brought up by a couple—Steven and Karen Jones—who'd protected her from the threats of her family's crooked connections.

She'd been told her Steele siblings died as well in the crash and the accident was such a haze, she'd believed it. Steven and Karen had insisted they were keeping Brea safe from threats existing in her birth father's world.

Finding out after the Jones's deaths that her real dad and her siblings were alive had been a shock, one that started a steamroll of questions about other things. Still, loyalty to Steven and Karen, who'd saved her, was tough to break. She'd told herself they lied about her siblings to keep her safe from her father, who'd orchestrated her biological mother's death. Brea still believed that to a degree. So much so that she could only envision meeting with the Steeles with lawyers present for her safety—and so she didn't end up in jail.

There was also the whole matter of her wrangling a job at Alaska Oil Barons Inc. under her fake name and leaking business secrets. She'd wanted revenge for their abandonment. Now she was beginning to realize things might not be that simple. But she still needed to be careful.

As the plane began its descent into Anchorage, she shivered. Afraid, but resolute. The time had come to face her past, to make peace so she could move forward free of any entanglements with the Steeles.

Free of the pain of realizing they never really searched for her.

Never could she be a part of the Steeles' world of lies and a fake sense of family.

Felicity found disentangling her feelings when it came to Conrad Steele was easier said than done. Their simple ride together had left her more confused than ever.

Fidgeting with her long, silver necklace, she looked at her half-eaten turkey-and-hummus sandwich. She contemplated grabbing it off the pile of vintage travel books she'd used to decorate her office. Unlike her coworkers, Felicity didn't have many pictures of family and loved ones plastered in every square inch of her office.

Not that she wasn't sentimental. Instead, she had a few handwritten cards displayed, pinned to a corkboard. These mementos helped her through the dark days, when the important work she did weighed heavy on her mind. Felicity needed reminders of light.

Compelled by memories, Felicity reached for the letter Angie, the social worker who made all the difference in her life, penned upon Felicity's acceptance of her first social worker job. She hadn't worked here long, but already files were piling up on her desk. The workload was heavy, but each day came with opportunities to touch lives. Already, she'd added a new note to her board, a thank-you from a young patient and her parents, alongside others from the past she'd brought from her other job.

She gathered up the files and stowed them in a drawer, trying to tidy up before Conrad Steele and Isabeau Mikkelson arrived. Felicity kneed the drawer closed. Her office wasn't as grand as anything in Conrad's work world, but she was proud of her new space, with a corner window. Her framed diplomas might not be Ivy League, but she'd finished with honors, the first in her family to attend college. She'd worked two jobs to put herself through. It had taken her an extra year in undergraduate school, as well as an extra semester to complete her master's in social work. But she'd never given up on her dream.

People like Conrad didn't understand what it was like to have no family support. She didn't blame him or resent him for that. However, she couldn't help but feel they came from different planets and he could never fully understand her journey.

A tap on her door pulled her from her thoughts. She smoothed back her hair on her way across the room. Nerves fluttered in her stomach at just the prospect of seeing Conrad. She willed herself to take three slow breaths, in through her nose and out through her mouth, the way she coached patients to do.

She opened the door. There wasn't enough air in the room to calm her reaction to the man on the other side of the threshold.

Conrad's broad shoulders filled out the designer suit jacket, his overcoat and Stetson in hand. "Isabeau's running a little behind. Her OB doctor was held up."

"Come in." Felicity gestured through, willing herself not to think about how much smaller the space was with him inside.

He hung his coat and hat on the rack in the corner before turning back to face her. "Isabeau said she should be here in about ten minutes."

They were going to discuss procedures for including more therapy dogs in the pediatric ward.

Felicity had seen amazing results from therapy dogs with children, but she wanted more information on channels for ensuring the dogs were the right fit. She knew enough to realize that just because a dog was affectionate didn't make it a therapy dog candidate.

Isabeau had information on programs that tested dogs and provided training to the therapy dog's owner. She'd also mentioned discussing the different levels of work, varying from simply sitting with a reading group to assisting someone in a recovery setting.

Conrad tapped along her note board and framed art from patients. "These notes and pictures are incredible."

"They've gotten me through some rough days at work."

He shot her a wide smile. "This beats my wall of fame, hands down."

"You won't find me disagreeing with that," she couldn't resist retorting, grinning back. "There's an indescribable thrill when my job works the way it should."

"I can hear that in your voice." He sat on the corner of her desk, the Alaska skyline stretched out behind him through the window. "That compassion is what makes you such a success."

She leveled a stare his way. "I'm also not won over by idle flattery. You don't know enough about my work to judge how successful I am or am not."

"I do know, from your wall there and your boss's confidence in you to represent the hospital with the charity foundation."

His words stopped her short, stirring confusion. She'd been so certain Conrad had orchestrated their working together on the program. "Oh, uh…"

"What?" he asked. "Is something wrong?"

"I'm just…surprised." She searched his face. "I thought you pressured my boss into choosing me for the project."

"Absolutely not," he said without hesitation. "You don't know me all that well or you wouldn't say it, much less think it. When it comes to business, I'm no-nonsense. My brother has the soft heart."

"He seems gruff and you're all smiles." She studied him for a moment longer even though she could swear she knew every handsome detail of his face, every line that spoke of experience. He was all man and she was far, far from unaffected. "And that's how you two catch people off guard in negotiations. People don't expect gentleness from your brother and ruthlessness from you."

He ran a hand through his dark, gray-flecked hair, hand stopping on the back of his neck. A boyish kind of charm that she hadn't noticed he'd possessed. Conrad—a complex man of many mysteries.

"Ruthless? Ouch." He clapped a splayed hand over his heart. "How did I go from all smiles and charm to ruthless so fast?"

She wasn't sure. Just when she thought she had him pegged, he surprised her. "I guess I'm learning to get to know you. Wasn't that your goal in pursuing me?"

"You could say that, although I was hoping for something more persuasive than *ruthless*."

"Ruthlessness can be a good thing, when channeled properly."

His blue eyes heated, the air crackling between them. "And do you think I've been channeled properly?"

She ached to lean in closer to him to see if the temperature continued to rise the nearer she came. And then she realized...she was being played.

Felicity angled back. "I ask questions for a living, you know, and it's to keep someone talking rather than having them do the asking."

"Busted." He shrugged unrepentantly.

Fine. She could go toe-to-toe with this man. "My training also makes me believe you only want me because I'm telling you no."

"Let's test your theory." He lifted her hand, the calluses on his fingertips touching her skin, arousing her. "Say yes to a date. See if my interest evaporates. It won't, by the way. But go ahead. Try."

"Now you've changed to charming again." She should pull her hand from his. Should. But didn't.

Instead, her imagination ran wild with the possibility of having his raspy touch all over her body. Her senses filled with the crisp, outdoorsy scent of him.

A cleared throat in the doorway broke the spell like a splash of chilling reality. She tugged her hand away quickly. But she was certain he didn't miss her guilty flinch.

Felicity took in a very pregnant Isabeau, whose slender hand rested gently on her baby bump. She wore a violet knit sweater dress, her shoulder-length red hair perfectly styled into loose romantic waves. Even in her eighth month, Isabeau had a chic style that she put to use in her PR profession. Felicity had been impressed with her when accompanying the Steeles to the ballet last month.

Isabeau looked at them with curiosity in her eyes. "I'm sorry to be late. Thank you for waiting."

Thank goodness Isabeau hadn't commented on, well, the obvious. Felicity adjusted the second chair so it was closer to the pregnant woman. "How was your appointment?"

Smiling her thanks, Isabeau sank into the seat with a sigh. "We're watching the baby's weight because of my diabetes." Diabetes could cause a baby to be larger. "But, thankfully, all appears to be on track. I'll finish up plans for the hospital dinner and still have two weeks to put my feet up before my son is born."

Isabeau and Trystan had shared the gender news, but were keeping the name a secret.

Conrad patted her shoulder. "That's great news from the doctor."

His concern was undeniable. And touching. He cared for his family. Felicity knew that already, but the reminder, especially right now when she was feeling vulnerable, made her edgy. She needed to distance herself. Work had been her buffer for years and she embraced that now as a way of understanding the people around her.

And she needed to maintain that sense of professionalism. She worried about appearances and letting her guard down around him.

She gestured toward Conrad's chair. "We have a lot to cover, so let's get started."

However, with her skin still burning from his touch, she knew she was only kidding herself if she thought it wouldn't happen again.

Ninety minutes later, Conrad packed his briefcase, the meeting drawing to a close. Felicity had kept the discussion businesslike, moving the agenda along at a brisk pace. Isabeau was already retreating toward the elevator, the office door still open.

Leaving Conrad alone with Felicity. Worries about Brea showing up and the unrest in the family dogged him. Being around Felicity felt like the only time he wasn't hounded by the sense that his family was on the brink of another disaster.

She thumbed through a stack of new children's

books on her desk. "I'm impressed with how seriously you and the committee are taking the reading selection. It's going to be incredible having therapy dogs sit with the children during story time."

"We're certainly adding to our family library for the little ones." Try as he might, he felt his gaze drawn to the curve of her pink lips. Natural beauty shone through in her delicate eyebrows, arching as she smoothed back a strand of brown hair.

"Naomi's twins were born here."

He nodded as he packed a children's book away. "And Glenna and Broderick's daughter, too. Her adoption is almost complete."

"Adoption?" Felicity passed him a stack with the rest of the books.

As she leaned forward, he noted the way her blouse hugged her body, suggesting well-appointed curves. Felicity had the kind of beauty that few possessed. It was about more than her looks. It came from her confidence, the way she carried herself.

Damn mesmerizing.

"It's complicated." He tucked the rest of the storybooks into his briefcase, keeping his distance for now. He wasn't going to push his luck. "Baby Fleur was abandoned on my brother's doorstep with a note from the mother saying she didn't know if the father was Broderick...or Glenna's first husband."

She raised an eyebrow. "I've dealt with some complex placements. That had to be so difficult for everyone."

"Turned out that Glenna's first husband had cheated on her just before he died." He wasn't sure why Felicity hadn't booted him out of the office yet. "The baby is, in fact, his biological child. But in the time waiting to learn the paternity results, Glenna and Broderick bonded hard with Fleur."

She leaned in, clearly invested in the story. He would take any opportunity—any conversation—to build a firmer connection between them. Stolen time. A date could still be possible. He could feel her interest crackle in the space between them. "And her biological mother?"

He should have realized Felicity's professional instincts would kick into gear. "Signed over her rights to them for a private adoption." He snapped his case closed and locked. "We couldn't love Fleur any more if she was Broderick's."

"That's how it should be." She tapped one of the framed thank-you notes.

"I agree. Naomi's twins were conceived with an anonymous sperm donor. Yet, Royce is one hundred percent committed to being their father. He even delivered them in a car in a snowstorm."

One of the crazier moments of the last year. But one that his family had welcomed and embraced with open arms. His family anchored him through hard times. With the Steeles so on edge, he found himself…searching.

A bad reason to want this date with Felicity so much? Maybe. But he wasn't giving up.

She angled her head, hair tumbling in front of her eyes. He fought the urge to reach across the desk and sweep it behind her ear. "How did I not know all of this about the Steeles and Mikkelsons?"

"We're a big family. There's a lot to know." He held her gaze for a moment before turning toward the door. He'd made more progress than expected today. And he was only getting started on his plans for seduction.

Only four days had passed since her meeting with Conrad, and Felicity was starting to worry that by the end of the week, she might not have any space left to move.

Her office was overflowing with gifts—Swiss chocolates, outrageously expensive Vietnamese coffee beans and two lavish floral arrangements. The scent of roses, lilies and freesia filled her office.

She needed to walk the flowers down to the children's ward for the nurses' station to share with patients who could use a pick-me-up. She felt decadent keeping them for herself even for the short term but it had been a hectic week, each day more stressful than the one before. And today had been the worst, starting early with eleven children being admitted to the hospital for neglect.

But pampering herself with candy and flowers

wasn't going to make that any easier. She needed to stop dwelling on thoughts of Conrad Steele.

She scooped up her cell phone to take with her and noticed she had somehow missed a call from Isabeau. Tapping Redial, she didn't have to wait long.

Isabeau picked up on the second ring. "Hi, thanks for getting back to me so quickly. I have a favor to ask."

"Let me pull up my file on our plans so I'll have it handy for reference." She typed in her password to bring the computer screen back to life.

"Actually, this isn't about business. It's a personal favor." Isabeau's voice was so heavy with concern it had Felicity sitting up straight with worry.

"Of course." Felicity turned away from her computer, her focus fully on the call. "What do you need?"

A pause filtered through the phone.

Felicity felt as though her heart became dislodged from her chest, climbing into her throat. Threatening to spill out on her desk amid budget requests and case files.

"Would you be willing to sit in when the family meets with Breanna?" The words fell out in a fast tumble with a nervous edge. "There will be lawyers present, as if it wasn't already going to be tense enough. I think they would benefit from having you there."

Felicity agreed that having professional help present

would be wise, but she wasn't as sure she was the right person since she knew the family. Not to mention, Isabeau was a Mikkelson, not a Steele.

And there was the whole crazy draw to Conrad to deal with. "What does the rest of the family have to say?"

A sigh signaled the weariness Isabeau felt.

"Jeannie agreed, and she's going to talk to Jack about it. He listens to her."

While she appreciated Isabeau's heart was in the right place, Felicity still wasn't sure she was the person for the task. "There are other counselors in the area. I would be glad to give you a list of recommendations."

"But we know you. You know us, and that's no small task, given our huge family tree," Isabeau said wryly. "But if you're not comfortable, I understand."

Felicity weighed her decision and chose her words carefully. Things were complicated enough, given her feelings for Conrad.

Feelings?

Felicity pushed aside the wayward thought and settled on a compromise. "If Jack and the others agree, then I'm glad to do what I can to help with any issues that may arise."

"Thank you. That's a huge relief." A shaky sigh whispered through the phone. "It's all just so...surreal. Brea coming...being alive, her being this Milla person who was out to harm the company."

"I realize this must be stressful for you. I hope you're taking care of yourself and the baby."

"Of course I am," Isabeau said quickly in a way that Felicity interpreted as the end of the conversation about Breanna. "My husband is waiting on me hand and foot, as is the rest of the family. All I have is this project to think about until my son is born."

Felicity laughed along with her, even through an ache that lodged in her chest over the woman's words as they finished the call. Her grip tightened on the silent cell until her fingers numbed.

There'd been a time when Felicity had dreams of being pregnant, with a doting husband as excited as she was. Yes, her ex had wanted children, but she'd sensed trouble in the marriage and wanted a steady home first. Something that never happened because her ex was a drug addict, hooked on prescription meds. She still couldn't believe how long it had taken her to discover his addiction. She was a counselor, for heaven's sake.

But he was that good of a liar, twisting her inside out over time.

In a last-ditch effort, she'd begged him to go to counseling together in addition to checking into a rehab center. He'd delayed and delayed until she realized he was never going to change. He didn't want to. Two weeks after she booted him out, he moved in with another woman.

Felicity knew she'd dodged a bullet. The heartache

would have only been worse the longer they'd stayed together. Still, sometimes, when she heard about other happy couples living the dream, it made her remember all that pain. The betrayal. And yes, it even made her question herself, although she knew in her gut she'd done everything she could.

Well, everything except having chosen someone different from the start. She could forgive herself for one mistake. But if she repeated the past? She would have no one to blame but herself.

The scent of roses drew her attention back to the arrangements from Conrad. She really did need to get them out of her office. And the staff would appreciate the chocolates. If only it was that easy to get the man out of her mind. But this was a start.

Juggling the two arrangements with the box of chocolates tucked under her arm, she made fast tracks down the corridor. She stepped out of the elevator on the floor for pediatric oncology...and stopped short as she caught sight of children seated in a circle in the play area. Story time? It appeared so. She'd forgotten the discussion about having readings here for patients too ill to go to the memory garden.

Or maybe her subconscious had nudged her this way.

Sighing at herself, she secured her grip on the flowers and chocolates. If Conrad saw her giving away his gifts, then so be it. Maybe it was for the best.

As she walked closer, she realized it wasn't a male

voice, but rather a woman's voice reading, a familiar voice. Her friend Tally, who was engaged to Marshall Steele, held up the kids' favorite book about the magical horse.

Felicity passed the flowers and candy to a nurse with a smile, her attention drawn to the children as Tally told them to go to the window for a surprise.

Curious, Felicity stepped closer, helping a little boy struggling with his wheelchair. Gasps and squeals of delight filled the air. She parked the wheelchair at the window that overlooked the parking lot.

And found a sight that tugged her heart far more than any roses or chocolate.

Below the window, Conrad Steele sat astride his horse just like the hero in the storybook, confident, strong…

And tipping his Stetson in greeting.

Four

Even from across the parking lot, on his palomino, Conrad could see Felicity was fired up. She charged through the sliding doors out into the elements. The wind tore at her cape as she picked her way past a pile of sludge a snowplow had pushed to the side.

From the scowl on her face, she wasn't happy.

Sexy as hell. But definitely not happy.

He guided his horse closer, anticipation sizzling through him with each step of Jackson's hooves. He hadn't planned on seeing her, but he was damn glad for the opportunity to square off with her, all the same.

Drawing up alongside her, Conrad gave a gentle

tug to the reins. "Hello, beautiful. How's your day going?"

"What are you doing?" Her words were soft, but steely.

"Hopefully, I'm charming a bunch of sick children." He lifted his Stetson and waved it at the windows where the children were lined up watching. His horse shifted his weight from front hoof to front hoof as if gearing up for a dance and show. Sometimes, he swore the palomino could read his thoughts as they formed.

Sighing, she tugged the hood of her cape over her ears. "And this has nothing to do with your quest to wear me down."

"You're assuming I planned on you seeing me, which I didn't since I expected you to be in your office." And that was the truth. It stung him that she still thought only the worst of him. Although if she already thought that of him, he might as well make the most of the moment. "But hey, if it dazzles you as well, then that's just a win-win. Let's give them a show."

She eyed him warily. "What do you mean?"

He extended a gloved hand. "Join me."

Picturing the scene now, he imagined the oohs and aahs of the children as he rode off with Felicity. A classic cowboy hero move. A movie brought to life on their doorstep. Some bit of light he could offer them.

And offer for himself, if he was being honest.

For a moment she didn't move. Just stood assessing him as he contemplated how to advance if this impromptu idea backfired.

Backing up a step, she hugged her cape tighter around her. "You're kidding."

Only one step back, though. She still seemed to be assessing, contemplating. Seizing the indecision, he pressed forward.

"Not at all. Ride with me." He might not have planned this, but suddenly he wanted her to join him as much as he wanted his next breath. "The horse trailer is just around the corner, but the children don't know that. You'll make their day without risking frostbite."

She chewed her bottom lip for so long he was sure she would say no and bolt back into the hospital. Then her chin jutted and she extended her gloved hand. He clasped it and as soon as she placed her foot in the stirrup, he gave a firm tug, maneuvering her in front of him in a smooth sweep. No question, she was at home on a horse. He hadn't expected to find this common ground with her. A pleasant surprise. And one he intended to make the most of.

As she straddled the horse, her bottom nestled against him in a sweet pressure that made his teeth ache. His arms slid forward to clasp the reins. Damn, she felt good, right here where she belonged.

He guided the horse forward with a quick *click,*

click. His thighs pressed against Felicity's legs. The closeness sent their chemistry into overload. His libido sure had a way of betraying him around this woman.

He knew this would be short-lived and she would raise those barriers in place soon enough. But for now, he let himself enjoy the sensations of being close to her, the rocking of the horse's gait generating a tantalizing friction of her body against his.

She glanced back at him, a wry smile on her face. "The children really did enjoy seeing you out here. Thank you for making the arrangement with Tally."

"I have to admit it was Marshall's idea when he heard Tally planned to read today. He said he would have done it, but he had an appointment." And now Conrad wondered if somehow his nephew had engineered this. Even if Felicity hadn't seen him out here on the horse, she would have heard about it. And while he was enjoying having her in his arms, he preferred to keep his family out of his relationships as much as possible.

Which posed a problem since Felicity was good friends with Marshall's fiancée. Hell, this was complicated.

He stopped Jackson to let a car ease past, the child in the backseat watching them with wide eyes. No doubt, the children in the hospital weren't the only ones noticing this impromptu jaunt.

"Well, thank you all the same for taking time off from the office to do this for the children."

Was it Conrad's imagination, or did she lean back into him more?

"I can work from home this evening." An image filled his mind of the two of them side by side on his sofa, laptops open. The thought caught him up short. That kind of shared time ventured into the relationship realm, something more than recreation or sex.

Jackson stopped at the end of the horse trailer, waiting. Conrad cleared his mind and focused on the present. He swung out of the saddle and held up a hand for Felicity, even though she could clearly handle a dismount on her own. He wanted to touch her again, to feel her fingers clasp his.

Then they were standing face-to-face, their breaths filling the air between them with puffy clouds that mingled, linked. He wanted to kiss her, but needed her to make the move. They were in her workplace and he knew better than to risk alienating her with a public spectacle.

He'd already pushed his luck with the shared horseback ride.

So he stepped back and took to heart the flash of disappointment in her eyes.

He removed the saddle and saddle pad from Jackson. To his horse's credit, he didn't need to slip the bridle off and tie him to the trailer. His palomino had no interest in bolting. He grabbed a hard brush, running it down the horse's strong frame. Jackson shook from ears to tail, seeming to enjoy the post-riding care. Grabbing the horse's halter, he unhooked the bridle, slid it down his arm. Conrad led Jackson into the trailer, aware of her gaze on him. She hadn't left, and that boded well. He didn't intend to let the opportunity pass.

"Can I convince you to warm up in the truck cab with me? I have a thermos of hot coffee." Latching the trailer door shut, he shot her a grin.

"Coffee…my weakness," she said with a rueful smile.

"I remember." He made a point of remembering everything about her.

And he intended to use whatever leverage he could in his quest to get her into his bed. Hopefully, sooner rather than later.

Climbing into Conrad's truck, Felicity wondered if *she* needed her head examined. As if things weren't complicated enough between them, now she had the meeting with Breanna to consider, too. Did Conrad know she would be sitting in? Still, she couldn't bring herself to ask him. She was enjoying this.

It was just a simple cup of coffee, she reminded herself. Except nothing about this man or her feelings for him were simple.

She was making just one reckless decision after another when it came to him. First, climbing on the horse—her body still tingled from the proximity. Then, agreeing to sit here in the close confines of the king cab, heater blasting and carrying the spicy scent of him.

But reason had left her right about the time she'd sat in front of him in the saddle, her body coming alive in a way that made her question her decision for distance. His effect on her was potent. Intoxicating. And damn near irresistible.

The truck wasn't the luxury SUV he usually drove. No, this was a working vehicle. While it appeared to be only a couple of years old, the truck had been used often and hard. The leather seats wore the look of many cleanings. Snow and ranch life had taken a toll.

His gaze landed on her toying with her lanyard. "That's a really pretty piece."

"Thank you. Lanyards are my weakness." She tried not to be aware of his eyes on her hand, which happened to be right at breast level. His look wasn't of the ogling sort or disrespectful, but it was…aware. "I have a collection of them."

He passed her a travel mug of coffee.

She let go of her necklace and took the drink, inhaling the java scent. "Heavenly. Thank you. I really needed this."

"Long day?"

She nodded, touched by his insight. "I was called in before breakfast for an emergency."

There had been an influx of eleven children admitted for signs of neglect after child services pulled them from a commune. The children would be placed in foster care. The intake had been emotional for all the staff, who had worked to reduce the stress for the already traumatized youths. Every time she thought she'd seen it all, she learned otherwise.

Conrad reached behind him to the backseat. "I have some power bars in my emergency kit."

"I snagged some fruit from the cafeteria. Thanks, though."

He dropped the bag back to the floorboards. "You're a tough lady to pamper."

"Or incredibly easy to pamper. Keep bringing me coffee like this." This wasn't hospital coffee. This was the good stuff.

And now she realized why she'd joined him. She needed this time away from the office and the strain of a rough day. Maybe it was unwise to indulge, but she wanted this momentary escape.

She searched for a way to extend their time together awhile longer. "Tell me what it was like growing up here."

Draping an arm along the back of the seat, he angled to face her. "Our dad and mom were busy building the business, so Jack and I didn't have a lot of supervision. Jack was expected to look out for me. Which he did. He took me horseback riding, fishing, hiking, kayaking. Wherever he went, he let me tag along."

"You two are close," she said, more to keep the conversation going than anything. She already knew how much his brother meant to him. His sense of family was one of the things that made him all the more tempting.

"We are. Although once he and Mary got married, because my parents were getting older, I was left to my own devices more."

"How so?" she asked, curious about Conrad as a little boy. She recalled there being about fifteen years between the brothers, so Conrad would have still been quite young then.

"Unlimited computer time. That's when I started playing the stock market."

"As a kid?" she asked in surprise.

A wry smile crossed his lips that she noticed more than she should.

"I used my father's profile."

"He didn't notice?" She wondered just how much he'd been left on his own. No wonder he'd reached out to his brother's family.

"Oh, Dad noticed…eventually. He saw the profit margins increase at a much higher rate." He shrugged. "So he set me up an account of my own and began loading it up with allowance money to invest—as long as I would give him tips."

"And that was the start of your company."

"Yes, ma'am."

He truly was a self-made man. She was impressed. *Surprised.*

"I seem to recall reading that you got a master's degree in engineering. But how did this young entrepreneurial side of you never make it into the press?" She swirled the hot coffee in the mug, tendrils of steam carrying a light scent of cinnamon and nutmeg.

"I prefer to keep a lower profile than my brother." He tapped her forehead. "What are you thinking?"

Her stomach fluttered at his touch, reminding her to proceed with caution despite the electricity he ignited in her skin. "I'm trying to decide if you're being honest or just trying to tell me what I want to hear."

His smile faded. "I'm always truthful. Always."

She realized she'd insulted him. He took his honor seriously. That…tempted her.

While she might have wanted to escape from the stress of work, this conversation was bringing a whole new host of problems. She was playing with fire.

Felicity drained her coffee and passed him the cup. "I should get back to work."

He took the mug, his fingers sliding around her wrist, holding her. "Felicity?"

The connection between them grew stronger, making her ache for more. Just a taste of him. Unable to resist, she swayed toward him, just a hint. But it was enough.

His head dipped and his mouth met hers, fully, firmly. He tasted of coffee and winter, of passion and confidence. And he set her senses on fire with a simple stroke of his tongue. As much as she tried to tell herself it was just a kiss…that her reaction was because of abstinence…this kiss, this man, moved her in a way she'd never felt before.

She gripped his coat and pulled him closer, the heat of him reaching even through his clothes, her gloves, into her veins. The world outside faded away, the truck cab a warm haven of isolation and temptation. Much longer and she would be begging him to take her home, and more.

Then a gust of warm air whispered between them and she realized he'd pulled away. She opened her eyes to find him studying her from the driver's seat. Unmistakable desire flamed in his gaze, but he was pulling away.

Giving her the space he'd promised?

That made her want him all the more.

He stepped out of the truck, walked around the hood to her side and opened her door. "I'll see you tomorrow."

His words were a promise.

One she couldn't bring herself to deny.

Walking away from kissing Felicity had been tough as hell.

But Conrad knew it was the right move. Aside from being in a public parking lot, he could sense she still wasn't ready to take things to the next level. He'd made too much progress to risk a setback by pushing too fast.

He was a patient man.

Patient, and frustrated.

Thank goodness he had the distraction of a family card game at his house. He'd rather play pool on his vintage table. There was something calming about the angles. Like riding, sizing up shots calmed him to his core. But today, he and his brother, Jack, opted to gather the Mikkelson and Steele men for cards. Chuck and his wife had moved to North Dakota, but they made use of the family's private jet for trips back to Alaska.

Playing games together was a carryover from Conrad's childhood when his brother taught him to play.

Jack Steele stood in front of the wet bar, whiskey glass in hand, talking on the cell phone to Jeannie.

Conrad moved to the high counter that separated Jack from him. The housekeeping staff had left an array of snack food on the tan-and-brown-flecked granite countertop. Grabbing a plate, Conrad shoveled some fresh Parmesan fries onto his plate, along with two Reuben sliders. He swiped a bottle of beer and made his way back to the table. He scooped fries into his mouth and chewed, trying to push the memory of Felicity's lips from his mind.

An unsuccessful venture.

Chuck filled his plate, pouring nuts and fries sky high. Opting for the sparkling seltzer water, he returned to the table.

Conrad sat in silence for a moment, listening to the cadence of his brother's laugh. It was good to hear that sound given the events of the last year and the strange reemergence of Brea. Conrad was grateful Felicity had agreed to sit in when Brea met with the family. He couldn't even begin to imagine what time apart from her birth family could do to a child who'd disappeared at her age.

A creak from the door to the game room cut through his thoughts. He cranked his head to the side to see a man in the door frame. Conrad did a double take as Royce entered.

Naomi's husband, a renowned, brilliant scientist who worked for the company, Royce was…eccentric and reclusive. He had proved a great father to the twins, but he tended to spend his downtime on solo activities rather than hanging out with the extended family.

His near-midnight-colored hair was slightly disheveled. Looked like he had come from hours of working out a formula. Knowing Royce's dedication to his work, Conrad's assessment was probably correct.

Conrad swiped the surprise from his face over the scientist's unexpected attendance. "You're joining us?"

Royce shrugged, dressed in a plain black sweater, opting for understatement always. "It's too cold for fishing." He looked at the spread, then moved for the fries and popped one into his mouth. "Hope you don't mind that I let myself in."

With Royce's showing up, all the men in the extended family were present. It would make for an interesting poker game. And a welcome distraction. "We rank better than freezing your ass off. Nice to know."

"I came for the beer." Royce nodded to Jack as he tucked away his cell phone and stepped behind the bar. "How's Aiden doing?"

"Haven't heard from him," Jack said tightly, pulling the tap handle down and filling the frosted glass.

Aiden had dropped out of college. The teen said he wanted to learn the family business from the ground up. His father had suggested working summers, then. Aiden had declined.

Conrad could see both sides.

Their dad had booted him and Jack out when they'd each turned eighteen. It had been tougher for Jack since he'd already been in love with Mary, ready to tie the knot. They'd started a family right away. Jack's education had taken long, hard hours.

Things had been easier for Conrad since he'd been on his own, using every free minute to study for higher scores, grateful his investment savvy could pay the bills. And he hadn't been providing for a family or reading bedtime stories to kids then.

Jack shot a glance Conrad's way. "Don't send him money."

Conrad held up his hands. "I have no intention of doing any such thing." He took a swig of his beer, savoring the hoppy notes from the seasonal brew. "I may take him out to dinner next time I'm on-site, but my wallet will stay otherwise closed."

As much as he'd filled his wish for kids with Jack's children, Conrad was 100 percent clear on who their father was.

At the poker table, Chuck began shuffling decks.

Conrad tipped his beer to Chuck. "How did the house hunting go?"

"We're going to build. We found the land we want, and now we're having an architect draw up plans. If all goes well, it should be done by the time our name comes up on the adoption list."

"That's great." Jack placed a plate of sliders and nuts on the table, his piercing eyes fixed on Chuck as he sat. "I hope you have a suite there for Jeannie, because once there's a grandchild, there'll be no prying her away."

Chuck smiled. "We're counting on it." He turned to his brother, Trystan, offering him the deck to cut. "How's Isabeau?"

"The doctor says she's doing well, but I gotta confess, her diabetes scares me." His hand shook as he stacked the cards again for Chuck to deal.

Conrad toyed with his chips in front of him as the cards were dealt. "If you need anything, just ask."

Trystan scrubbed a hand over his jaw. "Keep an eye on her during the meetings. Make sure she isn't overdoing."

"Consider me on it," Conrad said without hesitation.

Trystan smiled his thanks. "If there's anything I can do in return, let me know."

"I believe Marshall already beat you to the punch." Sliding his cards from the table, Conrad leaned back in his chair.

"What do you mean?" Trystan fanned the hand he'd been dealt.

"Sending me to the hospital to ride a horse during story time." Conrad slid a card to the center, while the others at the table looked on with undisguised interest.

Marshall tossed chips into the middle of the table. "I figured Felicity would either see or hear about it, which would bode well for you. Did it work?"

"She was impressed," Conrad admitted, memories of that kiss filling his mind.

Grinning, Marshall sipped the seltzer water. "I've always thought you two would make a nice couple."

Broderick leveled a shocked look at his brother. "Tally has certainly made a change in you."

Marshall swapped out two of his cards. "Uncle

Conrad has always been there for us. He deserves a family of his own."

"Hey," Conrad interjected. "We're talking about me dating Felicity. Neither of us is marriage material. We're married to our jobs, which makes us a good match for a relationship."

Marshall cocked an eyebrow. "Funny, but I always thought you were more self-aware than that."

Conrad scratched along the logo on the beer bottle. "I invited you all here for cards, not a gossip circle."

And in fast order, he won the hand. If only wiping the knowing looks off their faces could be that simple. Unlikely, since if he had his way, they would all be seeing a lot more of him with Felicity on his arm.

Five

Felicity fidgeted with her phone as she sat in the waiting area outside the Alaska Oil Barons Inc. conference room, the meeting with Breanna Steele still a half hour away. This confrontation had the potential for healing—but she feared that it was more likely to tear open old wounds. She'd arrived early to gather her thoughts, and be on hand to get a read off everyone as they arrived.

Nerves fluttered in her stomach over seeing Conrad, but she was determined not to let them distract her from helping this family. She still hoped to steer them to another counselor, but they'd reached out to her. The sound of footsteps drew her attention from her phone, unable to quell the leap of excitement over seeing Conrad today… Except it wasn't him.

Disappointment stung, too much. She'd definitely made the right choice in limiting her help to today's meeting. Objectivity was difficult around Conrad.

She forced a smile of welcome for Isabeau Mikkelson…and her friend Tally, who also happened to be Marshall Steele's fiancée.

The redheads could have been sisters. Certainly they'd formed a bond as future in-laws in the sprawling family. Did the Steeles and Mikkelsons know how lucky they were to have so much support not just from each other, but from their extended family? Hopefully Breanna would see that, too.

The weight of today's meeting returned to the forefront of Felicity's mind. While she had been trained to navigate difficult spaces such as this, her stomach knotted as she tried to imagine Breanna's position. Tried to unpack all the ways warring emotions probably tore at her.

All would be revealed soon enough.

Tally smiled with relief as she drew closer to Felicity. "Thank you for coming. It's reassuring to have you here."

Standing, Felicity tucked away her phone. "I'm glad to help however I can. There's no way anyone could be prepared for a situation like this."

Isabeau glanced over her shoulder as staff passed in the hallway. Pregnancy elevated her beauty, giving her the glow of a Madonna painting by one of the old masters. She sighed in her flowing maternity dress, her ruffled cap sleeves dipping down as her shoulders relaxed. She looked from Tally to Felicity, and said in a low voice, "The family is all so stalwart it worries me. They even scheduled a business meeting right after this to continue negotiations with the final candidate for the CEO position."

"It's not unusual for people to cling to the familiar when they feel other things are out of their control." Although Felicity had to question the wisdom of holding such an important business negotiation after what would undoubtedly be an emotionally draining meeting with Breanna Steele.

Isabeau eased down to sit in an overstuffed leather chair, one gentle hand atop her baby bump. Leaning into the plush leather with her other elbow, she rubbed her temple as she stretched her shapely legs. "We'll all feel better once the new CEO is in place. If our families can lock in a deal with Ward Benally, he's just the sort of take-charge guy who's needed right now. No one will need to 'babysit' him through the transition."

"I think he's got Marshall's vote, too. Although, speaking of take-charge guys..." Tally's mouth pulled up into a wily smile as she turned toward Felicity. Tally rested a hip against the reception table, her sleeve brushing against the arrangement of wildflowers. "What's up with you and Conrad? You can tell me to mind my own business and I won't be offended."

Felicity weighed her words and opted for simple and succinct, hoping to quell any matchmaking. "He wants a relationship. I need to focus on my career. There's nothing up."

Tally scrunched her nose and tapped Felicity's arm. "You know what they say about all work and no play…"

Isabeau laughed softly, her eyes twinkling. "And the chemistry between you two lights up a room."

Bracing her shoulders, Felicity needed to nip this kind of talk in the bud. She knew how to wield silence as well as words. After giving herself a moment to gather her thoughts, she continued, "Did you bring me here to help or to match-make?"

Isabeau's smile faded and she touched Felicity's wrist. "I would have asked you to come today regardless."

"Okay, then," Felicity said, Isabeau's words bringing the importance of this meeting back into focus. "Let's concentrate on that."

Voices from the corridor had them all sitting upright fast, heads swiveling toward the new arrivals. Felicity's skin tingled as she heard Conrad's deep timbre stroke her senses as he spoke to his brother.

The two men paused in the archway, immersed in discussion. Felicity's gaze was drawn to Conrad's profile. His handsome face was tense, lips drawn taut in a line as his features attempted neutrality. But she'd been trained to read people. She could feel the tension radiating from him over the confrontation to come. But he stood shoulder to shoulder with his brother, head dipped, listening to Jack.

That show of support touched her. Deeply. The ability to put aside personal pain to help another wasn't as common as it should be.

As if he could feel her watching him, Conrad looked up, his gaze colliding with Felicity's. The emotion in his eyes was so raw, beyond what she'd even suspected. She ached to reach out and comfort him. It was all she could do to keep her feet planted.

Tally cleared her throat. "Nothing up between the two of you, huh?"

Felicity glanced at her friend, realizing she wasn't fooling anyone, least of all herself. How ironic that only moments after she'd insisted her devotion to work precluded any relationship, she was so tempted by Conrad.

She hadn't been good about articulating issues to her ex-husband, so she'd been careful to face her problems—at work and in her personal life—head-on since then. But with Conrad, she'd been so certain that he was the problem and kept throwing herself in his path to deal with him. Only to realize Conrad wasn't the issue so much as her—she was damned attracted to him and there was no escaping that fact.

She needed to make it clear to the family that,

based on how things went today, she would make a recommendation for another counselor to see them through this tense time with Breanna.

Because in order to get Conrad out of her head, Felicity was going to have to confront the attraction head-on, sooner rather than later.

Brea was sick to her stomach.

Even knowing this meeting was exactly what she wanted, what she'd planned for, bracing herself to enter that conference room full of Steeles and Mikkelsons rattled her. Having her lawyer at her side didn't ease the knot of panic in her chest.

The last time she'd been here, she'd hidden her true identity. She hadn't relied on her family not recognizing her as an adult. She'd bleached her hair and wore colored contact lens. That disguise had offered a buffer between her emotions and her return, a protective shield. Now, with her real name revealed and her hair dark again, she felt exposed walking into a meeting as…herself.

Whatever that meant.

She'd once considered herself a Steele, first and foremost, part of a big, loving family. Then her world had been rocked by the accident. Doctors told her the concussion she'd suffered was severe, a part of what made processing all that happened immediately afterward so difficult.

But she couldn't deny the truth that someone connected to her family had killed her mother, and almost killed Brea in the process. She didn't know whom to trust. She only knew now that her adoptive parents were dead, and she was questioning everything.

And she couldn't rest until she had answers, safety and, most of all, resolution. She needed to move forward with her life and she couldn't do that until she made peace with her past.

She also needed to make sure the company didn't prosecute her for leaking corporate secrets. She hadn't planned on doing that when she'd wrangled her way into the organization undercover. She still wasn't sure how her better judgment had gotten away from her. She'd been so caught up in a need for revenge and wanting to strike back. That time was still a fog of frustration, betrayal…and heartbreak.

Somehow, she'd let her emotions get the better of her. Anxiety had her shaking in her ankle boots. Was she sweating? Her whole body felt on fire. But she didn't dare show her apprehension by dabbing her brow to check.

Throat running dry, her lips parched, she attempted to find something here and now to anchor her. Finding something here and now in this place though? That was part of the problem.

Hooking her thumbs into the sleeves of her black turtleneck sweater, she did her best to channel her alter ego, the one who had provided a degree of armor last time she was here. With her family.

With determination she did not feel, she gripped the stainless steel door handle leading to the Steele conference room. Her lawyer kept even stride next to her. Brea tried to imagine herself like some warrior princess striding into the battlefield with her loyal second in command.

She worked to keep her eyes off the faces of the people gathered at the long, dark conference table. People she'd once called family. She'd accomplished putting them out of her mind for the years she'd been away. She'd slowly stopped thinking of them in the interim. Her adoptive parents had helped her with that, reminding her that letting go of those connections was important for healing.

These people were all her enemies, after all. One of them was most likely responsible for the accident that had thrown her life into disarray and killed her mother. It was best not to linger on any good memories. She definitely couldn't afford to let emotions get the better of her now.

She continued her measured walk to the table. Chin high. Resolved. She fought down the rise of nerves that threatened to undo her calculated mask of neutrality and power.

Which became harder with the weight of their gazes on her. Unable to resist, finally, she looked into the eyes of her family.

She lingered first on her uncle Conrad. The strangeness of the supposedly familial connection chilling her blood. Images of someone else's life flashed in her mind. Her uncle helping her onto a paint horse, teaching her where to place her weight in the saddle. Her twin sister's peal of laughter and whispered secrets. Brea knew better than to let her eyes linger on Naomi, the toughest one of all to forget.

An avalanche of half-formed memories threatened to bury her alive. Right here. In the thick tan carpet of the Steele boardroom. Her eyes flicked away from her family members at the table, searching the visible Alaskan wilderness beyond the glass planes.

Part of her wanted to spin away and make a run for it. Cast aside all identities, all knowledge. Make her life in a small cabin in the woods. Become a recluse, take up knitting or writing. Avoid people and all the pain they caused.

But Brea bit down on the impulse to flee, made herself look at each person. But then her gaze landed on her father. His sharp blue eyes full of pain—and tenderness. The tightness in her chest intensified. She would do better to keep her eyes off those from her past.

She'd seen them all before during her time here working as Milla Jones. But this was the first time they'd *really* seen her, knowing who she was.

Would she have ever had the nerve to come back

if they hadn't run the DNA test and found out her true identity?

She honestly wasn't sure.

Stanley Hawkins, her attorney, pulled out a chair for her. With an outward control she was far from feeling inside, Brea sank into the chair. The young lawyer took his seat next to her, and the rest of the group followed suit.

Her attorney, who'd taken the case pro bono, gave her an almost imperceptible nod of encouragement before he placed a manila folder in front of him, his green eyes as wild as a jungle. Formidable for someone his age, Stanley did not back down. He cleared his throat after what seemed like years of suffocating silence.

"I have a statement prepared by my client." He passed pages around the table. "It details her life after the airplane crash."

A flash of pain chased across Jack's face. Real? Or affected for the others at the table? "Is this really necessary? I had hoped we could talk through what happened, rather than read about it."

Her attorney shook his head, as she'd been clear with him about what she wished. "My client is present and cooperating, in spite of her concerns about her personal safety."

She tried not to notice how many of those seated winced at his words. Could they really not know that fear for her life motivated her? She'd been so busy protecting herself, she hadn't really considered that her siblings could have been snowed by their father, as well.

Jack bristled, his chest puffing out as he held the paper in a white-knuckled grip. He clung to it the way someone would hold on to the edge of a cliff. One miscalculation would mean a tumble to certain death.

"I don't know what happened to you in the years we were apart, but I hope with time you'll remember how very much you were—are—loved by your family. None of us would do anything to hurt you."

In the space of half of breath, Stanley leaned forward in his chair, putting his hand on top of the folder. "And yet someone did. Hearing that a Mikkelson could be involved in that long-ago plane crash does little to put my client's fears to rest. Perhaps it's time to end this for today."

"Everyone, let's breathe." A woman in the back corner of the room spoke up. She'd been sitting in the shadows, and Brea had missed noticing her when entering the room.

Brea leaned to whisper in her lawyer's ear. "Who is that?"

Before the attorney could ask, the woman scooted her chair closer. "Brea, I'm Felicity Hunt, a family friend. I'm also a counselor."

Brea's shoulders braced defensively. "If you're

here to force me to change my plan for this meeting, you're not going to succeed."

Felicity held up a hand. "Actually, I think you're right to handle this in the manner that you're most comfortable. This statement is a good place to start."

Brea eased back into her chair, without relaxing her guard. "All of you went to a lot of trouble to track down Milla Jones." If only they'd put forth that effort into investigating the crash. "You've found her—me. I'm here to cooperate." For her siblings' benefit, in the event that some could be trusted, she added, "I don't want to give the impression that I'm less than understanding of how stressful this is for each of you."

Jack held the paper in a tight grip. "Are there questions you would like to ask us?"

Plenty. But she was shaking so hard on the inside, she feared she would fly apart if she spoke. It was tougher than she realized, seeing them all with the truth out there between them. So many of her child-hood memories were a jumble. She loved her adop-tive parents…but she'd once thought she loved the people at this table, too.

Now? She didn't know what she felt except afraid.

And determined not to let that fear show.

Brea did her best to school her features, keeping her tightly linked hands under the table. Anything to mask the whir of emotions and half memories threatening to steal air from her lungs.

Her eyes slid to Naomi. To her twin. To the bond that felt as real as the grain of the wooden table beneath her palm. As steadying, too. Somehow, despite everything.

Naomi's face softened slightly, her jaw loosening as an audible breath escaped her lips. She nodded, her ponytail bobbing.

Swallowing, Brea readied herself. "I have a question about a memory. Or what I think is a memory, anyway. Naomi, maybe you could shed some light here?" Brea's voice felt strange in this too-still room. All around the table, her family leaned in.

"Of course. I'll do my best," Naomi vowed.

Pursing her lips together, Brea attempted to articulate the memory as best she could. "When our mother would tuck us in at night, did she sing us a song about bear cubs that chased the northern lights?"

Naomi blinked, surprised at the question. There were harder questions floating around Brea's brain, but for now? Brea needed to find something real to hold on to. While Naomi's loyalty to the people at this table would be stronger than anything for a long-lost sister...the connection between them was still undeniable. It had drawn Breanna to the hospital the night Naomi's twins were born, even though going there had been a risk.

"She did. Then she would turn on a night-light that simulated the colors of the northern lights on the ceiling. We would fall asleep staring at it, talking about all our dreams." Naomi's voice was gentle, mournful.

Brea didn't trust herself to speak. She couldn't afford to show vulnerability. She tapped her attorney's foot with hers in their prearranged cue for when she was ready—or needed—to end the meeting.

Her lawyer touched the back of her chair, standing. "I want to thank you all for this initial meeting. My client has had enough for the day."

Brea kept her eyes forward, letting the room become a blessed blur as she pushed the chair back from the table. Turned toward the door. Stanley again in perfect stride.

"We'll be in touch soon," Stanley called over his shoulder to the murmuring Steeles, who were poring over the written statement.

Writing that document had been hellish. But it was easier than speaking the details. She'd kept it as factual as possible, telling of the couple who'd saved her from the wreckage, protected her and brought her up as their own in their off-the-grid community.

Taking a shaky breath, she willed her legs to move faster. Needing to be away from the claustrophobic space of that conference room. From the questions that gnawed at her.

As they turned the corner near the elevator, Brea's heart dropped from chest to stomach. She'd caught the figure only in her peripheral vision, but she'd known him from before. From when she pretended to be Milla Jones. A towering, charismatic man who drew her attention by the sheer force of his eyes. A dangerous attraction, given he was a driven power broker. Just the sort of man—like her family—whom she would do well to steer clear of.

Ward Benally—rumored to be the new CEO of the company—strode past. Brea pressed the button impatiently. Needing fresh air and open sky more than before.

Apparently, it was business as usual around here, in spite of a meeting that had her struggling not to sink to her knees. She should have known better than to give her so-called family the benefit of the doubt.

Conrad braced his hands against the wet bar in the conference room, not sure how he was going to get through the business meeting with Ward Benally. But it was the only time the CEO candidate had been able to meet. Conrad reached for the crystal pitcher and poured himself a glass of water.

He was drained. Completely.

His neck was tight, his whole damn body tense, from the post-Brea conversation. From the pain evident in his brother and his brother's kids.

Seeing Brea today knocked the wind out of everyone. Even Conrad, who prided himself as the man who could swoop in with a sincere, well-timed gesture to sidestep tragedy.

Not today. Not even close.

It should be so simple. His niece was alive despite all the evidence suggesting otherwise. The family was reunited. But somehow, something so joyous had taken a dark turn. Reopened old wounds for his family and dealt new ones.

Brea's decision to end the meeting so quickly had left everyone rocked. Naomi had voiced fears that her answer had triggered the reaction, blaming herself for the way the meeting unfolded. Jack had been deathly silent, reminding Conrad how close they'd come to losing him in a riding accident a year ago. How much more strain could his brother's body take?

A hand on Conrad's shoulder pulled him back to the present. He turned to find Felicity watching him through concerned eyes. He'd wanted her here for his family, but found himself grateful there was someone here who saw this was hell for him, too.

He set aside his water glass. "Thank you for being here today."

Her hazel eyes softened. "I don't know how much help I was."

"After Brea left, you said all the right things to help the family manage their expectations." The meeting had been frustratingly short, with little from Breanna. He was most grateful for how Felicity had handled things afterward, quietly talking them through the aftermath.

She took a step closer, her silky brown hair sliding forward along her face. He resisted the urge to test the texture of a lock and tuck it behind her ear.

Her citrus scent filled his breaths, the flowing bells of the sleeves of her dress brushing the air as she moved past. She was all he saw, despite a room full of family filling chairs on the other side of the room.

"Conrad, you're so worried about them, but this has to be difficult for you, too."

Her words alone were a comfort, but he needed to keep his focus on his family. "Today was a big step." He drew in a deep breath. "I need to get to work. Thanks again. I don't know how to repay you."

"You can take me out to dinner tonight."

Her offer stunned him silent. He looked at her, trying to read her expression and find a reason for her about-face. Was she simply offering to help him talk through today's stressful reunion? Or did she want to talk about the hospital dinner party?

Regardless, it wasn't an opportunity he would let pass. His day from hell was finally looking up. "Consider it a date."

He intended to make this next meeting the shortest ever. In his mind, he was already out the door early, more than ready to spend an evening with the most captivating woman he'd ever met.

Six

Jack Steele had suffered the worst blows from life nearly twenty years ago when the plane had gone down with his wife and daughter on it. Today should have been the best day of his life with the return of his daughter from the dead. Instead, it was his second worst.

The weight of that strained meeting, of Breanna's accusatory expression, chilled him to his soul. His eyes closed tight against the pain, his head fell to rest in his hand. He'd been in a fog afterward, lasting through the entire hour afterward when Ward Benally had come in.

Jack was struggling still.

It had taken everything inside him to convince

Jeannie she should still accompany Isabeau and Trystan to the ultrasound. But he'd known how important it was to her. Family was everything.

Sinking lower, he pushed back in his rolling ergonomic leather chair, stopping inches away from the floor-to-ceiling recessed bookshelves that formed the wall behind him. Pivoting in the chair, he looked at a family photograph beneath one of the spotlights.

From before. When his family—and heart—were whole. In the photograph, Brea slung an arm around Broderick. An innocent, toothy grin on her face.

The picture seemed like pure fiction at this point. Jack's normally steady resolve balked. Spinning the chair forward and around, he saw ghosts of Brea everywhere. Saw her as a baby crawling across the plush rug, Mary making sure she didn't travel to the tile floor. Saw her at eight with her sleek silver book bag excitedly chattering about her science class.

An avalanche of memories that seemed irreconcilable with his present life.

What had happened to his daughter to make her turn her back on her family so soundly? She clearly remembered them all. How could all those years in a happy family mean nothing to her? The fear and rage radiating from her had been soul crushing.

He couldn't believe—or understand—how the child he and Mary had loved so deeply could have turned against him. The rest of the family had seemed to take comfort from the counselor present, but Jack had been too numb, too stunned to process anything that was said.

A tap on his door sent him sitting up straight again, scrubbing a hand through his hair to shake off his mood. His younger brother, Conrad, appeared, a force to be reckoned with in his well-tailored black suit and slightly loosened red tie.

Ever since Conrad was a kid, Jack had thought his brother moved like a jungle cat. Slow, determined strides. Predatory instinct in the boardroom. A silence that commanded respect. It was part of the reason they made a good team.

Conrad tucked into the room with that familiar swagger. "I thought you were cutting back on office hours to spend more time with that beautiful new wife of yours."

Jack hadn't expected to find love again after Mary died, and he certainly hadn't expected to fall for the matriarch of a rival family. But Jeannie had stolen his heart. Completely. And he knew she was as torn up about the rumors surrounding her family's involvement in the crash as he was. "I'm heading out soon."

"I would ask if you're okay, but there's no way anyone could be alright after what shook down today."

True enough. "Having Felicity present was a good idea." Even if he hadn't been in the right frame of mind to listen. "I'm just sorry that Breanna didn't give us an opening to talk at all."

"Give it time. She's here. That's a start," his brother said wisely.

Jack pinched the bridge of his nose, his eyes stinging with tears. "I know. I have my baby girl back. That's what matters most. Knowing she's alive…"

Jack appreciated that Conrad gave him the space to regain control. His brother had always been intuitive that way, seeming to understand that an overt sign of comfort would only make things worse. This silent support, his brother's way of being there and helping, had carried Jack through some of the most hellish times imaginable.

"Thank you, brother. There's no way I can repay you for all you've done for me over the years."

"You'd do the same for me," Conrad said with a half smile.

Jack liked to think so, but had he missed opportunities, being so wrapped up in his own life? "You look like you're on your way out. I don't want to keep you."

"I can stay awhile longer," Conrad said, but didn't sit.

"I'm good. Really." He eyed his brother. "Big plans?"

Conrad looked to the windows on the west wall for a moment as if considering the question. He cocked his head back to Jack. "Dinner out with Felicity."

Surprise lit through him. "I thought she gave you the boot. Glad things have turned around."

Conrad shook his head dismissively. "Thanks, but

I'm not here to talk about me. How are you doing? That was one helluva rough meeting earlier."

His brother had always been a good listener, but talking wouldn't fix this. "I'm fine. Really. And you're right that I should go home to my wife."

Conrad lingered, his bright blue eyes sharp and searching. "If you're sure."

Jack closed his laptop for emphasis. "Absolutely. And thank you."

"Anytime," Conrad said, backing toward the door, closing it behind him on the way out.

Jack sagged back in his chair again, not ready to go home, in spite of what he'd said to his brother. Jeannie was the epitome of support, but he couldn't miss the tension in her over rumors that her brother, Lyle, had somehow been involved in the crash. Jack loved her and trusted her implicitly. However, he couldn't expect her to remain totally objective when it came to her siblings. It was best not to burden her.

He would have to deal with this on his own. He just prayed he would get his daughter back without further damage to his family.

Her heart racing, Felicity swept on mascara.

She still couldn't believe she'd asked Conrad out after all her vows of swearing off relationships. But that tragic family reunion had tugged at her every last heartstring until she'd found herself reaching out to him now rather than later as she'd originally planned.

Committed, she was going to look her best. She dug through the modest array of makeup in her teal bag. Lately, she'd simplified her daily routine to moisturizer and mascara for work. She couldn't remember the last time she'd reached for fancier products or performed a more elaborate routine. Not since her divorce.

That thought almost made her drop her makeup bag in the trash.

Felicity picked up the simple pearl drop earrings. They were her favorite pair. She'd splurged when she'd graduated from her master's program. They were among her most valued possessions, and she broke them out only for special occasions. Like nondate dates with a handsome man.

Stomach fluttering, she pulled out the shimmery metallic powder and swept it onto her lids. She blinked, satisfied with the light glow. She added a brush of color along her cheekbones, then gave her lips a pop after applying the neutral color, surprised to find she was smiling.

Surprised, and guilt-ridden as she reflected on the emotional turmoil of the day. She hoped the Steeles would accept her recommendation for a counselor. They were going to need all the help they could get to navigate this reunion to a peaceful resolution.

But that was out of her control now. She should be

focused on her dinner date. Although now that she thought about it, she wondered if it had been selfish to ask for tonight. His family might need him. She reached for her phone to call him and reschedule, or maybe she should cancel—

The doorbell echoed through her apartment.

Her stomach flipped like she was a teenager rather than a mature woman. Backing from the bathroom mirror, she snagged a long silver necklace and draped it over her head, the tassel falling to rest against her black sweater.

She was halfway across the room before she realized she'd been almost running. So much so that she practically stumbled into the tall bookcase on the wall in the living room. Rocked the books on social inequity within the child care system that stood as stalwart companions in her tiny one-room apartment. Smoothing her sweater, she did her best to regain composure, her heels clacking on the wood floors as she moved away from the kitchen-living room toward the door.

She wasn't sure going on this date was wise. But ignoring the attraction hadn't worked. She needed to face it, face *him*, head-on.

Willing her breath to even out, she pulled open the door.

Conrad stood in the hallway, a box of candy in hand. His gaze skimmed her up and down, lingering on her red leather boots before sliding back up to meet her eyes. "Has anyone told you lately how gorgeous you are?"

His words shouldn't have the power to send her heart into overdrive, but they did. The more time she spent with him, the more she desired him. Could the reality possibly live up to the expectation building inside her?

Now there was a strange thought—hoping for bad sex so she could get over thinking about him.

She'd given Conrad an opening by asking for this date, and she couldn't deny she wanted to spend more time with him—wanted *him*—but she still needed to be careful. "Thank you for the compliment. Let me get my coat and we can be on our way."

He followed her inside. "You aren't smiling at the compliment."

"I'm flattered, truly." She pulled her overcoat from the hall closet.

"But…"

She needed to make sure he didn't read too much into this evening out. Hugging her coat, she turned back to face him. "I want to be fair to you."

"How about you let me worry about myself. I'm a big boy."

"Yes, you are." And just that fast, she realized she'd revealed how drawn she was to him in spite of everything she'd said. She couldn't pretend tonight had been a simple dinner invitation. In fact, nothing had been simple since the first time she'd seen him two months ago when she'd given Tally a ride home from volunteering at the hospital.

She couldn't pull her gaze away from the allure of his clear blue eyes. He passed her the black foil box of candy, gold bow glinting in the bright hall light. Their fingers brushed, and the air crackled with awareness.

She skimmed a finger along the intricate bow without taking the box. "I'm not sure what to make of this."

"Romance," he said, his voice husky.

"I thought you were romancing me with donations to the hospital." Was that breathy tone hers?

"At the celebrity auction? Yes, I was. Now, my part in the hospital program has taken on an official and professional angle. I can't let my feelings for you interfere with the financial decisions I make."

"Oh." Her eyes went wide.

"That wasn't what you were expecting to hear."

"Not at all," she had to admit. "But it's a good answer. An honorable one."

Inclining his head, he gestured to the box of candy. That wit shining in his blue eyes. Crackling and collapsing her senses until her focus was solely on him, the way his lips moved as they formed words.

"Then you'll accept the chocolates."

She laughed, clutching the box to her chest. "Try to pry them out of my hands."

He grinned back at her. "Tally told me you had a weakness for chocolate."

Felicity placed the candy on the half-moon table next to a succulent plant. "It's no fair how you keep getting all the inside scoop. What's your weakness?"

His eyes flamed. "You."

Her breath hitched in her chest as his head dipped. His mouth slanted over hers, warm, firm. Tingles spread through her at the first touch. She clenched her fingers in his jacket, anchoring herself in the wash of sensation, the fine fabric of his lapels and the sweep of his tongue over hers. The deeper she sank into the kiss, the more he brought her body alive again, the more she realized she was right in thinking this connection couldn't be ignored.

He brushed his mouth along hers a final time, lingering for another toe-curling moment before he backed away. "We should go before we're late for our reservation."

Conrad hadn't expected dinner with Felicity to flow so effortlessly, from appetizers to desserts. The conversation had been easy, entertaining, distracting him from thoughts of his niece and fractured family for long stretches at a time. No doubt, Felicity was a brilliant and engaging woman.

And she entranced the hell out of him.

Conrad held out her coat for her while they waited for the valet to bring his SUV around. He draped the satin-lined dark wool over her shoulders, his fingers brushing along her neck. The light scent of flowers tempted him to indulge in touching her longer.

As she swept her hair free from the collar, she looked over her shoulder at him, smiling. "Thank you for a lovely evening."

Was that a promise of more in her eyes? He was learning this woman was beyond predicting. He pushed the restaurant door open and followed her outside into the bitter cold under the awning. "Then let's do it again."

"Why don't we wait to see how this night together finishes?" The curve of her smile had his full undivided attention as their footfalls crunched into the snow-flecked sidewalk.

Now he was certain that was a promise of more and that prospect stopped him in his tracks on the salted walkway.

At his abrupt stop, she grabbed his arm fast. Her feet slipped on a slick patch of ice. He caught her, his arms clamping around her, hauling her against his chest. His heart hammered at how close she'd come to falling. Her hair teased his nose and he could have stood this way all night.

If it weren't for the fact they would freeze to death.

He scanned for his SUV and found it in line behind three other idling vehicles, waiting. Without another thought, he scooped her into his arms and began walking to his red SUV.

"You're going to slip on the ice," she gasped.

"You already did that." Conrad secured his hold, enjoying the sweet press of her hands gripping the lapels of his overcoat.

"Yes, I did slip. And it hurt. Please put me down before the same happens to you," she pleaded as they strode by a stretch limo. The passengers climbing inside whistled and called out to him and Felicity.

"Are you okay?" he asked, alarmed and mad at himself for not checking her over right away.

"Just twisted my ankle a little." Her breath was warm against his neck. "I can walk, though."

"You'll only risk more damage to your ankle. And I'm not going to fall."

"You sound confident."

"At least you didn't call me arrogant," he said with a half smile. "Although, you wouldn't be wrong."

"Do all the Steele males act this way?" she asked as they stopped beside his vehicle.

The valet stepped from behind the wheel, engine still running, and opened the passenger door.

Conrad turned to the side and angled her into the leather bucket seat. "By 'act this way,' do you mean helping a wounded individual make her way back to the car safely?"

Her laughter floated on the brisk breeze. "I can't believe you managed to say that with a straight face."

He closed her door and settled behind the wheel, heater blasting. "I told you. I'm arrogant."

"And yes, I acknowledge that you're charming, too." Her eyes glistened with a lightheartedness that still knocked him on his ass.

"Glad to hear my hard work's paying off." He wanted to stroke snow from her hair, to kiss her. But he needed to know. "How does your ankle feel? Do we need to go to the emergency room?"

She unzipped her boot and flexed her foot a couple of times. "Only a little sore. It's going to be fine."

He hauled his gaze off the slim line of her leg and onto the road as, finally, the cars began moving forward. "Glad to hear. I imagine you didn't get much practice walking on ice in Texas."

"That would be an accurate guess. I thought I'd gotten better, though, having lived here for seven winters." She looked at him sidelong.

He steered the SUV onto the road, headlights streaming ahead, windshield wipers sweeping snow off the windshield. "How is it our paths have never crossed before you brought Tally home from the hospital when her car broke down last month?"

Her fingertips tapped the glass lightly.

"You and I don't exactly run in the same social circles." Her voice was dry.

And hinted at more of those reservations on her part he'd hoped to have already overcome tonight.

"That's been entirely my loss," he said, and meant it.

She shifted in the seat, angling toward him. "You just don't ever let up, do you?"

"I'm only being honest." He could feel himself losing precious ground with her.

"Let's just say I'm not an overly trusting person by nature."

A challenge? He accepted. "Then I'll have to work on earning your trust."

She toyed with a lock of her hair, and he sensed an opportunity opening up between them again, especially with the way she leaned toward him.

Her head tipped to the side. "How do you intend to do that?"

"Let's start now. Ask me anything," he invited her. "And rely on those counselor skills of yours to determine if I'm being honest."

"Do you ever wish you'd left Alaska?"

He wondered at her reason for asking. But he'd promised her the truth and he would deliver. "My family's here. My business is here. I'm able to travel as much as I wish."

"You didn't answer my question." She warmed her hands in front of the heater vent.

"Ah, you're good at this." He respected her intelligence, her devotion to her job, her quick wit...hell, so many things, other than the fact she had been so determined to push him away. Hopefully, that was changing. "The answer is no, I don't wish I'd left. I'm happy here. It's my home."

"What are your favorite childhood memories growing up here?"

Why did she want to know? He searched for a reason, so he could figure out the best answer to roll out that would win her over. While he wasn't certain of her motivation for that question, he did know she regretted not having a family. "Jack would take me sledding. He was well past sledding days himself. Yet, he was patient with me."

The memory scrolled through his mind. His much older brother trekking them out to the best hill on Steele land. He always made it an adventure. Named the animal sounds they heard. Would stay out in the cold for hours.

"Where were your parents?"

"Working long hours. Taking long business trips." He gripped the steering wheel. "Our parents weren't neglectful, if that's what you're implying."

"That's how you and your brother grew so close?"

Yeah. His brother had damn near brought him up. Even picked him up and dropped him off from school most days. They were a tight family unit. Family, their father always said, was the cornerstone of everything. "He looked out for me."

"And you felt like you owed him," she prodded. Gently, but he felt the pressure of the statement.

"It's not a matter of owing anyone anything. It's just what we do for each other." He shot a glance her way. "What? You don't believe me?"

"I completely believe you." Her beautiful face was earnest, basking in the glow of the dash light. "It's just…well… I read about this kind of bond and I see it with siblings sometimes. I just didn't expect to hear this from you. You're lucky to have each other."

"Yes, we are." He knew she'd been in foster care, but he hadn't given thought to her biological family. "Do you have siblings?"

"I do. Half siblings. We were split up before we even finished elementary school." She scratched a fingernail along the armrest, repeatedly, the only sign that relayed how the discussion upset her. She always kept her emotions close to the vest. "We tried to keep in touch for a while, but other than the occasional message online, we've gone our separate ways. Actually, I have more contact with my last foster family."

How she'd built a life for herself in spite of everything that had been thrown her way was admirable. Rare. "You're so damn incredible, you steal my breath."

Her mouth spread into a wide smile. "Well, that's a good thing. Because as much as I've tried to ignore the attraction between us, I'm not having any luck."

He struggled to follow her shift from discussion of family and admirable character to…attraction. "Felicity—"

She pressed her fingertips to his lips. "Time to stop talking and take me to bed."

Seven

Felicity had known from the second she issued the dinner invitation to Conrad that they would very likely end up in bed together. And now that they were stumbling through her front door in a tangle of arms and legs and passion, she couldn't bring herself to regret the decision.

Her fingers dug into his shoulders as he pressed her against the hall wall. She stroked her booted foot along the back of his calf, looking forward to no barriers between them. The press of his body to hers with the solid wall of muscles and thick ridge of desire stirred the need inside her higher, hotter. She breathed in the lingering scent of his soap—sandalwood, patchouli and *man*.

Sliding her hands under his custom-fit jacket, she explored the breadth of his back, her nails scoring along the fine silk of his shirt. In her restless roving, her elbow bumped the hall table. The box of candy he'd brought earlier slid to the floor.

At the thud, he looked to the side. A smile creased his handsome face. Easing back a step, he leaned down to scoop up the wrapped box. "It's my pleasure to indulge your weakness. I'd like to learn what else you have a weakness for."

The promise in his words and in his blue eyes set her on fire, leaving her eager to learn the same about him. His mouth pressed to hers again as they made their way deeper into her apartment. The warm glide of his tongue brought hints of their after-dinner coffee and how easy the conversation had been between them. He was a bold, brilliant man and that attracted her every bit as much as his well-honed body.

She steered him, her body against his, kissing and walking and wanting. She wrestled his coat off, and her cape slid to the floor as they moved. Shedding the layer didn't begin to cool her off, however. As she stumbled past her tufted leather sofa, foot catching on the rug, her desire for this man went from a blaze to a wildfire.

Why had she ever thought this was a bad idea?

The connection between them was combustible and undeniable. She would indulge. Her heart was on lockdown. She deserved this much for herself.

Felicity saw her living room only in glimpses as she charted a course for her bedroom, moving quickly past the bookcases full of professional reading and a collection of her favorite romance novels. She bumped open her bedroom door, her haven.

Her place wasn't a high-end mansion like those his family owned. But it was hers. A space for decompressing after the stress and weight of social work. The downy blush comforter in her room accompanied three rows of pillows—just like a posh upscale hotel room. Her bedside table sported a half-read book, open and facedown to save her place. And yes, in spite of her personal life where happily-ever-after had ceased to be an option, she still gravitated to romance novels, books where life turned out for the best in spite of obstacles. She needed that uplifting message after the stress of her work life.

Right now, she was far from wanting to chill out, and her little decadences in the room would serve a new purpose. From the high-thread-count sheets to the essential oils diffuser steaming sweet lemongrass.

He tossed the candy on the bed, the box landing with a thump an instant before the backs of her knees hit the mattress. She fell into the soft give of the comforter, the toes of her leather boots just grazing the carpeted floor.

Kneeling, he tugged the zipper down one of her red boots, inching off her sock and kissing his way along her calf. Peeling away her restraint along with the leather. She flung her arms back, her eyes sliding closed as she savored the sensation of his mouth on her skin.

Imagined his lips all over her.

Anticipation notched higher.

He took his time slipping her out of her dress, kissing her shoulders and murmuring sweet words in her ear as he unveiled new places to his touch. She told herself to savor the moment, to relish every touch, but her fingers grew impatient. Her hands twisted in his shirttails when she tugged them free. Her lips lingered on the hard planes of his chest when she slid aside the garment.

With a hiss of breath between his teeth, he threw aside the rest of his clothes in a haphazard array on the floor. She elbowed up to take in the naked magnificence of him, from his broad shoulders to his lean hips. To his thick arousal against his six-pack stomach.

A smile of sensual intent lit his face an instant before he dropped to his knees again. Between her legs.

Her breath caught in anticipation. He nudged her wider, dipping his head to nuzzle, then give her the most intimate of kisses.

A breathy sigh carried a soft moan between her lips as her eyes slid closed. Her elbows gave way and she sagged back on the bed, surrendering to the magic of his touch and tongue. His hands skimmed upward to caress her breasts, his thumbs teasing and plucking her nipples into tight, tingling buds. She twisted her fists in the sheets, tension building. All too soon, she soared toward release, her body arching into each ripple of sensation pulsing through her.

Air teased over her bare flesh, every nerve ending alive and in the moment. She struggled to gather her thoughts enough to give him the pleasure he'd brought her. She elbowed up just as he angled over her to kiss her neck.

"Hold that thought," he said just before he popped a truffle into her mouth.

When had he opened the box? She must have languished longer than she'd thought after the incredible orgasm he'd given her. She let the truffle melt on her tongue, the creamy chocolate and raspberry filling saturating her taste buds.

Conrad angled away and she clasped his arm. "Where are you going?"

"Not far." He reached for his suit jacket. "I'm just getting protection."

"I have some in the bedside table." She reached for the drawer, her elbow bumping a jar of sunflowers and daisies. They breathed life into this space, pulling together the pale metallic lamps with beaded lampshades that cast a dusky, beckoning glow on the bed.

"So you planned for this," he said with a smile, a condom packet between his fingers.

"I had a strong sense this was a definite possibility." She picked up the open candy box and placed it beside the lamp. She couldn't resist scooping out two more truffles.

"Just so we're clear... I need to make sure you want this."

Angling up to sit beside him, her hip against his, she popped a truffle into his mouth to silence him. "If you recall, I asked you on the date. I want this. And I know my own mind."

"You're one hundred percent right about that."

She put the other truffle between her teeth, drawing him toward her to share. The candy and kiss blended, their legs tangling as he rolled on top of her.

The hard planes of his chest called to her fingers, the heat of his skin searing through her palms. He stayed in shape, but she'd already known that from their outing riding horses and the way he'd carried her to his SUV. Still, feeling the cut and ripple of those muscles without any barriers between them outdid her expectations.

She nipped his bottom lip. "How do you know just what to do to have me melting faster than those chocolates on my tongue?"

"I'm just listening to you, to your body."

A man who listened. She could get turned on by

that alone. And yet he brought that and so much more to the bedroom.

She slid her hand between them, stroking the length of him, learning the hard, velvet feel of him. His low growl of appreciation spurred her on until he angled away, panting. He tore open the condom packet and sheathed himself.

The intensity of his gaze, the urgency in his taut jaw, echoed the feelings swirling through her. She stroked her feet up his calves on her way to hook her legs around his waist. Open. Eager. For him. He thrust inside her, filling her not just with his body, but with a fresh wash of sensation. Her nerve endings sizzled to life in a way she'd been so long without.

In fact, right now, she couldn't recall ever experiencing this incredible kind of a connection. He was everything and yet also had her wanting more. More of him. More of this.

Her hips rolled against his, her breasts teased by the hair bristling his chest. Conrad's husky moans matched hers, their whispers of pleasure and encouragement creating a sensual symphony between them.

Conrad threaded his fingers through the tangled locks of her hair, kissing her. Or was she kissing him?

Both perhaps, because this was a meeting of equals between them.

And already she felt another wave of release ready to crash over her. She did her best to hold back, to hold on to this moment awhile longer, because truth be told, trusting in the future was hard as hell for her. But the building passion couldn't be denied. The orgasm slammed into her without warning, stronger than the one before, wrenching a cry of bliss from her throat. Her nails sunk into Conrad's shoulders, biting in with half-moons.

His breathing heavy, sweat dotting his brow, he followed her with his own completion, the muscles along his back tensing under her touch. His pleasure launched another ripple of aftershocks through her already sated body. Her arms slid from him in an exhausted glide to rest on the bed.

The scent of them lingered in the air, filling her every ragged gasp.

Before the perspiration cooled on her body, she wondered what the hell she'd done. Because no way was this a one-time deal. And that realization rocked her. So much so, she needed space to deal with it.

She pressed a kiss to his temple before easing out from under him. Already, she had to resist the urge to climb right back into his arms. "I'll make us some coffee before you go."

He sat up, sheet wrapped around his waist, his chest sporting the light scratches she'd left on his skin in the heat of the moment. "You're booting me out of your bed."

"I thought you would be relieved."

"Hell no." He sat on the edge of the bed, studying

her through narrowed eyes. "I think we could have an incredible affair."

"I agree, but I've been clear there can't be feelings involved between us." She searched for the words to explain why she was sending him away. "Sleeping over takes this to a level that, well, I'm not comfortable with."

"Understood." He clasped her hand, tugging her closer until she stood between his knees. "I can't see us being able to ignore that while we're working together on the hospital dinner."

She could see his point. "What exactly are you suggesting we do about it?"

"Let's call these next few weeks a no-pressure window of time to see each other, to be together." His thumb caressed the sensitive inside of her wrist over her racing pulse.

"And when the event is over, we go our separate ways? Just like that?"

"If that's what you want, then yes."

Could she trust him?

She wanted to. And she also wanted to have more nights like tonight with him—while keeping her heart safe. "What if I agree to that, but we still take things one day at a time?"

"For another chance to be with you? I say, hell yes." He tugged her onto his knee, his other hand sliding up to cup her breast. "What do you say we make use of your stash of condoms before we have that coffee?"

Even knowing she might regret it later, she sank back into the covers with Conrad, already losing herself in another chocolate-flavored kiss.

The next day, Conrad pulled up outside his brother's waterside mansion. Nestled up against an iced-over lake, the impressive structure seemed to double in size, its dynamic log-cabin-inspired reflection flickering on the glass-like surface of the water. Wind tore through the lone pine tree near the water's edge. A shiver in the tree's spine as it bowed forward.

Over coffee at four in the morning, Conrad had asked Felicity to join him for this family gathering and he was surprised she'd agreed. Especially since she'd held firm to her decision that he couldn't spend the night.

He'd gone home to shower, returning to pick her up just before lunch. He couldn't deny he was pleased to have her by his side today, at this luncheon around the indoor pool. No question, his brother needed to have the support of his family. In reality, all of them needed this, a positive get-together, after the stressful meeting with Brea.

Conrad shifted his SUV into Park as Felicity gathered her pool bag. "Thanks for coming along."

"I enjoy your family." She angled across the center console to kiss him quickly. "Just no PDAs when we're inside, please."

"Understood."

Sex with Felicity had been even more incredible than he'd expected—and his expectations had been mighty damn high. He'd half thought she would boot him out, and granted, she'd tried. But he'd been given this window of time with her and he intended to make the most of it.

He exited the SUV, boots punching through the snow as he made his way over to her door. Conrad's eyes locked with hers, that electric recognition passing between them. Offering his hand, he helped Felicity out of the car. Regretted that they had to make their way to the house's side entrance, which would lead to a glassed room, heated indoor pool and people. Even in the subdued touch her leather gloves provided, Conrad hungered for more time alone with her.

She stepped through the threshold, Conrad following her into the din of noise. His family milled around the indoor pool area. His youngest niece, Delaney, sat on the gray stones that flanked the pool, feet casually moving in the water. Her infectious peals of laughter echoed in the glass and wood hall.

A large table filled with hummus, pita, kalamata olives, pineapple and strawberry spears, juicy moose burgers and garlic lime chicken wings drew the attention of the majority of his family. His older brother, Jack, handed a red plate to Jeannie as she smiled at some private joke. Across the pool, near the floor-to-ceiling glass wall sporting a breathtaking view of snowcapped mountains and feathering pine trees, Isabeau lay out on a lounger, fanning herself. She rested a hand on her pregnant stomach, a calm smile on her face as Trystan kept her well stocked with water and food. Her service dog was tucked under the lounger, head on her paws, ears and face alert.

"You made it!" Jeannie exclaimed across the pool, her eyes bright and welcoming. Marshall clapped Conrad's back in greeting on the way to the array of food. Royce and Naomi laughed with the twins in the pool, doting over them with care. Broderick and Glenna nudged little Fleur in her baby float, their daughter squealing in delight, kicking her chubby legs underwater.

Felicity waved to all as she dashed for the changing room. Conrad opened a beer, taking a swig before he ducked into the other changing area. He stepped back out just as Felicity rounded the corner to return. Conrad's heart threatened to jump out of his chest and skip across the room.

Sexy as hell, Felicity walked toward him in a sleek emerald green one-piece with a plunging neckline. Her curves perfectly highlighted threw him back into memories of their night together. The taste of her on his lips. The suit and her beauty reminded him of a mermaid, a siren, luring him in.

Picking up flatware, Felicity joined him in line. She scooped hummus and pita onto her plate before adding skewers of pineapple and strawberry. Conrad placed a burger onto his own dish, feeling Felicity studying him through narrowed eyes.

He glanced at her. "Is there something wrong?"

Smiling, she gently brushed shoulders with him. "I'm just curious. This doesn't seem like your kind of party."

"Maybe I'm doing research for the next kids' story to read to sway you with my Machiavellian plan."

"Is that true?"

His levity fled. "This is my family. They're here. I'm here." He couldn't help wondering. "Why are you?"

"My friend invited me."

She'd called him a friend. That was progress of sorts, given they were also lovers. "Well, what a smart friend I am for wrangling the opportunity to spend the day with you in a swimsuit."

"I could say the same." She snapped the waistband of his swim trunks playfully, then blushed, looking around quickly to see if anyone had noticed.

His fingers ached to touch her, pull her in for a kiss. Given the scenario, his throat hummed with a rumble of appreciation, eyes locking hard with hers.

Conrad leaned in to steal a quick kiss from Felicity, but the erratic barking of Isabeau's dog interrupted him. Tearing his eyes from Felicity to the lounger across the pool, he watched Trystan's expression fill with concern as he launched to his feet, leaning over Isabeau. Jeannie was already across the pool. Shouting mixed in with the dog's increasingly urgent barks, launching panic.

Isabeau was going into premature labor.

A half hour after the family departed for the hospital in a fast caravan of vehicles, Brea still sat in her car, where she'd hunkered down and watched with binoculars from a hidden vantage point as they'd partied. She hadn't lived in that home long, her father having built it as they grew older and needed more space. But she'd still had time to make memories there.

She should take the rental car out of Park and leave, but she was so caught in the past, she hadn't been able to make that move. Hours had passed since she pulled her little sedan into this hidden spot near the gates. Like a hawk, she'd watched the Steele mansion with a macabre interest. Unable to tear herself away.

Waves of memories presented themselves to her. As each receded, she felt more hollow and raw. Once upon a time, she had dared Broderick to hang from the rafters of the boathouse like a bat. He'd done it, stalwart and brave in the middle of the night.

Once upon a time, she'd wanted to be a mermaid with her sisters in the indoor pool. Brea made them stay in the water practicing synchronized mermaid dives until their hands turned pruney.

Once upon a time, she had been happy there as a

Steele. In that house that loomed so far from her. A pain lodged in her chest that felt much like a knife piercing her ribs.

How could they all be so happy, so unaffected, when her world had been blown all apart?

She couldn't help but think her reappearance hadn't rocked them all that much. Sure, they wanted her around, but she wasn't one of them anymore. They'd moved on. The bond had been broken. Any joy in seeing her was…out of nostalgia.

That confirmation of her suspicions should have reassured her, but it just hurt. More than it should. She couldn't allow the Steeles to have this kind of power over her.

A three-knuckle tap on her passenger window disrupted her thoughts. She cranked her neck to the left. Ward Benally's fox-like gaze met hers.

As if her emotions weren't raw enough.

She spotted his sleek SUV parked a few feet ahead. She didn't know a lot about him, but if he was now a part of the Steele and Mikkelson corporate empire, then she'd best keep her guard up around him.

Tipping her chin, she rolled down the window, the cold air washing over her. Centering her as she met his deep blue eyes, which she cursed herself for noticing so acutely. "Yes?"

"Mind if I climb in with you before we talk? I'm

freezing my ass off out here." He glanced pointedly at the empty passenger seat.

She studied him for a moment, resisting the urge to tell him to go back to his own vehicle. The more she learned about him, the safer she would be. He wore a well-tailored coat that showed off his finely toned body. His brown hair covered mostly by the black stocking hat making him somehow even more attractive.

Since he'd already seen her lurking around, there was no need to bolt. The damage had been done. She might as well make the most of the inside scoop he could offer her on her family's world.

She tapped the locks and gestured to the passenger seat of her rental car. After he climbed in, she turned off the low-playing radio and turned up the heat. "So you're the CEO who's going to take over my father's company."

He folded into the bucket seat, his large frame a tight fit in the compact vehicle. "The business belongs to the shareholders, from both the Steele and Mikkelson corporations."

"I stand corrected." She conceded that point, but nothing more. He was an outsider and the Jack Steele she'd known growing up would never have turned his business over to a stranger. Another mystery. "You owe both my father and stepmother for your advancement."

"It's my understanding that none of your siblings

or your stepsiblings could be convinced to take on the job." He nodded, his angled jaw flexing.

She sat up straighter. "Are you implying there's a reason no one will step up?"

"A lot of reasons, I imagine." He fell silent, his eyes on her.

"What?" she asked, fidgeting uncomfortably.

That fox stare of his pinned her again. "I'm trying to figure you out."

"Why?" she fired back. "Are you interested?"

Whoa. Where had that come from?

"Only interested in the chaos you're causing." He tapped the dash decisively. "My first priority, if I decide to accept the job, will be getting this company on stable footing again. What is your priority?"

Brea let her smile turn as icy as her Alaskan birthright. "What do you think?"

He removed the stocking cap, his textured brown hair standing on edge. Disheveled in a way that made Brea want to run her fingers through it.

His hands squeezed around the knit hat as he casually said in a gruff voice, "I'm guessing some kind of self-interest."

That surprised her. And intrigued her. "I appreciate how you don't tiptoe around me like my family does."

"That's because I don't care. And they do. Sadly. Because it doesn't seem like you give a damn about them."

"You don't know the first thing about me."

The heat in the air crackled between them as they stared at each other. His pointedness magnetized and enraged her.

"I know you've been avoiding the Steele family." He gestured to the mansion with his hat. "So I think it's strange that you're out here spying on them."

Spying? She didn't like that word at all. Or the sense that's how he saw her, as someone who lurked and stalked. "What you think isn't of significance to me. Is there something I can help you with?"

"Actually, yes. I need to find out where everyone is. I need to drop off some paperwork and no one's answering at the gate."

A tart laugh burst from her lips. She angled toward him, lowering her voice conspiratorially. "That's because they all just hauled out of here in a caravan of cars."

"And you're still hanging out because?" He didn't miss a stride, leaning in with a dramatic whisper of his own.

She blinked. She wasn't giving him any more information than necessary.

He lifted his hands innocently. "Okay, none of my business. Except for the fact that—as you said—I'm a lock to be the new CEO of Alaska Oil Barons Inc. And as the head of that company I think it's in my best interest to make sure you don't intend to do something that harms the business."

"Is that a threat?"

His head snapped back. "No. Not at all. I had no intention of giving off that impression."

"You can understand I'm not too trusting of the people around here."

He cocked an eyebrow. "And I'm sure you can understand why people around here aren't too trusting of you right now."

"Point made. Get out of my car."

"Can do. I need to figure out where that caravan of Steele vehicles was heading anyway." He tugged a lock of her hair. "Nice chatting with you, Breanna Steele."

The door slam vibrated the car and she wished she could have attributed the tingle she felt to the gust of wind that had blasted through. But she knew full well it was from that infuriating man.

A man she couldn't allow to distract her. Not now. Not when her future, her life, her sanity, was at stake.

Balancing a tray of coffees and a bag of pastries, Felicity channeled her college waitressing days as she moved into the waiting room. Carefully maneuvering around the green chairs that had seen better days, she distributed the sweets and coffee to Conrad's family. Appreciative nods and murmured thanks lifted up from all around.

Food and coffee would not mitigate the risk Isabeau was in as she labored a month early. The baby was coming, and the road to the safe delivery of the child would be hard fought.

Still, sitting idly by had never been Felicity's style. So she did the best she could to offer temporary distractions.

Felicity's heart was in her throat for this family as they worried about Isabeau. Trystan had been beating himself up for not insisting she never set foot out of bed, even though the doctor had assured them all had looked well at the last appointment.

They would feel better when that baby was in the world and Isabeau was healthy.

Marshall scooped up the last apple pastry, and Felicity slumped in one of the green chairs by Conrad. She'd sat here a year ago with the sister of one of her clients. A flashback to that day involuntarily played in her mind's eye, along with memories of her own marriage. About the time she'd wanted to start a family, her relationship had begun crumbling. She hadn't understood why then. But later realized that was when her husband's drug use had started.

She'd beaten herself up for a long time, not understanding how she—counseling professional— could have missed the signs. Only later, with some distance and proof, had she realized he was just that adept of a liar.

Tears stung her eyes as she stared at the board of baby photos from ward deliveries, all those healthy babies and happy families, all the joy around them now with other relatives getting news that everything went alright. She prayed for similar news today for this family as she watched nurses in scrubs scurry down the hallway.

Conrad blew into his cup of java. "Thank you for this. I appreciate your sticking around to help here."

Her hands moved on their own volition to stroke behind his ear. He leaned into the touch, settling into the chair more. Somehow, despite all the signs for why she didn't need this complication, she found herself unable to leave.

No. That wasn't quite right.

She didn't want to turn her back on this man. This kind, complicated man.

Felicity gently massaged his temple, hand tracing circles in his dark hair. "I figured you would want to sit with your family for updates, and if I hadn't come, you would have been the one making runs for coffee and pastries."

"Probably so." He let out a chuff of air, nodding.

A chime of bells dinged—an indication a baby had been delivered. The whole family turned toward the double doors. Waiting. But no doctors came. The room's collective hush faded. Whispers of conversations started again in their private nook where they couldn't be overheard.

"I enjoyed myself earlier." Felicity scooped her legs underneath her. She leaned against him. Their shoulders touching. "You're so good with the kids.

I know you say you've wanted to be there for your brother, but…"

"Why am I not married?" He supplied the obvious question.

"I don't mean to be rude or pushy…"

"You're certainly not the first to ask. It's a reasonable question and given the shift in things between us, you have every right to ask. I almost made it to the altar. We had the reception hall reserved…and she got cold feet."

She'd heard he'd had a very serious relationship in the past, but hadn't realized things had gone so far. She felt selfish thinking she'd had the corner on the market for painful pasts. "I'm sorry to hear that. What happened?"

"Why does it matter?" He bristled.

"I guess my career makes me ask questions without even thinking." She dunked a piece of the pastry in her coffee.

"Or as a means of keeping people from asking about your life. Maybe if I had asked more questions before, I would have understood you better."

She chewed the bite of pastry, grateful for the pause it gave her before answering. Conrad may not have her training, but he was sharp. Attentive. And perhaps all too close to the mark.

She cleared her throat with a sip of coffee, knowing she owed him the same kind of answers she sought from him. "I believe I was clear when I broke things off last Christmas. I had a rotten first marriage. I'm focused on my career, now more than ever, with the new position at the hospital."

He stretched his legs out in front of him, crossing his feet at the ankles. "Surely you can't think one bad man represents the entire male population. Your career must tell you otherwise."

"If that's true, what if I just don't like you? It's not like we went out for very long."

He laughed, locking eyes with her. "I believe we're past that now."

A blush heated her face. "Point taken."

He patted over his heart. "I think that may well be the nicest thing you've said to me."

"Considering I've pushed you away more often than not, I don't think that's saying much." A hint of regret stung as she thought of how forceful she'd been. She'd been pushing him away because of her own shadows.

"Then make it up to me by letting me take you home when we finish here."

As she weighed her answer, the bell chimed. A new baby. The doors opened and a nurse walked through, calling for them. "The doctor wanted me to let you know Isabeau is fine. And the baby boy is doing well for a preemie."

An eruption of cheers rivaling any college touchdown echoed in the waiting room. Felicity was swept into the movement of this family, exchanging hugs with not just Conrad, but the rest of the clan. A beautiful, happy family moment, and she cherished it. Felicity was caught right up in the middle of the celebration. If she wasn't careful, she would get caught up in this family the same way she'd gotten caught up in the man.

Eight

Three hours later, as she stepped into Conrad's home, Felicity wasn't any closer to stemming the excitement singing through her. There was just too much beauty in the day for the moment to be denied. The happiness made her realize how long it'd been since she felt this way—not bracing herself for the next storm life had to offer her.

After buffering herself from life for so long, this new ease and happiness had been unexpected. Strange, even. But she wasn't ready to let it go yet. She decided to savor it just awhile longer. Tomorrow would come all too quickly.

Right now, she wanted to ride the joy of knowing

the baby was okay. And yes, it had been a wonderful afternoon with Conrad.

Shrugging out of her red wool coat, Felicity stepped farther into the entryway. Drank in the small details she now recognized as Conrad's signature, understated style.

A wall of windows on the far side of the living room boasted a stunning vista of snowcapped mountains, eliminating any need for art. The room was dominated by nature, with sleek silver cliff sides jutting through and tall trees that fluttered in the wind. Even now, the view still took her breath away.

"This is…quite a place." Her whole apartment would fit in the living room with space to spare.

He tossed his Stetson on a coatrack hook. "Are we going to discuss my overprivileged life again?"

"No, I understand you made your own fortune." She passed her coat to him and placed her bag on the leather sofa.

"And I understand that my home life was stable, giving me advantages you didn't have," he said, his eyes cautious.

She couldn't help but think that despite all of Conrad's charm, he moved as warily through relationships as she did.

She did appreciate that he was trying to show her he'd heard her concerns, but she didn't want to hash through that now. She wanted to live in the moment. "How about we just deal with the present?"

"Sounds good to me." His hands fell to rest on her shoulders, massaging lightly.

She swayed nearer, drawn to the heat of his touch. "We'll be working together on the hospital event even more closely now that Isabeau's had her baby. Let's keep our focus on that, rather than the past."

His thumbs stroked along her collarbone in sensuous, slow swipes. "I'm not going to pretend last night didn't happen."

"Me either." She couldn't. What they'd experienced together was rare, and absolutely unforgettable. Still, she needed to be clear with him before she could feel comfortable indulging that attraction again. "But please understand, I'm not walking back on what I said about not being in the market for a long-term relationship."

"I heard you." His hands glided up to cup her face, fingers spearing in her hair. "And I also remember you suggested that since we can't avoid each other for the next three weeks, we might as well make the most of that time."

She couldn't agree more. Stepping into his embrace was so easy. So natural. Felicity arched up onto her toes just as his head lowered, their mouths meeting with ease and familiarity now, a perfect fit that stirred anticipation. Their bodies were in sync, the attraction so tangible neither of them seemed able to resist.

She wasn't sure how long it would take to see

this through, but she was determined to take all she could until then.

He tasted of the berry cobbler they'd had for dessert, topped with the best vanilla ice cream she'd ever had. Everything about this family brought the best of the best to even the simple pleasures of life. They weren't pretentious, but they were privileged. Quickly, she pushed away the thought that threatened to chill her and wriggled closer.

His hand slid down her arm in a delicious glide until he linked fingers with her, stepping back. "Follow me."

"What do you have in mind?"

"Trust me," he said, blue eyes full of irresistible intent.

Conrad tightened his grip on Felicity's hand. Leading her through his home, his mind set on exactly where he wanted to take her. During the entire party at his brother's place, Conrad had fantasized about getting Felicity into his own pool. Preferably, naked.

Images of her curved body, dark hair slick on her breasts, set his heart racing. Feeling her quickening pulse in their laced hands, he maneuvered through the living room, winding around the sectional and leather recliners. Her footfalls were soft against the thick rug on the hardwood floor as they passed the large dining table, which saw use only when he'd hosted holidays for his brother the year after he lost his wife and daughter.

Conrad pushed the thought aside, as he smoothly opened glass sliding doors to his own heated, enclosed pool area.

The space was private, even with glass walls. The tint was one-way, with an incredible view overlooking a cliff and snowcapped mountains in the distance. No one could approach from that side.

Felicity turned in a slow circle to take it all in, her red leather boots clicking on the mosaic tile flooring. "This space is breathtaking."

Her smile pleased him.

He couldn't take his gaze off her. "*You* are breathtaking."

A fire lit in her eyes as she stepped back to peel off her sweater dress. Inch by inch, she bunched the knit fabric up, revealing creamy skin one breath at a time. She whipped the dress the rest of the way over her head, tossing it onto a pool lounger and shaking her silky hair back into place. Static lifted strands in a shimmery electric halo around her slim face.

She was bold and beautiful as she stood in a black lace bra and panty set, still wearing her red leather boots.

His pulse hammered in his ears, all the blood rushing south. Fast. Leaving him hard with desire, his feet rooted to the spot as he watched her.

She reached behind her, unhooking her bra. The

straps slid forward along her arms, the cups holding on to her breasts for a moment before the scrap of lace fell to the tiled floor. She shimmied her panties down her legs and stepped out of them.

His breath hitched in his chest. Her beauty, confidence and sensuality lit up the room. Moving forward, he lifted both hands to sketch a finger along her collarbones, down to her breasts, the tightening buds encouraging him to continue. He traced farther, farther still until he dipped to stroke between her legs. Already, she was damp and ready for him. Her knees buckled and she grabbed his shoulders, her eyes sliding closed with a sigh.

He reclined her onto a padded poolside lounger to remove her boots as he'd done the first time they were together.

"I don't think I could ever grow tired of this." Her eyes blinked open, the hazel depths full of shadows that reminded him of the time limit she'd put on their affair. The last thing he wanted was for her thoughts to already be jetting toward leaving.

He touched her lips, silencing her, before he stepped back to toss away his own clothes in a speedy pile. He snagged a condom from his suit pocket before lowering himself over her. She beckoned him with open arms, her knees parting. He didn't need any further invitation. Stretching over her, he pressed between her legs, inside her welcoming body.

Her sighs, the roll of her hips, the caress of her

skin against his—all of it teased his senses. The water feature tapped an erratic symphony that matched his speeding heart—her answering heartbeat against his chest.

He lost himself in sensation, in her floral scent and the mist of salt water from his pool. The glide of their bodies against each other as perspiration dotted their skin. He waited what felt like an eternity to get her into his bed since the first time he'd laid eyes on her. In reality, it had barely been two months. But time had shifted in that moment when he'd seen her, his every waking and sleeping thought leading him to pursue her.

And he didn't intend to let up. This woman was one in a million, a class act with sex appeal that seared him clear through. He thrust deeper, her legs hitching up and around his waist, drawing him closer still as her hips encouraged him on.

A flush spread over her skin, her head pressing back into the cushions from side to side. Seeing the oncoming tide of her completion sent a fresh surge of pleasure through him. Her moan grew louder, becoming a cry of bliss. The warm clasp of her pulsed around him, bringing him to a throbbing finish that rocked him to the core. His arms collapsed and he fell to rest, blanketing her. His orgasm shook him once more, a shudder racking through him. Her hands on his back, his butt, teasing every last bit of sensation from his tingling nerve endings.

Once their labored breaths slowed, he hefted himself off Felicity and lifted her in his arms. She smiled up at him and looped her arms around his neck without a single protest, seeming to trust wherever he intended to take her.

He strode toward the pool, the tile cool against his bare feet. Carrying her down the steps, he plunged them both into the heated waters, the stone fountain feature spewing a shower into the deeper end. A saltwater pool, there was no chlorine to sting the air or skin. Just the glide of soft, warmed waves over them.

Neither of them spoke afterward. He smoothed her hair back, his forehead resting against hers, their breaths mingling. It had been an intense couple of days, with Brea's return, making love to this woman, the emergency C-section of Isabeau's baby boy.

And he couldn't deny having Felicity by his side had made all of it easier. She'd supported him. It was also an unusual dynamic since he was more often on the giving end. He wasn't quite sure what to make of that. And he wasn't in any state of mind to untangle those thoughts.

Felicity had a hold over him that exceeded anything he'd felt for any other woman. And that scared the hell out of him.

Felicity stared at her lover as he slept, his head denting the pillow beside her. After they had sex by the pool, they'd swam playfully, then showered together. Her body was mellow and sated, her still-damp hair gathered in a loose knot on her head.

She hadn't meant to stay through the night, but time had slipped away as they'd made love again and talked into the early hours. The long dark nights of an Alaskan winter had made it all too easy to lose sight of the approaching morning.

In the gentle rays of moonlight streaming through the window across his room, Conrad looked peaceful. Sexy and chiseled, but the light revealed a softer side of him. The kind of light that sent her mind wandering, probing possibilities. A seductive space to imagine.

Combing her fingers through his coarse hair, she could swear that he leaned into her touch. She took in the strength of his body as she sank into the down feather pillows. For the span of a breath, she allowed herself to picture an impossible future. One where she moved through this space—Conrad's space—dressed in this room of cool grays and breathtaking views. Shared a bed and a life with this bewitching man. What it might be like. What that life would taste like, fresh berries, his lips, mountain air singed with pine scent... Incredible sex, a shared interest in supporting and bettering others.

She'd prided herself on dating people with less traditional good looks. But there was no denying that Conrad had a movie star face, with his strong cheekbones and jawline.

Even the hints of gray in his hair grew in with perfection, just the right amount sprinkling at the temples.

He was a handsome man, completely comfortable in his own skin.

Given he was the younger brother of an immensely successful businessman, Felicity marveled all the more. She would have expected a younger brother to struggle at least a bit to find his place in the world.

Not Conrad. He'd built his own business, while still supporting his brother's business and personal ventures. Maybe that was why Conrad had never tried marriage again after the failed engagement.

Who the hell would have time for more? His life was packed.

Or maybe she was just giving herself a convenient out for keeping barriers between them.

Sliding out of the bright white, high-thread-count sheets, she landed gently on the tan carpet. Toes luxuriated in the softness as she gathered her clothes from the nearby chair.

Before they slipped into bed last night, Conrad offered her a tour of his place. She'd never been in a home quite this large or extravagant. No question, the home was amazing, from the pool to the media room. He even had a workout area and indoor basketball court, perfect for enjoying during long Alaska winters.

She knew her worth. Understood that she was a smart woman with a great career. A catch in her own right.

Still, there were times she wondered what drew Conrad to pursue her so intensely. He could have anyone he wanted. Certainly, even someone much younger. She'd half expected that after their first time together, the thrill of the chase would fade for him and he would walk away.

But he hadn't.

The previous morning had brought the invitation to join him at his family's get-together. And then here, as well. He'd been attentive, while giving her space, a difficult balance to achieve.

Slipping into her black lace panties, she cast a casual glance back at Conrad. His chest steadily rising and falling.

She wasn't sure what to make of him.

And until she figured that out, she needed to maintain some distance between them. Sitting to hook her bra behind her back, she willed her mind and body to sync.

She needed to hold strong to her decision to keep this simple. She would not—could not—linger for a romantic breakfast.

She tugged on her sweater dress, then resecured her damp top knot. Hair she'd defiantly grown out after her messy divorce. Her ex had preferred her with a shoulder-length bob. When the divorce process started, she'd resolved to do something small and symbolic for herself. So she let her hair grow long and wild. A reminder to herself she'd never be compromised or caged like that again.

A rustle of the sheets gave her only a moment's warning before he spoke.

"How about coffee before you leave? I wouldn't want you falling asleep behind the wheel." He swung his legs from the bed. "Or better yet, I'll call for a driver."

His hair was mussed from her fingers, his jaw peppered with a five o'clock shadow. He was every bit as appealing as when he was decked out in a custom-fit suit. She needed to get moving or she would be tempted to crawl back into that bed for the rest of the night...maybe longer.

"There's no need for that." She pulled on her fluffy socks and tall boots, ready to find that distance she'd been thinking about. "I didn't mean to wake you."

"More like you were sneaking off. No need to do that. I heard you loud and clear about your 'no sleepovers' rule."

"Well, technically I did sleep over, even if I didn't fall asleep." She dropped a quick kiss on his mouth. "But I also meant what I said about making the most of this time while we're planning the hospital event. Avoiding the attraction would make those meetings miserable."

"I'm glad we're in agreement on that."

She pointed to his phone. "Could you check for any message about Isabeau and the baby?"

"Of course." He scooped his cell off the dresser and thumbed through. "All's going well. He's still on oxygen, but is eating well and alert. Would you like to see some photos?"

"Yes, please." She rushed to his side and leaned in to look at the screen. The pinkish newborn had oxygen tubes around his tiny face in the stark white warmer. A fighter already. At five and a half pounds, so tiny, but bigger than they'd feared. A sting of regret pinched her as she thought of the children she'd once dreamed of having.

"They've named him Everett, which means strong."

She touched the screen lightly. "He's beautiful. Congratulations, Uncle Conrad."

"Great-uncle. Good God, that makes me sound old," he said, although he showed not the least bit of vanity. Just a wry laugh.

"You're a good bit younger than your brother. You could still have children of your own." How had she let that loaded statement slip from her lips? Especially when she'd vowed to keep things simple between them. This was not a simple question, by a long shot. Yet she couldn't help but wonder how he felt about not ever being a father.

"What about you?" he dodged her question, his face inscrutable.

She weighed her answer, trying to decide whether to speak or run far and fast. She opted for the truth. "I've considered adopting an older child. The timing just hasn't been right."

He stroked a strand of her hair back, cupping the side of her face. "You would be a phenomenal mother."

The tender sincerity in his words touched her in a way that stirred her heart, too much.

"Thank you." She passed back his phone. "But this conversation has gotten entirely too serious for our ground rules about this affair."

He cupped her hips and drew her close. "Then by all means, let's not lose focus."

She laughed, appreciating that he didn't push the point. "I'll take that coffee, thank you."

"Lucky for you, I know exactly how you like it."

That wasn't the only preference he'd taken note of, and it didn't escape her attention. Was he that thoughtful? Or was she being played?

She hated being suspicious, but her instincts in the romance department had led her so horribly astray, she couldn't bring herself to let her guard down.

Living in the moment was far safer. She kissed him once more. "I'll take that coffee to go, please."

Jack rubbed the back of his neck, exhausted.

The day spent at the hospital visiting baby Everett, helping Trystan and Isabeau, had proved to Jack more than ever that it was time to hand over the reins of the business. He wanted—needed—to focus on his family. The sooner he could wrap up this call with Ward Benally, the better.

Leaning against one of the windowpanes on the wall of windows, Jack searched the lake while listening to Benally on speakerphone. Fading sunlight filtered through the blinds in Jack's private library, casting the room in a weary twilight glow. It matched his mood. His fingers rested on the blinds, opening up the view ever so slightly. As if there'd be a magic answer out there about winning back Brea if he could just see better.

If only it were so simple. If only anything made sense to him anymore.

Benally said his goodbyes on the other end of the phone.

"Thank you," Jack said. "Yes. We'll talk soon."

He placed the cell phone on the vintage desk. It had belonged to Jack's great-grandfather. A man Jack remembered in flashes. Images mostly, if he were being honest. But his grandfather had built and carved the wooden desk. Embedded scenes of the Alaskan tundra into the wood—elk, bears and cresting mountains. The well-worn wood gave Jack a sense of solidity.

The library served as a refuge for Jack and Jeannie as their ever-expanding family filtered in and out of the common areas of the house. He didn't mind retreating here. The walls were warmed by shelves of books and a plush, red Oriental rug. A crystal chandelier descended from a recessed point in the ceiling. Years ago, he'd painted that ceiling sky blue. A reminder of hope in the days after his family suffered unimaginable tragedy.

Jack was a detail man.

"Jack?" Jeannie called from the sofa, where she sat with boxes of papers at her feet. "Who was that on the phone? Was it something to do with Isabeau and the baby? I should get back to the hospital."

Jeannie gathered her blond hair—streaked with glistening gray—into a ponytail. A move Jack had learned to associate with action, unrest and intervention. Jeannie's bright blue eyes turned cloudy as worry set in her jaw.

He made fast tracks across the room to rest a hand on her shoulder, to reassure her. "Relax. That wasn't Trystan."

She pressed a hand to her chest in relief. "Thank heavens."

The NICU allowed only a limited number of visitors and Trystan and Isabeau had made it clear they wanted the nighttime alone to bond with their baby. Odds were in the infant's favor, but a tiny preemie was still a frightening proposition for all.

A call to come to the hospital would likely only mean the worst.

The fire crackled, adding warmth to the cool, fading light from the overcast sky. Snow fell harder, in bigger chunks outside as night approached. While he would drop everything to be at Trystan and Isabeau's side, a small pang of guilt and relief passed through him. Relief, because no call from the hospital meant the baby's stability. Guilt because he'd merely exchanged one crisis for another.

Their joint families could not seem to catch a break or a breather. His heart was heavy. The contents of Brea's written statement had only made things worse as she detailed the off-the-grid family who had rescued her at the crash site, then brought her up as their own.

The people who'd saved her had stolen her, and that was eating him up inside.

Jack dropped to sit beside Jeannie on the sofa. He would rather talk about anything except that damn statement. "That was Ward Benally. He had some questions for the board. He's a tough negotiator. We'll be lucky to get him."

Jeannie smiled warmly, her pink lips pressing together. She turned her head, running gentle fingers through his still-thick hair. "And you're truly alright with giving over control of the company to an outsider?"

She stroked from his head down to the nape of his neck. With an expert touch, she massaged him softly.

"Are you?" He brought her manicured hand over his lap, massaging her palms as he knew she enjoyed.

She leaned her head against his shoulder. "Well, none of our children seem interested in the position."

"They're forging their own paths. That's admirable." He tapped the boxes at her feet with his boot. "What's all of this?"

"I'm sorting through old letters from my brother and sister." She glanced at Jack with pain-filled eyes. "I don't want to believe that Lyle and Willa could have anything to do with what happened to your family. But I can't bury my head in the sand."

Her fear cut through him. While he wanted— needed—answers about the crash that had torn apart his family, he couldn't ignore how explosive those discoveries might be.

He leaned toward the box, sifting through the contents, aged paper brittle to the touch. As fragile as the future. "What are you expecting to find in these?"

"I don't know exactly. Maybe something that places them in the wrong place at the wrong time. Or even some hint that one of them had a connection to the airplane mechanic involved."

It had been quite a blow to realize Marshall's fiancée's father had been the mechanic who'd worked on the plane that fated flight. Tally's dad had killed himself out of guilt, so now they couldn't ask him if his role had been deliberate or accidental.

And if it had been deliberate, why? At whose instigation?

"Have you found anything?"

"Nothing concrete, I'm afraid. But there's a lot

here to sort through." The words practically leaped out of Jeannie's mouth.

"Can I help?"

"You could, but I'm not sure it's the best idea. You don't know them the way I do. You might miss a subtext, or a reference to something in our past that seems innocuous."

Suspicion lit. Was she trying to keep him away from those letters for another reason?

There was no denying that Jeannie's siblings had sketchy pasts. Her brother had been mixed up in shady deals more than once. And Willa had man problems and drug problems that had led her to give up her son, Trystan, for Jeannie to raise, and Jeannie had embraced the boy into the fold unreservedly. Most didn't even know he wasn't her biological son.

One thing Jack was certain of. If Jeannie's family had been in any way involved in that crash, Jeannie had no knowledge of it. He trusted her.

If only he could say the same about her siblings. Hell, even about her first husband.

And although Jack trusted her, how would any negative news about her family affect his children? Affect how they felt about Jeannie?

He'd thought the worst of their families' feud had passed once he and Jeannie had married. There was no way he could have foreseen anything like this.

A knot formed in Jack's throat. He'd been given this second chance at happiness, one he'd never expected to find. And he'd been so damned grateful. But how could he have guessed that the Mikkelson-Steele divide might have far darker depths than old mistrust or even corporate espionage?

Because he'd also never imagined that the return of his long-lost daughter could threaten to tear his marriage apart.

Nine

Conrad intended to make the most of the time he had left with Felicity planning the hospital charity dinner. Sleeping together had in no way eased the sensual tension during those working sessions. In fact, it only increased since now he knew just how good they were together.

Sitting beside her at the table in the Alaska Oil Barons Inc. boardroom, he reviewed the financial spreadsheet while she finalized the seating chart now that the RSVPs were locked down. Felicity left work early once a week for them to hammer out details for the event. The rest was accomplished between them by text and emails. This would be their final, in-person meeting since the hospital dinner was scheduled for the end of the week.

The gust from the heater vent carried the floral scent of her shampoo, tempting his every breath. The same scent that clung to his pillow after they were together.

For the past two weeks, he'd done his best to romance her out of bed, as well. Time was running out.

He'd taken her on a dinner cruise, with stunning glacier views. Another night, they'd gone to a dinner theater. He could still hear the melodic sound of her laughter echoing in his head, reverberations calling to mind her soft skin, her supple lips.

He stole a sidelong glance at her. She swiped along her tablet, rearranging the seating chart graphic with one hand. With the other, she popped chocolate-covered pretzels into her mouth. A gift he'd sent her. It made him smile to see he'd chosen well.

"I'm glad to see you stopped giving away my gifts to the nurses' station." He stole a chocolate pretzel from the dish.

She grimaced, hair falling in front of her slender face, calling attention to her angled jaw. "I didn't mean for you to know that."

"It was the nicest way I've ever been rejected," he said with a grin. "I'm glad we've moved past that, though."

For how long?

"You're spoiling me so much, I've had to double my time on the treadmill." She pulled the dish closer. "Not that I'm giving these up."

Her playfulness reignited the barely banked fire in him. He was enjoying the hell out of getting to know the different sides of her. "I'll have to look into chocolate coffees."

"You're going to melt me." She stroked her foot along his calf under the table, out of sight of anyone who might walk by the conference room.

He slid a hand down to caress her leg, the linen of her suit warmed from her body. "That's my intention."

Footsteps and conversation from the hall broke them apart quickly.

Part of the rules—no one could see them. No PDA. Felicity had held hard and fast to this.

Withdrawing his hand to the top of the long table in the Steele building, he already missed the feeling of her. She leaned forward in her office chair. Imperceptible to outside eyes. But a secretive flick of her eyes told a different story. Ever so slightly closer to him without arousing any kind of suspicion.

Fire burned in his blood.

He glanced at the seating chart. With the board of directors for the hospital and the Alaska Oil Barons Inc., with their plus-ones and special guests, the dinner party included just over one hundred. It would also mark the first official function for Ward Benally as the new CEO.

"What do you think of Ward Benally?"

"What I think doesn't matter." She swept her finger along the screen, shifting the table placements, swapping around the location for the musicians' stage. "The decision's already been made to move forward with the hire."

"So you don't like him?" he pressed.

"I've barely met the man," she answered. Evasively? Or diplomatically?

He'd learned that her years of social work made Felicity's face sometimes hard to read. She knew how to bury emotions and feelings. To center her features in an expression of neutrality. Conrad had learned to treat her unguarded emotions as a treasure.

"I'm curious about your impressions of him. You have good instincts." He meant what he said. The more time he spent with her, the more he enjoyed her beyond just sexual attraction. "Maybe it's from your training. Or maybe it's innate in you and that's what drew you to the profession. Regardless, I'm curious what you think."

Pushing her tablet away, she rolled back her chair, turning it toward him. "You want tips on how to handle him as the head of the company."

"Partly," he admitted, but couldn't deny it was more than that. "I also want to protect my brother. I'm not sure he's at the top of his game right now."

Her bright eyes met his. He felt her intelligence sparking as she nodded.

"That would be understandable for your brother, given the shock of finding out his daughter's alive—and that by her own admission in her written statement, she chose not to contact him."

Conrad had trouble wrapping his brain around Brea's recounting of having lived with a family off the grid who had claimed her as their own. It was… too much. He needed to focus on what he could handle, control and change.

The present.

"I need to be sure Benally is the right person to take over this company my family has poured their hearts into."

Felicity splayed her hands on the table, her voice soft yet empathetic. "As I understand it, the recommendation may have come from your brother, but you told me the board had to vote. The process of checks and balances is there for a reason."

True enough. It was still difficult to see his brother step down and pass over the company to someone out of the family. Although it felt hypocritical to complain when Conrad wasn't willing to take the helm either.

"Then what do you think of Benally?"

"Cutthroat businessman. He'll do well for your company," she said without hesitation.

"That simple?"

"He's the type who lives, eats and breathes the job. That's my impression."

Relief swept through him. "Okay, then. I can rest easy that the company will thrive."

"You trust my opinion that much?" Her mouth curved into a surprised smile.

He did. Her brain was every bit as sexy as the rest of her. "That's why I asked."

He lifted her hand and pressed a kiss to the inside of her wrist, giving her fingers a quick squeeze before letting go.

Her pupils widened in response. A surge of desire pumped through him, along with a vow to kiss every inch of her later when they were alone.

She cleared her throat and rolled her chair back to the conference table. "What are we going to do about entertainment since the string quartet bowed out?"

The cellist had come down with influenza, which had progressed into pneumonia. The others in the group were showing symptoms of the flu. Even if they recovered in time, the risk that one of them might be contagious was too great. The last place they needed to be performing was in a hospital full of vulnerable patients.

Conrad spun his smartphone on the conference table. "I called Ada Joy Powers and she tentatively committed as long as her agent confirms the scheduling works. Ada Joy was a big hit at the steampunk gala last November."

"Are you sure we can afford her and stay within budget? She's such a big name and the steampunk gala was a huge affair." Felicity studied the budget sheet before looking back up at him.

He hesitated before answering, but then she would find out eventually anyway. "I'm going to cover the cost. That will give us more money to apply to the menu."

"That's very generous of you."

"Something needed to happen fast. I took care of it. The expense is minor."

She laughed. "To you maybe." She tipped her head to the side, her silky hair fanning forward. "So you have Ada Joy Powers's personal number…"

Was she jealous? "Is that a question?"

"I know I've said I'm not interested in a long-term relationship, but I don't take sleeping together lightly." She clasped her hands together so tightly her knuckles went white. "I expect exclusivity for the time we're together."

Of all the things he could have predicted she would say, this wasn't on the list. But he was damn glad to hear it. "Good. Because so do I."

Her gaze locked with his, and he'd been with her long enough now to read her expression with total clarity.

She wanted him. Now. As much as he wanted her.

To hell with work.

He slid back his chair at the exact same moment she did the same. And he knew just where he intended to take her.

* * *

Felicity hadn't even known there was a penthouse apartment in the Alaska Oil Barons Inc. headquarters. Conrad told her it was for the occasions when one of the family had to work late.

He'd also said it was the nearest, fastest place he could bring her, this luxury condo with towering ceilings and an incredible view of the icy bay. Even this emergency stopover for the Steele and Mikkelson families could easily fit three of her apartments. Her heeled boots reverberated on the hardwood floor that connected the living room to a recessed kitchen and dining area. Intricate stonework on the walls framed the window overlooking the bay. And that was as much attention as she wanted to give the place.

The man in front of her was far more enticing.

She stroked the back of his neck as he tapped in a code locking the door. He continued to type along the panel, the fireplace glowing to life. The makings of an idyllic evening. The flames crackled, an echo she felt in the way Conrad's blue eyes fell on her. Even through his button-up shirt, Felicity could make out the suggestion of the hard planes of his chest. Over the past two weeks, his body had become seared in her memory. She craved him. On so many levels.

Enticed, she drew his head down to hers, his kiss intoxicating. His briefcase thudded to the hardwood floor along with her purse. They walked deeper into the living room, their legs tangling as they tugged at each other's clothes. His fingers made fast work of the buttons on her blouse. She swept aside his suit coat and tugged his crisp shirt free of the waistband, sighing with pleasure as she reached bare skin, stroking up his broad back.

Nibbling his way to her ear, he whispered, "I take it to mean you approve of the place."

She loosened his tie, then tugged it off. Slowly. One seductive inch at a time.

"Have you brought anyone else up here before?" She hated the words the moment they left her mouth, much like when she'd asked about Ada Joy. A spiral of doubt and pain opened beneath her, threatening the here and now. Years of hurt from her failed marriage screamed in her ears.

Felicity shut down the thoughts before they threatened to steal this moment from her. Time was running out until the dinner, her deadline for this relationship. She shouldn't care about his answer. What they had was casual.

She pressed her fingers to Conrad's lips. "Don't answer. Just kiss me."

She was a stronger woman than that. She didn't need affirmations.

He pulled her hand from his mouth. "I have not brought anyone here. Anytime I stayed in this place, I stayed alone."

His answer mattered. Too much. And the affirmation filled a hollow place inside her.

She forced herself to breathe. "Well, I'm happy you thought of it now."

"You're an inspiration."

"Get ready to be majorly inspired."

Her mind filled with possibilities, a list she intended to put to good use. She lost herself in the power of his kiss, his touch, pausing only to snag a condom from his wallet. The urgency pumping through her veins surprised her, given how often they'd been together over the past weeks. But rather than dulling the edge, sating the need, her desire for him ramped up. She couldn't get the rest of his clothes off fast enough. His discarded garments mixed with hers in a trail over the thick Persian rug until they were both bare, skin to skin.

This man undid her in so many ways. Keeping her boundaries in place around him was a constant battle, to the point she sometimes wondered why she bothered. He was so good at sliding right past them when she least expected it. Like when he'd asked her what she thought of the new CEO hire. As if he deeply valued her opinion.

Damn it. Enjoy the here and now.

She let go of the thoughts and just held on to him. She tapped him on the chest, nudging him toward the large-striped club chair.

Grasping the armrests, he sat, his gaze a blue flame heating over her. Setting her on fire. She stepped between his knees and took her time rolling the condom into place, savoring the feel and heat of him.

She straddled his lap, her hands flat against his chest. Her eyes locked on his, she eased herself down, taking him inside her. His chest rose and fell faster under her palms, his pulse quickening against her fingertips.

He gripped her hips, guiding her as she met him thrust for thrust. Deeper. Faster. Their speeding breaths synced, sweat glistening and slicking their flesh. Desire built inside her, crackling through her veins as hotly as the flames in the hearth. Her breasts grazed his chest, his bristly hair teasing her overly sensitive nipples to taut peaks.

This man moved her in a way none had before. Not even her ex-husband.

Again, she pushed away thoughts of the past and focused on the present, on taking the most from this moment. Savoring every blissful sensation. The future could be faced later.

She deserved this, wanted this, craved more. Everything.

And he delivered, intuitively knowing just where to touch and stroke her to the edge of completion, easing up, then bringing her to the brink all over again until she was frenzied with need. Unable to restrain herself any longer.

Her head fell back, her cries of pleasure riding each panting breath as her orgasm built, crested, crashed over her in a shimmer of sensation. He thrust once, twice more, his hoarse groan mixing with her sighs, his finish shuddering through him.

Sated, she sagged against his chest. His hands stroked along her back, quiet settling between them with an ease that should have been a good thing. Instead, it made her uneasy.

She rested her head on his shoulder, the scent of him so familiar now. They were sinking into a relationship, a real one, in spite of all her attempts otherwise. He was getting through to her. And as much as she wanted to trust him—to trust herself—that was easier said than done. Her heart had been broken beyond repair.

Felicity tried to enjoy the steady rise and fall of his chest. Tried to let the happiness of this moment touch her. Conrad ran a gentle hand up and down her spine, wrapping closer to her.

But she couldn't shake the fear of what came next. Of the way the boundaries needed to be drawn before irreparable damage touched her soul again.

She couldn't risk losing herself in this man. Not after how hard she had fought for her peace, her quiet but meaningful life.

She needed to get through to him—and herself—that this couldn't last.

An hour later, Conrad drew Felicity to his side, their legs tangled in the sheets. He'd been honest with her about never having brought anyone here before. He'd never been one to mix business and pleasure.

Something about Felicity had him throwing out his personal rule book from the first time he'd seen her.

The sex between them had been as amazing as ever, but he sensed something was bothering her. And with their timing running out, Conrad knew he needed to attend to the issue now.

She shivered against him and he pulled the downy comforter over them.

"Is that better?" he asked. A second fireplace sputtered dulled orange flames, bathing them in subdued light. The night sky glowed with winking stars and remnants of northern lights. He couldn't have asked for a better, more romantic setting on the spur of the moment.

"Perfect," she said, tipping her head back to smile at him. "I'm glad you brought me here."

Her words reassured him. Maybe he was just imagining that she was pulling away, just a flashback to his ex, which wasn't fair to Felicity. "And just in time. The place will be going to Ward Benally once he starts with the company. He made it a condition of accepting the job. Apparently, he's that much of a workaholic."

She laughed softly. "And you're not?"

His hand slid to cup the sweet curve of her bottom. "Work is the last thing on my mind right now."

"Luckily, we're on the same page." She teased her fingers along his chest.

"Hold that thought," he said, dropping a quick kiss on her lips before easing away. He slid from under the comforter, leaving the bed to get his briefcase from the living room. He returned, enjoying the way her eyes followed his every move.

"Is it something with work?" She sat up, hugging the sheet to her breasts.

Her loose hair in the firelight made her look like a statue of the goddess of the hunt. But this goddess was all flesh and fire.

He shook his head, dropping the briefcase on the foot of the bed. He typed in the password, then pulled it open. Anticipation pumped through him as he pulled out a long jewelry box with a ribbon.

"Another gift?" Her eyes lit with curiosity as she tentatively stroked the ribbon. "You already gave me the chocolate pretzels today."

"And I helped you eat most of them." He laughed a bit sheepishly as he sat on the bed.

She squinted at him, the blanket falling from her slender shoulders. Shadows danced across her bare body. His gaze skimmed from the soft curve of her breasts to the smile on her face. Damn. *Mesmerizing* didn't even begin to explain the effect Felicity had on him.

"We shared." She took the package from him tentatively. "Thank you. You're going to spoil me."

"I'm certainly trying." In countless ways, this woman astounded him.

She helped so many people; he enjoyed pampering her. He waited while she tugged the ribbon slowly, taking her time like a kid drawing out the excitement. She creaked open the box to reveal the gift.

A pearl lanyard for her hospital badge.

Her eyes lit with surprise—and appreciation. "Oh my goodness, this is so gorgeous. And truly thought-ful."

She drew the lengthy strand out of the box and slid it over her neck. The necklace settled between her breasts, the pearls luminescent against her creamy skin.

Conrad joined her in the bed again, knowing he would carry this vision of her in his mind every time he saw her wear it. "I'm glad you like it. I saw it when I picked up a gift for Everett." He grinned, thinking of the newest member of his ever-growing family.

"What did you choose for him?" She linked her fingers with Conrad's.

"A silver bank shaped like a bear." The baby had improved beyond even the doctors' best expectations and was going to be released from the hospital by the end of the week.

"That sounds precious." She draped a leg over his, leaning against the leather-padded headboard with him. "I know you've been a huge part of your nieces' and nephews' lives. But do you ever wish you had children of your own? You didn't answer when I asked earlier."

An image of a very different time clouded his mind. When he'd lain in bed with his fiancée, kissing her as they dreamed about having a full house, at least four kids, she'd laughed as she kissed his ear. How full his heart had been in that moment.

Despite the pain, Conrad considered Felicity's question. After a moment, he answered in a quiet voice. "My fiancée and I had planned on a large family, but when she walked away..." He shrugged. He hadn't been interested in revisiting an emotional shredder.

"It's not too late for you. Men have less of a biological clock than women."

He couldn't help but wonder... "Are you asking me to father a child with you?"

"No!" she said quickly, almost insultingly so, "no. I was just making conversation." A flush creeping over her face, she pulled back, swinging her legs off the bed. "I'm going to get something to drink. Can I bring something for you?"

He recognized her move for what it was—avoidance. He clasped her elbow. "Wait. Let's keep talking about this. You mentioned wanting to adopt an older child. Did your ex-husband object to that?"

She hesitated so long he thought she would leave anyway.

Then she sat on the bed again, hugging a pillow

to her stomach. "He was on board with as many children as I wanted."

"But…?"

Pain flashed through her hazel eyes, so intense it weighted the air and had him reaching for her.

She shook her head, her hold on the pillow tightening. "He was a drug addict."

Her grip on the pillow intensified. Even in the dull light, Conrad could make out the whites of her knuckles as her fingers dug in.

Shock stilled him. He'd known their marriage was troubled, but he never would have guessed this. He stayed silent, sensing she was on the edge of bolting if he said the wrong thing.

She chewed her bottom lip, then continued, "I didn't know for a long time because he was also an incredible liar. We'd been going to counseling for years and he even managed to fool the professionals…for a while. I know too well how a person can be manipulated into believing falsehoods. The lies are so insidious over time, the liar hones their skills, you start to doubt yourself and your perception of reality. It's frightening. And it's real."

The strength of her conviction—the old anger—leaped from her words, a hint of what she'd been through. He touched her arm, feeling inept to deal with the depth of her pain. Wishing he had more to offer. He barely stemmed the need to find her ex and make the bastard pay for hurting her.

"Felicity, I'm so sorry."

"That's not my point. I'm sharing it now to help you understand Brea as well—"

"We're not talking about Brea. This is about you."

"That's my past." She blinked fast, her face molding into the neutral expression that he'd seen her adopt for work.

In the past? Clearly it wasn't given how insistent she was on keeping him at arm's length.

"Are you so sure about that?"

She raised an eyebrow. "You're not in a position to preach about letting go of the past." She held up a hand. "Never mind. Forget I said that. I need to go home."

The pillow carelessly discarded, Felicity moved past him. A coldness descended in the room. A draft that rivaled the Alaskan weather outside. She walked back to the living room, and he followed to find her gathering her clothes.

He considered calling her on her avoidance, but outright confrontation didn't seem in his best interest, given the set of her shoulders. "It's late to be on the road."

"I'm an adult," she said, stepping into her panties and pulling on her bra. "I know how to drive in snow."

He could see the determination in her eyes, but no way was he letting her get behind the wheel when she was this upset. "And I'm a gentleman. I'll drive you."

She exhaled hard, deflating the pain as she gave a small nod.

Even as he saw the acceptance in her expression, he knew without question, when he took her home, she wouldn't be inviting him inside. He recognized the distancing look in her eyes all too well. He'd seen it before.

In the eyes of his ex, just before she'd walked out of his life.

Ten

Intellectually, Jack understood that he and Jeannie had so much to celebrate with the grandbaby's recovery and the company soon to settle in with a new CEO, which would give them all more time to enjoy their growing family.

Unfortunately, the intellectual understanding didn't reassure him the way it should.

As he sat in the hospital cafeteria with Jeannie for lunch, waiting for the doctor to finish checking Everett, Jack struggled to will away the impending sense of doom dogging him since he'd come across Jeannie sorting through that box of old letters. With each day that passed and no word from Brea or her lawyer, the frustration grew.

He needed to do something to fix things with his family. He just wanted peace and normalcy for all of them.

Cradling his coffee cup, Jack focused his attention on his wife. "Would you like me to get you something else to eat?"

Stress lined Jeannie's face, dark circles under her eyes as she picked at her salad. "This is fine, thank you. I'm just not that hungry."

"We can try somewhere more appetizing after we visit Everett."

She nodded noncommittally, dodging his gaze. Then her eyes widened as she looked past him and waved.

"Felicity?" Jeannie called, appearing grateful for the distraction. "Come join us."

The hospital social worker paused at the elevator, then strode toward them, carrying a small blue basket. She stopped at their table, lifting the gift. "I was going to drop off some things for Trystan and Isabeau, snacks and a little present to welcome Everett."

"That's thoughtful of you," Jeannie said. "We're going to plan a baby shower after Everett's released and settled in. I hope you'll be able to attend."

"I would like that, thank you." Felicity smiled warmly, but there was something…off…in her eyes that Jack couldn't quite pinpoint.

Something to do with Conrad?

A buzzing incoming text distracted Jack from

their conversation and he glanced at his cell. A message from Brea's lawyer. Jack's heart hammered with wariness.

He read through the message, then read it again in surprise.

Hope tugged at him like a magnet. Unease and mistrust jerked him back. The warring emotions cinched his shoulders tight, jaw tensing.

Jeannie touched his wrist. "Is everything alright?"

"It's a text from Brea's attorney." He tucked his phone back into his pocket, his body on autopilot. "She wants to attend the hospital charity dinner."

Jeannie gasped, pressing a hand to her chest. "I don't know what to say, what to think." She turned to Felicity. "What's your opinion?"

Felicity cradled the basket in her lap, her eyes concerned. "Are you asking me as a friend?"

Jack leaned forward with a heavy sigh, wanting to believe this was a positive sign but remembering too well the unrelenting anger in Brea's eyes. "I would welcome your feedback based on experience."

Felicity looked from one to the other, waiting as a couple walked past. Once their conversation was private again, she said, "Just so we're clear, I'm offering an opinion as a counselor, but not as your counselor."

Jeannie pushed away her salad. "What do you mean by not being our counselor?"

"I'm too close to you all to step into that role," she said apologetically. "I thought I made it clear when

I attended the first meeting that it was with the understanding the family would look into long-term counseling with someone else."

"And we will," Jack reassured her. "Once we're all a family again, we realize we will have a lot to work through."

Felicity leveled a steady, no-nonsense stare at them. "Sooner rather than later would be best for everyone. Every time you see her is going to be fraught with stress for all of you and you're going to regret it if you feel you haven't done everything possible to get through this."

Jack heard her, but still wrestled with why this needed to happen now. Brea was back and reaching out. "We understand she's not thinking clearly...but given time, now that she's heard the truth..."

"Jack," Felicity said, her voice taking on a professional calm. "She has been gone from you longer than she was with you. She was so young when she lost you all. Keep in mind it's highly doubtful her adoptive parents didn't hear about your family's tragedy. It's my impression the crash was big news in that area."

"Yes..." He remembered the days after the crash in flashes. Headlines. Newspaper clippings. Sound bites on local news sources. A horrifying reel of images from the wreckage.

"But do you understand she was in essence a kidnap victim?" Her blunt words sliced through the antiseptic air. "Just because we have no reason to believe she was physically abused by them, that doesn't take away from the psychological trauma. Have you heard of Stockholm syndrome?"

Jeannie gasped. "Brainwashing by a captor?"

"Basically, yes." Felicity nodded, leaning closer. Careful to keep her voice low so it wouldn't echo in the room. "How you behave now is more important than I think you realize, not just for getting her back, but for facilitating her healing."

Her words resonated, deeply, offering Jack the first real hope he could actually do something. Strange how he hadn't thought of how counseling for himself and his family could help Brea. He'd been more focused on her needing to seek a professional.

Felicity pushed back from the table. "You have an incredible family. I know you're facing some unthinkable challenges, but together? My money's on you all."

Smiling her reassurance, Felicity stood, grasping the gift basket to leave.

As she walked away, Jack turned his attention back to Jeannie. "I think it's time to take Felicity up on the offer to speak with someone about how to reach out more effectively." He squeezed Jeannie's hand. "My heart is being torn in two thinking about how scared my little girl must have been, how those people took advantage of that and stole…"

His throat closed with anger and pain just talking

about it, affirming all the more that he needed help seeing this through.

"Jack, I'm here for you," Jeannie said, holding tight. "Whatever you need, however I can help. We'll face this together."

"Thank you," he said, so grateful not to be alone any longer thanks to his beautiful wife, always at his side. How had he gotten so damn lucky? "Jeannie, have I told you lately how grateful I am you took a chance on me?"

He stroked a thumb along her wrist, their wedding bands glinting.

Smiling, she stroked his cheek. "I seem to recall you saying it a time or two."

"I just want to make sure you know that no matter what happens with Brea, I love you." He couldn't imagine a future without her.

Tears filled her blue eyes. "Even if—God forbid—it turns out my brother and sister had something to do with that awful tragedy?"

The words clawed at his soul. It would hurt if that was the case. And he could see it already hurt her. He couldn't bear to see her in this kind of pain. Felicity was right that he hadn't fully grasped the toll this was taking on all of them. He needed to rectify that. Jeannie—and what they shared—was too precious to risk.

"No matter how much our family means to us, we can't control their actions. I do know that if they are guilty of something, you had no knowledge of it. That's all that matters. Whatever shakes down, we'll deal with it. Together."

He lifted her hands to his mouth, pressing a kiss over her ring with a promise of forever he looked forward to fulfilling.

With Jeannie at his side, he could face whatever the future held.

Felicity sank down into her chair behind her desk, her emotions raw from visiting baby Everett. Seeing Trystan and Isabeau's happiness had blindsided her in a way she hadn't expected. She didn't begrudge them their joy, but it made her think of those dreams she'd had during her marriage. Reminded her of the depth of her ex-husband's betrayal.

Of course, seeing the baby was only half the reason for the resurgence of those emotions. The bigger part of the equation was her exchange with Conrad about having children. He was getting under her skin, burrowing his way toward her heart, making her feel things she couldn't afford to feel.

She gripped the edge of her desk, willing her nerves to ease. She'd taken a couple of days away from Conrad in hopes of regaining some distance, some objectivity. Because he was becoming too important to her, too fast.

A tap on the open door drew her eyes upward. Conrad stood in the void as if conjured from her thoughts. The man before her was no trick of the imagination or hallucination. His solidity—his existence and presence here—ignited some spark deep in her soul.

When she felt the flames within her, she knew the time for the affair had expired.

She was interested in him on so many levels beyond just the sexual and that made her vulnerable. She could get hurt. By indulging in these dates over the past few weeks, she'd opened herself up for pain.

He leaned a shoulder on the door frame, his hands surprisingly empty of any gift. Not that she needed presents. But she couldn't help but wonder. Was he easing off the romance?

"Hello," she said, staying behind her desk, moving two files around as if she was busy and not just sitting around daydreaming about him.

"You've been avoiding my calls." His expression was inscrutable. But his words were crystal clear.

"Could you close the door? I don't want to broadcast my personal life at work." She waited until he stepped into her office and sealed them alone together inside. She held up the two folders. "I've been swamped. But everything's in place for the event."

"That's not what I meant, and you know it." He rounded her desk, but didn't touch her, just leaned against the window.

Guilt pinched. She wasn't being fair to him. She

stood, flattening her hands to his chest and giving him a welcoming kiss.

A kiss that seared her to her toes and threatened to weaken her resolve to give herself time to sort through her feelings. She smoothed his lapels. "Things have been intense between us."

A half smile twitched at his mouth, but didn't quite reach his eyes. "I'm glad to hear you admit that."

Drawing in a shaky breath, she searched for the words to make him understand how this was tearing her up inside. "I just needed some space to get my thoughts together."

"And did you intend to at least tell me that rather than just ignoring my calls?" The first hints of anger clenched his jaw.

She braced her shoulders, anxiety tightening her chest. "I've never lied to you about where I stand. You knew from the start that I'm not ready for a serious relationship."

"You're too busy lying to yourself," he shot back.

Anxiety turned to anger. How dare he patronize her and her concerns.

Her hands fell from his chest. "That's not fair."

He lifted an eyebrow. "But it's true."

"No, no… You don't get to talk to me that way." She held up a hand, putting arm's length distance between them. Away from him and temptation. "But if we're going there, then what about you? You play at being a father to your nieces and nephews because it saves you having to commit to something that might actually be a risk to your heart."

He crossed his arms over his chest, his blue eyes snapping. "Sounds like you have me all figured out. Why are you so afraid of an affair with me if you're certain I'm never going to commit? Or was that part of the draw? No risk to your heart? And as a bonus, I come with this great big family you always wanted growing up."

She gasped, pain slicing through her. "How dare you use what I shared about my ex and my child-hood against me."

Her past rose like a monster from the bay. A night-mare where ghosts wandered. She could taste years of loneliness on her tongue. Feel the weariness settle in her bones and joints.

She recalled the time when everything she owned collapsed into a small pink backpack. The time in fourth grade when the most popular boy in junior high laughed at her because she didn't have parents to talk at career day. And yes, her upbringing had made her all too vulnerable to her ex-husband's false charms and empty promises of family.

Pain threatened to steal her resolve to stand up for herself as she did her best to shove down the mem-ory of shuffling from foster home to foster home.

"I'm only calling it as I see it." The anger eased from his face, and he shook his head, sighing with frustration. "You spout off about getting help and moving on and yet you won't take your own advice."

Tears burned behind her eyes, but she would be damned if she would break down and cry in front of him. "If I'm so broken, then you're better off without me." She strode to the door and opened it, gesturing out into the hall. "Just go. Get out of my office."

She stood stone still. Unflinching, with an apparent resolve she didn't come close to feeling.

He searched her expression silently for so long, she thought he might not leave. Just when she was about to weaken and say something, he nodded tightly. He strode across the office and out the door, angling through, careful not to so much brush her.

The silence after he left was deafening, the weight of what had just happened sweeping over her in the aftermath. Numb, she let the door close behind him, unwilling to let anyone see her like this. Her legs folded and she sank into a chair, stunned at the depth of her anger. Her grief. Her pain over having pushed Conrad out of her life.

She wanted to trust what they had together. She wanted to believe that a real relationship was possible for her, but she didn't know how to reconcile her own past. He'd been uncannily correct in that regard. She felt like a hypocrite, touting the benefits of therapy to deal with such a monumental issue when she couldn't get past her own ghosts.

Unable to fight back the tears, she let them flow.

How had things gotten out of control so quickly? Sure, she'd given herself a couple of days apart to get her emotions under control. She'd thought she was making progress, until today when she kept running into Steeles and Mikkelsons at every turn.

And it wasn't likely to get much better with their active role in charitable endeavors at the hospital. If she hadn't just changed jobs, she would have seriously considered a move. Even now she found herself considering it. There was a time she'd thought her job was everything. Yet…it didn't feel like nearly enough.

And now she had nothing else left.

Conrad couldn't believe how badly he'd mismanaged the confrontation with Felicity. Everything he'd planned to say had flown out of his head. So much for being the rational businessman. But nothing about his feelings for Felicity was rational.

Their fight had gutted him, leaving him shaken and clueless on how to fix things. He wanted to believe the break wasn't permanent, but Felicity had been wary from the start. And she'd been pulling away for days.

His drive to cool down landed him on the road to his brother's house. A sign that Felicity was right about his using Jack's family as a substitute for having one of his own? There may have been some truth to that.

As he turned the corner to Jack's driveway, he lowered the radio. A classic rock song's guitar riff faded in favor of the distinctive crunch of tires on hardened snow and gravel.

If he was honest with himself, he'd been on edge after taking the gift to Everett. All the talk with Felicity about having children came flooding back. He'd genuinely thought he was okay with his decision not to become a parent. Now? If he couldn't have a family with her...

The thought threatened to swamp him. He pushed it aside, trying his damnedest not to think about the woman who meant everything to him.

Hopefully hanging out with his brother and the horses would provide the distraction he needed so desperately right now.

Pulling through the security gate, he spotted his brother outside the barn and shifted his SUV into four-wheel drive. Alongside the pasture fence, he put his vehicle into Park.

Jack's barn mirrored the rustic mansion, reminiscent of a log cabin. The facade of the interlocking wood panels seemed to reflect the red hues of the setting Alaskan sun.

Stepping out into the compacted snow, Conrad yanked his gloves from the passenger seat. The sun grew heavy in the horizon, beginning to sink behind the trees and mountain line across the lake. Shrugging his coat on, he walked through the snow, moving toward his brother, who was wearing a puffy winter coat, focused on the horses playing in the pasture.

Conrad pulled on the gloves, fingers thankful for the reprieve from the quickly dropping temperature.

When Conrad was about ten feet out, Jack turned around. A vague surprise danced in his brother's half smile.

Jack nodded, his black Stetson obscuring his brother's normally inquisitive eyes. "What brings you out this way?"

Two feed buckets jutted from the snow, dinner for the horses that currently cantered in the white pasture. Abacus, a bay quarter horse, circled wildly around a lone pine tree at the center of the turnout. He let out a bellowing whinny that reverberated across the property.

Conrad stuffed his gloved hands into the pockets of his jacket as a gust of wind rolled off the bay. "Just at loose ends and thought I'd swing by."

"Uh-huh," Jack said even though his face was clear that he wasn't buying it. Still, he stayed silent, waiting.

He offered his brother one of the pails of feed. Conrad grabbed the red bucket, following Jack to the feeding troughs. They plowed through the snow. Silent except for the sudden attention of Abacus and his paint counterpart, Willow.

The horses circled, galloping for the feeding area.

The strong muscles of the horses working overtime as they raced each other. Almost like brothers, siblings engaged in play.

Conrad's mind filled with images from decades ago, of Jack teaching him to ride when their parents had been too busy. He was lucky to have those memories and so many more. Yet he'd deliberately hurt Felicity by throwing it in her face that she didn't have any such memories of her own.

He felt like a selfish ass—for what he'd said to Felicity and for bothering his brother when Jack had heavy burdens.

"How are you doing with all the Breanna mess?" Conrad inspected the feed in his bucket, knowing his brother didn't buy that he was telling the whole story or that he'd come to talk about Breanna.

Jack glanced over at Conrad, pouring the feed in Abacus's feeding trough. "I'm fine. Jeannie and I have contacted a counselor to help us through. I've been leaning on you too much and that's not fair to you."

Conrad nodded, dumping the contents of his bucket into Willow's trough. Going through the motions of feeding the horses only proved to him how empty his life was. "I want to be here for you. I'm your brother."

The two horses broke their gallop, relaxing into an enthusiastic trot. Ears perked forward, excited for their evening meal.

"And I want to be here for you. So let me." Jack stroked the paint's neck. Willow snorted into his food, chomping loudly. "Now tell me. What really brought you here?"

Conrad hadn't intended to burden his brother, but Jack's face showed he wouldn't back down.

And Conrad was confused as hell, to say the least, and he could use his brother's feedback. The man had somehow managed to have two good marriages when Conrad hadn't been able to manage one. "I've screwed up."

"What happened?"

The fight with Felicity flooded his mind again, her every word and his own unguarded responses. "Felicity gave me my walking papers."

On instinct, Conrad reached out to touch Abacus's neck. The bay looked up from his food, stretched his long neck, leaning over the fence so Conrad could scratch him. The horse's tongue hung out to the side as Conrad tried to find comfort in the silken coat. His usual ritual wasn't cutting it today. The ache over losing Felicity still consumed him.

"I'm sorry to hear that. You two seemed like a great couple. Any hope this will blow over?"

Abacus chuffed, returning to his food. "She was pretty clear." And he'd bungled the whole conversation. He rubbed the kink in the back of his neck. "Her ex-husband really did a number on her."

Guilt flashed through him because he'd just done a number of his own, throwing her past in her face.

"Like your ex did a number on you," Jack said.

"Worse." And he felt guilty as hell for using what she'd shared against her. He prided himself on being a better man than that. He'd lost his mind in the exchange. Lashed out at her in the most unproductive way.

Jack grabbed the discarded feed buckets, stacking them together. "Must have been bad, then, since what happened to you kept you from committing for so long."

His head snapped back. But he couldn't deny the truth of what his brother had said. Conrad had allowed that one rejection to taint all his future relationships. How much worse it must be for Felicity with all she'd been through.

She'd been honest with him about her wary heart. And he'd pushed anyway. "You don't pull any punches."

"We're brothers. You've always been there for me, and I'm trying to be better about being there for you." Jack clapped a hand on Conrad's shoulder, squeezing. "Jeannie and I took Felicity's advice and contacted the counselor she recommended. So you don't need to worry about me. I'm grateful for all you've done. Now, it's time for you to have your own life."

Felicity had spoken with Jack and Jeannie? She

was doing more for his family than he was, and she hadn't said a word. More guilt stung him.

Having devoured their meal, the horses waited at the gate. Abacus pawed the snow-covered earth, digging a trench with his front right hoof.

Jack tossed one of the halters and lead lines at Conrad. He caught it, the action as natural and familiar as breathing. How many times had they done this routine over the years?

Conrad thought about Felicity's words again about using Jack's family as a substitute for his own. As a way to protect his heart.

And it was past time he accepted there was truth in that.

For the first time in two decades, he allowed himself to want that future. With Felicity.

"What if I can't win her back?"

"What happens if you don't try?"

Fair statement. But that didn't help Conrad with the *how*. "What do you suggest I do? I've romanced the hell out of her."

"I'm sure you have," Jack said.

Conrad followed his brother, securing Abacus in a halter. They moved back toward the barn, the horses eager to be out of the cold.

"Just like you did with all the other women you've had affairs with over the years."

"She's different," Conrad said without hesitation, the truth of that resonating deep in his soul. He led

Abacus into the stall, unhooked the halter and gave the horse a pat between the ears.

His brother, who had finished putting Willow into the neighboring stall, appeared at the gate. "Then why are you treating her the same? Tell the woman that you love her."

The obvious truth of his brother's simple advice broadsided Conrad.

His time with Felicity had been about more than romance and sex. He was mesmerized by her intelligence and compassion. The confident way she faced life, whether it was at work or riding a horse. Everything about her called to him at a soul-deep level.

Somehow, Felicity had slipped under his radar and stolen his heart.

He was completely in love with her.

Now he had to convince her he was worthy of her trust.

Eleven

Felicity wished she could blame her exhaustion on prepping for the party. However, even though she had worked herself into the ground getting this hospital dinner under way, her lack of sleep came from a broken heart.

And in this ethereal, romantic landscape with the memory garden full of flowers and twinkling lights in the trees?

It made her heart cinch, balking under the pressure of hopes and whims she had done her best to smother to keep herself safe. Futile efforts, though, she realized, as she gazed up at the elaborate centerpiece. Cherry blossoms with pink tea roses weighed heavily from the center of the table, making the glass-enclosed space seem like a fairy garden, filled with possibilities.

Except Felicity felt only a pang of regret as she smoothed the white shimmery tablecloth in front of her.

Two days had passed since her argument with Conrad, and her sadness only intensified, especially when she'd seen him this afternoon as she'd finalized the last of the setup. Thankfully there had been enough traffic with the caterers and florists to help her keep her distance.

The event was going off without a hitch, and she should be celebrating. She swirled a glass of sparkling wine, taking in the flickering lights strung from the ceiling, which gave the appearance of nested constellations.

Slow, sensual piano chords melted under the roaring conversation among guests.

As she leaned back in her chair, her eyes wandered to the boughs of pink and white flowers blanketing the stage where Ada Joy Powers would offer her soulful crooning after the keynote speech that should be starting soon.

Dinner had passed over her lips. The blackened salmon, rich mashed potatoes and vegetable medley as nondescript as water even though the caterer was without peer and her dining companions raved. Food simply lost its appeal as her heart sank further, her emotions taking up all the space in her mind. Replacing her hunger with nausea and dizziness.

Felicity did her best to smile at her tablemates, offer polite conversation. Words left the aftertaste of ash, and the longer she stayed at this event, the more the lump in her throat swelled, her chest tightened. Maintaining a smile of neutrality took all her effort.

It seemed like she had to actively remind herself not to cry every few minutes. She paid such attention to her own internal mantra she barely noticed her waiters dressed in crisp white uniforms clearing her plate, bringing her dessert.

The event moved forward.

Felicity felt stuck in the moment of her fight with Conrad. Forced to replay the scene in her mind again. And again.

Now, the event was in full swing, the keynote speaker behind the microphone and dessert under way. Grateful she didn't have to make small talk with the strangers at her table any longer, she felt able to breathe for the first time since Conrad had left her office.

Her sorbet sat untouched in front of her, berries beginning to float in the melting treat. She'd made a last-minute change to the seating arrangements, ensuring she didn't sit with any of the Steele or Mikkelson family. She just couldn't make small talk with them, not even with her friend Tally. The last thing they needed was more tension, given how stressed they all had to be about Brea Steele's surprise request to be present tonight.

Felicity's gaze trekked to Brea's table, where the woman sat with Conrad and her lawyer. The rest of the table was filled with Steele and Mikkelson siblings since Jack and Jeannie had to sit at the table of honor with the new CEO, Ward Benally.

All had their attention focused on the podium.

The voice of the keynote speaker floated through the room. Thomas Branch, the lead actor from the hit wildlife show *Alaska Uncharted*, leaned on the podium. His voice as rich and gravelly as the outdoor landscapes he showcased to scores of viewers. The rugged, dark-haired actor had first made his name in action movies, but he'd left the big screen for television after the death of his wife, to be more available for their newborn son. Conrad had secured the speaker, just as he had the vocalist.

Unable to resist, Felicity stole a look at Conrad since no one would notice with their attention focused on the dynamic speaker. Conrad took her breath away. He appeared every bit as comfortable in the tuxedo as he did in jeans and a Stetson. He was a brilliant, magnetic—and compassionate—man.

When she'd taken her new job, she'd thought her world was on track. How could Conrad have worked his way into her life so completely in such a short time until her days felt empty without him?

She thought back to what he'd said about her only

wanting him for his large family. And she couldn't deny how much she'd enjoyed getting to know them. But she knew in her soul there had been more to her relationship with Conrad than that. It had been real and powerful, despite her efforts to keep her emotions in check.

Blinking away tears, she forced herself to focus on the speaker as a distraction before she embarrassed herself by losing it altogether.

"I'm honored to be here tonight for the renaming of the children's oncology ward, a testimony of hope for the future. This project is a beautiful tribute to the Steele family and their strength. Like Jack and Jeannie, I lost my spouse. She died too young, and I know how hard it is to get over that. Yet, Jack and Jeannie have found a way to honor that love while embracing the future with a new happiness…"

Felicity pressed a shaky hand to her mouth. She'd chosen the wrong time to pay attention to the speaker. Her heart was in her throat. She couldn't keep her gaze off Conrad any more than she could hide from the truth of why she'd pushed him away. She'd been terrified. Not of loving him, because she had already fallen for him, deeply, irrevocably so.

She'd been afraid of what would happen if he loved her back.

If that happened, there would be no hiding from taking a chance on a future with him.

The speaker's words rolled around in her mind,

chastising her for not having the courage to risk her heart a second time.

Her gaze lingered on Jack and Jeannie, seeing the love between them against all odds. More than anything, Felicity wanted to be the kind of person who continued to grow and love, instead of the kind of person who let a bad experience keep her in a shell of self-doubt forever.

Brea sat in the darkened corner of the greenhouse party, preferring to watch unobserved, with her back to the wall. So far her identity had been kept a secret from everyone except the family—and Ward Benally, since he was taking over the company and they all thought she was some kind of corporate spy.

Three bold piano notes resounded in the enclosure, and an eruption of applause animated the air with palpable energy. Ada Joy Powers slunk onstage in a swanky, vintage floor-length violet gown. Her hair cascading over one shoulder, pink lips outlined in a sensual Cupid's bow. Looking like a princess from another world as the spotlight accented her curves.

Ada Joy smiled brightly, thanking the audience. "Count me in, will ya?" she called to the piano man. He flashed a toothy grin of his own, responding with a "three, two, one" before loosening his fingers on the keys. His hands played a lively tune across the ivories. Soon, a violin joined the fold.

"Give me…" Ada Joy belted. "Give me the moon and shadows. I'll keep you…"

Brea twisted her napkin in her lap to occupy her twitchy hands under the cover of the table, resisting the urge to bolt. She was through running.

No. She would stay. Learn to stay, at any rate.

So much of her life felt punctuated by movement. Shifts that still left her reeling.

What might happen if she stayed put for a change? If she let herself unwind in this space, near the people she'd once called family? She could simply trace the contours of her old life. See how it felt.

Except the problem was Brea had no idea what might happen. But her heart urged her to find out. To favor stillness.

She'd come to this event against the advice of her attorney. And she still wasn't certain what had compelled her to ask to be present. Part of her had been sure her request would be denied since they wouldn't be able to control her here. She could definitely make a scene and ruin their event if she chose. However, if that had been her goal, she could have accomplished it long ago.

Returning to Alaska last year and then coming back now had been about something else altogether. A search for more than safety.

Because safety would have been best achieved by staying away.

She was in search of peace.

The sense of being watched made her jump with nerves. She turned quickly to find... Ward Benally.

She searched for her attorney, but he was nowhere in sight, and the rest of her table's occupants had taken to the dance floor. How could she have been so preoccupied? So careless? And if her family had been keeping their distance because of her lawyer, then why hadn't they come over once he left? The fact that they were giving her space instead of pushing like they had after the first meeting surprised her. She wondered what had caused the change.

Ward dropped into an empty chair beside her. "Thank God your lawyer finally had to use the restroom. I was starting to think I would never find you alone."

Well, that explained where the lawyer went. "Unless there's a line at the men's room, which there never is, he'll be back soon. You should go."

Brea kept her eyes fixed forward on Ada Joy, whose arms raised as she delivered an elongated high note.

Ward didn't budge. "I'm curious why you're still around. I thought for sure you would disappear into another country, this time one without extradition."

"You're rude," she snapped, turning away from the stage to look at him hard.

He seemed so relaxed in his custom-fit tuxedo. He flexed his jaw. Arrogantly. "Just curious why you're sticking around if you intend to hold everyone at arm's length."

That was actually a good question, not that she intended to give this arrogant man a compliment. "We all need answers and this seems the best place to get them."

Her gaze drifted to the table where Naomi, her twin, sat with her head turned toward the stage. Naomi's hand reached for Royce. An embrace of love, one Brea could recognize from across the room.

So many years had separated her from her twin. And yet...

She felt a pull toward her sister. A tether that connected them beyond typical familial lines. A deeper connection, a deeper version of love.

Yes. That is what she felt when she looked at Naomi. The kind of love that only existed between sisters, intensified by their twinship.

That alone made Brea's presence here worth it. She'd known returning was the only option the day she snuck into Naomi's room to see her nieces.

"Why now?" Ward leaned forward, his voice a whisper against Ada Joy's powerful vocals.

None of his business. If she wasn't telling her family, she sure wouldn't tell him. "I understand that you're looking out for the company, but don't you think this is between my father and me?"

Ward crossed his arms over his chest, leaning

back in his chair, his gaze too perceptive. "That's the first time I've heard you refer to him as your dad."

His observation stole the wind from her lungs. Except she couldn't deny he was right.

She sipped her champagne. Swallowed, bubbles tickling her nose. Took a second to gain her composure.

"Facts are facts. He *is* my father," she said with more nonchalance than she felt. "And the facts are going to show I have done nothing to harm the company."

"You didn't leak secrets to cause chaos during the consolidation of the Mikkelson and Steele companies?"

She gave herself a moment with another strategic sip of her champagne. "I may have spoken to the press and stirred the pot. And I may have shared more than I should, but I didn't do anything near what I've been accused of."

"Okay." His dark eyes focused on her lips. A faint blush threatened to stain her cheeks.

"You believe me?" She nearly buckled under this moment of unexpected softness.

His sarcastic laughter cut through her.

So much for that. Brea felt heat and anger rise in her throat.

"I believe you're not going to tell me anything more." He scraped back his chair. "I see your watchdog is back, so I'll go now."

His fingers lingered on the back of her chair as he moved past, just grazing her bare shoulders. The scent of musk and spice hung in the air, staying with her in ways that simultaneously intrigued and infuriated her.

What had he hoped to accomplish with this chat other than to get under her skin? If so, he had succeeded.

She'd said far more than she'd intended, and he'd gotten her to question her own motives with only a few words. She could understand why he'd been chosen to head the company.

But she wouldn't make the mistake of letting her guard down around him again. Important to know, since she'd made a decision tonight.

She wasn't going anywhere anytime soon.

Conrad wondered how much longer this dinner party could continue.

He'd been waiting for the right moment to approach Felicity. He wanted to stack all the odds in his favor. But even if his plan to win her back was a bust, he wasn't giving up. He intended to prove he could be trusted with her heart.

As if drawn by a magnet, Conrad's eyes found Felicity in the buzzing crowd. Her black, floor-length dress stopped his breath. Flowing material gathered in a suggestive arch on her left shoulder, plummeting into a deep V that accented her breasts. Her other shoulder was bare, the asymmetrical cut further deepened by a deep slit in the hem that revealed her well-toned legs.

Try as he might, he couldn't take his eyes off her. His mouth dried, heart pumping overtime. A helluva woman.

Her gaze met his across the room, holding, the air between them crackling with awareness. She didn't look away. Instead she took a step forward. All the encouragement he needed. He strode toward her, shouldering through the crowd until he reached her. Or rather, she met him halfway in the middle of the dance floor.

He hadn't planned that part, but then he hadn't expected to see the relief and wary joy in her eyes either. He held out his arms in an invitation to dance.

Again, she surprised him by stepping into his arms without hesitation. He gathered her against his chest, the feel of her familiar and so very welcome. He rested his head against the top of her head, breathing in the scent of her shampoo and losing himself in the slow music with her.

His hand roved up and down her back in time with the jazz tune. "The party's almost over, but I don't want what we've shared to end."

There.

He'd begun to lay his thoughts bare. Knew he needed to fight for this intelligent, sexy woman.

"I don't want to keep having an affair," she said, her breath warm against his chest.

But her words chilled him. "You're still breaking things off with me?"

His heart sunk. Was he too late? He knew his words the other day had found their mark. Dealt her pain. Conrad wanted to take them back. Spend his days proving that moment wrong.

"No, not at all." She looked up at him, her heart in her eyes. "I'm saying I want more than an affair. I want us to have a future."

Her admission filled him with so much relief, he refused to let the opportunity pass. He would do his best to reassure her. "I'm happy to hear that, because…" He drew in a bracing breath, about to utter the most important admission of his life. "I've fallen in love with you. And I want the opportunity to prove you can trust my love will last."

Her arms slid up around his neck and she stepped closer into his embrace, swaying. "That's so wonderful to hear, because I've fallen in love with you, too."

Of everything he'd imagined she would say back to him, this hadn't been on the list. But he didn't intend to complain.

"You're making this too easy for me. I owe you an apology for the way I spoke to you. I was speaking to you from my own fears, and that wasn't fair to you."

"I said some hurtful things to you, as well."

"Wait. I need to say this. You were right about so

many things." He swallowed hard but refused to give her anything less than his best. "It rattled me seeing Trystan and Isabeau, and realizing that without a doubt I'd buried my own wish for kids in my relationship with my nieces and nephews. But I don't want to hide from my own future anymore."

Her eyes showed no condemnation, no *I told you so.* Just quiet acceptance and love. Best of all, love.

He held her closer, her body a perfect fit to his. "I deserve a happy future, and more importantly—to me—so do you. Starting now."

"Right now? I'm intrigued." She smiled up at him, her hazel eyes warm as a Texas summer. She whispered in his ear, her breathy words sending shivers down his spine. "You can still romance me. I won't complain."

He knew she appreciated his gifts, but this time together meant more to her. As he mulled that over, it made sense. She'd received precious little attention from the people in her life, instead always giving hers to them.

He intended to make up for that, spoiling her in every way possible.

"Just what I wanted to hear." His heart fuller than he'd even dared hope, he guided her off the dance floor, exchanging a look with his brother. Jack had agreed to take care of the party wrap-up if Conrad persuaded Felicity to leave early. Which he had. "Come this way, my love."

He snagged their coats on the way out, their path down the corridor lined with potted trees covered in small white lights. He couldn't wait to get her alone. The sliding doors opened to the outside.

Where his horse—Jackson—waited in the parking lot.

Felicity gasped in pleased surprise. Damn straight, he still intended to romance her. Conrad took the reins from the groom and swung into the creaking saddle. The smile in her eyes rivaled the glistening stars.

He reached a gloved hand down for Felicity, and she clasped it without hesitation. He drew her up in front of him, then took a blanket from the groom and draped it over her legs. He set the horse into motion, the clop, clop of the hooves echoing his heart hammering against his rib cage at having her close again.

Tucking her head under his chin, she hugged the blanket tighter. "You weren't kidding when you said you planned to keep romancing me."

"I've been thinking we should pick out your next gift together. Something along the lines of a ring with a diamond so big it rivals the northern lights."

She stilled against him, tipping her face up to look at him. "Are you…?"

"Proposing?" While he hadn't planned that part, it felt right. "Yes, yes, I am. I want you to marry me, to be the mother of those incredible older kids we're going to adopt. To be my wife, my partner for life."

"Of course I will." She sealed her answer with a kiss, before whispering against his lips, "You are the love of my life. You are my future. And I look forward to making our dreams come true together."

A sigh of relief and happiness racked through him. He'd hoped this would be her answer, but had intended to be patient if she'd said no. Now, knowing that she was his and he was hers...his dreams had already come true, thanks to her.

She slid her arms around his waist. "I've been thinking."

The gesture felt right. Natural.

"About what?" Conrad squeezed his calves slightly. Jackson perked up, his ears attentive as they maneuvered toward the deserted side road. The clop of Jackson's hooves softened, cushioned by the fresh powder of snow.

They moved farther down the road. Snow clung to the pine branches that flanked the road. A giant moose moved through the shadows of the trees. Illuminated only by the silver moonlight.

She leaned closer. Settled into him, deepened her seat in the saddle. A whisper leaped from her lips. "Let's elope."

Had he misheard? "As in get married now?"

She laughed softly, her breath puffing into the cold night air. "That's generally what *elope* means."

The more he thought about it, the more her proposal felt right. "You're sure?"

"I'm sure that I love you," she said, staring up into his eyes with all that love shining through, "and that I don't want to wait to spend the rest of my life with you."

He also realized she was offering this to alleviate any fears he might have of a repeat of a broken engagement. He needed to be certain this was right for her, though. "And you trust me?"

"I trust *us*."

Smiling, he lowered his mouth to hers, kissing the woman who would soon be his wife, who would forever be in his heart.

* * * * *

*Passion and turmoil abound in the lives of the
Alaksan Oil Barons!
Nothing is as it seems.
Will Brea finally return to the family fold?*

*Find out the answers and so much more in the
final story starring the Steeles and Mikkelsons!*

The Secret Twin
(available February 2019)

*And don't miss a single twist in the first six books
of the Alaskan Oil Barons from*
USA TODAY *bestselling author*
Catherine Mann:

The Baby Claim
The Double Deal
The Love Child
The Twin Birthright
The Second Chance
The Rancher's Seduction

COMING NEXT MONTH FROM

HARLEQUIN® Desire

Available February 5, 2019

#2641 LONE STAR REUNION

Texas Cattleman's Club: Bachelor Auction

by Joss Wood

From feuding families, rancher Daniel Clayton and Alexis Slade have been star-crossed lovers for years. But now the stakes are higher—Alexis ended it even though she's pregnant! When they're stranded together in paradise, it may be their last chance to finally make things right...

#2642 SEDUCTION ON HIS TERMS

Billionaires and Babies • by Sarah M. Anderson

Aloof, rich, gorgeous—that's Dr. Robert Wyatt. The only person he connects with is bartender Jeannie Kaufman. But when Jeannie leaves her job to care for her infant niece, he'll offer her everything she wants just to bring her back into his life...except for his heart.

#2643 BEST FRIENDS, SECRET LOVERS

The Bachelor Pact • by Jessica Lemmon

Flynn Parker and Sabrina Douglas are best friends, coworkers and temporary roommates. He's becoming the hardened businessman he never wanted to be, but her plans to run interference did *not* include an accidental kiss that ignites the heat that has simmered between them for years...

#2644 THE SECRET TWIN

Alaskan Oil Barons • by Catherine Mann

When CEO Ward Benally catches back-from-the-dead Breanna Steele snooping, he'll do anything to protect the company—even convince her to play the role of his girlfriend. But when the sparks between them are real, will she end up in his bed...and in his heart?

#2645 REVENGE WITH BENEFITS

Sweet Tea and Scandal • by Cat Schield

Zoe Alston is ready to make good on her revenge pact, but wealthy Charleston businessman Ryan Dailey defies everything she once believed about him. As their chemistry heats up the sultry Southern nights, will her secrets destroy the most unexpected alliance of all?

#2646 A CONVENIENT SCANDAL

Plunder Cove • by Kimberley Troutte

When critic Jeff Harper's career implodes due to scandal, he does what he vowed never to do—return to Plunder Cove. There, he'll have his family's new hotel—*if* he marries for stability...and avoids the temptation of the gorgeous chef vying to be his hotel's next star.

YOU CAN FIND MORE INFORMATION ON UPCOMING HARLEQUIN® TITLES, FREE EXCERPTS AND MORE AT WWW.HARLEQUIN.COM.

HDCNM0119

Get 4 FREE REWARDS!

We'll send you 2 FREE Books
plus 2 FREE Mystery Gifts.

Harlequin® Desire books feature heroes who have it all: wealth, status, incredible good looks... everything but the right woman.

FREE
Value Over
$20

They'd never talked about how they were always overlapping each other with dating other people.

It was an odd thing to notice.

Why had Sabrina noticed?

Sabrina Douglas was his best girl friend. Girl, space, friend. But Flynn felt a definite stir in his gut.

For the first time in his life, sex wasn't off the table for him and Sabrina.

Which meant he needed his head examined.

After the tasting, Sabrina chattered about her favorite cheeses and how she couldn't believe they didn't serve wine at the tour.

"What kind of establishment doesn't offer you wine with cheese?" she exclaimed as they strolled down the boardwalk. Which gave him a great view of her ass—another part of her he'd noticed before, but not like he was noticing now.

Not helping matters was the fact that he didn't have to wonder what kind of underwear she wore beneath that tight denim. He knew.

They'd been friends and comfortable around each other for long enough that no amount of trying to forget would erase the image of her wearing a black thong that perfectly split those cheeks into two biteable orbs.

"What do you think?" She spun and faced him, the wind kicking her hair forward, a few strands sticking to her lip gloss. He reached her in two steps. Before he thought it through, he swept those strands away, ran his fingers down her cheek and tipped her chin, his head a riot of bad ideas.

With a deep swallow, he called up ironclad Parker willpower and stopped touching his best friend. "I think you're right."

His voice was as rough as gravel.

"You're distracted. Are you thinking about work?"

"Yes," he lied through his teeth.

"You're going to have to let it go at some point. Give in to the urge." She drew out the word *urge*, perfectly pursing her lips and leaning forward with a playful twinkle in her eyes that would tempt any mortal man to sin.

And since Flynn was nothing less than mortal, he palmed the back of her head and pressed his mouth to hers.

Don't miss what happens next!
Best Friends, Secret Lovers *by Jessica Lemmon,*
part of her Bachelor Pact series!

Available February 2019 wherever
Harlequin® Desire books and ebooks are sold.

www.Harlequin.com

  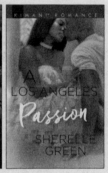
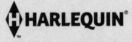

He leaned over her now, his voice a deep rumble. She could feel his breath on her face, and the broad outline of his body seemed to cast a shadow over her. They were in full view of anyone in the garden, but Lord Blackthorne behaved as if they were alone.

She found her voice. "Lord Blackthorne, I have been honest with you about everything. And if your pride is causing you to have doubts—"

"*My* pride? Madam, it is becoming clearer every day that I am not the only one who's proud in this marriage."

"It's not a true marriage," she said between gritted teeth, still trying to pull free.

But he didn't allow it.

"No? It was a marriage when you wanted access to your money."

"I know!" She felt confused and guilty and flustered. "But now—I don't know what I want."

Her breathing was erratic, and to her surprise, his gaze suddenly dipped to her breasts. For just a moment, she could have sworn his dark eyes actually smoldered with heat.

GAYLE CALLEN

PAPL
DISCARDED

RETURN
OF THE
VISCOUNT

AVON

An Imprint of HarperCollinsPublishers

AVON BOOKS
An Imprint of HarperCollins*Publishers*
10 East 53rd Street
New York, New York 10022-5299

Copyright © 2012 by Gayle Kloecker Callen
ISBN 978-0-06-207606-9
www.avonromance.com

First Avon Books mass market printing: August 2012

Avon Trademark Reg. U.S. Pat. Off. and in Other Countries, Marca Registrada, Hecho en U.S.A.
HarperCollins® is a registered trademark of HarperCollins Publishers.

Printed in the U.S.A.

10 9 8 7 6 5 4 3 2 1

To Kris Fletcher, one of my Purple buddies: thanks for dropping everything to read a synopsis or brainstorm. This book wouldn't have happened without you. I so admire your dedication to family and friends, and feel blessed to be included in that special circle.

RETURN
OF THE
VISCOUNT

Prologue

Appertan Hall, Middlesex, 1 September, 1841

Dear Sergeant Blackthorne,

Allow me to introduce myself. I am Lady Cecilia Mallory. We have not met officially, and there are some who would feel that my writing to you is inappropriate due to my unmarried state. But I feel a connection to you from my father's letters, and the disparity in our ages should put aside all gossip. You notified me of my father's death and sent kind words of condolence. I knew the military life was what he wanted, and his death in battle could not be altogether unexpected. My mother always feared this ending, and in some ways, I'm grateful she passed out of this life first, so she did not have to suffer this terrible grief.

My brother is now the Earl of Appertan at the young age of eighteen, but I have faith that he will take his duties seriously. He has left his stud-

*ies at Cambridge, and, like any young man, he is
eager to prove himself as an adult.*

*But, Sergeant, how are you? My father's death
surely was not easy on you. His letters were filled
with words in your praise, ruminations on your
long talks together. You must keenly feel the loss
of his friendship. Do write and tell me how you
fare.*

Yours in shared sympathy,
Cecilia Mallory

Bombay, India, 20 October, 1841

Dear Lady Cecilia,
*You did not need to respond to my letter, but
I am grateful you did. It eases me to know that
your brother has assumed the earldom with dedication. If he is anything like your father, he will
take good care of you. Do not worry needlessly.*

*I understand the grief of a father's death.
When it happened, I was separated by con-
tinents from my family, and it is easy to feel
alone in your sorrow. But you are not alone. In
memory of your father, I will always be interested in your welfare.*

Your concern for my well-being was surprising. I assume by your words that you wish to continue this correspondence, so I will do what I can to alleviate your worries.

Your father spoke proudly of the years your entire family accompanied him to follow the drum. A woman's life is hard here, and I admire your mother's courage for keeping you all together as a family. My own family was not so understanding of my choices. My father thought that I, as the eldest, had a duty to remain in England. But I felt more keenly my duty to my country, and this estranged me from him. My younger brother, Allen, has always been up to the challenge of seeing to our family property. We correspond regularly and make decisions together. It is good to have a sibling, is it not?

Now please tell me more of your life at home. It comforts me to think of you doing everyday things, to know that there is more to the world than unrest and the threat of war.

Your faithful servant,
Sergeant Blackthorne

Several letters later . . .

Appertan Hall, 1 March, 1842

Dear Sergeant Blackthorne,

I truly enjoyed your last letter about the holidays in India. It reminded me well of the friendships our family formed there, the gay parties. And yes, I remember the eager young ladies who came to find husbands in Civil Service, but I'd never heard the term "three-hundred-a-year-dead-or-alive-men." So a pension to a widow was the same as a husband's yearly salary? Love cannot be a part of every marriage, of course. After what I have told you of my life so far, you surely know that I am practical by nature.

Your gossip makes me laugh, and I must admit, I have been doing little of that these days, confined at home in mourning. I have not spoken much of my brother, and your words from several letters ago about your closeness to your own brother gave my heart a pang. I envy you, Sergeant. I'm trying to help my brother, but he is having difficulty dealing with our steward. Oliver is still so young yet, and I alone seem to under-

stand that. I have come to appreciate my father even more, knowing that he controlled these estates from India.

Soon I will be out of mourning, and I know there will be men who wish to court me. I cannot believe I am writing of this to you, my father's friend, but I find it easier to put my thoughts into words rather than speak them, even though I know my dearest friend, Hannah Webster, would understand. She is happy for a man's notice, whereas I wish I could remain anonymous. You must know I have a generous dowry, and I cannot help believing that this matters more than what kind of woman I am. My parents' marriage was not what it looked like from the outside, and I would never allow myself to be this unhappy. Oh, please do not think their sad marital state was my dear papa's fault—it was not. I'm not even certain what I'm trying to say in this letter or if I have advice to ask of you. Thoughts of marriage trouble me, and I sometimes wonder if I should marry at all.

Now see the silly things I am saying? Surely that is due to the influence of my guardian, Lord Hanbury, a cousin to my mother. He and his wife are happiest in the country, and their grow-

*ing anxiety about chaperoning a debutante in
London is surely irritating my nerves.*

*Your sincere friend,
Cecilia*

Bombay, India, 15 May, 1842

*My dear Lady Cecilia,
I am humbled that you wish to confide in
me. Know that I would be honored to assist the
daughter of my commander and friend. I am concerned to hear that your brother is having difficulty adjusting to his new role. Maturity will
help, of course. If your steward is the same as
the one employed by your father, then yes, young
Lord Appertan is in good hands. But if, as time
goes on, things do not improve, please confide
this in me. For the sake of your father, and my
friendship with you, I would help your brother
however I could.*

*As for marriage, although I am not married
myself, allow me to say it is not to be entered
into lightly. But I sense from your letters you are
not a flighty young lady, given to making rash
judgments. I, too, have sad history in my family,
which is probably the reason I have not married.
And, of course, I am but a noncommissioned of-*

ficer, which is hardly the life for a young lady. I am a career military man, Lady Cecilia, and I plan to remain in India, where my country needs me. You have your own difficulties, of course, and it is never easy to be the daughter of an earl, to be expected to marry within your station. You will meet young men, and you will make the right choice if you listen to your head as much as your heart. Marry on your own terms, not simply to satisfy another. Then you will be happy.

Your faithful servant,
Sergeant Blackthorne

Bombay, India, 30 August, 1842

My dear Lady Cecilia,
Do not think me presumptuous, but after corresponding regularly for over a year, the absence of a letter from you leaves me puzzled and apprehensive, especially after you shared your concerns about your future. Please write when you are able. Surely you are in the midst of your reintroduction to Society.

Your faithful servant,
Sergeant Blackthorne

Appertan Hall, 19 October, 1842

> *Dear Sergeant Blackthorne,*
>
> *Please forgive my lack of correspondence. You have written to me faithfully, and I have allowed my own concerns to override my behavior as your friend. I have sad news to report. No sooner did I emerge from mourning, than did my dearest friend Hannah tragically drown. I have been comforting her younger sister, Penelope, as well as her parents, even though my own brother requires more and more of my attention. I am feeling constrained by my guardian, who will not grant me access to my own inheritance until I turn twenty-five.*
>
> *Unless I marry. Sergeant, you will surely think my next words mad, but please listen to my reasoning. Would you consider marrying me? Neither of us has anyone we are promised to, and every young man of my acquaintance is so shallow and immature compared to you. I know you plan to remain in the Dragoon Guards for life, and I would be perfectly content with that. We could marry by proxy, as has sometimes happened when military men are stationed out of the country. I will remain here, helping my brother*

with the Appertan estates, while you remain in India. If this favor is beyond your ability to grant, I understand, and know that I will continue to be your faithful correspondent—

Cecilia

Chapter 1

Middlesex, England 1843

At the pounding on the front door, Lady Cecilia looked up from the letter she'd been writing at the little desk in the drawing room at Appertan Hall. The afternoon was so overcast as to seem like dusk, and a lightning flash illuminated the curtains while giving off a crack of noise. Who would be out and about on such a day?

She briskly got to her feet and strode toward the cavernous entrance hall of the castle, reaching it at the same moment her white-haired butler, Talbot, opened one of the massive double doors. A broad man stood silhouetted briefly by another flash of lightning, and she couldn't see his face. A blast of mist blew in around him, and she smelled the rain.

"Good afternoon, sir," Talbot said in a dignified voice, even though he had to raise it to be heard above the storm.

The man leaned heavily on a cane and nodded to Talbot. "Good afternoon."

There was something about his deep voice that seemed . . . different, that made her more alert.

"I need to see your mistress," he continued.

"May I ask who is calling?" Talbot said with reserve, as if he would be the stranger's gatekeeper and judge.

"Sergeant Blackthorne. She will know the name of her husband," he added.

Cecilia covered her mouth, feeling a surge of shock and disbelief. Sergeant Blackthorne? Here in Middlesex? He had assured her he never planned to leave his regiment in India, and she'd assumed she might never meet him.

He took a step across the threshold, and she saw the broad, strong hands of a young man, the unbowed shoulders. Her late father's supposedly closest friend could not be more than ten years her elder. How was it possible that she'd made such a wrong assumption about his age? She'd married him by proxy six months before, thinking she was making a perfectly rational decision about a husband she'd never wanted.

She must have made some sort of sound, for both men turned to look at her. Talbot said nothing, surely realizing the next decision was hers.

"Please do come in, Sergeant Blackthorne," she said with more calm than she felt.

He swept off his hat and limped inside, and she

wasn't surprised when he stared at her for long moments. She knew she was pleasant to look at, but his regard seemed more intense than any she'd ever felt before.

"Shall I send a footman for your bags, sir?" Talbot asked.

"And a groom for my horse."

"Of course, sir."

Talbot closed the door behind Sergeant Blackthorne. "Shall I send a tea tray, Lady Cecilia?"

She cleared her throat. "To the drawing room, Talbot. Thank you."

With his hat off, she could see Sergeant Blackthorne more clearly, brown hair disheveled and damp. His face was broad and harsh, stark cheekbones beneath intelligent, impassive brown eyes. He had a square chin and jaw, and eyebrows that seemed like slashes on his skin. With his cane against his thigh, he swept off his wet cloak and handed it and his hat to Talbot, who then silently melted away into the gloom.

Sergeant Blackthorne had a soldier's body, none of the lean grace of the refined men she was used to. She could see the expanse of muscles in his arms and thighs, as if his civilian clothes no longer fit quite properly. Heat rose into her cheeks with her unusual awareness of him.

And then she remembered she'd invited him into the drawing room. She turned, her skirts swirling, and led the way. The drawing room had once been the great hall of the ancient castle, but over the years, her ancestors had refined it, with clusters of sofas and chairs scattered about, and a pianoforte in one corner. But there was no civilizing the massive fireplace as tall as a man, and no one had ever suggested removing the swords and shields dominating the high expanses of the walls although large landscapes and portraits hung below.

To ward away the autumn chill, she'd been sitting near the coal fire in the hearth, and she led him there.

"You must be damp from your journey," she said, trying to find polite conversation when her mind was racing.

He stood near the coal grate for a moment, both hands braced on the cane, his head lowered to the warmth. Then he glanced at her from beneath his dark, heavy brows, and she felt as if a thread went taut between them, connecting them there, alone together in the storm-darkened room.

"Forgive me for arriving unannounced," he said in a low voice. "A letter would have traveled at the same speed. I did not intend to return to England anytime soon, but then I was injured, and ordered home until my health improves."

"You are recovering, Sergeant?" She clasped and unclasped her hands while she studied him too closely.

"I am."

He did not elaborate, so she continued on, "I hope

your wounds were not serious." For a man who could write interesting letters, he did not speak easily although she didn't need the sound of his voice to feel his very presence taking up the space all around her.

"Shrapnel. There were several pieces they could not remove from my leg without risking further damage. The cane will become unnecessary soon enough, then I will be able to return." He paused and slanted a look at her. "Normally, such a wound would not merit this much recovery time, but my superiors knew of the circumstances of our marriage and insisted."

She bit her lip, then sat down at last, smoothing out her skirts with trembling fingers. *The circumstances of our marriage* indeed. He'd gone along with the marriage—at her request, of course. She'd desperately needed access to her funds. Sergeant Blackthorne had seemed like the perfect solution in those desperate, sleepless hours when she'd paced the nights away. She hadn't wanted to marry, couldn't risk being controlled by any of the men of her acquaintance. They'd all seemed so eager when they saw the riches of Appertan Hall—or when they'd admired her form rather than shown interest in any conversation. With Sergeant Blackthorne, she'd thought she was marrying an elderly compatriot of her father's, one who would die sooner rather than later, to be blunt about it.

But, this . . . this healthy, intimidating, overpowering man upset every decision she'd made for herself.

She couldn't stop staring at him, and he seemed to be feeling the same way. It heated her skin, sweeping up from her chest to flood her face. She'd never blushed so much in her life.

Why had this *young* man so easily agreed to marry her?

She gestured to the chair across from her. "Please sit down and rest, Sergeant."

He did so, very slowly, as if the ride there had stiffened his leg, and she regretted his discomfort. But at least she could breathe again, now that there was a small table between them.

Except that he stared at her so very intently. "Your miniature does not do you justice, my lady," he said softly, as if he did not often make such a statement.

"You are too kind." Her fingers clenched in her skirts. She didn't want him to admire her face or form, to assume . . . oh, she couldn't even think it. "But I have never seen a portrait of you, sir. I must confess, I thought you much . . . older."

He arched one dark brow. "Did I do something to give that impression?"

"My father's letters about you made you seem such a close friend. I made assumptions."

Thunder rolled deeply outside, startling her.

"You wanted to marry an elderly man?" he asked. "I did not know anything more was required of me than my very presence releasing you from your guardianship. I wanted nothing of you but the chance to help. I asked for no dowry, no control of your finances."

"And I thank you again for your generosity and discretion."

She'd been picturing an older man at the twilight of his life, wanting only to assist the daughter of his late close friend. A young man in his prime, without title or fortune, could very well have other motives.

She always prided herself on her intelligence and sensible nature, but she was as flawed as any other desperate woman. And she'd given this stranger power over her.

Or had she, she thought, swallowing back a desperate hope. Marriages by proxy were risky and were sometimes invalidated. But she didn't want to go back to being a woman under a guardian's control, her money withheld as if she were a child, all say in her own life restricted.

She would have to consult her lawyers—but how to explain herself to her relatives and friends? She'd already said she'd fallen in love with the sergeant's letters. It would be fickle to say that now that she'd met him in person, she'd changed her mind.

His expression remained impassive. She was used to men who showed their emotions freely—her father's happiness and passion for life, she remembered sadly; her brother Oliver's moody outbursts. But, of course, he hadn't always been like that, she thought, stark, sad

memories teasing the edges of her mind. She could remember playing games as she chased him through the
gardens of their bungalow in India, their footsteps on
the crushed shell path, their laughter.

"Since I was in England, I wanted to see to your
welfare, my lady," Sergeant Blackthorne said. "I could
not in good conscience visit my mother without seeing
how you fare first."

"I appreciate your consideration, Sergeant." She
prided herself on being able to judge a person's character, but in so brief a time, Sergeant Blackthorne seemed
utterly blank to her, except for the very cloak of masculinity that made him so different from her. The letters
from him she'd once enjoyed now seemed foreign to
her.

She mustn't forget his history with her father. He'd
opened himself up to her in his letters, granted her request though it had cost him his freedom from a marriage of his own choosing. She should be grateful—but
she could not banish her suspicion.

"You are the daughter of my commanding officer,"
Sergeant Blackthorne continued, "a man I held in the
highest esteem. His death—" He broke off from whatever he meant to say, and his gaze went to the window,
where the rain streaked down in rivulets. "He taught
me what it was to be a man and a soldier. I will never
forget my debt to him."

He'd obviously looked up to her father, as had she.

But she'd also resented his dedication to his regiment, the Eighth Dragoon Guards, for the many sorrows it had caused. It had made her mother miserable, and the older Cecilia got, the more her mother had confided that misery.

"So you consider me a debt," she said slowly.

"No," he said, then spread both his hands. "What am I to you?"

She stared at him, and was glad when Talbot himself, rather than a gawking maid, came into the room with a tea tray. Cecilia could only imagine how the servants' hall was buzzing with news of her mysterious husband's arrival.

"Since dinner is some hours away," Talbot said to her, "I had Cook prepare sandwiches for Lord Blackthorne."

"You are using an incorrect title, Talbot," she said absently, still obsessed with staring at the sergeant.

Talbot hesitated. "I have served this family for long years in London, Lady Cecilia, and I have always prided myself on my knowledge of Society. I recognized Lord Blackthorne's name and heritage, but if he wishes me to use his military title, then I shall. I acquiesced to your retention of 'Lady Cecilia' as your title, thinking you had personal reasons. I now regret my silence."

"My mistake was not your fault, Talbot." Cecilia turned back to the man she'd married. "Sir, you have a title I know nothing about?"

"It was in the marriage papers. You did not read them all? I hold a viscountcy."

Talbot once again made himself scarce. Sergeant-Lord Blackthorne was not just a soldier; he was a peer, a man with even more power than she'd thought. She'd never heard of the title although she'd never had much time for London Society. She regretted that her lawyers had the marriage papers.

"You're a viscount," she began slowly, "yet you are a noncommissioned officer. I don't understand."

"I did not feel qualified to be an officer without the knowledge to lead. I wanted to earn my fellow soldiers' respect before I expected them to follow me into battle."

"So you enlisted like any ordinary man." She'd never even heard of that being done by a peer. "And you call yourself sergeant? I don't know what to think."

"I don't believe your thoughts occurred to me, my lady, considering I didn't even know of you when I made my decision years ago. I would have thought my being a viscount might have appealed to you, might even have helped explain our unorthodox wedding. The fact that you didn't realize it makes me very curious."

"Curious?" She forced a smile. "That is the least of what I'm feeling about this awkward situation."

"It seems we are beginning this marriage on the same footing."

She willed her hands not to tremble as she poured his tea. "How do you prefer yours?"

"Plain, Lady Blackthorne. Thank you."

She flinched at the use of her new title, then watched him sip his tea and eat several wedges of ham sandwiches.

At last he sat back and regarded her. "So, where do we stand, my lady?"

She truly was his lady, not just his wife. Their mutual stare seemed charged with awareness, a knowledge that they were man and woman—joined, at least legally, as husband and wife. It was an intimacy she'd never imagined. She got to her feet. "I don't know what to say, my lord. I had never planned on marrying—I am far too busy here with the Appertan estates."

He rose with a slow, graceful agility that suddenly made them too close. She stepped back.

"That is a strange sentiment for a woman. And yet you are now married to me. You cannot want an annulment," he added, as if they were discussing the weather.

Then she'd be a ward again, at the mercy of her guardians, and without the power she needed. He knew that. "I need to give this . . . situation consideration. If I decide to end this, then it could be scandalous that you lived here within the house. Please take no offense, my lord, but would you sleep in the dower house? It is just across the western lawn."

For the first time, she watched his gaze move slowly down her body, taking in the flower-sprigged muslin. She suddenly had trouble catching her breath.

"So now I am a horse to be examined before a sale?" she asked quietly.

His brown eyes met hers once again. "I never said you were, my lady. Do you have other rules I as your husband should be aware of? No referring to my embarrassing military title, no looking at my wife."

"I never said I was embarrassed by your military title," she protested. "You earned that above other enlisted soldiers, and the accomplishment must be a source of pride."

He bowed his head gravely. "You do me honor. But you also seem to believe I will meekly acquiesce to whatever you want, regardless of how reckless it is. No, I will not reside in the dower house."

She tensed, but he spoke before she could reply.

"I am your legal husband, and I assume all of your friends and neighbors know. It would cause a terrible scandal and harm your reputation if you were to cast me off."

"I would not be casting you off," she insisted, striving to be calm. "If my lawyers say a proxy marriage is invalid, then we would have to abide by it."

"You'd be making the marriage invalid by treating it that way. Now that I've met you in person, I know something must be drastically wrong for you to marry a man sight unseen, even if I do write interesting letters," he added dryly.

Her mouth opened and closed, but her brain couldn't

seem to settle on the right response. This man was insisting he knew what was best for her.

"I would be happy to continue this discussion at dinner," he continued, "but first I should change out of these damp garments."

"Of course. I will have Talbot show you to your bedchamber. I hope you understand that you will not be sharing mine."

"I assume you have a spacious apartment, Lady Blackthorne. Give me whichever of your rooms you'd like. I would never force myself on you. I will gladly give us time to know one another. And it is no one's business but ours."

She let out her breath. "Thank you. I will see you at seven when we dine."

He bowed. "Until then."

She watched him limp across the drawing room, and it wasn't until she glimpsed him meeting with Talbot, that she stumbled back to sit on the sofa and close her eyes. *Oh God, what have I done?*

Michael, Viscount Blackthorne, followed the butler up into the mansion that had obviously once been a cavernous castle. Part of his mind memorized the route to his bedchamber, as any good soldier would, but another part of him was still stunned by his first encounter with Lady Blackthorne.

His wife.

For the rest of his life, he'd never forget his first sight of her, the lightning illuminating her beautiful, bewildered face, surrounded by a blond crown of hair. He'd been stunned, having convinced himself that only a truly ugly woman would need to marry as she had. Instead, he'd been astounded by her flawless features, the high cheekbones, the golden tones of her skin that hinted she was a woman of the outdoors. Her eyes reminded him of the petals of the Indian blue poppy, so vivid that he could have lost himself in their depths. Her figure was just as captivating, curves barely contained by her corset. He was still amazed he'd managed to speak to her coherently.

Talbot opened a door, and Michael preceded him into a spacious bedchamber, the chill of disuse now combated by a fire in the coal grate. The massive four-poster bed dominated although it was complemented by a wardrobe, writing desk, washstand, and several different chairs. He wondered if the door at the far side led to a dressing room—or his wife's chambers.

"My lord, a maid will arrive soon to unpack your bag," Talbot said, apology in his voice.

Michael nodded, barely noticing the butler's departure as his thoughts returned to his wife. His very reluctant wife—he could see that now, and it surprised him, after the desperation that had hovered beneath each word she wrote. He couldn't blame her for holding him off. They truly didn't know each other but for words on paper. The instant connection he'd felt with her made them seem more intimate than they really were. If she felt it, she was fighting it, for he saw no hint that she might be as instantly smitten as he was. Her letters over the last two years had been the bright point of each month. He'd read them several times each, smiling at her lightheartedness, understanding that she tried to distract him with cheerful stories from home.

After the first few letters, Michael had assumed that Lady Cecilia was doing well enough, though in mourning, of course. His few friends in London had reported that the estate thrived, and that she had a dowry to attract any man she wanted.

But something had gone terribly wrong, and Michael, half a world away, had not seen it until the friendly letters were briefly silenced. The fact that she'd only come to him, a stranger, had made him feel concerned rather than flattered, and now, upon meeting her, his concern was only heightened. She'd experienced true desperation for some reason, and Michael felt keenly the vow he'd made to her father to protect his children.

He owed Lord Appertan so much he could never repay. His commander, a man more like a father to him than his own, had died in his arms. It would have been his last engagement; he'd wanted to return home to his children. With a bloody hand, Appertan had held Michael's own and begged him to take care of his family.

So when Lady Cecilia, a lively, intelligent, amusing

correspondent, needed help, he'd agreed to marry her. He'd thought for certain she was exceedingly plain and that she must not trust any man who'd want to marry her. There were fortune hunters out there, as he well knew—his own family bore the scars of such disastrous marriages. He wasn't going to do to a woman what had been done to the women in his family: used for their money, not respected in any other way. His own father had been guilty, his mother a victim, and as a youth, Michael had seen his father planning for Michael's own marriage to a wealthy girl, beginning to ensnare her family with lies. It was one of the reasons he'd enlisted at eighteen, forgoing even one Season in London. There were honest ways to earn money to restore his estate. Marriage would have been what he made of it if he married at all.

Michael had learned never to let himself show interest in a woman when he lived at home. He had held back, never giving himself the chance to know someone too well, too deeply. He'd never realized how much that continued through his twelve years in the army—until he'd begun to receive her letters. He'd been able to glimpse the life and heart of Lady Cecilia, and for the first time, he'd felt a yearning for a woman he could never have.

She was so lovely that he could barely look upon her golden beauty without wanting her with a desperation he'd never felt before. He remembered all those men who used to follow his beautiful mother around like rutting dogs. He didn't want to be one of them either. Thank God the late earl hadn't known how Michael would lust after her.

He remembered the shock on her face when she beheld him—old and infirm, she'd thought him, uninterested in a marriage bed. He'd done for her what no other man would do—denied her dowry and any claim to her inheritance.

But she worried he had ulterior motives, and the truth of the rash proxy marriage she'd asked for now stared her in the face. For a woman of intelligence, she'd not thought further than her own desperation.

He walked to the window and looked out, past the rain-streaked glass to the Appertan land, which must stretch to the horizon. He knew from her father the vastness of the estates scattered all over England and Scotland. He imagined even though she was now married, men still flocked to her.

Patience was the only card he could play. If necessary, he would dive into cold rivers every day to keep himself from seducing her before she was ready. She wanted a distant marriage—or no marriage at all, now that she'd met him.

He'd vowed to marry on his own terms, without the involvement of money. His service in the Eighth Dragoon Guards—his rise in power, even without a purchased commission—would add enough to the estate to guarantee the stability of his family, along with the small investments in shipping and exporting he'd begun to make. As a cavalryman, his dedication to work mattered more than his lack of inheritance.

Michael would do his best to be a good husband, for he'd already seen every mistake a family could make and had learned from them. But first he had to find out why the lovely sister of an earl, who could have married advantageously, was so desperate to control her own wealth.

"Cecilia!"

A woman's light, cheerful voice called to her, and Cecilia pasted a pleasant smile. "In here, Penelope!"

Miss Penelope Webster was their nearest neighbor. Her parents leased a small manor house from the Appertan estate. She breezed into the drawing room, her black hair in perfect ringlets about her olive-toned complexion. She had cat green eyes that projected mischievousness, and moved with grace, considering her abnormal height. Her older sister, Hannah, had been Cecilia's dearest friend growing up, and when Hannah drowned last year, Penelope had become the little sister Cecilia never had. Cecilia was grateful for her cheerful presence, for now that she dealt with the estate, she didn't have as much time to devote to writing letters to old friends.

Penelope's sisterly relationship with Cecilia's

brother, Oliver, had changed with maturity, and now they were engaged. Privately, Cecilia thought Oliver was too young at twenty years of age, but who was she to judge someone's marital fitness? Penelope tolerated Oliver's wild ways, and perhaps she could help change him for the better.

"Did you miss the rain?" Cecilia tiredly patted the sofa beside her.

Penelope flounced onto it, her white skirts spreading all around her. She gave Cecilia a quick hug. "Oh, I was already here, in the library with Oliver."

"The library?" Cecilia repeated hopefully. Oliver had never been one for studying, and the moment he'd inherited the earldom two years before, he'd gladly left Cambridge. She had spent her life being tutored privately, and she would have given anything to attend university. But she could not force her beliefs on Oliver; she could only help him and was gladly doing that.

"We were looking up a title in *Debrett's*." Penelope giggled, and when Cecilia didn't follow suit, her smile faded. "Is something wrong? I saw the stranger your butler was leading away. You have a visitor?"

She'd meant to tell Oliver first, but it hardly mattered. "A stranger yes, but only in one sense. It seems my soldier husband decided to visit me."

Penelope's green eyes went wide. "No! He didn't inform you he was coming?" She put a comforting hand on Cecilia's arm.

Cecilia covered it with her own. "No. He was injured, and the army sent him home to recover. And it also seems I should have read my marriage papers more closely before handing them over to my lawyers. I am the wife of Viscount Blackthorne, not simply Sergeant Blackthorne."

"So you are Lady Blackthorne!" Penelope cried, clapping her hands together. "You deserve to marry into a title and lands, Cecilia." For a moment, Penelope looked confused. "I thought I received an impression from you that your husband was older, but I never heard you tell others such a thing. I must have been mistaken. Now things have happened as they should. You work so hard—you need someone to work hard to take care of you!"

But that wasn't going to happen, Cecilia knew. She was going to continue to take care of the Appertan properties until Oliver was ready to grow up and give up his wild friends and his drinking. Even a fiancée couldn't stop Oliver from doing that.

Sometimes, she thought Penelope didn't even *see* Oliver's flaws. She made more excuses for him than Cecilia did. But basically, they were both hoping Oliver would mature—soon.

"So what did you think of your husband?" Penelope whispered, looking over her shoulder as if Lord Blackthorne were eavesdropping.

Cecilia sighed. "I—I don't know. I was so shocked

when I heard his name. I don't think I've yet recovered."

"Is he finished with the army and come to sweep you off in romantic bliss?"

Cecilia blinked at Penelope, who broke into laughter that gradually faded when she realized Cecilia hadn't joined her.

"Oh dear," Penelope murmured. "Do forgive me. It is all so strange. I thought to . . . lighten your mood."

"I don't think that's possible. You've been in love with Oliver—forever."

"But you fell in love with Sergeant-Lord Blackthorne's letters!"

"But it's not the same thing as meeting him in person," Cecilia insisted. "He's my husband, a man with whom I exchanged so many letters"—none of them romantic although he'd been kind and considerate—"yet he's a stranger. I . . . I don't know if I've made the right choice."

Penelope gripped Cecilia's hands and looked into her eyes with determination. "Don't be hasty, my dear. His letters moved you—that man is inside there somewhere. Perhaps he's nervous and confused, too."

"He doesn't seem confused," Cecilia murmured, thinking about how intently he'd stared at her.

"Men are good at hiding such things."

Cecilia bit her lip, trying not to smile at her friend's earnest certainty. Oliver never hid a single thought he was thinking, regardless of how inappropriate—yet Penelope didn't see that.

Penelope leaned closer. "Have you told Oliver? As your brother, he'll want to make sure you're protected."

"You can tell him, Penelope. I think . . . I think I need to rest before dinner. If he has any questions, he can find me in the study."

"And that's resting? You'll bury your face in account books, and the servants will have to remind you to eat!"

"But it's restful to me, honestly."

"Very well," Penelope said, as they both rose. "I'll explain things to Oliver. Maybe he'll go find Lord Blackthorne's room and talk to him. He is . . . sharing your apartments?"

"He is. I made certain he knows I am uneasy about our marriage."

"But a man assumes . . ." Penelope trailed off again, growing pink.

"I know what a man assumes. But this man was my father's dearest friend. He has offered to give me time."

"Probably not much time," Penelope warned. "He's a soldier, after all. Now I must go speak with Oliver."

Cecilia kept a smile on her face as Penelope left her, then it faded away. How long *would* he wait?

Chapter 2

Cecilia was almost late to dinner, when usually she was the most punctual one in the house. But she'd paced the study for two hours, the account books not bringing their usual focus, her mind whirling about her dilemma even as she imagined her "husband" exploring her rooms. It was Talbot who gently announced—for the second time—that their guests had already gathered in the drawing room, and dinner was about to be served.

Breathless from hurrying, Cecilia found Oliver leaning against the massive hearth, eyeing Lord Blackthorne with undisguised indifference, which pricked her with sadness. His disheveled blond hair was darker than her own, his eyes a bloodshot gray, his frame lean and gangly with youth. Beneath his brown coat, he wore plaid trousers that set off his dashing red waistcoat. He seemed so young when compared to Lord Blackthorne's military bearing and air of quiet confidence. He *was* young, she reminded herself.

Lord Blackthorne, neatly, conservatively, dressed

in dark coat and trousers, stared back at Oliver, nonplussed. She didn't know if she expected him to wear his uniform, but she was relieved he hadn't. Oliver didn't need to be reminded of their days in India—and frankly, neither did she.

Penelope's worried frown cleared upon Cecilia's arrival. "There you are! And aren't we all just starving? Lord Blackthorne must be, after his journey from London."

"It's not that far from Town," Oliver said sullenly. "A few hours by horse."

"The weather and his injury might have affected his travel, Oliver," Cecilia said. "But why don't you lead the way."

She was paired up with Lord Blackthorne, who held out his arm, and she placed her hand on it. She could feel the tight, hard muscles of his forearm, and it made something strange swirl around in her stomach. Never had touching a man seemed so fraught with intriguing danger. Releasing him as soon as was proper, she allowed him to guide her chair beneath her.

The table could easily seat fifty people, but they sat together at one end. She wondered if Talbot had ignored the family dining room to make sure that Lord Blackthorne understood the importance of the family he'd married into.

"Sit at Oliver's left, my lord, as our honored guest," Cecilia murmured.

He nodded, and she slowly let out her breath as he walked away and sat down opposite her. Penelope perched on a chair to her right, her expression fond as she looked at Oliver, then hesitant, perhaps even eager, as she studied Lord Blackthorne. Cecilia wondered what Penelope had said to Oliver because his sullen dark glances were no true indication, and she felt another twinge of sadness. As the earl and host, he might have begun the conversation, but he said nothing, only eating the first course, acting as removed as a little boy.

She saw Lord Blackthorne studying him, and she felt a flare of embarrassment and exasperated tenderness all at the same time. In some ways, Oliver had been more her child than her mother's, especially after the death of his identical twin when they were only children. She touched the locket she always wore, with the miniatures of both her brothers laughing as if to each other.

It took her a long moment to get beyond that memory. "Lord Blackthorne, how was your journey from India?"

"Uneventful, thank you, Lady Blackthorne."

"The steamships make the journey in only six weeks or so, which is far more pleasant." She gave a faint shudder. "I remember the six months' journey on sailing ships. My mother had a delicate constitution and spent much of the time in her bunk."

Oliver casually said, "So, Blackthorne, tell us the real reason you married my sister, sight unseen."

"Oliver!" Cecilia cried.

Michael had been expecting this, so he wasn't all that surprised. Young Lord Appertan *should* be concerned about his sister—but Michael sensed there was so much more going on. The young man seemed immature and didn't even attempt to hide it. It was hard to believe he was the son of a military hero. But, then again, Appertan's father had not often been a part of his life the last ten years or so.

Her face a pretty pink as if with embarrassment, Cecilia said, "My marriage is none of your concern, Oliver. You weren't my guardian."

"But I am your brother, and the earl."

Michael answered honestly, "I married your sister because she asked me to."

Cecilia winced.

By letter, she had seemed to him to be a woman who did what was necessary, even when it meant marrying a stranger. But she didn't want her brother to know the details? Michael began to wonder who was in command here.

"You're that easily wed, Blackthorne?" Appertan demanded, smirking.

"I had no immediate plans to wed. But I considered your father a friend and mentor. With his death, I wanted to assist your family in any way I could.

Frankly, I assumed Lady Cecilia was a plain spinster, who felt she could only attract a suitor with her fortune."

Lady Blackthorne gasped, Miss Webster covered her lips to hide what was obviously a grin, and Appertan's mouth dropped open before he barked out a harsh laugh.

Michael glanced at his wife apologetically. "You must concede that is a fair assumption."

"I told you I didn't want to be under the control of my guardian, Lord Hanbury," she said.

"I admit, I was surprised when I first beheld you," he said, looking upon her lovely, flushed face.

She seemed more exasperated than angry. Other women might react differently, and he was relieved she was not the kind to take offense easily. It was almost off-putting to meet the woman behind the letters and see if reality could improve upon the sweet, caring disposition she'd shown through words. He wasn't disappointed—he was intrigued, for he sensed depths she'd kept hidden from him.

Miss Webster turned to her. "What did you think your husband would be like?" she asked eagerly. "After all, you felt you knew him well from his letters."

Michael was very curious to know what Lady Blackthorne had told other people about them.

"I will admit, I did not picture his face," she began slowly.

She avoided meeting his gaze, to Michael's amusement.

"I just knew he was a kind man, who honored Papa in every way, who was a hero in battle."

"I am not a hero," he cut in, ignoring the darkness of memories that so easily welled up inside him. "I did my duty, as did many men."

Lady Blackthorne stared at him with obvious interest but didn't ask for an explanation. Perhaps she had too many of her own secrets.

"But she *thought* you a hero," Miss Webster said dreamily. "I found it all so romantic."

Romantic? Perhaps through a young girl's innocent eyes. It had practically been a business agreement, where Lady Blackthorne received the reward of financial freedom, and he received her gratitude—and the knowledge that he'd assisted the daughter of his late commander. It had been enough for him, but not anymore, now that he'd met her.

"I don't care how romantic it is," Appertan said in a bored voice. "I don't know you, Blackthorne, and your presence in Appertan Hall offends me."

"Then Lady Blackthorne and I will remove ourselves to the Blackthorne estate," Michael said.

As his wife gaped at him, Michael calmly took another spoonful of his oxtail soup. It was really quite delicious after army fare and shipboard provisions.

"Cecilia doesn't even know you!" Appertan answered with outrage. "How could you insist she leave?"

Michael met his gaze. "I am not insisting, Lord Appertan. You are."

Appertan's gray eyes narrowed, and his lips twitched, but he obviously couldn't refute that. "I would never allow my sister to leave with a stranger."

"And I don't intend to make her leave her home since I'll be returning to India soon. But I understand that Lady Blackthorne needs time to become acquainted with me, and I intend to give her that time."

Her flushed face took on a darker hue, and he wondered if she was embarrassed to be discussed so freely—so familiarly. He already knew she wasn't a woman given to standing by while others made decisions about her life, and he admired that.

"Very well," Appertan said between clenched teeth. "I'll accept that, as long as I never hear Cecilia complain in any way. How long do you plan to remain?"

"My schedule is flexible. Other than visiting my family, there is little I need to do in England."

"You are so anxious to return to India?" Lady Blackthorne asked. "We experienced much of it as children, including traveling up the country with our father's regiment. It was hot and wet and unpleasant."

It could be all of that. But was she so unadventur-
ous? he wondered with disappointment. "The climate
has its disadvantages, but the views can be pleasant.
All of that is of little consequence to me. I am a soldier
for the queen."

"You're not an officer?" Appertan asked, looking
curious for the first time that evening.

"I am a noncommissioned officer."

"That makes no sense." Appertan shook his head. "I
would never want to make things so hard on myself."

No one answered that, and Michael guessed that
Appertan made certain nothing was very difficult in
his life. How could one not relish a good challenge?
That thought momentarily changed the direction of his
thoughts, and his gaze slid to his wife. Now *she* was a
challenge.

After several minutes of silence while they continued to eat, Michael said to Appertan, "From what I
could see of the grounds during the storm, they look
well cared for. Your father would be pleased that you've
continued his excellent management."

He shrugged, lounging in his chair. "The servants
know their duties. Whatever else comes up, Cecilia is
perfectly capable of handling it. It's not that difficult."

Michael saw Lady Blackthorne inhale and briefly
close her eyes, as if she was embarrassed that Appertan
proved his own ignorance. Michael was more and more
disturbed every time the young man opened his mouth.

He kept remembering the pride with which the late Lord Appertan talked of his son—did he know Oliver at all? Sadness and frustration warred with each other in Michael's mind, and he knew how disappointed his commander would be, how conflicted Lady Blackthorne must feel, torn between the gentle pursuits of a lady, and the practical concerns of her family estate. He'd begun to think she was a woman too used to controlling everyone around her—even himself—but now he wasn't so certain.

"You must have an excellent steward yourself, Lord Blackthorne," his wife said, "considering that you're hardly ever home. Wait—now I remember that you wrote about your brother handling such duties."

He couldn't help the way his gaze swept over her. He was feeling possessive, and defensive on her behalf. "We keep in regular contact. But it is nowhere near the size of the earldom."

Suddenly, he wondered if other people saw him in the same light as Appertan, both of them peers who allowed others to take control. Much as he knew their situations were vastly different, it bothered him, made him wish there was something he could do to help Appertan see the error of his ways.

"No wonder you agreed to this marriage," Appertan said.

Michael felt the slur, saw Lady Blackthorne give a start and look away with embarrassment.

Michael regarded him impassively. "I did not accept your sister's dowry, nor do I have access to her funds. You can be certain I will not abuse her finances."

Appertan's contempt seemed to fade into puzzlement, then he shrugged again and started a conversation with Miss Webster about a party they would be attending. Lady Blackthorne finished eating, keeping her eyes on her plate.

At last, Appertan rose and tossed his napkin down. "I'm off to Enfield for the evening."

Michael was relieved his new brother-in-law didn't ask him to accompany him. Michael might have to call him on his behavior, not a way to win the young man over.

Miss Webster smiled at her fiancé. "I'm sure Papa has already sent the carriage for me." She looked back at Lady Blackthorne, and said, "But if you'd like me to stay . . ."

His wife smiled. "You mustn't keep your parents waiting, my dear. Have a good evening."

When Miss Webster and Appertan had gone, Michael sat back down.

Lady Blackthorne, hands on her armrests as if she meant to rise, paused to ask, "Is there something you wish to discuss, my lord?"

"I have no business asking personal questions of Lord Appertan, but I have some for you if you would humor me."

She dismissed the footmen, and they closed the doors as they departed, leaving the two of them alone again. She carefully drew her gloves back on. Did she wear them all the time, or did she choose this moment to bow to propriety?

After folding her hands in her lap, she spoke calmly. "I'll answer what I can."

"You married me for access to your funds, but from what I've been able to see, you aren't in London enjoying your freedom."

"I'm grateful for the favor you did me, and I'm using my financial freedom as I see fit."

"Taking care of your brother and his estate," he pointed out.

Her shoulders were stiff with tension, and he guessed she wanted to tell him to go to hell—in a lady-like manner, of course.

"My brother is very young, only twenty years of age. He inherited the title at eighteen, while all of his friends were—and still are—enjoying their youth. He needs to experience the same, just like any other young man."

"So does his steward report to him?"

"He reports to me."

"And the lawyers and bankers for such a vast estate?"

"They come to me."

He steepled his fingers, and he saw her glance at his bare hands. "And this pleases you? Do you plan to continue in this capacity?"

"Of course not." She leaned across the table toward him, and her eyes softened with earnestness. "It's only temporary, until he's a bit older."

He arched a brow in surprise. Was she truly naïve or just telling herself this? "You don't think you run the risk of him enjoying your coddling so much that he never behaves as a man?"

"You do not know this family, Lord Blackthorne," she said mildly.

"I knew your father well. Would this arrangement please him?"

"It would. I respect and admire the long tradition of my ancestors. These grounds and every estate in the earldom deserve the best care, and I'm devoted to them."

She spoke with such pride and fervor, as if the estates and its people meant everything to her. He admired her devotion, even as he knew she would someday be disappointed with this foolish path she'd chosen. She needed her own life, not that of her brother.

"You must be devoted," he said quietly, "to beg a stranger to marry you."

Cecilia knew she was blushing again but couldn't refute his words. She'd been devoted—and desperate. She had no choice but to go forward and minimize the damage. If she could just outlast his curiosity, surely her lawyers could somehow extract her without her losing everything.

"And Appertan's guardian?" he asked.

"He is a busy man and trusts me with the day-to-day affairs. Once a month he visits and examines everything. He's due in less than a week." She hoped Lord Blackthorne would not ask more—it was none of his business, after all. Lord Doddridge had been Oliver's idea—handpicked as a friend of their father's, yet one who was so busy with his own estates and Parliament, he would permit Oliver much leeway. As the new earl, Oliver had been allowed to choose his own guardian, and he'd thought the Hanburys far too rustic to oversee a prominent peer. Cecilia had no such choice and had been stuck with the Hanburys, to the distress of everyone involved—until she'd married Lord Blackthorne.

Lord Doddridge had control of the vast Appertan properties, but he was content to allow Oliver—and hence Cecilia—to oversee its management, as long as he received regular reports. But he held the purse strings tightly, something Oliver hadn't counted on. She couldn't explain that she'd been acting in Oliver's place to her own guardian, so conservative he would have surely contacted Lord Doddridge and ruined everything. She needed access to her own money, another reason to marry a man who would allow her that control.

As if reading her thoughts, Lord Blackthorne said, "I assume you needed your funds because your brother is quick to spend his own on pleasure rather than the estates?"

"You don't know what his life has been like," she said in a low voice.

"Regardless, in your opinion, Appertan cannot deal with his own estates, and you do not trust a man of business to do it for you. Does Appertan have any responsibilities at all?"

She leaned toward him, hands braced on the table. "Our father died, and Oliver has suffered with his grief."

"All while you managed more than your own duties—along with your grief."

"He is my responsibility, my lord. I gave my promise to my parents that I would see him well. Surely, having a younger brother, you understand that."

"I do. But you do him no favors in this, madam. You need to rethink his future, and your own."

"Are you threatening me, Lord Blackthorne?" She was proud of her soft, dignified voice.

"Why would I threaten you?" He sounded genuinely surprised. "I offer my advice as an objective person outside the family."

"Objective? For right now, you're my husband. I'm not sure how objective you can be." Now that he'd seen the impressive castle that was her country home, perhaps he was beginning to realize how much money he'd given up by allowing her her freedom. "Please tell me the truth—why did you marry me? You say you honored my father, but that cannot be the sum of it since you renounced the money I might have brought you. You're a viscount—you could find a perfectly lovely wife all by yourself."

"I'm a career soldier, Lady Blackthorne. Until this point, my regiment has been my mistress and wife. I only planned to marry under my own terms, for I needed no heirs, since my brother is perfectly adequate for that task. In that regard, you and I are well matched since you seem too busy to want children, should we not be blessed."

She blanched, for she never let herself think about children. And she didn't want him thinking about the *creating* of children.

"I believe, in marriage, we suit each other's purposes. You need access to your money . . ." His voice faded as he frowned.

"And you, my lord?" she whispered. "What do you need?"

He hesitated, then spoke in a low voice. "I thought I needed to help the children of my commander. I tried to write to you about how much he meant to me, but words are not often my forte. But there was something in your letters, my lady, that called to me in a way I'd never imagined."

She found herself barely breathing, staring at him, but he did not continue with the words that flattered even as they confused her.

He rose slowly to his feet, reaching for the cane hooked in the arm of his chair even as he cleared his throat. "As for your brother, Lady Blackthorne, I had to express my concerns."

"Then I hope you can be objective, my lord." She paused, realizing she could not make a grand exit—he could simply follow her right to their rooms. Modulating her voice, she said, "I know the evening is still young. I will be reading in the drawing room if you wish to join me."

"I thank you for the invitation, but I am fatigued from the journey. I'll retire for the evening."

She kept her breath held, afraid she'd let it out in a big sigh of relief, knowing that most men would insist they retire together. Feeling grateful for his consideration, she said, "I wish you a good evening, Lord Blackthorne."

They stared at each other, the silence fraught with the new awareness she now associated with him. He bowed his head and left her alone in the dining room. The silent footmen entered as if on cue, and, feeling numb with relief, she watched them work. She'd thought she had everything in hand—she was helping her brother until he was old enough to take over, she was in control of her own money, and had miraculously found a husband who wouldn't intrude in any way at all, except as a convenient reason she wouldn't have to tolerate other suitors. She wasn't going to be like her mother, so desperate to cling to her husband, to make sure he remained faithful, that she dragged her children on military campaigns in a country that ended up being the death of her and her son.

But now Cecilia's world was starting to unravel. Oliver's behavior was growing worse instead of better, and her absent husband had decided to involve himself in her life.

And she was fascinated by him—overwhelmingly, completely, helplessly fascinated.

Closing her eyes, she told herself she would get through this. She just had to be patient. Oliver would realize his responsibilities, then she'd be able to trust him with everything their ancestors had built. And Lord Blackthorne had come right out and said he was returning to India as soon as possible, hopefully leaving their marriage as it was.

She would consult her lawyers, but until she received a reply, she had to do her best to steer clear of Lord Blackthorne.

After an hour alone in the library, Cecilia reluctantly retired to her bedroom, trying to keep as quiet as possible. Her lady's maid, Nell, took the hint and asked nothing about the husband ensconced nearby in her apartments. Cecilia knew the girl's silence would only last so long, but for now she appreciated it. When she was alone, she pressed her ear to the door of the dressing room that separated their bedrooms, but she heard nothing.

At last she crept to her bed, where she read almost until midnight, not feeling the least bit tired. After finishing her novel, she lay down, but her eyes refused to close. Sighing, she put on her dressing gown, picked up a candleholder, and went out into the shadowy corridor. There was supposed to be a lamp lit at each end, but apparently the footmen had forgotten. Shaking her head, she held the candle higher. The library was on the ground floor, and as she approached the main staircase dominating the entrance hall, she slowed her step, for the darkness overtook the cavernous room where the corridor opened out into it, and her tiny candle gave off little light. But she knew every inch of her home well.

Just as she reached the balustrade, her foot hit something hard, pitching her forward into the darkness. The candle went out, her hands flailed for the balustrade, and a feeling of terror overwhelmed her. The bottom seemed to drop out of her stomach as she began to fall.

Chapter 3

Cecilia's feet hit the first couple steps, but she was pitching forward, unable to right herself, terrified and helpless. Just as she would have tumbled headfirst into the blackness, her hand connected with the balustrade and gripped it hard to catch herself. She felt pain at her shoulder as her body came to a jerking stop, but she didn't let go. Collapsing against the rail, she remained still, eyes closed, breath heaving in her chest as she hung there.

Slowly, she tried to stand up on the stair, and felt a mild twinge in her ankle that was nothing compared to what might have happened if she'd fallen all the way to the bottom.

She might even have broken her neck.

The candle had gone out; she could see nothing and certainly didn't want to find the library in the dark. Gripping the balustrade, wincing from the pain in her shoulder, she limped up the few steps to the top, then bent down, trying to feel what she'd tripped over.

Frowning when she discovered nothing, she dropped to her knees and widened the search with both hands. Still nothing. Had she just tripped over her own feet?

But her toes were sore to the touch, and she could swear they'd hit something hard. Shaking her head, she felt her way back down the corridor and into her room, where the candlelight was a relief. She washed her perspiring face with hands that still shook and couldn't stop thinking about what might have happened if she hadn't been lucky enough to catch herself. Propping her foot on a pillow in bed, she picked up the book she'd just finished and, with a sigh, started from the beginning.

When Nell arrived with a tray before dawn, Cecilia debated telling the girl about her midnight accident but knew everyone would put up a fuss. She wanted to get on with her day, not be coddled. Her ankle felt better already, and she was determined to go on her usual long walk. As Nell styled her hair, Cecilia waited with resignation for the questions to begin. She didn't hear anything from the dressing room.

Nell had seen her glance. "Only you, Lady Cecilia," she said, shaking her head. "I guess I should say Lady Blackthorne."

"Pardon me, Nell?"

"Only you would marry a man ye'd never seen, from halfway round the world, and be lucky enough to land a handsome one. We all thought ye crazy, beggin' yer pardon, but ye come up smellin' like a rose."

Cecilia reluctantly smiled. "You know his features don't matter at all, Nell."

"Hmm, so ye say." Nell continued to brush out Cecilia's long blond hair. "But I will tell ye somethin' ye might find interestin'." She leaned closer before glancing out the window. "That husband o' yours, who ye didn't spend a wedding night with—"

"Nell, we don't even know each other!"

"—he's a proud man, that one. Said he didn't want a valet, that he was used to takin' care o' himself in the army."

That gave Cecilia pause. Lord Blackthorne had been raised as a gentleman—surely he was used to servants.

"When he needs laundry done, I'm sure he'll give us a call." Nell sniffed. "A strange man. Maybe you were right to make him wait on ye for a while."

In the mirror, she met Cecilia's eyes with her own wide ones.

"I mean, beggin' yer pardon, milady."

But there was a smile at the corner of the girl's mouth; she knew what she could get away with.

"Nell," Cecilia began hesitantly, "were the lamps lit in the corridor outside my room last night?"

Nell frowned. "Aye, they lit me way to bed. Why do ye ask?"

Cecilia shrugged and forced a smile. "No reason. I couldn't sleep and didn't see the flicker of light beneath my door, and I was just curious."

The storm must have sent a draft through the old castle and blown out the lamps.

After Nell helped her into a plain morning gown—"Blue to match yer eyes!"—Cecilia ate a quick piece of toast with her hot chocolate from the tray Nell had brought, then took a shawl and went outside. The sun was only just above the horizon, the ground glittering with autumn dew, the leaves beginning to turn orange, yellow, and red. Though the breeze was brisk, it promised to be a lovely day. She followed her usual route, one that led her past tenant farmers and the mill, the stables and outbuildings, where people knew they could speak to her if they needed to. She avoided the soggy patches left over from the storm, even as gardeners were already picking up broken twigs.

She'd no sooner left the formal gardens when she pulled up short in surprise. Lord Blackthorne, limping along with the aid of his cane, had come to a stop when he saw her. For a moment, they stared at each other beneath a glorious sun. Though he was still dressed plainly, conservatively, nothing could hide the very maleness of him. He made her far too aware of him as a man—as her husband. She couldn't help feeling that he wanted to look at her in a more thorough manner but stopped himself. She was used to the admiration of men, but this seemed . . . different, brazen, dark, with maybe a touch of possession.

She thought of Nell calling him handsome. It seemed too tame a word for him. He was too unfashionably . . . large. He wasn't wearing a coat, only his shirtsleeves and a waistcoat above his trousers, a simple cravat tied at his throat. Now she could see that he needed no padding in his clothing, that he was broad through the shoulders, even barrel-chested, yet narrow through the hips. She felt herself blushing, remembering how she'd protested when he looked at her in the same manner.

He briefly doffed his hat. "Good morning, Lady Blackthorne."

"Good morning, Lord Blackthorne. I am surprised to find you exercising your leg. Should it not be healing?"

"Your concern is appreciated, madam, but the leg will stiffen if I don't use it. The stronger it gets, the less I'll need to use the cane."

"But . . . the shrapnel?"

He shrugged. "The doctors say the pieces of metal might work themselves out on their own, or they might not. I'll just have to become used to whatever the outcome."

She hesitated, wishing she could say she preferred to be alone but knowing she couldn't. "I am walking toward the stables, if you'd like to join me."

He nodded. She expected to slow her pace to accommodate him, but he moved along briskly. He had obviously been in fine physical condition before the wound, and that must stand him in good stead.

"You are going riding?" he asked.

"No, I walk every morning. The stables are simply one stop on my way. Did you plan to ride?"

"I did enough of that yesterday. It made my leg quite stiff."

Another awkward silence grew between them. She looked into the distance, at the green rolling hills, the occasional cottage.

"I love this land," she found herself saying. "I wasn't born here, and we did not spend much time here at all until Oliver returned to go to Eton, when Mother and I came with him. But there is something about the place of our ancestors that calls you to do your best to maintain it." *But not Oliver,* she thought with a twinge of sadness.

"I understand," he said. "I have been improving my estate to bring it back to what it once was."

She gave him a curious glance but didn't feel she could question him.

He accompanied her from building to building, and she realized ruefully that in less then twenty-four hours, the news of his arrival had spread far and wide. People turned out in droves to see Lord Blackthorne, and many boldly introduced themselves. What would happen when she had the marriage invalidated? There would be a scandal, of course, but her servants knew they had not spent the night together. And Cecilia didn't care what other people thought, she told herself.

Lord Blackthorne proved a knowledgeable man about every position on the estate; if only she could discuss things like this with Oliver. As she answered various questions the staff asked about a grain shipment to London, or which cattle had been selected to be delivered by train to market, she felt the uncomfortable stare of her husband. He watched her like a falcon watched a rabbit, intently, single-mindedly, and it was like an itch she couldn't reach, couldn't scratch. By midmorning, she wished he would just go away so she could feel herself again, but he followed her into Appertan Hall and right into the study, where the steward and secretary both waited. She introduced her husband to the men, and was gratified when they did not begin directing their estate questions to him, as some men might have.

She spent another two hours dealing with estate matters and correspondence, and she kept waiting for her husband to leave, but he seemed interested. Even when he was leaning on his cane, staring out the window, there was an alertness about him that kept drawing her attention. More than once, she was distracted by him and lost her train of thought. The steward and secretary shared amused glances but wiped away their smiles when she frowned at them.

At last, the two employees left, and she sat back in

her chair behind the desk and met Lord Blackthorne's contemplative gaze.

"Go ahead, say what you need to," she said briskly.

He perched one hip on the edge of the window seat. "Tell me about Lord Appertan."

She frowned. "I thought I already had. And surely my father spoke of him often."

"But I want to hear your thoughts."

She wanted to say that her brother's life—her own—was none of his business but didn't want to antagonize him. She had already written to her lawyers, asking about the proxy marriage and what options she had. But she had to bide her time until she received a response.

She sighed. Anything she told Lord Blackthorne about Oliver could be gotten from any family acquaintance, after all. "As I said, we were born in India and had a home in Bombay. We spent summer in the Hills to escape the worst of the heat."

"I am surprised your mother did not spend more time in England."

"She did not want to be parted from my father." Cecilia spoke impassively, but inside, her stomach churned with the memories that wouldn't go away. How, as she grew older, her mother confided more and more in her as if she were a grown woman, about her fears that Appertan would find a mistress to shame her if she left him alone. Once or twice at a dinner party, she even forced Cecilia to follow her father, as if he might sneak away from the card room for an illicit affair. The constant neediness and dread and pessimism wore away at Cecilia, until she realized she could escape into her studies, into her books. And that also helped her escape the memories.

"You went on campaign," Lord Blackthorne said, and it wasn't a question.

"We followed the drum, a military family." She forced a smile, her fingers playing restlessly with a quill on the desk. "When Oliver was younger, he played with all the other boys, and it didn't matter whose father was a sergeant or whose was a colonel. But as he grew older, their different circumstances began to play out among even the children. When Papa decided it was time to return to England, for Oliver to attend Eton, I thought things would be better for my brother."

"Eton can alter a boy," Lord Blackthorne said. "I noticed it among my friends."

But not himself? she wondered, but didn't ask.

"It's supposed to build character," she continued, "or so I heard. But the friends he made weren't the kind I would have chosen for him. They now like to drink too much and . . . socialize with the wrong element. He is immature, and I wish my father were still alive to take him in hand."

Lord Blackthorne briefly looked away. He must miss her father, and she would try to remember that.

"Every young man goes through such a period," he

said. "But Appertan has not come out of it, and, forgive me, but I don't think you're helping by managing everything for him."

"I'm doing what I must," she said coolly.

"Then I have a suggestion. Let me become involved." He left the window seat and limped toward the desk, sitting opposite her.

She stiffened. "I am managing the estate just fine, my lord."

"I don't mean the estate—with Appertan. Let me get to know him, to guide him. I have a facility for instructing young men. I was often in charge of the new soldiers. And I have a brother, too. When I became the viscount, I, too, needed a guardian, but when I reached my majority, it was Allen, at twenty, who assumed much of the mantle of the Blackthorne estates. I know exactly what Appertan is going through. Although Allen and I are closer in age than your brother and I are, I do understand the competitiveness that can exist between men."

Though he made a persuasive argument, she was ready to refuse. But at the last moment, her common sense overruled her feelings of defensiveness, and she remembered her situation. If Lord Blackthorne was busy befriending Oliver, she would have more time to make a decision about the marriage.

Surely, Oliver could deal with Lord Blackthorne. She remembered her father's constant praise of the man, his ability to negotiate a compromise with even the most stubborn of enemies. It was almost like a character reference for a new employee.

"I do not know if this is a good idea," she said slowly. "You are at least ten years older than Oliver."

"Ten years exactly, my lady."

"I have matchless deductive powers," she said, forcing her voice to be light.

He nodded, so focused on whatever task at hand, even if it was just talking to her. When his dark eyes looked into hers, she felt as if she were the center of the world at that moment, very different from when her suitors used to fawn over her. It was too intense, even threatening to her very way of life. This man could wield so much power over her if he chose. She'd given him that power; she'd have to find the best way to take it back.

"If I allowed you to . . . work with Oliver, what would you do?" she asked.

"Spend time with him in masculine pursuits—hunting, riding, even socializing. I imagine it would help to meet and understand his friends. Then I should be able to see why he so resists the responsibilities of his title."

She bit her lip, trying not to smile.

He tilted his head. "Did I say something amusing?"

"Forgive me. I am trying to imagine you with Oliver's fellow young bucks."

His lips curved in the faintest hint of a smile, and he relaxed back in his chair. "I am well aware of the mentality."

"Are you? Does that mean you went through such a period yourself?"

"Not a very long one. I enlisted at eighteen, and although men off duty often embarrass themselves in drink, that did not appeal to me."

"I am not surprised," she murmured, studying him just as intently as he liked to study her. "Are you and your brother close?"

His eyes seemed to focus inward. "We are. Although it has been twelve years since I've been able to spend much time at home, we were always playmates as children, and our letters have deepened our friendship as adults."

"I find myself envious," she murmured, her eyes stinging.

"It is not too late, madam." He hesitated. "You can have such a relationship with your brother. With your parents gone, you need the closeness of family."

Her throat was tight with the emotions she didn't want to reveal. His kindness had shown through in his letters, and now, seeing it in person, made her feel so very confused.

"So I have your approval?" he urged.

"Are you asking for it?" She spoke softly, wondering about the kind of husband he'd be.

"He is your brother."

"So if I asked you to leave him alone, you would?"

He regarded her solemnly. "He is in need of an older male influence, but yes, I would abide by your wishes."

She realized she'd been holding her breath, and she let it out slowly. "Very well. You have my permission to attempt the battle of Oliver."

His head tipped back as if in surprise. "He's been as bad as all that?"

"No, no, but it is you who make it seem like he's your new campaign."

"I am a soldier; I see much of life like a battle to be mastered and won."

"And do you often win, my lord?" she asked softly.

"Almost always, my lady."

He'd lowered his voice until it was a deep rumble that reverberated through her. Again, she felt a twinge of intriguing danger, which she would do her best to ignore. She was responsible for Oliver, and she'd vowed never again to fail a member of her family.

The door swung open, and Penelope entered like a floral spring breeze. "Hello, Cecilia!" she trilled, then came to a stop upon seeing Lord Blackthorne, her happy smile fading to pleased curiosity. "Oh, I am interrupting you."

Lord Blackthorne rose stiffly to his feet. "Good morning, Miss Webster."

"You are always welcome, Penelope," Cecilia said, finding herself relieved.

Hesitantly, the young woman said, "Did you remember that we were going to paint the autumn colors of your garden after luncheon? But we don't have to, of course. Circumstances have obviously changed." She gave Lord Blackthorne a bright smile.

Cecilia knew Penelope was thrilled with the revelation of Lord Blackthorne. But then she was very much like her sister, Hannah, who'd been a firm believer in true love. For a moment, melancholia rose inside her at the senseless drowning of her dear friend. Every death seemed to buffet Cecilia in a new direction.

"Of course we'll still paint," she said, grateful that she had the other woman to remind her that there was more to life than business.

"Oh, I'm glad," Penelope said. "Talbot asked me to tell you that luncheon will be served in half an hour."

Cecilia glanced at the mantel clock in surprise. The morning had passed swiftly. "We'll be there."

She expected Lord Blackthorne to follow Penelope out of the study, but after a couple limping steps, leaning heavily on his cane, he turned back to her.

"Miss Webster was introduced to me as Appertan's fiancée. For a young man still living wildly, the engagement seems unusual."

"They grew up in constant contact, as the Websters have long leased a manor from the estate."

"And Miss Webster was determined she would be the next countess?" Lord Blackthorne asked.

"I never had that feeling," Cecilia said, blinking in surprise.

"Then whose idea was it?"

She rose to her feet. "When my brother announced the engagement, I did not question what had gone on privately between them. I trusted their feelings. Oliver plans to wait until at least his twenty-first birthday to set a wedding date, which will give them time to decide if such a match truly suits."

"He is not certain of that yet he already asked for her hand in marriage?"

"You make quick judgments, my lord," she said coolly. "I wrote to you about Penelope's sister, my dearest friend, who drowned in a pond near their home. Such tragedy often brings people together, and they no longer want to waste time alone."

"Then it is good that I know these circumstances, madam. They might affect how I deal with your brother."

"Be compassionate with him, Lord Blackthorne," she said in a quieter voice, sinking back down into her chair.

"I do not believe compassion has helped him much, but I won't forget that you requested it of me."

He limped away before she could respond, closing the door behind him. She finished filling out her report to Oliver's guardian about the daily management of the estate. But it wasn't easy to think of business. Lord Blackthorne's belief he knew what was best for her brother disturbed her. Was it that she herself should be able to help Oliver and couldn't seem to find the way? Or was it that she found herself attracted to such a strong-willed man?

Chapter 4

Luncheon was a grim affair. Cecilia watched Lord Blackthorne study Oliver's slow recovery from a night of drinking and waited for her new husband to change his mind. But he didn't, only kept talking to Oliver about upcoming issues for the next session of Parliament, as if Oliver knew or cared.

But he should care, Cecilia reminded herself. There was no use being upset at Lord Blackthorne because he was right. Yet she wanted to believe her brother would overcome the tragedies of his young life eventually. Lord Blackthorne had obviously kept abreast of political issues through his family and friends while on the other side of the world. Oliver should be able to do the same.

After the meal, Penelope met Cecilia's gaze and gestured with her head toward the windows, where a rare sun was shining.

"Excuse us, gentlemen," Cecilia said, coming to her feet.

It was obvious Lord Blackthorne had to struggle to stand, and Oliver seemed to do so reluctantly. She imagined his pounding head made movement painful. Why would one self-inflict such suffering? Except, perhaps, to forget for a while . . .

"Penelope and I have an engagement in the garden," Cecilia continued. "Do not let us keep you from your discussion."

Oliver's brows lowered disapprovingly over his bloodshot eyes, but she ignored him.

Outside in the formal gardens, Cecilia found easels already waiting for them, and they placed them near a stunning view of the gurgling fountain in the foreground and autumn-tipped trees swaying behind in the park. They mixed the ground powder of their chosen paint cakes in water, chatting about color and detail and nothing in particular. But once they were briefly quiet in concentration on the scene, Penelope seemed to start speaking as if she'd been awaiting the right moment.

"Cecilia, Oliver told me he spent an evening out with his friends again last night."

She couldn't tell from his bloodshot, wincing eyes? Cecilia wondered.

"We'd had an engagement to walk this morning, but he slept through it. I am . . . concerned about him." She gave Cecilia the pained yet eager look of a puppy hungry for a treat.

"I know," she answered on a tired sigh, gazing un-seeing on the colors she was mixing on her palette.

"We had discussed waiting at least a year to marry, but perhaps . . . setting an earlier date would help."

Cecilia glanced at her in surprise. "You and he have discussed this? It is after all a personal matter between the two of you, and perhaps your parents."

"I know, and no, we have not discussed it. I wanted your opinion first." Penelope bit her lip and looked away. "I thought perhaps marriage would help him to . . . settle down."

It was as if she'd heard the discussion between Lord Blackthorne and Cecilia. Or perhaps Oliver had forgotten one too many "engagements"—as if he'd forgotten their engagement to marry.

She wondered if Penelope was clinging to her fiancé, soon to be her husband, desperate to be with him, to change him. Cecilia felt a momentary twinge of dismay at the thought of Penelope's becoming like Lady Appertan.

"Although my opinion doesn't count—" Cecilia began.

"But you're his sister! Of course anything you say counts!"

Cecilia smiled and touched her arm. "Thank you. But you know what I mean. Only the two of you can decide what's best. But . . . I don't believe marriage will help settle Oliver. Only maturity, and the realization that other things are more important than his pleasure, will truly help him. You have to trust that he will gradually come to this conclusion. Most men do." She hoped. Although she was afraid to trust Lord Blackthorne regardless of her father's praise, she found herself saying a silent prayer that he could help her brother be a better man, a better husband.

Penelope kept her eyes downcast as she nodded. "I appreciate your opinion."

"But regardless, I'll stand by whatever the two of you decide."

"Just like you stood by us when we became engaged." Penelope smiled.

"You didn't need my support. Your mother was happy for you."

Penelope giggled. "Thrilled, you mean. She always hoped I would catch the eye of a peer."

"What mother doesn't wish that?" Cecilia said with a chuckle.

"Surely yours wanted the same for you? And you've succeeded."

Cecilia hid a wince. "My mother . . . yes, you are right, she wanted the best for me." *Was that even true?*

"Lord Blackthorne is a knowledgeable man of the world."

Cecilia eyed her with faint amusement. "Are you saying you think Oliver should become such a man?"

"Oh, no! Oliver is a man comfortable in England, at

ease in drawing rooms or in the countryside. I think he still fights the memories of his time in India but wants to overcome them."

"And Lord Blackthorne? Tell me your impressions of him."

"I think you were very brave and in love to marry a man you'd never met."

"You may say it without hurting my feelings, Penelope—you wouldn't have done the same."

"I am not brave like you. Lord Blackthorne . . . he seems a stern man, with a strong feeling of duty to his country. He will go wherever his regiment sends him, and you'll be separated once again. Have you ever thought of traveling with him?"

Cecilia's eyes widened. "No, my dear, my place is here. I had enough of India."

"Then you will be separated much of the time."

"He writes compelling letters. We will get by." If she even stayed married to him.

Late that night, Michael came awake with a start. He didn't know where he was at first until the shadowy gloom revealed the bedroom where his wife had banished him.

His very skittish wife.

But he couldn't fault thoughts of his wife for why he awoke in the middle of the night. It had been happening long before he met her. Dreams clung to the corners of his mind like cobwebs. He saw his friends, the three his military decision had doomed to death. In his dreams, they were alive again, even Lord Appertan, taking his son in hand and making a man of him.

With a sigh, Michael slid his legs to the side and sat on the edge of the bed. These dreams weren't nightmares. No one haunted him, or berated the decisions he and his superiors, the Duke of Rothford and the Earl of Knightsbridge, had made in all honor.

But the sadness of those lives cut short could not be denied, and he felt a debt of honor—not one of guilt, as Rothford and Knightsbridge foolishly insisted on feeling—to try to help those left behind. Guilt had no place, once a battlefield decision had been made to the best of one's knowledge and ability. And he would never allow himself to be ruled by emotion.

Lady Cecilia's family had been altered by a decision he'd help make: Three men had died because Michael and his fellow soldiers had thought it was noble and humane to release prisoners—including women and children—about to be tortured for information in a secret encampment. He, Rothford, and Knightsbridge had turned their backs while their prisoners slipped into the jungle, and thought themselves making the honorable choice.

But their regiment had been attacked by the prisoners they'd released, and three soldiers—good friends and mentors—had died. Rothford and Knightsbridge had returned to England to make amends to the families of the other two dead soldiers. Young Appertan was too soon the earl, without his father's guidance and knowledge. Michael could help make that right.

Lady Cecilia had written that the new earl had left Cambridge University to assume his duties. Like a man, Michael had thought at the time, now realizing he'd only made assumptions without knowing the facts. The young Lord Appertan seemed to be a spoiled, arrogant boy who put his own pleasures above duty and responsibility. Weak and selfish, he left the burdens of the earldom on his sister, enjoying all the money and the pleasures for himself.

Michael could see what kind of woman Cecilia was: hardworking, selfless, beloved by her servants and tenants. And if he worried it was love of power that drove her to exercise control over the estate, he'd soon been able to tell that she was just as open to suggestions from the people below her and would change her mind. She wasn't afraid of stepping in something unpleasant in a barn or taking a laborer's dirty hand. He'd watched everyone on the estate consult her even as they praised her to him, her new husband. He'd almost felt proud, as if he'd had something to do with it. In one sense he had: he'd enabled her to have access to her own funds, to do as she needed to guide the earldom. He long ago heard of the late Lord Appertan's pride in her, and now he knew it was justified.

And he was still astonished by her range of knowledge about every aspect of the estate. She must have been tutored at Appertan's side in mathematics and even agriculture rather than simply learning the feminine studies of languages, domestic skills, and artistic endeavors like painting. Although she'd probably mastered those as well from what he'd been able to observe so far. Their written conversations could lead to even better discussions—if she allowed it.

But there was a sadness deep within her that surprised him. Did others see it, or did they simply want to believe that she was content with her life?

First, he would make her life easier by teaching her brother to be a man. This should help her soften her regard for him and hasten a more normal marriage. He hoped it would happen quickly because sleeping so near Cecilia might surely destroy his peace of mind.

Michael awoke in the morning, feeling tired from his restless night. He'd bathed the night before, so he dressed for the day, looking out the window. He knew who he was looking for: his wife. Perhaps she thought of him, even longed for a man's touch. He knew what *he* was missing, after all. He might not be reckless, but he'd had the occasional night with a willing woman. Of course, he had no idea how far things had gone with her suitors before she married him . . .

Hearing a knock on the door, he went to answer it.

Cecilia stood there, hands linked together with casual elegance, fresh as sunshine in her cream-colored gown. He wanted to bask in the warmth of her, and his body, long starved for a woman's attention, flared to uncomfortable life once again.

She didn't cross the threshold. "I thought I would accompany you to the breakfast parlor."

"Very well." Picking up the book he intended to return to the library—the nights were long with Cecilia so nearby—he limped into the corridor, and she walked at his side. Her floral scent drifted to his nostrils, and he inhaled deeply, silently, half closing his eyes. But when she glanced at him, he regarded her impassively. In the breakfast parlor, he placed his book on the dining table.

She glanced at it. "You enjoy reading, my lord?"

"It is a comfort to me in the field, when there are few others."

"Military history," she mused, studying the title. "Oliver does not read. He had access to the best education, but he treated it lightly, squandered it." She turned away and helped herself to eggs and toast.

He heard the envy and frustration in her voice and wondered if she sometimes wished she'd been born a man and the heir. He certainly did not; her beauty was a soft grace on a tired morn. He thought of waking up at her side and reminded himself that he'd never needed soft comforts; he could wait for them now.

He filled his plate with fried trout, along with the eggs and toast. Their gazes met, and he saw the clear, intelligent blue of her eyes. Did she guess his thoughts? If she did, she would run away.

"You have offered your help with my wayward brother," she continued, carrying her plate toward the table. "And you're dealing with me, a reluctant wife. Why?"

He came to a stop across the table from her. "Your father earned my loyalty every day, Lady Blackthorne. He taught me strategy and ruthlessness; he taught me patience. He guided me in the ways of diplomacy and negotiation, helping me to understand the dark hearts of men." Except that last time, when Michael had missed the signs, been fooled so utterly. Through a clenched jaw, he finished, "He saw in me a worthwhile soldier when my own father thought my calling was a mistake. I will not forget Lord Appertan's belief in me." Feeling that he'd revealed too much, he tried to lighten the mood. "Perhaps he was preparing me all along to come home to you."

She rolled her eyes. "That is not true."

"How do you know? He talked about you constantly, and your brother, of course, but the focus was always you. It was as if he knew we would suit each other."

She bit her plump lip, and he almost forgot the point he was making, so instantly did he wish to lean across the table and steal a kiss.

"Now you are deluding yourself, hoping to persuade

me to change my opinion of our marriage. My father and I often discussed my various suitors, and never once did he show a preference. He trusted me to make my own decision."

"Believe what you will."

"However he trained you to be a soldier," she said, going back to the original, safe topic, "he didn't give that to Oliver."

"He never got the chance. He was about to come home when he died."

He heard her gasp, saw her eyes moisten as she sat down heavily. In that moment, she was a vulnerable daughter, not a commanding woman.

"I—I didn't know," she whispered.

"It was to be a surprise." His voice was gruff in memory as he took his seat. He hadn't wanted his commander to retire, felt he could still learn from him. Those choices were taken away by one battlefield decision—a wrong one, made in good conscience. But Lord Appertan had always taught him to move on, that the past was the past.

"Thank you for telling me that," she said softly.

She searched his face for a moment, and he kept his expression impassive, a lifelong study and so easy now, he didn't have to think about it. They silently ate their breakfast.

When at last she rose, he knew she was leaving on her walk. "May I accompany you this morn?"

"I would prefer to be alone today if you do not mind." She spoke firmly.

"Of course."

He followed her to the door of the breakfast parlor and stood in the doorway, seeing two maids and a page cease whispering and look away with guilt. Cecilia would have to accept their marriage soon, both for the benefit of her reputation—and for his tenuous hold on his control.

Chapter 5

Cecilia spent the morning with her head in a whirl, finding it difficult to concentrate on her daily tasks. Even her walk brought her no relief. Lord Blackthorne was so difficult to read, his eyes calm rather than snapping with whatever emotion he felt. In such an offhand manner, he'd revealed that her father had been on his way home to them.

It hurt deep in her stomach to imagine that by one extra day, he'd lost his life, his chance to retire from the army. She wanted to be angry at God for such cruel fate, but every day, people suffered life's traumas. She was no different.

Lord Blackthorne had surely acted out of honor and duty by marrying her; she should be grateful, and she was. But for the first time, it bothered her that she was someone's idea of a debt, she, who'd been the toast of London her first Season, who had already been proposed to several times. Ah, she was a vain creature after all, that she'd want a convenient husband to confess he'd fallen in love with her letters, like the fictitious story she told others about their relationship. She'd boasted they'd debated books and art, that they'd even shared amusement over the mundane topics of raising sheep versus cattle. In reality, she'd told him about her life on the country estate, just hoping to have him keep writing more about the military world that her own father chose over his family.

At luncheon, there was a strained tension coming from Oliver toward Lord Blackthorne, whose topic of conversation left Parliament behind and switched to horses. Oliver reluctantly told him about several new additions to the stables, and they discussed the breeding of horseflesh for a while, from the demands of a military horse all the way down to what a lady required. Cecilia contributed where she wanted to, for she knew all about the cost of Oliver's new horses.

"Lord Appertan, would you show me about the estate by horseback?" Lord Blackthorne asked. "I would like to continue this discussion and see more of the land your father described to me in such detail."

Cecilia saw the suspicious glance Oliver gave him, as if Lord Blackthorne shouldn't be curious. He was her husband, after all.

Her temporary husband, she reminded herself.

"Of course, Lord Blackthorne," Oliver said at last. "I have time to ride this afternoon."

He sounded as if he had a rigorous schedule that he

could hardly interrupt, Cecilia thought, briefly lowering her gaze to hide her amusement.

"Cecilia," Oliver said, "I will be having several friends over tonight for an evening of cards. Would you speak to the housekeeper and make whatever arrangements are necessary?"

She withheld a frown as she considered him. He'd always met his friends elsewhere for whatever drunken fun they had. Was the sudden change due to the arrival of Lord Blackthorne?

"Oliver, I will see that you and your friends have whatever refreshments you need." She barely knew his friends, only one or two of whom were from local families, and the others up from London on occasion.

"We'll use the billiard room. Oh, and you might have the maids prepare several guest rooms, just in case."

She nodded, not wanting drunken young men falling from their horses. He did not ask Lord Blackthorne to join them, and Cecilia gritted her teeth at his rudeness. She was about to speak, when she could have sworn Lord Blackthorne almost imperceptibly shook his head, as if he had other plans for her brother.

She'd agreed to this, she reminded herself. She'd wanted Lord Blackthorne to focus on someone other than herself. When the men left on their ride, she told herself she was relieved to be free of the both of them.

* * *

That night, well after midnight, Cecilia could hear the drunken laughter of Oliver's friends echoing through the castle. She was in her room but not undressed; servants kept sending messages via the new page, Francis: "Are you certain we should provide more brandy, Lady Blackthorne?" "They are roaming the corridors, Lady Blackthorne, making a terrible mess in more and more rooms!"

She had greeted their guests earlier in the evening, of course. They'd grinned as they each bent over her hand, eyeing her too boldly, making her feel uncomfortable and embarrassed. They made what they thought were sly jokes about her as if she were too simpleminded to understand the crude references. They'd already been imbibing and were hardly witty as a result.

Strangely, she'd found herself wishing Lord Blackthorne had been present, as if she needed to remind the men that she had a husband who might take offense. But her "husband" had spent the evening in the library after his long ride with Oliver. She'd seen him limping stiffly away from the stables, wondered if perhaps he'd overexerted his injured leg. But one could never tell a man so.

Oliver's friends had been upsetting the household more and more as the evening advanced. Susan, the upstairs maid, had heard something crash, and when she went inside the billiards room to investigate, she'd been indecently handled by one of the guests. That was the last straw, as far as Cecilia was concerned. If Oliver didn't see that his friends were abusing his hospitality, then *she* would make them understand.

After sending Susan to bed, Cecilia moved through the darkened house, carrying a candleholder, the sounds of revelry growing louder and louder as she descended to the first floor. Something else crashed, and she could hear a roar of laughter.

She approached the billiard room from the rear of the house rather than the front public rooms. The way was darker, and to her surprise, lamps were once again extinguished, which made her progress slow. With her candle, she could see a short distance before her, but every alcove or corridor became a gaping hole of darkness once she passed. She shook off her uneasiness—she was only reacting this way because she'd tripped at the top of the stairs the other night.

Just as she reached the closed double doors to the billiard room, she heard a rush of air behind her, then a man's arms closed around her. She cried out, but the sound was lost against the loud voices from the billiard room, even as the candle fell from her hands and went out before it hit the floor.

Stunned, she felt the man's hot breath against her ear, his moist lips moving. "We've been waiting for you. But maybe you'd like to play a bit first."

And then he was dragging her away from the billiard room. She struggled, appalled and offended and a little bit frightened that she could be overwhelmed so easily—that decent men could lose their heads like this under the influence of strong drink. And these were the kinds of men who befriended Oliver? He was so gullible that perhaps he gave them whatever they wanted, money, liquor, his influence.

Not loose women, surely, she thought, not in this house. She opened her mouth to demand her release, but he clamped his damp palm over her mouth as if he sensed her intent. The lit edges of the billiard-room door receded into the darkness, and she had her first moment of real fear. If she could not make this drunken brute realize his error, she wasn't sure what might happen.

She tried to bite his hand, but he gave her a tight squeeze around the ribs that made her groan instead.

"Be a good girl, now. You'll get your money at the end of the night."

Then she heard the strangest sound, a growl of rage from nearby that made her assailant pause. They weren't alone anymore.

"Unhand *my wife*!" barked a voice in the commanding tones of a man used to being obeyed.

Lord Blackthorne, she thought with relief. She couldn't see him in the darkness, but neither could her captor.

The man laughed. "She's no one's wife, except one for hire. Wait your turn."

She felt the rush of air beside her, heard the sound of flesh meeting flesh, then a man's grunt. The hold on her loosened, and she ducked away, crying out as her hair, brushed out for the night, was caught from behind.

"Damn you!" Lord Blackthorne grunted.

She felt him lunge past her. She flung back the door to the billiard room, and yellow, flickering light spilled out into the corridor, illuminating the shadows. She whirled about and saw Lord Blackthorne in his shirt-sleeves, trousers, and boots. He knelt above her assailant, pummeling him. The man—she now recognized him as Sir Bevis Fenton from London—threw a couple punches of his own, but Lord Blackthorne had him pinned to the floor. Helplessly, Cecilia picked up his cane, not knowing what else to do.

Oliver staggered to the doorway and was bumped from behind by several other curious men, who stood on tiptoes to see past him.

"Hey, who's that attackin' Fenton?" one of them cried, beginning to push Oliver aside.

She stepped into the light, knowing she looked wrinkled and wild, with her hair falling all around her. The men pulled up in surprise. One of them actually lost his balance and fell backward onto a chair, gaping openmouthed like a fish.

"He's getting what he deserves," she said coldly. "He attacked me from behind."

She saw Oliver's grin falter and fade, and he glanced

again at Lord Blackthorne, who was now dragging the nearly insensible man to his feet. In the shadows away from the door, Lord Blackthorne's eyes gleamed, but his face remained vague and full of menace. His big body controlled Sir Bevis with ease, his movements precise yet full of power. If his injured leg bothered him, he didn't show it. She could imagine what his opponents saw on the battlefield: a brutally strong, angry foe, a man who'd show no mercy. He dragged Sir Bevis toward the open doorway, limping slightly, and the younger men fell back.

"I say, who is that?" one of them whispered to Oliver.

"Lord Blackthorne, my sister's husband." His voice was wary but laced with more respect than he'd shown so far.

Lord Blackthorne dumped her assailant on a sofa near the door, where the man groaned softly as his head lolled to the side. Her husband turned around and regarded the gathering of a half dozen young men with a cold impassiveness edged with disdain.

"Lord Appertan, this is your home and these"—he nudged the man's boot with his own—"are your guests. But they abuse their welcome when they dare attack *my wife*."

She wasn't his possession, but a woman he'd married in name only. Yet he *had* saved her from assault, she reminded herself.

"I'm certain Fenton didn't realize she was my sister,"

Oliver said with a touch of belligerence. "You are well, Cecilia?" he asked belatedly.

She put her hands on her hips, the cane bumping her thigh. "I wouldn't have been for long. I believe Sir Bevis was expecting other women to this party tonight?"

Silence was her only answer, and she saw the beginning of resistance rise in Oliver's eyes.

"This is a gentle household," she continued, "not a bachelor establishment. Surely you gentlemen should meet elsewhere from now on, where you can conduct yourselves as you see fit."

Oliver's tension ratcheted another level, and he was close to belligerence. She should never have challenged his authority in front of his friends, but she'd begun to shake with the aftermath of the attack. Oliver might not notice that, but Lord Blackthorne did, approaching her, eyes narrowed. He took the cane from her and leaned against it.

"Madam," he began, "are you well?"

She found herself looking again at Sir Bevis, who seemed helpless on the sofa but had been very real, very menacing with his arms about her, handling her as he wished. Her lips were trembling now, and she pressed them together. Hearing voices in the corridor, she knew some of the staff had gathered to await orders. She could not appear so weak in front of them.

"I am fine," she said briskly.

But at least she had Oliver's attention now, and he was studying her with curiosity. "That's enough billiards for the night," he said. "Let's hie to Enfield and see what entertainment there is."

Their cheerfulness at his idea seemed forced.

Pointing his cane at Sir Bevis as if it were a sword, Lord Blackthorne said coldly, "Take *that* with you."

As the men began to file out, he took her arm. "Allow me to escort you to your bedchamber, madam."

She was still stunned by all that had happened, and could only stare up at him and nod. He gripped her arm firmly, and even though he still limped, he could be menacing and frightening. She was glad of it this night, of course, for something far worse could have happened to her. But for the first time, it made her wonder if he would amicably agree to end the marriage when she insisted.

A footman handed them a candleholder, and Cecilia tried to smile at him but failed. She felt unlike herself, her calm certainty in the world and her place in it as upset as a toy boat in a stormy pond.

Lord Blackthorne remained a silent presence, his grip firm and warm and unsettling. When they reached the door to her bedroom, he opened it and guided her inside as if he had every right. And, technically, she'd given that right to him.

A man had never been in her bedroom before. It felt all wrong—the whole evening felt wrong. One man had tried to drag her off to a darkened corner, and now another man—her husband—had her alone.

"I am fine, my lord," she murmured, knowing it was a lie.

"You experienced your first battle. It is only right for you to be upset."

"My first battle?" She stared at him in bafflement.

"You fought for your honor."

"Well, I may be upset, but you certainly weren't," she said.

"I was sixteen when a thief attacked me with a knife as I rode my horse, not far from my home. The world seemed a much darker place after that."

"At least you rescued yourself. I could do nothing. I am not used to feeling . . . helpless." She looked away from him, hating that she couldn't stop trembling.

"Yet you must have felt that last year, after it was apparent your brother was not up to managing the Appertan estates. You found a solution and triumphed."

"Triumphed?" she echoed, glancing at him.

He was staring at her intently, the shadows flickering over half his face. She couldn't place why her stomach fluttered and her pulse raced.

"You found a solution to your problems," he replied. "You did it yourself."

"With your help," she said dryly.

He briefly bowed his head in acknowledgment.

"Why were you downstairs tonight?" she asked.

He looked grim. "To see what happened with your brother's friends."

"Did you think I should not have permitted the event?"

"Was that your decision?"

"No." She sighed. "He is the earl. I fear I antagonized him in front of his friends tonight."

"He deserved it." He practically growled the words. "I regret that I was not close enough to intercept that fool who frightened you."

"You stopped him. I am truly grateful. I'm sorry I did not yet say those words to you."

Michael stared at her, masking his surprise. She'd suffered a trauma, yet she still tried to be polite, as if he were a stranger rather than her husband. He was both, he realized. "I did not take offense."

And still he stared at her, this woman who was his wife yet not his wife. In the candlelight, her hair gleamed like a beam of moonlight, cascading down her back and around her shoulders like a cape. She was made to be worshipped, and, out of honor, he could do nothing.

And he could do little to comfort her either. He saw that she kept touching the locket she always wore around her neck, like a touchstone that helped orient her.

He needed to focus his mind back on his mission. "Will Lord Appertan be affected by what happened here tonight? Or will he take it in stride like a child who always wants what he wants?"

He saw her back stiffen, even as she turned away to pour herself a glass of water. Her hands still shook, and he yearned to hold her.

"You don't understand him," she said softly. "He has seen too much death at too young an age."

Michael frowned. "Your mother didn't die all that many years ago."

"No, but Oliver's twin, the first heir, was only ten when he died."

Startled, Michael stared at her somber profile. "I did not know you had another brother. How did he die?"

"An accident, in India."

He wanted more details but did not press her. There were things he didn't choose to discuss either. Yet it surprised him that her father had not confided in him.

"Oliver was close to Gabriel, and when he died, Oliver . . . changed. My mother became even more possessive of him, and my father thought it was time Oliver went to Eton, to . . . get away. In some ways, I think my father should have waited a year, given Oliver time to grieve. He thought the change would do him good." She glanced at him with faint amusement. "I think that is a male trait. A woman will usually let herself experience the grief until it lessens, while a man wants to forget it."

But she wasn't letting go of the grief, he saw that now. The sadness he'd sensed wasn't just about her father, but the deaths of her family one by one. She didn't want to control so much as to protect. She nourished a deep love for them, and the only one she had left was Appertan.

"It doesn't mean a man forgets the tragedy itself," he said.

"Oliver's behavior is his own reaction to everything that's happened," she continued, "his own kind of grief."

Michael arched a brow. "So selfishness and immaturity should be excused?"

She frowned at him. "He's only twenty." She held up a hand before he could speak. "And I know what you were doing at twenty, a man's work in the army. But . . . Oliver isn't you."

"You are being too lenient with him," Michael said in a sober voice. "You expect nothing of him, so he gives you nothing."

"He is still practically a boy," she insisted.

He realized she was going to continue to protect her brother because of the death of Appertan's twin. She was a woman of many layers, and, for the first time in his life, he wanted to see beneath, to find out everything about her.

"Appertan is your brother," he answered, giving her a brief bow. "You know him best. I'll take my leave."

And he walked out of her room before he did or said something he'd regret.

Chapter 6

It had taken a long time for Cecilia to fall asleep. In the morning, she felt fuzzy and drowsy going through the estate ledgers, startling easily whenever someone knocked at the study door. She kept hoping Oliver would come apologize for what had happened, but he didn't—of course, he probably wasn't awake yet. He'd come home in the wee hours, according to Talbot.

Cecilia's mood only worsened during luncheon. Lord Blackthorne joined them for the meal, and he was watching her every time she glanced his way, as if he thought she would break down. Oliver coolly asked to speak with her afterward, and Lord Blackthorne left, signaling to the footmen as he went to shut the doors for their privacy. Oliver glowered at her when they were alone.

She sighed, knowing she wasn't going to get an apology for his friend's behavior the previous night. "Is something wrong, Oliver?"

"I permit you to do as you wish with the estate," he said crossly, "but my entertainment is my choice. I did not care for how you challenged my authority in front of my companions last night."

She gaped at him, feeling sad and frustrated. "Oliver, how can you speak to me that way after what Sir Bevis did?"

He reddened. "It was uncalled for, I know. But it was an accident. It had nothing to do with—"

"It had *everything* to do with my own reaction!" She threw down her napkin. "How can you think I'd want such a man in my house? He may have misunderstood my identity, but he was about to force an unwilling woman to . . . to . . . be alone with him!"

Oliver's gaze sidled away. "I know. And it was wrong."

"Are you even grateful that Lord Blackthorne intervened? Or did that embarrass you, too?"

"Of course not. He was right to do so. Perhaps I wish *I* could have been the one to help you."

She stared at him, her anger and indignation deflating and the first tears springing to her eyes. "Oh, Oliver," she whispered. "I know what happened wasn't your fault. And it is kind of you to wish you could have been the one to make things right. But regardless, you must understand why I don't wish such entertainment in our home."

"I'll explain your concerns to my companions," he

said after a long hesitation. He used his knife to trace a pattern across his dirty plate. "About Blackthorne."

She tensed. "Yes?"

"What do you plan to do about him? He seems to be—hanging about, intruding on everything. I don't like his superior airs."

"He is my husband—for now. You know I've written to my lawyers to discover my options. Until I hear back and make a decision . . ." Her voice trailed off.

"He knows he's unwelcome. If he were any kind of man, he'd leave."

"Leave?" she replied, bewildered. "He's injured, Oliver. And he promised Papa he would see to our welfare."

"By his clothing, he doesn't have any money to do so," Oliver said with a faint sneer.

"He's been in uniform for years." She felt suddenly tired. She'd been defending Oliver to Lord Blackthorne, and now she found herself defending Lord Blackthorne to Oliver. "And it's not about money. You know that." But there was always a deep part of her that worried that maybe money really did play a part in Lord Blackthorne's sudden appearance. "Be patient, Oliver. I appreciate your spending time with him. He has little enough to do here, and I don't wish him to be bored."

"If he's bored, he'll leave sooner."

"No, he won't. Surely you see that. He believes that it is best we stay married."

"Of course he does," Oliver said with sarcasm.

"Perhaps if you spend time with him, you could help me make the decision about my marriage."

"That's easy. Annul the thing."

"You know it's not that easy. I like being an independent woman rather than a ward to my guardian, which I'll be once again if my marriage is ruled invalid. Surely you can understand that since you're about to reach your own majority." Then a guardian wouldn't be the one giving Cecilia permission to manage the estates—it would be Oliver. He could take it all away from her even if he wasn't ready for the responsibility. She thought she had time, but truly, it was less than a year. Lord Blackthorne's concerns about Oliver were valid.

Oliver frowned, then said reluctantly, "I do understand. But if he stays here, you won't be independent for long."

"That won't happen," she said quickly. "He's a career man, Oliver. The only thing keeping him in England is his injury."

"And perhaps you, Cecilia," Oliver said, narrowing his eyes. "You have much to interest such a man, and not just your money. I've seen him looking at you."

"What do you mean?" she demanded, her voice suspiciously weak.

Oliver rolled his eyes. "You know you're comely, Cecilia. Don't make me compliment you."

She almost smiled.

Someone knocked on the door to the family dining room. She gave a start, and Oliver called for the person to enter.

Talbot stepped inside and bowed. "Lady Blackthorne, you have visitors, several ladies of the neighborhood and Miss Webster. I have escorted them to the drawing room."

"Thank you, Talbot," she said. "I'll be there momentarily. Please send tea and whatever cakes Cook has made today."

He bowed again as he left the room.

Cecilia found herself watching Oliver's face and felt relieved when his smile seemed to relax on hearing his fiancée's name.

"I could tell Penelope you'd like to see her," she said.

He shook his head and grimaced. "Wish I could, but I promised Blackthorne I'd shoot with him."

She smiled. "Thank you for keeping the peace, Oliver. I knew you would."

He shrugged and left, and she followed him out, listening as the footmen filed in behind and began to remove the dishes.

Cecilia followed the wide corridor to the public drawing room at the front of the castle. She heard the ladies even before she arrived, their voices carrying out into the entrance hall, echoing up the two floors. She smiled, feeling calmer than she had that morn.

As she entered, all four ladies looked up with varying expressions. Mrs. Webster was Penelope's white-haired grandmother, a formidable woman who'd made herself important in the town social life by sheer will. She never let the lack of a title in the family impede her. Miss Jenyns was Mrs. Webster's constant companion, plump and reticent and on the shelf for decades, who took her social cues from the other two ladies. Lady Stafford was far more congenial, with a twinkle in her eye that suggested one was in on her little jokes. She was just reaching her middle years, her dark hair glinting with strands of gray that she swore came from trying to find a husband for her daughter.

"Ladies, how nice of you to call," Cecilia said.

Miss Jenyns blushed furiously and couldn't meet her gaze. The spinster was able to compose herself when a maid entered the room pushing a tea cart, where iced cakes were displayed to entice.

They made small talk about parish events while Cecilia poured the tea and handed out refreshments, but she couldn't help noticing that Penelope seemed . . . nervous. Or maybe she was just distracted. After all, her beloved was somewhere on the premises, and perhaps she wished to be there.

But then she realized the cause of Penelope's tension, when her grandmother set down her teacup and fixed Cecilia with a pointed gaze.

"Lady Blackthorne," Mrs. Webster said, "I must

admit, when I first heard several months ago that you had married a soldier who was still in India, I was . . . surprised at your choice."

Miss Jenyns watched her mentor with earnestness, while Lady Stafford gave Cecilia an encouraging smile, as if they both realized it was none of their business, but even she would like to hear the details. Cecilia had been permitted to get away with vague answers before, but now the actual man had arrived.

She sipped her tea and debated how to respond. "Mrs. Webster, after the tragedy, Lord Blackthorne's letters gave me comfort. He had been with my father at the end and could explain so much. We shared sympathy and temperament, and I found I could write my feelings to him in a way I'd never cared to express with another man." And that wasn't a lie, she reminded herself.

Penelope was watching her with a soft expression, as if she hoped to share even a part of such wonder with Oliver.

Lady Stafford leaned forward. "That is a noble sentiment, my dear, and one we all can understand. But we're so curious—what was it like when you finally met him? He just . . . arrived at your door unannounced!"

Cecilia kept her smile relaxed and confident, knowing that her next answer would make its way about Enfield, and even into London itself. But she felt anything but confident, a new experience for her. She explained about Lord Blackthorne's injury and his need to recover. "Surely he shouldn't have languished in London, in pain, waiting for a letter from me?"

"No, no, of course not," Miss Jenyns mumbled as she dabbed a crumb from her lips.

Mrs. Webster looked doubtful but held her remarks.

"And when I saw him . . ." Cecilia began, trying not to laugh as all four ladies leaned toward her, "I felt that all my father's praise of his kindness and honor showed right there on his face."

"Is he a handsome rascal?" Lady Stafford asked.

"Some would think so."

"Including me!" Penelope almost squealed, and the other ladies chuckled.

Before Cecilia could continue, she caught sight of Lord Blackthorne through the open terrace doors, approaching the drawing room. His coat flapped open in the breeze, and his hair was unruly. Perhaps he only just realized that she had guests, for when their eyes met, he gave her a nod and backed away. But she wasn't certain he actually left the terrace.

"But," Cecilia said, before anyone could speak, "our marriage was by proxy, and my lawyers wish to ascertain the validity."

"So he agreed to your reluctance," Lady Stafford said, eyeing Cecilia with closer interest. "And?"

"He is a soldier and a gentleman," Cecilia said simply. "This affects both of our lives, and we want to make certain everything is legal." Then she wanted to wince, and Penelope actually did. It almost sounded like Cecilia was afraid he was after her money. But she could hardly protest that he'd done the exact opposite, requesting nothing. If only that didn't seem so suspicious, now that she'd actually met him, a young man in the prime of his life, not an elderly grandfather.

"A soldier," Lady Stafford mused, exchanging a look with Mrs. Webster, who looked through her lorgnette at Cecilia as if she were a bug. "We cannot help being curious. It has been a long time since someone mentioned the Blackthorne viscountcy."

"He doesn't come to London," Mrs. Webster explained. "He's never attended a Season although his father used to, quite frequently, until he landed Lady Blackthorne."

"'Landed'?" Cecilia said. "That is not very complimentary."

Mrs. Webster sighed. "I did not want to be the one to tell you—especially since I assumed your marriage was legal, and it was too late. But if there's a chance that your lawyers say that you would have to wed here in England, you might want to think carefully."

Cecilia spoke coolly. "What are you saying?"

"Only that his father was a fortune hunter, and it was much whispered that his mother was *very* unhappy in the marriage."

"That can be said for many Society marriages," Cecilia said sternly. "My father had nothing but the highest praise for him. Only an honorable man would feel that he wanted to enlist and learn to be a soldier before becoming an officer."

If Lord Blackthorne was eavesdropping on this, she could only imagine what he'd think of her staunch defense—or what kind of ideas it would give him.

"Then it's true, he didn't purchase a commission?" Lady Stafford asked, eyebrows rising. "I can see the family's financial difficulties have continued."

Cecilia never condoned gossip and refused to be drawn into intrigue. "Upon meeting him, you will see that he is a decent man, a soldier injured in service of the queen."

"We would very much like to meet him," Mrs. Webster said.

Cecilia stood up. "Then I shall make it happen. Enjoy the cakes, dear ladies, and I'll return in a moment."

She strode across the drawing room to the open French doors and went outside, where the autumn sun still shone down with startling warmth. She shielded her eyes, looking across the gardens, wondering if Lord Blackthorne was still exercising his leg, or if he'd already gone to meet Oliver.

"Looking for me?"

She turned her head upon hearing his deep voice and found him right beside the doors, leaning against the rough stone wall of the castle, the shadows almost obscuring his dark garments and hair. She pretended to walk slowly along the terrace, as if still looking for him.

But the moment she was out of sight of the drawing room, she quickly closed the gap between them and leaned up into his face with rare indignation. "You were *eavesdropping*."

"We would call it spying in the army," he said dryly. "It has its place."

"But on a ladies' tea?" She threw her arms wide in outrage.

He looked down her body. "I did not know you could be so dramatic. I like it."

She resisted the urge to fold her arms over her chest. "Please answer me."

"I came upon your party quite accidentally. I heard your spirited defense of my character and could not tear myself away."

The teasing strummed her like a bad guitarist. "If you'd been caught, it wouldn't reflect well on your status as my husband." Without realizing it, she poked him in the chest to emphasize her point.

He caught her gloved hand and didn't let go when she tugged.

"Madam, you have made certain I don't know what my true status is."

He leaned over her now, his voice a deep rumble. She could feel his breath on her face, and the broad outline of his body seemed to cast a shadow over her.

They were in full view of anyone in the garden, but Lord Blackthorne behaved as if they were alone.

She found her voice. "Lord Blackthorne, I have been honest with you about everything. And if your pride is causing you to have doubts—"

"*My* pride? Madam, it is becoming clearer every day that I am not the only one who's proud in this marriage."

"It's not a true marriage," she said between gritted teeth, still trying to pull free.

But he didn't allow it.

"No? It was a marriage when you wanted access to your money."

"I know!" She felt confused and guilty and flustered. "But now—I don't know what I want."

Her breathing was erratic, and to her surprise, his gaze suddenly dipped to her breasts. For a just moment, she could have sworn his dark eyes actually smoldered with heat. He let her go, and she took two fast paces away.

"So what do we do?" he asked.

He spoke as if he'd never allowed her the briefest glimpse of . . . something.

"For right now, you meet our guests."

"Perhaps you should take my arm. I am a wounded soldier of the queen."

She rolled her eyes at his repetition of her own words. When she would have walked past, he stuck out his elbow, almost catching her in the chest.

"My lord!" she fumed.

"Yes, I am. Please take my arm and help me inside. I am feeling the need for some feminine sympathy, and I'm not finding it out here." He added the last with a touch of humor in his voice.

She pressed her lips together and slid her arm through his, waiting as he adjusted his cane to the other hand. She only realized she'd become cold in the shade of the ancient castle when his body seemed so very hot near hers.

Together, they walked through the glass doors. Penelope smiled, casting sidelong glances at the other ladies for their reactions. Mrs. Webster had her lorgnette closely affixed to her eye again, and Cecilia wondered if it was Lord Blackthorne's turn to feel as inspected as horseflesh. Lady Stafford just smiled and looked him over, a bit of surprise shown, then hidden away. Miss Jenyns blushed and lowered her face to sip at her tea.

"Lord Blackthorne," Cecilia said, "allow me to introduce my dear friends, Lady Stafford, Mrs. Webster, and Miss Jenyns."

He bowed, then sat in a chair across from their little

group. Cecilia felt she had no choice but to take the chair at his side. He seemed so very masculine, his hands dwarfing the teacup he accepted from her.

"I fear I know little of your ancestry, my lord," Mrs. Webster said, peering at him now through her lense. "What part of England do you hail from?"

"Buckinghamshire, Mrs. Webster."

"And your family?" she prodded again.

"My mother still resides in our country seat, along with my unmarried brother."

"And you never came to London for the Season?"

"No, madam, and neither has my brother."

"Eligible bachelors, connected to a title, ignoring Society?" Lady Stafford mused, her eyes glinting with humor. "How very rare."

Lord Blackthorne said nothing, merely took another sip of his tea.

Miss Jenyns ogled him with occasional glances from the corner of her eye. Penelope kept looking back and forth from Cecilia to her husband, as if she awaited something really interesting to happen. Cecilia suddenly felt a twinge of sympathy for him.

"Lord Blackthorne was in the Eighth Dragoon Guards under my father's command," she said.

"Ah, a cavalryman," Mrs. Webster said with apparent relief, as if she held to the standard belief that a mounted soldier was far superior to one in the infantry. "And where did you serve, my lord?"

"Most recently in Bombay, India, madam."

"Did you see much action?"

He glanced at his leg. "Some, but it is nothing I would discuss in the company of ladies."

"War must be . . . quite ferocious," Miss Jenyns murmured, her eyes wide. "I heard about all those poor soldiers who died in that massacre in Afghanistan."

Cecilia watched Lord Blackthorne's face, and saw the faint touch of sadness like a ghost in his eyes. Thousands and thousands of soldiers, women, and children had died, picked off by Afghani sharpshooters in the mountain passes during the retreat from Kabul. The newspapers had claimed it one of the worst defeats in the history of the British Empire.

"A soldier is trained to handle all manner of tasks," he said, "and actual battle is only one of them. Often it is more a matter of perfecting skills while simply waiting."

He didn't want to speak of those who'd died—perhaps he'd known too many of them.

"Then patience is important to a soldier," Lady Stafford murmured. "I imagine that helps when one is newly wed."

Cecilia tried not to blush, for that comment could be taken so many ways—as Lady Stafford probably intended.

Lord Blackthorne only nodded.

"You must have been anxious to meet your new wife," Mrs. Webster said.

It was as if the ladies were taking turns trying to get something—anything—out of him. Cecilia felt tense as thread in a loom, realizing that she and Lord Blackthorne had never discussed how they should explain their marriage.

"But I understood he had a duty to perform," Cecilia said, trying not to sound like she'd cut him off before he could speak. "I was content with his letters until such time as we could be together."

"A good writer is rare," Lady Stafford said. "Lord Blackthorne, you must be exceptional to win the heart of our practical Lady Cecilia—pardon me, Lady Blackthorne."

"So romantic," Miss Jenyns said.

Lord Blackthorne glanced at Cecilia, and with the slight arch of his brow, it was as if she could read his thoughts: *I wrote romantic letters?*

"And there were so many men she could have chosen from," Penelope spoke earnestly. "She's been sought after since she came out of the schoolroom at seventeen. Oh, the proposals from besotted men—"

She broke off when Cecilia stared pointedly at her. Lady Stafford lowered her amused gaze to the cake she nibbled, while Mrs. Webster regarded Penelope with fond exasperation.

"Then I am lucky to have won Lady Blackthorne's

regard," Lord Blackthorne said, setting down his teacup. "Ladies, I must take my leave. Lord Appertan is waiting for me in the park."

"He told me you're shooting together," Penelope said. "He is quite the shot."

Lord Blackthorne nodded at her pleasantly enough, but Cecilia could only imagine that a trained soldier would be far superior. With the aid of his cane, he rose to his feet, then surprised her by lifting her hand to his lips.

"Have a pleasant afternoon, my lady wife."

He spoke the words so close to her gloved hand that she could swear she felt the warmth of his breath through to her skin. His dark eyes met hers, and she couldn't decide if he laughed at her or was trying to please her.

She watched him as he limped across the room and out onto the terrace. When she turned back, all four ladies' gazes were fixed on her with varying degrees of interest.

"I knew he was romantic," Miss Jenyns murmured.

They only stayed for another half hour, but it felt interminable. Even Penelope abandoned her, saying she wanted to watch Oliver and Lord Blackthorne shoot. Her grandmother gave her permission, after reminding her they would be leaving soon.

At last, Mrs. Webster said they had other calls to make and rose stiffly from the sofa, turning down Cecilia's offer of assistance. Cecilia accompanied them to the entrance hall, where Talbot waited with their bonnets and wraps. He stood patiently as they adorned themselves, his gaze turned away with respect.

Cecilia saw the change come over Talbot's normally impassive face as he glanced up to the first floor, open to the hall below. To her shock, he cried, "Watch out!" dropped the garments, and launched himself at Cecilia, pushing her backward. She fell onto her backside and he tripped over her legs just as a bust that had sat upon the balustrade fell and cracked into a thousand pieces.

Right where she'd been standing.

Chapter 7

After the loud crash had settled into a frozen, shocked silence, Miss Jenyns screamed and covered her face. From her place on the floor, Cecilia vaguely heard people beginning to come to life all around her, the rustle of the ladies' skirts, and the vague cries from other servants nearby, but she could only gape at the ruined bust shattered on the marble floor.

"Lady Blackthorne!" Talbot cried, crouching beside her in an undignified manner for the proper man. "Are you hurt?"

"No, no, I'm fine." She let him help her to her feet and didn't protest when he still clutched her elbow. "What happened?"

"I do not know," he said, looking bewildered. "Out of the corner of my eye, I saw movement and realized something was falling."

When he looked up to the first-floor balustrade, she did the same. They both saw the head and shoulders of Susan, one of the upstairs maids, her cap askew as she gaped down at them between the giant potted ferns that framed the opening. Then she promptly burst into tears.

"Oh, Lord Blackthorne, I'm so sorry!" the girl wailed.

Then Lord Blackthorne leaned over the balustrade at her side. "Is anyone hurt?"

Cecilia should have answered at once; she should have reassured him. But she kept staring at him, wondering why he wasn't out shooting with Oliver.

Lord Blackthorne's frown could have frozen a winter pond. "Madam? Are you well?"

"I'm—I'm fine," she said, then cleared her throat. She refused to sound weak although, at that moment, her knees began to wobble. A strange little shiver seemed to work its way up her back until her neck ached. She put a hand there in distant wonder.

"Damn, stay still," Lord Blackthorne called.

She swayed again, and Lady Stafford surged forward to grab her arm.

Cecilia blinked at her. "I'm all right. Truly I am."

"You are too pale, Lady Blackthorne," the other woman said, not releasing her. "I think you should sit down."

Cecilia had no choice, as Lady Stafford and Talbot guided her backward until she sat on an overstuffed chair. She could hear her husband's quick, uneven steps as he came down the marble staircase far too fast for a man with a cane.

She looked up as he limped toward her. "I am well," she said, unable to stop staring into his concerned face.

Why had he been on the first floor near the maid? How could that slip of a girl have knocked over the bust? It had been created in homage to her distant great-grandfather, wreathed in jowls, as the man had been. The maid almost would have had to throw her shoulder against it and push.

"My lady?" Lord Blackthorne said, crouching before her chair. "Are you going to swoon?"

She straightened her spine. "I do not swoon."

"I didn't think so," he said dryly. He glanced at Talbot, who stood on the other side of her. "What did you see?"

Talbot licked his lips and spoke sincerely. "Nothing except the bust falling forward. And Lady Blackthorne—" He broke off, his eyes a bit wide.

Cecilia touched his arm. "I will be fine. I'm simply in shock."

"Nice of you to diagnose yourself," Lord Blackthorne practically growled.

Then he lifted up both of her arms and turned them over, examining them as if she were a doll. She tried to pull away, but he ignored her, taking her whole head in his hands and running his fingers along her scalp, dislodging strands of her hair.

"I say!" she cried. "Is this necessary?"

The three older women stood together in a little knot and gaped at Lord Blackthorne's familiar handling of her.

"I wanted to make sure you're not bleeding." He examined his bare hands. "No blood."

"I could have told you that. I felt nothing."

Nothing at all, except the surprise of seeing Lord Blackthorne right where the bust had been.

"What did you see, my lord?" she asked.

He grimaced. "Nothing. I'd greeted the maid as I passed, and then I heard the screams below."

She stared up at him, unable to look away. Twice since he'd arrived, accidents had almost harmed her—almost killed her.

He ran a hand through his hair, closing his eyes for a moment. "I must have startled her. It's not her fault."

Cecilia realized she could still hear someone sobbing. "Oh dear, I must go to Susan."

She tried to push past Lord Blackthorne, but he caught her shoulders. "Your devotion to your servants is admirable, Cecilia, but you are as white as a flag of surrender. You should rest."

Surrender? Hardly. "I'm fine."

He released her only to take her elbow until she was on her feet.

"Susan?" Cecilia called.

The sound of the maid's name set off fresh wailing

from the far side of the entrance hall. Mrs. Ellison, the tall, thin housekeeper with spectacles perched on her nose, stood beside Susan, the plump maid who huddled on her chair clutching her dust rag. Giant tears seemed to smear the freckles that dotted her face. Mrs. Ellison kept a firm hand on her shoulder, and Cecilia realized with relief that it was meant to comfort.

Susan raised great wet brown eyes as Cecilia approached. On a hiccup, she said, "L-Lady Cecilia, I don't know what happened. I—I never meant—" Sobs overcame her again.

Cecilia caught her chin and lifted her face until their eyes met. "No one blames you, Susan. It was an accident. Do you remember what happened?"

"I didn't think nothin' happened!" she cried. "I don't remember bumpin' into anythin'. I was dustin' the railin', and I heard a man's voice. I turned around, and there was Lord Blackthorne, havin' just passed by. And then I heard the shouts."

Just like her husband had said, Cecilia told herself, trying to calm her own breathing, although her lungs still felt too big for her chest, as if she couldn't get enough air.

"Maybe your skirt caught on the bust," Mrs. Ellison said in a kind but firm voice. "Can you remember that, Susan?"

The girl shook her head. "No, mum. It's all awhirl in me head."

"It's all right," Cecilia said, stepping back. "Why don't you go have something to eat and drink in the kitchen, Susan? A good cup of tea will calm your nerves. Take the rest of the day off."

Glumly, she mumbled, "Ye mean the rest o' me life."

"Of course not. You are a good maid. This was just an accident." Maybe if she repeated it enough, she'd believe it herself.

Mrs. Ellison led the stoop-shouldered maid away, and Cecilia watched them retreat down the wide corridor. The quaintly dressed subjects of the portraits seemed to stare down, frozen in time, waiting for what would happen next.

Slowly, Cecilia turned and saw Lord Blackthorne regarding Talbot, who'd brought in the page to clean up the shattered stone. Her husband seemed to feel her gaze, for he met it with his own.

"I only returned because I'd left my pistol in my bedchamber," he said, shaking his head. "I was on my way when . . ." He trailed off, pointing at the mess.

"Oliver and Penelope must be waiting for you," she finally said. "Go tell them everything is all right before they hear it from the servants and think the worst. I'll be fine."

Mrs. Webster, Lady Stafford, and Miss Jenyns then crowded around her, patting her like a lost little girl, leading her back into the drawing room for more tea. She *felt* like a lost little girl. Her mind was whirling with terrible thoughts, contemplating awful conclusions. It was just another accident, one part of her kept insisting. Another, deeper part of her whispered that she'd had *two* such accidents since her husband had arrived. But that could only be a coincidence.

The sun was shining in streaks through the French doors, dust motes floating like birthday decorations. The ladies kept up a steady chatter, and things began to seem more normal.

During the first accident, she'd tripped in the dark, she reminded herself. This time, a maid had been right there, dusting up above. These were accidents, they had to be, because it was impossible that her father would have spent years with Lord Blackthorne, in fierce battle and in quiet moments of dreadful anticipation, and not known what kind of man he was.

After the ladies had departed, Cecilia retreated to the study—once her father's domain—and sank down in the leather chair that still smelled faintly of her father's cologne and snuff. Or so she often told herself. She was surrounded by familiar and normal and comforting, and took several deep breaths, her hands on the ledger she'd been working on that morning.

Her mind felt blank, yet at the same time so full she couldn't pull anything free. She was almost relieved when the door burst open with Oliver's characteristic disregard of her work.

"What happened?" he asked brusquely, going straight to the bottle of brandy kept on the sideboard.

She let out a soft sigh. "I imagine you must know since you're here."

"Blackthorne went back for his pistol, and when he returned, he said you'd had an accident. The bust of Great-Grandfather Mallory sprouted wings or something. Mentioned it was his fault—something about distracting the maid? Made no sense." Oliver took a deep sip, then sighed his satisfaction.

She calmly filled in the details, even as her brother collapsed into a deep chair and regarded her.

"Were you frightened?" he asked.

She gave him a faint smile. "Afterward, certainly. It was a close call."

"Good old Talbot to the rescue." He saluted her with his glass and took a deep swallow. "Why did you earlier keep Blackthorne from our shooting match?"

"The neighborhood ladies descended."

"The three witches?"

She tried not to laugh, but it escaped her in a snort. Oliver eyed her with amused satisfaction. In these moments, she could forget her worries about him, the press of duty and responsibility. But he kept sipping his brandy, and her smile faded, knowing how the drink would affect him as the day wore on.

"They wanted to meet my husband," she said at last.

"Can you blame them? *You'd* never even met him."

She sighed. "Did you get in any shooting?"

"A few rounds, but Blackthorne seemed distracted, and after ruthlessly proving his domination, he came back to the Hall. He said he couldn't concentrate."

"Did he . . . say anything?"

Oliver went to refill his glass, and his movements were already slower. "He said he learned to shoot as a boy, that the army improved him, and I could get better with practice. No need to do that, of course. I have servants to put birds on my dinner table."

She nodded wryly. "But aren't you men usually competitive?"

He shrugged. "Why? Too much effort. I have better things to do."

"Like what?" she whispered.

He didn't hear her, only saluted her again with his glass and took himself and his drink from the study.

That night, Cecilia paced her room, one end to the other, over and over again, trying to exhaust herself so that her mind would quiet and allow her to sleep. She kept replaying the day in her mind, remembering how Mrs. Webster had said the late Lord Blackthorne had been a fortune hunter. Cecilia's husband hadn't bought a commission—did that mean his family was short of funds?

But he'd asked for nothing from her.

It didn't matter. Lord Blackthorne had no access to

her funds, and even on her death, nothing would go to him but a small stipend. *But does he know that?* a voice whispered as if from a quiet hiding place inside her.

She was being foolish. There were many little things bothering her, but none of them added up to the serious crime of attempted murder.

She heard a knock from the dressing-room door and called, "Come in, Nell."

The door opened, but it wasn't her maid. Her husband stood there, paused on the threshold, wearing trousers and boots, in shirtsleeves with an open collar. His neck looked so . . . exposed, from the deep hollow of his throat, to the bump of his Adam's apple. And once again, her body reacted with heat, even if her mind told her not to.

"You're not Nell," she said dryly, realizing she wore only her nightgown, with a dressing gown belted over it. Her hair was loose in anticipation of a good brushing, and her feet were bare.

He leisurely studied everything she wore. He was her husband—she'd claimed him as such when it suited her but wanted to deny it now that he was here. She'd spent so many years in control of herself and her home that the threat of losing even part of that was so very real.

"Am I disturbing you?" he asked quietly. "I could hear you pacing."

"All the way from your room?"

"No, of course not. I'd come into the dressing room. But I wouldn't have knocked if I thought you were asleep."

And he still hadn't even stepped inside but was waiting there.

"I could tell you to go," she said.

"You could. And I'd go." He leaned forward, one hand braced on the cane, the other on the doorframe. "I promised to give you time, and I'm keeping to that. But today . . . I wanted to make certain you were all right."

She gave a sigh. "Come in. But I trust you'll tell no one you were here."

He arched a brow as he limped forward and closed the door behind him. "I'm not certain what that would prove one way or the other. I'm your husband, and they'll all believe—"

She held up a hand. "Stop. I don't wish to discuss this tonight."

He paused, as if gaining mastery of himself, but any struggle did not show on his face. It was remarkable how well schooled his features were. She wasn't used to it, wanted to see every emotion written there—if he even had any deep emotion.

"Then we won't discuss our marriage," he said.

"We could discuss my brother. He said you offered to shoot with him, but after my accident—"

He grimaced. "He and I were both distracted. Mistakes happen that way, and I didn't want to take that chance."

She leaned both hands against the back of her dressing-table chair, feeling a bit foolish keeping the chair between them. "You have spent some time with Oliver. Do you feel like you've helped at all?"

He walked the few paces toward the window and looked out upon the full moon. "He is very young still, and I see his kind often, brash and arrogant, feeling entitled to do as he pleases from position and wealth."

It hurt to hear his assessment, but she knew it was true—partly. "You don't yet see the whole picture," she said. "I've told you of the deaths, that Oliver wasn't even meant to be the earl. Don't you think that matters?"

"I do. I'm simply telling you the image he projects to the world."

"Do you know he felt very bad that he wasn't the one to rescue me from Sir Bevis?"

Lord Blackthorne glanced over his shoulder, surprise widening his eyes. "That is an interesting comment from him. And it shows promise. But he didn't fling the man from Appertan Hall, and he still left with him."

She bit her lip. "They'd all been drinking. I wish he'd stop. He uses it to forget."

"That is part of it—some men would rather forget what hurts, what they can't change, using alcohol to do so. It is a childish thing, like covering your ears and pretending you can't hear bad news."

She sighed. "What do others do to forget?"

"Strong people—like you—do just what you've done, go on with their lives. They don't forget, but they learn to accept and put it in the past, since most things can't be changed."

She wondered if he spoke from experience, imagined the horrors he'd seen—maybe even participated in.

"So what do you do to forget?" she whispered. "What are you doing when you're not with my brother, or not annoying me?"

"Annoying?"

Again, she thought she saw the faintest smile curve his lips, and it caught her breath, making her wonder how truly handsome he might be if he gave in to a softer emotion.

Oh, she didn't want to think like this about him. He'd promised to stay on the other side of the world, after all. But for the rest of her life, even if they separated and never saw one another again, she'd remember him there in her bedchamber.

"I cannot possibly annoy you like your many suitors used to do," he said. "Were there dozens of marriage proposals you turned down in your day?"

"You make it sound like I'm ancient." But she was trying not to smile, even as she took another step closer. "And there were certainly not dozens."

"A half dozen?"

She didn't answer. It had been a long time since she'd bantered with a man, a year of mourning, and soon after, her marriage. They were alone in her room, and no one knew. She was surprised at the forbidden pleasure of it, had never imagined that this might attract her.

It was the danger, she realized, and felt a little shiver. He could do . . . anything. And yet she didn't ask him to leave, nor did she flee. A single candle kept him in the shadows, his broad shoulders filling the window frame.

"Tell me, Cecilia," he murmured.

Again, she felt the lure of the familiar way he said her Christian name. She'd heard him use it just after the accident. It made her feel . . . close to someone, not so alone, with the weight of so many responsibilities on her shoulders. Responsibilities she wanted, she reminded herself. And she was strong enough to accept them. But to Lord Blackthorne, she was a woman.

"You don't want to hear about my suitors," she said, finding herself at his side. They stared out on the moonlit gardens, where the pale light illuminated the strangest shapes, making it not the grounds she knew so well.

"Why wouldn't I?" he asked. "They are all the men you turned down, so you could choose me."

She almost choked out a laugh. "Choose" him? She'd turned to him in desperation. "Some were simply too young, others too old. And I loved none of them."

"I didn't realize you cared about such an emotion. I

thought maybe you didn't even believe in it, as if you were so very different from other young women."

She shrugged, still not looking at him. With a prickling awareness, she realized he'd silently stepped behind her, and now she could see his face reflected in the window, above and behind hers.

"Love—love doesn't matter in the management of great estates," she said.

"So cynical for one so young."

He very gently rested his hands on her shoulders. She tensed, but when he did nothing else, she didn't pull away.

In a soft voice, he continued, "But others obviously believed that you married me because of my letters. Aren't they misleading themselves into thinking that's love? Or did you tell them something else?"

"I was vague," she admitted. "I told them your letters were . . . meaningful, and I allowed them to believe what they wished."

"But I hear I was romantic."

She was hot with embarrassment, with his nearness, with the crazy feelings that were surging inside her very blood. "You know you weren't. You're a practical man, Lord Blackthorne."

"I'm sure others believe the opposite, that one would have to be very romantic to woo such a sensible woman as you into a wedding ceremony performed on the other side of the world from the bride."

His hands weighed heavy on her shoulders, and without her skirts keeping them apart, he was able to stand very close behind her. She thought she could feel the brush of her dressing gown against his legs. She almost wanted to sway with abandon.

He was not making love to her with his words, but there was something about being alone with him, on the edge of danger, that made her realize now why good girls didn't allow themselves to be alone with a man.

"Tell me the things that a romantic man would write," he said, his voice growing huskier. "I have no experience in courtship, unlike you, with your half dozen suitors."

He was moving his hands on her shoulders now, very gently squeezing, and it felt . . . strangely relaxing. At the same time, she couldn't imagine being any more awake and aware. His long fingers spanned her collarbones, dangerously close to the rise of her breasts. She could see in the window that his head was bent, as if he watched his own hands upon her. She couldn't move—the moon and the night and his presence enthralled and held her captive.

She had to speak; surely that would break the spell. "I guess . . . you could have written about the moon. That seems to captivate young lovers."

"The moon," he mused. "You think imagery would lure you into marriage?"

"Others were ready to believe it so."

In the window, she could see his head lift as he gazed out on the English moon that loomed over the land with distant benevolence.

"I remember the moon," he murmured, "shimmering in the night heat, rising over the ruins of a temple that was being swallowed up again by the jungle."

It was difficult to swallow, difficult to find moisture, when her lips wanted to part. She didn't remember India that way and didn't like that he could conjure up such a vision with only words. She cleared her throat. "That imagery . . . wasn't bad."

She wanted him to chuckle, to keep things light between them, but he didn't. He was studying her in the window just as much as she was studying him. And then she realized that the dressing gown she'd clutched to her throat had now separated, the belt sagging, her neck revealed, along with the dark valley at the tops of her breasts. It was nothing he wouldn't have seen as they danced a waltz in a ballroom, but they were so very alone in the night—in the bedchamber that by law he should be able to share with her.

Her trembling started again, and he must have felt it, for his hands slid to her upper arms, and he began to rub up and down, slowly, so slowly.

"Tell me more," he said. "I want to learn what pleases you."

Chapter 8

Michael wanted to take back the words as soon as he said them. Everything was so perfect here in the dark with Cecilia—his wife, the wife he never thought he wanted. But his words of pleasing her called up in his mind the sensuous slide of her clothing from her body. He could imagine touching her, the erotic thrill of her telling him what pleased her. He barely kept himself from pressing into her from behind, trying to find relief and delicious pleasure.

But she would pull away. She was angry that he disturbed her perfect little world, perhaps even frightened of all the changes. He knew it was easier for her to be in control than to let emotions overwhelm her.

But she didn't pull away, only stared at him in the window with a faintly curious look. Maybe she didn't even understand the double meaning of his words.

"What romantic words please me?" she murmured, sounding confused, turning her head to the side as if she could no longer look at him.

The fall of her golden hair was like a curtain drawn across the classic beauty of her face, with its slanted cheekbones, the sultry mouth made to form to a man's—to form to his.

"What else should I have written?" He had to whisper, afraid to trust his voice. He didn't want to sound harsh and frighten her when it was taking every ounce of his control not to draw her back against him, to cup her breasts, to part her gown. She was wearing so very little, and all of it of the finest silk. He could see her nipples, hard for him, though she might not realize it.

"You could tell me about the nautch girls," she said.

He glanced back at her face in surprise.

"A long time ago, I was at the court of a rajah," she murmured. "I remember little of it except feeling . . . captivated by their dancing."

He inhaled the warm scent of her and closed his eyes. "I would write that their beauty was nothing to yours, even in their jewels and glittering fabric. Their long scarves of gold floating about them in time to their dancing would be dim in comparison to your hair."

When she said nothing, he murmured, "How was that?"

"Adequate," she said after a long pause.

He was still moving his hands slowly up and down her arms, could feel the faint sway of her body, saw her eyes half closed as she succumbed to the magic of the moonlight and their nearness to one another.

He wasn't certain, but he didn't think she'd ever been touched, ever been kissed—or maybe he just wanted to believe that she'd saved even the first caress for her husband.

But that couldn't be true, not with a half dozen proposals. He knew every other man who beheld her must have succumbed to the same dazed longing. But it wasn't just her beauty—he admired her determination, her belief in herself, the very intelligence that let her stand toe to toe with any man.

He leaned closer, felt the strands of her hair against his face as he imagined baring her throat for his kiss. He inhaled deeply, smelling warm woman, fragrant with something exotic, as if she'd brought it back from the Far East.

He let his hands drift lower down her arms, no longer knowing what he meant to do. He encircled her wrists with his fingers, wanting to draw her arms up so that her head would fall back against him, that long, supple hair spill down his body—

"What are you doing?" she whispered.

He froze, hearing a thread of unease in her voice. He couldn't express his lustful thoughts—not without frightening her. His mind scrambled and latched on to the first thing he remembered—the thing that had haunted him all afternoon and evening.

"I can't forget your near escape today. I feel like I need to make certain nothing is broken."

Very slowly, he released her wrists, then silently cursed as she straightened and moved away from the lure of the moon and the apparent threat of his body. She touched the locket at her throat as if for comfort. He stood still for a moment, eyes closed, breathing deeply, evenly, calming himself, as he had such practice doing—although usually for a very different reason than the ache of pleasure thwarted. He told himself that this was promising, that Cecilia wasn't immune to him, that perhaps she might come to realize staying married to him was the best thing for her.

She stood indecisively in the middle of her own bedroom, as if she didn't know where it was safe to go. Her gaze hastily avoided the four-poster bed, with its luxuriant hangings meant for warmth but so intriguing when used for privacy. The counterpane had been turned down, the pillows plumped, already bearing the indentation of her body.

He began to perspire, never imagining what a fine line he'd walk, trying to get close to his skittish wife.

She rubbed her arms almost absently, as if she didn't quite remember what he'd done to her. "I'm fine," she said too firmly. "It was only an accident."

"I don't like to imagine a woman in danger."

She turned then and studied him with an earnestness that caught him by surprise. He didn't know what she was looking for but remained transfixed in her spell, off balance. And then he realized he didn't have his cane. He had to look for it, so he didn't further damage his leg by letting it collapse underneath him.

"It's leaning against the window frame," she finally told him, as if reading his mind.

He heard the faint amusement in her voice, and something in him relaxed. "I had no memory of where I put it. I think I was trapped in your notion of romantic letters when I set it down." He reached for it, then knew what he must do. "I'll bid you good night then."

"Good night," she murmured, even as she turned away.

Disappointed, Michael went into the dressing room and closed the door behind him.

Cecilia didn't even bother climbing into bed. She practically ran to her writing desk and began to search the little drawers until she found what she'd been looking for: the letters her father had written from India.

She hadn't read them since he'd died, tying them away with ribbon because it was too painful to see his sloppy cursive, realize that the faint scent of his snuff was gone.

But she could no longer delay. Today had shown her too many things about Lord Blackthorne: the ridiculous, momentary thought that he might be trying to harm her, then that his voice and his presence could make her forget everything else except her longing to succumb to his touch.

She put her hot face in her hands and groaned aloud. What had she been thinking? The moon? Dancing girls? Where had all that come from, and why hadn't she simply asked him to leave?

But no, apparently she had a weakness she'd never guessed. She'd spent so many months as almost the master of Appertan Hall and all of the earldom's lands that she'd never realized she hadn't thought of herself as a woman.

Lord Blackthorne made her remember what it felt like when she'd first come out and experienced the admiration of a man. She didn't want to feel like this, disturbed and intrigued and strangely languorous all at once. And maybe, regardless of what he'd led her to believe, he might not like that she was in control of her own life, that she no longer needed him.

Her father managed to mention Lord Blackthorne in almost every letter. "Blackthorne was a good sounding board today," "Blackthorne's bravery is never rash," "Blackthorne should have left the wounded enemy behind, but wouldn't." Her husband sounded like a saint, she thought with exasperation. Then she found an incident where her father didn't envy Lord Blackthorne's decision, and she forced herself to slow down. An enemy was running at them, firing, using a woman as a shield. Lord Blackthorne reluctantly ordered his men to fire in order to save the company, and the woman ultimately died. When her father counseled

Lord Blackthorne on how to handle his guilt, he said that although he regretted the action, he felt no guilt. He had to save his men and would have made the same decision all over again.

Cecilia stared down at the words, rereading them. Yet Lord Blackthorne was also a man who tried to help a wounded enemy. He was a contradiction, and the letters only made her even more frustrated. She got the sense that her father respected Lord Blackthorne's abilities as a soldier. In the last one she read, her father mentioned that he'd never met a man more trustworthy, so she eased her misgivings with those words.

Sleep proved elusive, leaving her to pen invitations to the dinner party she would host when Oliver's guardian arrived—and the first that Lord Blackthorne would attend at her side.

The next morning, Cecilia had to wonder if Lord Blackthorne had deliberately waited for her to go on her walk because he caught up to her before she'd even left the terrace.

"Cecilia," he called.

She was forced to stop, surprised to find herself most reluctant to face him after their encounter in her bedroom. Under an overcast sky, he was still a dark presence in his sober garments. He walked with a cane and didn't even have a smile for her. All those things should have kept her removed from him.

Instead, she could only remember the way he'd stood so close behind her in the night, the gentle way he'd touched her without pressing her too far, how he'd left when she asked him to. In the light of day, she shouldn't be thinking those things, knowing she'd blushed more in the last few days than ever in her life. She'd had a wealthy duke pay her homage, not to mention a foreign prince. But her husband, a cavalryman and a viscount, left her flustered.

He stopped before her, so tall and commanding that she kept her shoulders back, as if to measure up to him. "Yes, my lord?"

"It's a blustery day." He squinted out over the gardens. "I took my walk as dawn broke and was almost blown off course."

"I'll remember to clutch a tree when I need to."

A corner of his mouth turned up—was that his version of a smile? For a moment, she felt pleased with herself.

"I was wondering if I could have your permission to rouse Lord Appertan from his bed at a more decent hour."

"That would be quite a feat," she said dryly. "But I don't understand why."

"I would like him to accompany us into town this morn."

"'Us'?" she echoed. "Why do you need me? You insist that Oliver is *your* mission while you're here."

"Frankly, he will be more likely to accompany the both of us than me alone. I will have a better understanding for how others see him, and what I might do to make him see the same."

She considered only briefly, knowing she could not refuse if she wanted Oliver to improve.

"Very well. Do what you wish," Cecilia said. "I will be very curious to see if you can persuade him."

To her surprise, when she returned to Appertan Hall an hour later, Oliver stumbled out of the breakfast parlor, shadows under his eyes, his lips shaping a sulky pout.

"I can't believe you're insisting I attend you," he said, folding his arms over his chest.

She was about to protest that it wasn't her idea when she noticed that his hands were trembling. She bit her lip, then glanced at her impassive husband, now limping into the corridor.

"It will do you good to get out during the day," she said. "We could eat our luncheon at the old inn, just like we used to."

"You're living in the past," Oliver grumbled. "Since the railway came, that old coaching inn has seen better days."

"All the more reason we should patronize it. I'll be with you shortly." In her bedroom, she changed into a morning gown, and found herself not too frustrated when Nell insisted on fussing with her hair.

"Ye have to make a good impression, milady," Nell

mumbled between her lips, where she kept pins dangling at the ready.

"Whom do I need to impress?" Cecilia demanded, as if she didn't already know the answer.

"Yer husband, o' course." Nell tsked and shook her head as if her mistress were a lost cause.

When at last Cecilia stepped out onto the front portico near where the carriage waited, both Oliver and Lord Blackthorne turned toward her. Lord Blackthorne stared for a moment too long, nodding at last, while Oliver looked from one to the other and frowned before heading to the carriage and grumbling under his breath. Each of them was playing her on his own behalf, and she was caught in between.

Then she saw Oliver's horse tied to the rear of the carriage, and when she turned to say something to her brother, he beat her to it.

"I don't know what my plans are for this evening, so I'd best be prepared. And besides, I might not be able to stand being alone with the two of you."

Wearing a frown, Cecilia allowed Lord Blackthorne to assist her inside. Oliver crowded in beside her, then smirked at Lord Blackthorne, who had to sit across from them. Her husband simply rested both hands on the top of his cane where it leaned on the bench between his thighs, and regarded her brother.

The coachman guided the carriage away from Appertan Hall.

"What?" Oliver demanded, folding his arms across his chest. "You insisted I accompany you into Enfield; I am coming. You cannot expect me to be pleased at getting so little sleep."

And then he looked out the window, as if any conversation they had would bore him.

"And how are you feeling this morn, madam?" Lord Blackthorne asked.

He was studying her as if he expected to see an answer written across her face.

"I am well, my lord. You know I was not injured yesterday."

"But it must have upset you greatly to have such a close call."

She almost said, *It is not the first,* but caught herself in time. "Regardless, I will not be thinking about it again."

Oliver glanced at Lord Blackthorne. "And are you not upset on your wife's behalf, Blackthorne?"

"Upset? No. Concerned, yes. A terrible tragedy could have befallen your family yesterday. I believe you don't realize how important your sister is to you, the last member of your immediate family."

"I mean no offense, Cecilia," Oliver said with a smirk, "but I guess you haven't told him about our many cousins, and the fact that I could do so much good—your words—with the money I'd inherit should you leave this earth. You didn't mention that in one of your letters?"

Cecilia took a deep breath and eyed her brother. "I don't find your sarcasm amusing today, Oliver."

"And I find you disrespectful," Lord Blackthorne said.

"Then I guess you need to learn about my sense of humor," Oliver shot back.

"That's enough," Cecilia insisted. Part of her was relieved that Lord Blackthorne knew where her money would be going should she die. She imagined if she stayed married, the lawyers would be pressing her to change her beneficiary, but he didn't need to know that.

They reached Enfield, and although Cecilia tried to proceed directly to the inn, Lord Blackthorne would have none of it. She found herself paraded about the cobbled market square, then the park along New River, with her husband and brother. They were the center of attention, and the brave immediately approached for an introduction, while the shy held back and gawked. Cecilia knew everyone was curious, but she wished she'd forgone this adventure. Soon she might be having the marriage invalidated, and all along, she'd told herself it didn't matter, that she didn't care what Society thought of her. "Society" had been nebulous in her thoughts, the people in London she'd once socialized with.

But what about all these people who respected her, the people she spent her life with? Cecilia hoped they wanted the best for her, that they would understand.

Lord Blackthorne was gravely respectful to everyone he met, but she felt uncomfortable with the way he studied the townspeople's reactions to Oliver. She noticed, too, their reserve, the almost quick dismissal of Oliver in favor of a more open pleasure on seeing her. She felt embarrassed for her brother and wished she knew if her husband could help him.

In a private dining parlor at the inn, Oliver picked at his meal, then seemed relieved when he looked past Cecilia into the corridor. "I see Rowlandson. I'll return soon." And then he escaped.

Lord Blackthorne shook his head once Oliver had gone. "Your brother does not like me."

"Then you are giving up so quickly?" she asked.

"For a woman who was so reluctant to accept my help, you sound disappointed."

She wanted to look away from the intense focus of his eyes, but she couldn't. "If he keeps going as he is, he'll have no one's respect, including his own. And I am . . . at a loss." She broke a piece of bread apart in her hands but couldn't bring herself to eat it.

Lord Blackthorne leaned closer and lowered his voice. "It costs you much to say that. You are not a woman who easily admits defeat."

"I never have to," she said with indignation.

To her surprise, he lightly touched her ungloved hand with his own. "I like that you are a decisive woman, that you don't wait for things to happen but take charge."

She could read nothing in his face, not even this "admiration" he professed. He continued to touch her unexpectedly, and it troubled her that he knew how it would affect her. "Most men would not prefer such a woman."

"Which is why you turned down so many proposals."

She shook her head. "You think you know me, my lord, but that is only part of it. There are not many men who want a woman to so actively involve herself in her family estates."

"Which is why we suit," he said. "I need a woman who's not afraid of doing things on her own. A wife cannot always be at a soldier's side."

"And there's where we don't suit. I never promised to be at your side, especially overseas."

He studied her. "I know. Once I met you, I thought I might change your mind."

Now it was her turn to lean toward him. "That will never happen, my lord. Understand that."

He didn't answer, and she now knew she had another reason for ending this marriage. She was never returning to India, to the place where her family had fallen apart.

The serving maid arrived with their next course of food, and Cecilia noticed that the young woman's cap was askew and her sleeve torn.

"Is something wrong?" Cecilia asked.

The girl met her eyes with her own full of tears. "I'm

sorry, milady. I . . . displeased a gentleman. 'Twas me own fault."

Cecilia didn't recognize this girl, but a pang of foreboding chilled her. "What happened?" she demanded in a quiet but insistent voice. "I'd like to help."

"Oh no, milady, you mustn't," the girl cried.

The door opened, and Oliver walked in. Cecilia's stomach seemed to rise into her throat as she prepared herself to handle a terrible confrontation, but the girl actually relaxed when she saw it was Oliver. Cecilia felt Lord Blackthorne watching her, knew that he'd been thinking everything she had. But they were both wrong—of course they were. But she couldn't stop feeling terribly ill that she'd believed the worst of Oliver. The maid finished refilling their glasses with a trembling hand, then bobbed a curtsy and left.

"Something dreadful happened," Cecilia said to Oliver.

Her brother drained his glass of wine and refilled it himself. "Rowlandson is still down from London, and his night of drinking isn't over yet."

"But it's the middle of the afternoon!" she cried, looking to Lord Blackthorne as if one of the males in the room had to make sense.

Her husband was studying Oliver, absorbing everything without interfering. "What did that maid have to do with it?" he asked in a voice that portrayed indifference.

But she didn't believe it. He'd taken on Oliver as his project, and from her father's letters, she knew that Lord Blackthorne never backed down from a challenge.

She was his challenge, too.

Oliver shrugged. "Rowlandson tried for some enjoyment with the maid. She didn't take kindly to it."

"Like your sister didn't take kindly to Fenton?" Lord Blackthorne demanded. "What kind of friends do you have?"

Oliver narrowed his eyes. "My friends are none of your concern, Blackthorne. Remember that you are only in my home because I allow it. Do not cross me."

She was about to dress down her brother when she felt her husband grip her knee, hard enough to make her round on him. But he wasn't looking at her, only at her brother. He didn't want her interference, but Oliver was her responsibility.

"I am not crossing you, Appertan," her husband said. "But it is my right to keep Cecilia safe, especially after what Fenton did."

"Rowlandson would never do that," Oliver said dismissively. "He's down on his luck and wanted a little fun. When the girl refused, he backed off."

"Down on his luck?" Cecilia whispered. "And that gave him the right to . . ." She couldn't even finish her sentence, as the memory of her fear at the hands of Sir Bevis returned to her. It was rare for her to experience such helplessness—and this poor maid must feel it often.

"No, he stopped it," Oliver insisted forcefully. "Nothing happened."

Except that a young girl's confidence in herself and the world had been shaken. And that didn't seem to matter to Oliver. He didn't meet her eyes.

"He's my friend, and he asked me for help," he continued between bites of his beef pie. "Needs a place to stay. I told him it wouldn't work at Appertan Hall."

She silently let out a shaky breath.

"Rowlandson was upset, of course," Oliver continued, "but I made him understand that you wouldn't have it."

She was practically a target again because of his thoughtlessness in blaming her. Lord Blackthorne stiffened, and now it was her turn to touch his leg although she did so only briefly.

"I offered him a few nights at the inn at my expense," Oliver said, "until his monthly allowance was released. Everything is fine now."

He seemed pleased with himself, convinced that he had handled the situation, and she didn't know what to feel. She didn't like his "friends" so close—and was dismayed that Oliver didn't seem to understand why. Or he didn't *want* to understand. Would he feel any different if Penelope had been the one attacked by these friends of his? Maybe not, Cecilia thought sadly.

Her brother briskly finished eating, and all she could do was push her food around on her plate. At last she gave up.

"Since we're nearby, I'd like to visit the milliner." She tried to sound more enthused than she felt. "I've had nothing new since I emerged from mourning."

Lord Blackthorne pointedly rubbed his leg. "I fear I need to rest. Lord Appertan, would you mind escorting your sister? I will join you soon."

Oliver sighed and agreed, but Cecilia looked over her shoulder as they left the private dining parlor, knowing that her husband wasn't telling the whole truth.

Chapter 9

rue to form, Oliver stepped one foot into the milliner's shop, saw the display of dozens of hats and
many pairs of interested feminine eyes, and turned
around to wait outside. Cecilia hid a smile, but she did
feel some relief. She needed a moment to herself, surprised that the maid's dilemma brought back all her
uneasiness, even her worry over the accidents that had
happened to her.

She strolled through the displays, trying to picture
the gowns she wanted new hats made for, but it wasn't
working.

"Cecilia!"

Startled, she turned and saw Penelope coming
toward her, dressed in a smart shawl and matching
bonnet, towering over the other customers. They held
hands briefly.

"Did you see Oliver outside?" Cecilia asked.

"I did not." Penelope glanced out the window but
didn't rush away.

Cecilia appreciated that. "He must have returned to the inn." She hid her worry, hoping that Lord Blackthorne had finished whatever he needed to do before Oliver arrived. If there was a confrontation . . .

But no. Lord Blackthorne was a soldier, not a fool, at least according to her father.

"Cecilia, you seem . . . upset," Penelope said, worry creasing her brow. "Is there something I can do to help?"

Cecilia studied her friend's face, and in that moment, she was so tired of bearing the burden of her worries. It was almost a relief to lead Penelope into the small garden behind the shop and quietly tell her about the *two* accidents that had happened.

Penelope took both her hands and squeezed. "My dear Cecilia, I wish you'd told me sooner! Surely you're worried for absolutely no reason."

"I honestly thought I tripped over something going down the stairs, but I couldn't find it, as if . . . whatever it was had been removed. It sounds ridiculous, I know, and I put it right out of my mind. But then the bust almost hit me—*me,* not any of the other people in the entrance hall, as if someone had *waited* for me to be perfectly in place."

"But everyone loves you, Cecilia! I cannot believe you'd think a servant would want to harm you."

"Perhaps not a servant," she whispered, looking over both shoulders. But they were surrounded by bushes and trees, then a high fence. No one could overhear.

"Then who—no!" Penelope reared back in her melodramatic fashion. "You can't mean—Lord Blackthorne?"

Cecilia sighed. "I know it can't be true. He has no reason to harm me. He didn't search for me, I kept writing to *him*. And he asked nothing of me—which is why I'm even entertaining such foolish uncertainties. What man wants no dowry, no control of his wife's money?"

Penelope patted her hand. "Not everyone needs to feel so . . . in control, Cecilia. Look at Oliver. I think we suit well because he's content to bide his time, learning what he needs to from you and his steward."

Cecilia barely held back a sigh. She wanted to help Oliver, she truly did. But her defensiveness about Lord Blackthorne's helping him truly bothered her. Was she letting her suspicions cloud her thinking, or was she so afraid of losing control that she pretended Oliver was all right?

She thanked Penelope for listening and reassured the young woman that she was well even though she didn't quite reassure herself. Together, they enjoyed a very feminine exploration of the millinery, and Cecilia bought a lovely ready-made beribboned bonnet and ordered another, more elaborate one. When they exited the shop, they found Lord Blackthorne and Oliver seated on a bench near the market square and seemingly engrossed in conversation.

Penelope glanced at Cecilia, eyes wide. "Well, well," Penelope said, beginning to smile.

Cecilia smiled, too, telling herself that Lord Blackthorne was doing what he thought her father wanted, trying to help Oliver. And Oliver was doing as she'd asked, going along with Lord Blackthorne on her behalf. It was all such a muddle.

When Oliver saw both women, he stood up and gave Penelope a grin. "I didn't know you were in Enfield today."

She shrugged, her eyes brimming with flirtation and excitement. "Well, I am. Will you walk with me, so that I may display my fiancé?"

He chuckled and held out his arm. Penelope took it and looked over her shoulder at Cecilia, smiling her encouragement, even as she risked a glance at Lord Blackthorne. He was commanding in black, solid and broad to Oliver's litheness. Cecilia had always thought she should find her own happy young man, but something about them always seemed . . . frivolous. Perhaps she was judging young men on the basis of her brother, which wasn't fair.

She looked up at her husband. "It seems Oliver had good reason to bring his horse," she said.

Lord Blackthorne nodded. "Are you ready to return?"

She was, but suddenly she didn't want to know what might have happened at the inn, and she wanted to delay questioning him as long as she could. So, instead, she asked him to accompany her to the bookshop, then to the grocer's, where she bought a set of lovely, fragrant soaps, all under the watchful eyes of Lord Blackthorne—who was under the watchful eyes of the townspeople. At last, Cecilia allowed him to call for the carriage. He climbed up and sat beside her, forcing her to slide farther away.

When the coachman closed the door, and the carriage jerked into motion, she faced him with resolution. "What happened at the inn after I left?"

He glanced at her, a brown eyebrow cocked as if in surprise.

"Do not play coy, Lord Blackthorne. It doesn't become you."

"Play coy?" he echoed. "Is that not something virginal misses do to intrigue a man?"

"You know what I mean." She tugged her shawl higher about her shoulders and glared at him. "What did you say to Mr. Rowlandson? You were not resting your leg. You walk for miles every morning, after all."

"Perhaps I reinjured it on my walk."

"Or it stiffened in the carriage, another good excuse. I cannot believe it could suddenly be so bad."

He leaned toward her. "As my wife, it is your right to see my wound, to decide what should be done about its care."

Her mouth fell open as she had a sudden image of

his very naked leg, and how little clothing he would have to wear for her to see it. She'd nursed injuries before, but . . . he was her husband, whom she was keeping from her bed.

Her temporary husband.

She lifted her chin. "Your injury happened months ago, my lord. I imagine your care was adequate since you're recovering."

He was watching her mouth as she spoke, and his eyes seemed light with amusement.

She didn't want to be the source of his humor. "You're trying to distract me. It isn't working."

"Very well, I admit your brother's behavior at luncheon disturbed me."

She clutched her skirts in her hands, hoping he couldn't see.

"He attempted to seem so unconcerned about the attack on the maid. I wondered if he was beyond hope, if our efforts would even matter in the long run."

"I can't believe that," she whispered, feeling tears of despair prick her eyes.

He lifted his hand and cupped her cheek, and she closed her eyes, feeling connected to another person in her misery. She could feel the warmth of him through his gloves.

"I don't truly believe it either," he said in a low voice. "Appertan wouldn't meet your eyes, and that's the look of a man who feels guilty on behalf of his friend and is trying to pretend it's fine when he damn well knows it isn't."

She searched his face, wondering if he only told her what she wanted to hear. She touched her locket and moved away from him. His hand slowly fell back to the bench.

"Thank you," she whispered.

They were silent for a few minutes, their bodies jostling gently to the same rhythm. It was strangely intimate, riding with this man, when she'd done the same thing with others hundreds of times.

"I did run into Mr. Rowlandson in the taproom," he admitted.

"*Run into?* Did you knock him to the ground?"

"I wanted to. And it would have been so easy. But I simply warned him to be on his best behavior since he was your brother's guest in town. And I might have implied that I would develop a relationship with the innkeeper, who would keep me abreast of any abuse of his servants."

She slowly smiled at him. "I appreciate your restraint."

"You're welcome. I am capable of it, when necessary. Life here is not the same as on a battlefield."

He studied her from beneath lowered eyelids, his focus once again making her feel like she was the reason for everything he did. Even with daylight streaming in the windows, it was as if they were alone, with darkness enveloping them, hiding them.

"I know you are confused about this marriage between us," he began in almost a conversational tone, letting their shoulders touch. "How do you expect to make a decision?"

She couldn't seem to think, so captivated was she by the mysterious depths of his brown eyes. "I . . . imagine by coming to know you better, interacting as we've been doing these few days."

"Interacting," he said dubiously. "Last night was our first time interacting alone."

"That is not true," she insisted.

"Alone with you in your bedroom, as a husband should be. I put my hands on you."

"You shouldn't have." Though she tried to look away, he touched her chin, tilting her face back up to his.

"We should feel something about each other when we touch," he said softly. "Indifference would be the mark of people who do not suit. I don't feel indifferent, Cecilia, and I don't think you do, either."

"That is not a reason for marriage." Her mouth felt so dry she licked her lips, then gave a little start when his eyes seemed to heat.

"Money is your reason for marriage," he said.

"Yours is duty," she replied, narrowing her eyes. "Do you think I want to be a man's duty? Neither is a motive for a lasting relationship."

"There are many who would disagree, of course, but you aren't the type of woman who would settle for those motives. And duty was never my only motive. So can you not explore other reasons to be married? Or are you afraid to?"

She stiffened. "I am not afraid of you."

"I think you might be afraid of *feeling* something for me."

They stared at each other, and she didn't know how to respond, she who was gifted at handling every difficult situation. She had to look up to meet his eyes, and he seemed to loom over her. For just a moment, she wanted him to kiss her.

Hastily, she turned away and looked out the window. "Believe what you want, Lord Blackthorne, but wishing won't make it so."

Michael had pushed too hard with Cecilia, and that had been a mistake, he thought that evening as he watched her dine. She had to be slowly brought along in their marriage, like a new recruit.

In India, he'd remained outside British society, not taking advantage of the dances or dinner parties. He was focused on his regiment. But now he made no secret of his admiration of her fine figure, of the gentle, ladylike ways she comported herself. Staring at his wife made him realize he'd forgotten the softness of a graceful woman, the way just being with her made him ignore everything bad in his life. He frowned and glanced down at his plate. He wasn't a man who needed to forget the decisions he'd made, the deaths he'd caused. It bothered him that suddenly he *wanted* to forget.

But he couldn't stop looking at her whenever they were together. And tonight he could be even more obvious, for they dined alone. She'd retreated to her study after returning from Enfield. Although he could have followed her there, he'd given her some time alone to regroup. She was the kind of woman who preferred to show the world only her strengths and hide her vulnerabilities and emotions.

Part of what would soften her was if he could help her brother, so he let her prattle on about London Society, as if either one of them cared, then interrupted at last.

"Forgive me, but I must cut this meal short."

The footmen had only just begun serving some kind of tart, and now they froze, looking to Cecilia.

"Do you have an engagement, my lord?" she asked civilly.

"I will be joining your brother in Enfield this night."

She blinked at him, her only show of surprise. Then she thanked the footmen and dismissed them. "Does Oliver know you're joining him?"

"No, but since he has previously invited me, and my leg is feeling much better—"

"After your fireside rest at the inn," she interrupted dryly.

He gave a slow nod. "So I will join him. Since the townspeople had such a reserved reaction to the earl, I decided I should see why."

"A reserved reaction," she mused, resting her chin on her palm, a touch of sadness in her eyes.

"If he changes his ways soon, they will attribute his behavior to youth, and forget it."

"I hope so." Now she eyed him, wearing the faintest hint of a lovely smile. "Will you be able to tolerate a group of such young men?"

"You forget I am a sergeant in the dragoons. I see such young men every day, and I mold them into the soldiers they need to be."

"But Oliver doesn't need to be a soldier."

"He needs to become a man. There are some similarities."

She bit her lip, resisting a smile, he knew. She would continue to resist everything about him until he made her see that it was futile. He was ruthless in pursuit of a goal.

"Take care," she said, when he rose to his feet. "The roads are winding, and you do not know them well in the dark."

"Concerned for me, Cecilia? You would think if I broke my neck, you would be well rid of me."

Instead of smiling, she paled and put a hand to that locket she always wore.

"Forgive me," he said. "That was dark humor of the sort not used among ladies."

"But used among soldiers," she murmured.

"We talk often of death, as if we might keep it away with words alone."

Her gaze remained troubled. He couldn't put the image of her out of his mind on the ride into Enfield. Was there something wrong he didn't know about?

He found Appertan and his friends at the same coaching inn taproom, and they were already in full drunken splendor. Several loose women had wisely been brought in to focus their merriment. Michael remained on the fringes, assessing each young man, and several not so young, old enough to know better but obviously hanging on to the coattails of the foolish earl. Michael felt decades older than most of the young pups.

Appertan noticed him at last, and after a weary roll of his eyes, sent over a drink. Soon, he was introducing Michael to the other men, and they all began to ask for bloodthirsty stories of fighting in the mountains of Afghanistan. He obliged them with a few, and even

Appertan looked impressed. But it was difficult to talk of that time, when his regiment had been sent back to Bombay after the taking of Kabul, and those left behind were slaughtered a few years later while fleeing Afghanistan through winter mountain passes.

If Fenton, the man who'd attacked Cecilia, had been there, he'd made a quick departure before Michael could see him. As it was, Rowlandson seemed to have forgotten Michael's threats and acted as if they were old friends.

One by one, Appertan's compatriots either sank beneath a table or disappeared into a back room, where they gambled over card games and dice. Appertan himself kept studying Michael as if he wanted to say something but couldn't make up his mind. At last, he brought a brandy to Michael's table, plopping it down until it sloshed over on his hand. He laughed and licked it off, seating himself as if he were a sack of grain ready to spill open.

Michael silently saluted him with the brandy and tossed it back in one swallow.

Appertan laughed, then rested his elbows on the table and leaned forward. "So did m'sister send you to be my nanny for the evening?"

"No, in fact, she was concerned this might not be a good idea."

Appertan sipped from his glass, nodding as if in deep contemplation, when he was probably so drunk he had to take time to formulate words. "It's a good thing you're here," he mused, wiping at a spot of port on his chin. "If Cecilia is in fear of her life, I should keep an eye on you."

Michael reminded himself that the other man was drunk. "What do you mean by that? Is someone threatening my wife?"

"I don't know. Are you?" Appertan hiccoughed and chuckled.

"Explain yourself."

He raised both hands. "Calm down! They were just accidents. Cecilia knows that, really."

"'They'?" Michael stressed the words in a low rumble. "She's had more than one accident?"

"Penelope said she shouldn't have told me, but Penelope tells me everything. Seems Cecilia almost fell down the stairs a couple nights ago, caught herself on the balustrade. She probably tripped and doesn't want to admit that she could be as imperfect as the rest of us."

Michael barely resisted taking him by the collar and giving him a shake. "Go on."

Appertan shrugged. "Penelope said Cecilia thought something actually tripped her, but she couldn't find it. Of course not, because she just missed a step in the dark."

Teeth clenched, Michael glowered at the foolish young man. Cecilia never exaggerated or misspoke—he already knew that about her, and if Appertan were sober, he'd remember that as well. So Cecilia felt that she'd been deliberately tripped. "She didn't fall all the way down the stairs," Michael said slowly. "Or otherwise . . ." He restrained a rare shudder at the thought of her body broken at the bottom of the stairs.

"Or otherwise . . ." Appertan used his finger to mark a line across his throat. "She only told Penelope. I'm a little offended." He snorted a laugh into his glass of port. "And, of course, it was an accident. Everyone *loves* Cecilia."

He didn't bother to hide his sarcasm—or his jealousy, Michael thought. "And then the bust fell on her in the entrance hall."

"Another accident. The maid was right there, dusting. Cecilia is just being overly dramatic."

"And have you ever known her to be overly dramatic?" Michael demanded.

"She's a woman, after all." He stood up unsteadily. "I'm tired of talking about her."

Michael almost pulled him back down, but knew it was pointless to interrogate Appertan when he was drunk. "I'm heading back to Appertan Hall. Would you care to accompany me? Cecilia said the roads are hard to follow at night."

"You're so easy to read, Blackthorne," Appertan said, shaking his head and wearing a foolish grin. "You're just trying to get me to make an early evening of it. It's only one in the morning, and there's more fun to be had," he added after squinting at the clock on the mantel. He slurped the last of his port before slamming down the glass. "As if a soldier couldn't find his way back on good English roads," he muttered, walking away with a noticeable lean to one side.

Michael no longer cared if Appertan made it home. All he could think about was Cecilia alone and un-protected, fearing for her life—and maybe with good reason.

Chapter 10

Cecilia wasn't certain what woke her. She'd been exhausted when she'd fallen asleep after an evening of pacing. Now, as she rose through the depths of slumber to awareness, something wasn't right.

She didn't open her eyes—couldn't. Her breathing was shallow with sudden fear, but she controlled it, controlled herself, when she wanted to fly from the bed.

The floor creaked. Someone was in the room, and she knew it couldn't be Nell, who hummed when she worked.

Cecilia debated what she could use as a weapon. The letter opener was on her writing desk across the room. All she had nearby was a candleholder of heavy pewter. How could she reach for it without attracting notice?

The steps didn't come closer; someone hovered, watching her, and she felt a strange, tingling awareness. She was so helpless, so vulnerable. But she couldn't lie still and simply let her assailant do as he wished.

Slowly, she opened her eyes the slightest crack. She was relieved she'd left the curtains open, so that faint moonlight glimmered, giving everything a ghostly hue.

The shadowy outline of a man stood unmoving near the open dressing-room door. The moonlight reflected off something—a polished cane. Lord Blackthorne's cane.

Suddenly, he sat down in a chair and leaned his head back. His eyes were black hollows in the moon-touched planes of his harsh face. He gave a great sigh, his wide chest lifting and falling.

"You're safe," he whispered.

Safe? Why would he say such a thing?

Her breathing calmed, and she silently berated herself for her momentary fear.

But perhaps her husband felt compelled to claim his marital rights. She had heard her friends whisper that a man *needed* a woman, that it was painful for him if he did not . . . if she didn't allow . . .

She could no longer pretend to sleep, stirring as if awakening. He stiffened but remained where he was; he didn't care if she saw him.

She came up on her elbows first, doing a masterful job of acting drowsy and confused, or so she thought. "Is someone there?"

He didn't hesitate. "I am. I did not mean to frighten you."

She pushed up onto her hands, only realizing that

her blankets had fallen around her waist when his gaze dropped down her body. Her nightgown covered her well, but it was of a fine, thin fabric, and she felt almost naked in it compared to the layers of garments she wore like a shield during the day. She pulled the blankets back up and tucked them beneath her arms, across her chest.

"Why are you here?" she asked.

"I was worried about you." He hesitated. "It was . . . a strange feeling, one I can't explain."

"I did not hear you knock; nor did I invite you in." The faintest scent reached her. "I smell . . . strong spirits." She wondered if drink lowered his every inhibition?

He grunted. "I did not drink nearly as much as your brother. Considering his thin build, I am amazed that he still functions at the end of the night."

"He returned with you?"

"No. He said he had more entertainment to enjoy."

"But not you?"

In the gloom, she could see the shrug of his big shoulders.

"I am too old for such pointless endeavors. And I never did like wondering what I said or did while inebriated."

"But surely you've been in that state a time or two," she said, scooting back to lean into her pillows.

"Every man has. And I know Appertan is still a very

young man, but one with many responsibilities that he cannot continue to ignore."

"You are a viscount, with your own responsibilities. Surely you should not have overimbibed."

He rested his cane across his thighs. "My father was still alive when I enlisted. He was embarrassed by my decision and furious with me, but just to prove myself, I decided to drink like a man with the other soldiers."

"You showed him," she murmured, fighting to keep from smiling.

He sighed. "I certainly did. I wasn't even ten miles from home. We drank so much and brawled to show our fighting prowess that the tavern owner complained to our company sergeant. The man had great pride in wearing the uniform and thought little of someone who dishonored it. And I was wearing my uniform—when you're enlisted, you have to, at all times."

"But surely a few drunken soldiers weren't all that unusual."

"But I was a drunken baron, my courtesy title. The sergeant dragged my ass—forgive me—he dragged me back to my father and threatened to discharge me then and there."

She winced. "And proud man that you are, I imagine you did not take well to that."

"I was humiliated, and it was all my own fault. Never again did I embarrass myself that way." He hesitated. "It was the last time I ever saw my father. I inherited

the viscountcy six months later, when he had an apo-
plexy and died."

"I'm sorry your last memory was a poor one. Surely
he was proud of you, that your letters—"

"It was six months before I arrived in India. By the
time I posted my first letter, he was already dead."

She shouldn't speak, but the words tumbled out of
her. "I hope the letter informing you of his death was
as kind as yours was to me."

Old sorrows hung between them like laundry abandoned on the line.

"I only spoke the truth about Lord Appertan," he
said quietly. "He was a great man."

She thought of Lord Blackthorne's many letters to
her since, asking how she did, telling her of his daily
life without revealing much bloodshed. But she had
begun to know his letters well, and could read between
the lines, the tension of a border dispute, the endless
waiting and worry when he'd sent a detachment into
danger. He'd not been sentimental or full of flowery
phrases, but clear and concise and reliable.

Such a man could not want her dead. He would have
had to plan it from the moment of her father's death,
crafting his letters to appeal to her, planning to visit
her all along.

Squeezing her eyes shut, she leaned back into the
pillow with a sigh.

"You are tired," Lord Blackthorne said as he rose.

She tried not to tense, remembering how he'd touch her—how she'd allowed it, dwelled on the sensation. He limped toward the dressing-room door.

"Good night, my lord," she called softly.

"Sleep well," he answered, and shut the door behind him.

She told herself she was relieved.

At dawn, Michael walked the rolling hills of the Appertan estate, needing to exhaust himself each day just to sleep at night. He'd never imagined that being so close to a woman would enthrall him, having thought himself above such weakness. But no, his wife was like a siren to a sailor, luring him in even though it might not end well.

And now she might be in danger, and every protective instinct in him demanded that he spend the nights with her now, but she would only think he wanted to bed her. When he'd stood above her, saw her sleeping peacefully, a great weight had felt like it crushed his chest, filling him with an aching tenderness and worry and a helplessness he wasn't used to feeling.

She was his; he would protect her with his life. He'd been naïve to think that making himself a husband in name only, from the other side of the world, wouldn't change him or his life. Her sweet letters had drawn him in, until he couldn't stop wondering about the real woman behind the words, the one who needed money to protect herself and her people when her brother couldn't do it. The moment Michael had been ordered to recover in England, he hadn't protested, not one bit. He'd wanted to meet her, this woman who thought she had all the answers. And she hadn't disappointed him.

But Cecilia didn't want him, or the devotion of a husband, and he wasn't the sort of man to force himself on a woman, regardless of his rights by law.

It might have begun with words on paper, with her kindness toward a lonely soldier. She'd put aside her own pain, and now he knew she did that for everyone she cared for, from family to servants. Her fright at almost dying beneath a shattered bust didn't matter as much as the poor maid's fears of being let go. She gave up her chance at a normal young lady's life to help her brother. And someone might be repaying her kindness by trying to kill her. By not thinking of herself first, didn't she increase the danger?

She'd had two accidents, so minor that she only mentioned her concerns to Penelope. But the fact that she felt any sort of trepidation made him believe her, for she wasn't the type of woman to imagine things. He'd almost told her what he knew, then thought better of it. She wouldn't want his help, and if she forbade him from looking into it, he'd only anger her by going against her wishes. So for now, he would keep silent, helping her behind the scenes, keeping her safe, trying to find out if there was anyone who might wish her harm.

And the first one to question would be her brother.

The people closest to the victim were often the ones involved. And Appertan certainly had the most motive: Cecilia controlled everything he owned. Under his permission, yes, but what if he was beginning to chafe? With the approach of his twenty-first birthday and the withdrawal of his guardianship, perhaps he thought it wouldn't be so easy to dissuade Cecilia. What if he didn't give a damn about his responsibilities, his estates—and he'd certainly shown that so far—and simply wanted access to whatever money he could? For all Michael knew, Appertan was not only a drunk but a gambler, as so many young men were. Most would simply ignore the wishes of his sister, but Cecilia was a powerful force—a representative of their father, whom Appertan had disappointed.

But for now, he would question Appertan about other suspects and see what happened. Michael went to the kitchens first, and the respectful cook followed his directions and mixed him up the soldier's antidote to a night spent drinking. Then he carried the foul-smelling glass to Appertan's apartment, pushing past the protective valet, who insisted that ten in the morning was far too early to awaken the earl.

Appertan was sprawled across the turned-down bed, his clothing askew, boots placed neatly on the floor—due to the valet, Michael presumed. The room stank of alcohol, and Appertan snored louder than the worst military band.

Michael set down his glass on the bed table, then shook the other man's shoulder. Appertan didn't even stop snoring.

"He is a sound sleeper," said the valet from the dressing-room doorway.

"A bad trait in my line of work." Michael shook him harder, tempted to toss a pitcher of water in his face.

At last, Appertan frowned and sputtered and stirred, blearily opening one eye, then closing it again. "Go 'way."

"I'm not going anywhere. I need to talk to you about Cecilia. And I brought you something that will help you recover."

Appertan tried to drag a pillow over his head as he rolled over, but Michael pulled him back.

"Do you want me to feed you like a child? We need to discuss something important!" He spoke each word with clipped force.

After several more threats from Appertan about expelling Michael from the castle, the young man at last sat up and reluctantly took a sip of the thick liquid.

He gagged. "What the hell—!"

"Plug your nose if you have to, but get it down."

Appertan choked and gasped until it was all in his stomach, where it only remained for several minutes, until his eyes went wide, and he ran for the chamber pot.

Michael was waiting patiently beside the bed as Appertan collapsed on it.

"You're trying to kill me!" the earl groaned.

"If I were trying to kill you, you'd be dead. You're an easy target. I need to talk to you about who might be targeting your sister."

"It's all in her head." Appertan clutched his own and moaned softly.

"Even *I* know she would never imagine something like this. Talk to me. This is important."

At last, the other man allowed his valet to fluff his pillows, where he reclined with a sigh, crossed his arms over his chest, and glared at Michael. "You really think someone is trying to kill Cecilia? It's just—preposterous!"

"Maybe. I hope you're right. But I'm not willing to take that chance. Now get yourself together and think."

Appertan gave a dramatic sigh. "Really—who would have anything against Cecilia?"

"She's taken on a man's role, and there are some who don't appreciate it."

Appertan stiffened. "What are you saying?"

"I don't know—I'm talking out loud, trying to come up with a reason someone would resent her. Any disturbance with servants? Any let go recently?"

He closed his eyes. "Not that I know of. But as long as the staff functions well, I don't pay attention."

"Because Cecilia does," Michael said dryly. But there was an edge to Appertan's voice that seemed . . . wrong, but he couldn't place why. Perhaps there was something to the idea of a problem with servants.

"The household is always a woman's domain," Appertan shot back.

"You're right. I'll have to speak with someone more knowledgeable about that."

"What about Cecilia? Have you talked with her?"

"No. She hasn't confided in me, and I don't want to make our tentative relationship worse."

Appertan narrowed his eyes. "Perhaps I should ask about your relationship."

"I understand your suspicions. You and I are both closest to her, and anyone seriously investigating would think we both have motive. But I've asked nothing of her, so what motive could I have?"

"And I've asked for her help—why would I want to make my life harder?"

Michael crossed his arms over his chest and stared down at Appertan. Was he telling the truth? He didn't know the man all that well, and what he knew he didn't particularly respect. But attempting to murder one's own sister? It seemed . . . far-fetched.

"If it wasn't you or me," Michael continued, "and perhaps not a servant, although I'll look into that, who else?"

"We can't even come up with names! Of course no one's trying to kill Cecilia."

Michael leaned over the bed and pointed his finger at Appertan's face. "She's almost died twice! I will damn well keep looking into this until I'm satisfied that they were both accidents." And how suspicious was it that Appertan was trying to talk him out of the investigation. "Now *think,* man!"

The earl swung his legs off the bed and sat up, briefly holding his head in his hands. "Oh, very well, give me a minute to do all this thinking. Too bloody early," he added in a mumble.

"Any suitors?"

"Dozens of those. Could have beaten them off with a stick and hit several at once."

Michael eyed him. "Violent image."

"Oh please," Appertan said with a grimace. "You know what I mean. Stupid men fawning all over her, begging for a dance, begging to be noticed. I would never do that to a woman."

"You don't have to. You're an earl. The women must have come begging to you."

"True."

"Is that why you became engaged at such a young age? To avoid debutantes and their annoying mothers?"

Appertan shrugged again and dropped his head back in his hands as if he didn't want to meet Michael's gaze. "Not really. Knew Penelope would do and saw no reason to wait."

"What an ardent declaration of love," Michael said dryly.

"None of your business, Blackthorne."

His voice had the sharp ring of command, sounding much like his father, and Michael was reluctantly impressed. If only the pup would mature into a man who could use such strength of command wisely.

"And I never heard of you declaring your love for my sister."

"That's because I didn't." Michael kept his voice mild. "She asked for my help to access her funds, and I gave it to her."

"So selfless."

The sarcasm in Appertan's voice wearied Michael rather than offended. But Michael wasn't about to confess his growing feelings for Cecilia to her brother. "You keep veering off track. Her suitors? I need a list."

"I can't keep them all straight. But several live nearby and most certainly will come to our monthly dinner."

"We have a monthly dinner?"

"*We* have a monthly dinner, not you. My guardian visits us—tomorrow, incidentally—and he enjoys the camaraderie of our neighbors. Several local men thought they had a chance with Cecilia, and one or two even proposed."

"I hear there were six," Michael said, unable to keep the antipathy from his voice.

Appertan fell back on his elbows to look up at him. "Six? You should feel honored that she settled on you in her desperation."

Michael gritted his teeth, surprised to find it was difficult to ignore the provocation. "So these suitors will be here soon."

"Yes. And besides, what will it get them to harm her now, when she's already married?"

"Revenge?"

"There are other heiresses."

"None like Cecilia." Had he actually spoken those words aloud?

He must have, because Appertan gaped at first, then chortled. "You've only been here a few days, and already you're under her thumb. Pathetic."

Michael ignored him. "What about *your* friends? I already know that two of them are men who think nothing of harming women they deem beneath them."

Appertan's head sank between his shoulders. "Their behavior was unconscionable—they know it. They've learned their lesson."

He spoke meaningfully, as if the behavior of his friends really did bother him.

"But what motive would they have to harm Cecilia?" Appertan continued.

"She's spoiling their amusements, after all, controlling your money, restricting their use of the house."

"She's not controlling my money, only that of the estate," Appertan growled, obviously offended.

He would only keep defending his friends, so Michael altered tack. "What about her steward? He works closely with her."

"And with my father beforehand. Why would he want to deal with me?"

"He'll have to eventually." And Appertan would be far easier for an employee to manipulate. "Any close friends besides Miss Webster?"

"Penelope's sister, Hannah, died last year. She was Cecilia's closest friend. She wasn't a strong enough swimmer, and all those clothes women wear . . ." He shrugged.

"So you were there for Miss Penelope Webster in her grief."

Appertan came to his feet with surprising speed. "Are you saying I took advantage of her?"

Michael looked down upon the shorter man. "Strange that you would interpret my words that way."

"I'm done with this foolishness—I'm done with you. You can leave now."

"And I don't receive any thanks for improving your head and stomach this morn?"

Appertan ignored him and stalked to his dressing room, slamming the door behind him.

Chapter 11

O liver didn't often join Cecilia for luncheon—he was usually either still asleep or just having breakfast. She was surprised when he arrived, and relieved, too, so she didn't have to spend the meal alone with Lord Blackthorne. Her husband watched her too closely, and she kept remembering being alone with him in her bedroom and feeling far too intrigued.

Oliver looked from Cecilia to Lord Blackthorne, then rolled his eyes. "This newlywed shyness is beginning to bother me."

"Shyness?" she asked archly. "I have never been shy a day in my life."

"You wouldn't guess it from the way you behave around Blackthorne. You contracted this marriage, sister dear, so deal with it."

Affronted and embarrassed by his frank language, she said, "Oliver! This is none of your business."

"You're making it my business by having him live in my house."

"You just haven't given each other enough time." Cecilia tried to remind Oliver with her narrowed eyes that he'd promised to help her with Lord Blackthorne.

"We don't seem to care for the same entertainments," Lord Blackthorne said, leaning back in his chair to watch Oliver.

"You're men," she said. "Do something—manly!"

They regarded each other, Lord Blackthorne impassively, Oliver full of sulky defiance. What had happened between them? Only last night, Lord Blackthorne thought that Oliver might be redeemable. But not if they couldn't find a way to spend time together.

"A manly sport might do the trick," Lord Blackthorne said at last, "but I imagine a young man who drinks and socializes has not made the time."

"I fence!" Oliver practically snarled.

"No sharp weapons," Cecilia said. "I don't trust either of you."

"Do you box?" Lord Blackthorne asked. "My brother Allen and I often passed an afternoon testing each other's defenses."

Oliver straightened and slowly smiled, as if he knew the best secret. "It just so happens, I do box."

"But then again, you are much younger than I am," Lord Blackthorne continued. "Allen and I were close in age, almost equals. It made for interesting fights."

"And my youthful energy will negate your experience, old man," Oliver shot back.

If Oliver thought he could box, let him try, Cecilia thought wearily. "Then your afternoon entertainment is taken care of, gentlemen. I will occupy myself."

"That's wise," Lord Blackthorne said. "Such a sport isn't for a lady's eyes."

His implication that she couldn't handle it mildly stung. "Indeed? I would faint at the sight of all that blood, is that what you're saying?"

"I promise not to drain too much from his veins," Oliver said smugly.

Cecilia wanted to wince at his attitude. Couldn't he see how much . . . larger Lord Blackthorne was? Her husband was a cavalryman—trained to fight!

But the two men both seemed quite pleased with themselves, and she was the irritated one. When at last she finished her sturgeon and peas, she went to her study. Though she tried to concentrate on the projection of sheep to be driven to market this fall, and the eventual profit, she kept speculating about Oliver's boxing ability. He did spend time in London, and men seemed to enjoy that sort of exercise, or so they often told her when trying to impress her at dinner parties.

At last she gave up any attempt at concentration and left her study. She still felt uneasy roaming the corridors of her own home, but after two "accidents," she was doubly attentive. She hated feeling vulnerable, nervous, and almost felt like she was skulking from room to room. Or was she just being foolish, as even Penelope thought?

She found the two men in the green drawing room, with ceilings two floors high, just like the entrance hall. She was able to hide within the small curtained balcony overlooking the room. She was relieved that she didn't hear the sounds of an audience cheering, for it wouldn't do to have servants watch their master should he lose. The two men had rolled back the carpets and pushed furniture out of the way. They'd already removed coats and waistcoats, even collars and cravats. Lord Blackthorne had tugged his sleeves up to his elbows, and she saw his brawny forearms, which surely were the size of Oliver's biceps—or so she remembered.

She wanted to groan at the foolishness of men, who couldn't just have an intelligent conversation to discuss their differences—no, they had to prove it with their fists.

They faced each other, fists raised, Oliver circling, lighter on his feet than her limping husband, who basically stood in place, favoring his wounded leg. How could this be a fair contest? Oliver jabbed with his right, but Lord Blackthorne blocked it easily. Oliver tried a few more punches, and when he couldn't get past his opponent's defense, settled back and circled again, obviously waiting to see what would happen.

They were both sweating, their fine shirts beginning to cling. Swallowing, she couldn't help noticing once again that Lord Blackthorne had a soldier's body, hewn for combat, all threatening muscle. She wanted to be wary of him, but, instead, she was full of admiration and curiosity and an unsettling almost-ache that she couldn't define.

At last Lord Blackthorne punched Oliver, but even she saw it coming, and her brother blocked it easily, grinning. Then Lord Blackthorne hit Oliver in the ribs, so quickly she barely saw the blur of his arm. Oliver grunted and danced back out of reach. Lord Blackthorne didn't grin or taunt or do anything other than look focused and intent—deadly.

She remembered the story her father had written, about Lord Blackthorne's ordering his men to fire although a woman might die. He'd honed himself into a weapon on behalf of England. He was dedicated to guarding the lives of his men. Her father's daughter, she knew the costs of war, even in her own family.

Let the men play their little games; she enjoyed her work. Lord Doddridge, Oliver's guardian, would be arriving the next day, and there were preparations to see to for the dinner party. Searching for the housekeeper took her down a floor, into the main public rooms—past the door to the green drawing room.

To her surprise, she heard the voices of two footmen and the new page as she approached.

"—a lot of blood," one of them said, followed by the boy's snicker.

"Blood?" she cried, glancing into the now-open

doors of the drawing room and seeing that Oliver and Lord Blackthorne had gone.

The two footmen, Tom and Will, brothers alike in height, blond good looks, and gold-buckled livery, exchanged a glance even as they straightened like soldiers to attention. Francis, smaller and darker, copied their behavior, sticking out his chest.

"Who was bloody?" Cecilia demanded, staring each of them down.

"Lord Blackthorne had a lot covering his shirt, milady," Tom volunteered. "He and Lord Appertan helped each other off to their rooms—we think."

Helped each other? she thought, aghast. Had Oliver somehow hurt Lord Blackthorne? How much blood were they talking?

And then she saw red droplets scattered on the floor, and for just a moment, she remembered the crash of marble, and how close she'd come to having her own blood seep onto that floor.

"Lady Cecilia, are you well?" one of them asked.

She didn't answer, could only think of blood. And then she started running.

She practically flew up the stairs, through corridors that seemed endless, to the family wing, where she passed her own door and the dressing-room door, before flinging open Lord Blackthorne's.

Standing in the middle of the room, leaning heavily on his cane, he seemed to move so slowly as he faced her. And then she saw all the blood staining his shirt, could see nothing else.

"Oh, God, oh, God, where are you hurt?" she cried, running toward him.

She felt frantic as she pulled at his shirt, heard a button pop.

"Cecilia," he murmured, trying to cover her bare hands.

She pushed him away, pulled his shirt apart, imagining a terrible wound to cause so much blood. This time, her husband trapped her hands flat against his warm chest, then spread them wide so that she could see.

"I'm not injured," he said quietly. "Your brother had a bloody nose."

She blinked at his chest, still feeling shocked rather than relieved. Beneath her hands, she felt the contours of muscle, the faint brush of chest hair. This was what a man's chest really looked like beneath his garments? She'd never visited museums in London, but Hannah used to write of such things to her, and Lord Blackthorne's chest seemed to match those long-ago descriptions.

"Cecilia, why are you so upset?"

He pulled her closer, her hands still spanning his chest, her body pressed against his.

He whispered, "Tell me what is wrong."

And in that moment she almost confided everything in him, that someone might be trying to kill her. Everything would change then. He'd never leave her alone, and she'd be trapped in this marriage for all time.

She raised her gaze from his chest and up to his face. He was leaning over her, holding her against him, closer than a waltz, so imposing and dangerous, but she didn't want to run away. She could feel the beat of his heart beneath her palms, the rise and fall of his breath. Her own breath was coming too quickly, her lips parted. He was staring at her mouth, his gaze full of a stark hunger that shocked even as it lured her.

And then he leaned closer, until their lips almost touched, and his whispered words mingled with her own breath.

"I'm going to kiss you."

She had a moment to stop him, knew he was giving her that choice. But she didn't turn away, only trembled as his mouth gently touched hers, soft kisses that dampened her lips, explored them, but never frightened her. She swayed into him, and he pulled her even harder against him until she was standing between his spread thighs, her skirts all tangled about them.

The kiss's very restrained gentleness drew her more than wild passion, as if this strong soldier reined himself in just for her because she was precious to him. It was she who couldn't seem to get close enough, she who began to part her lips, not knowing if she wanted to taste him or devour him.

And that very feeling of wildness shocked her back

to herself. She broke the kiss to stare up at him, breathing hard, feeling faint. This was all wrong; it couldn't be natural.

"Release me," she whispered, her voice hoarse.

He did so at once, and she took several steps away. He stood still, as if she were a wild animal he didn't want to frighten, his bloody shirt ripped open as if she truly were an animal.

"Oh God," she breathed, covering her mouth with both hands.

"Cecilia, that was a kiss, not a defiling," he said with the soft tones used to calm someone out of control.

Like her. She didn't know herself anymore.

"It doesn't mean you've decided anything about our marriage," he continued. "But how will you know what we can share if you don't try the occasional kiss?"

"Share?" She almost choked on a laugh. "That sounds . . . too gentle for"—she gestured toward him with a fluttering hand—*"that."*

Once again, she drew out of him the faintest of smiles.

"I've not heard my kiss described in such a way."

"And have you kissed that many women in your soldier's life?" she demanded.

"A few."

"Did they all throw themselves at you, maybe even ripping open your shirt?" She groaned and briefly closed her eyes. What kind of woman was she becoming?

"I was not so lucky. In India, one could have an Indian mistress, but I chose not to. Too many soldiers left illegitimate children behind, who fit into neither parent's world. I couldn't do that to a child. Of course, there are plenty of British women who come looking for husbands, but a man should be serious if he dallies with one of them."

"And you don't dally."

"No, I don't." His voice softened. "But I would kiss my wife every day."

"And I'm supposed to enjoy feeling so . . . reckless, so swept away?" she demanded.

His eyes suddenly seemed to darken, and his voice grew husky. "I would make certain you enjoyed it."

Just the sound of him sent a shiver of need twined with pleasure through her. "But I don't want that, Lord Blackthorne," she whispered, feeling helpless next to the desire he evoked in her. "I've told you so."

"I can wait until you change your mind." He straightened and put his hands on the ruined shirt. "I'm going to change now, but you don't need to leave."

He shrugged the shirt down his shoulders, and she gaped a moment too long, seeing the ridges of his abdomen and the faintest line of dark hair disappearing into his trousers. She turned and fled, silently insisting she wasn't a coward, that she didn't want to tease him when they had no future.

* * *

After Cecilia slammed the door behind her, Michael leaned one arm against the mantel and squeezed his eyes shut. The tender kiss was all he'd imagined it might be, full of her sweet breath and gentle yearning. It had taken every ounce of control honed over years of warfare to stop himself from taking more, from plundering her mouth to explore. Those brief tastes only hinted at what they could share. He knew that going too fast, showing her his powerful desire, would only scare her off. Gentle kisses had frightened her, but she hadn't left immediately, had gifted him a few more minutes of time alone with her. Somehow, he would win her trust.

Because she was so frightened by her fears of attempted murder, she'd panicked when she heard what happened at the boxing match. And it was all his fault—he'd deliberately lured her to the fight, implying that, of course, as a lady, she couldn't handle the sight of a boxing match. He'd had two reasons, only one of which was to keep her nearby; the other was so that she would look at him as a man. Sometimes it was difficult to remember he would eventually be free of the cane.

From the moment she'd entered the balcony up above, he'd known she was there, feeling her presence and her gaze so vividly, he'd momentarily lost track of what he was doing. He'd punched Appertan harder than he'd meant to, bloodying his nose. And while he forced Appertan to stand still while he made sure it wasn't broken, blood had soaked both of them.

Michael rang for a bath. He'd started out living in this castle trying to be his own man, without needing a valet. But he'd definitely succumbed to the luxury of having a bath brought to him instead of submerging himself in a cold river.

He had a new purpose for every servant he encountered—finding out something about his wife, and if there might be someone within the household who wished her harm. So when the footmen carried in the bathing tub, he began what might be a long attempt to win their favor.

When the two of them returned with the first pails of water, he commented that they must be brothers, and they sheepishly nodded agreement, admitting that they were named Tom and Will. Practically the only way he could tell them apart was a faint scar on Tom's cheek.

"Weren't the both of you outside the green drawing room?" he asked, when they'd brought in the last buckets to fill his tub.

They glanced at each other. "Yes, milord," they said in unison.

"I hope you do not think I deliberately tried to harm your master."

"No, milord," said Tom.

And Will added, "'Tis none of our business, milord."

"You live in this household; it would seem all its

residents are your business. But then again, I imagine it is Lady Blackthorne who is more the mistress of the house than her brother is the master."

They said nothing, just exchanged uneasy glances.

"It must have been quite frightening for the staff when she was nearly injured by that falling bust."

"Susan didn't mean to—" Tom began.

Michael held up both hands. "I know she didn't. And it was all my fault for distracting her; I told Lady Cecilia that."

"And we're grateful, milord," Will said, giving his brother a warning look. "We're her only family, our sister she is, and if she was to be dismissed . . ."

He let his words die off, and Michael well understood the plight of servants. "Does Lady Blackthorne let servants go?"

"Oh, no, milord, never," Tom said, ignoring his brother's frown. "She's fair to everyone, and has even added to the staff."

"How long have you both been here?"

"Five years, since we were pages," Will quickly said, perhaps attempting to control his brother's side of the conversation. "We've lived in Enfield our whole lives."

Then they knew Cecilia's family well, perhaps even down through generations. Hopefully, that made them trustworthy. "So who are the new servants? I will make certain to appreciate their work."

Will's smile was faintly suspicious but grateful.

"Our sister, Susan, o' course, and the new page, Francis, and another watchman for the grounds."

"Name's Parsons," Tom supplied.

"I hope the new servants enjoy working here."

"Oh, they do, sir," Tom gushed.

Will had begun to roll his eyes at his brother's behavior. Was that because of Tom's kowtowing to Michael, or because his assurances about the servants weren't true?

"I'm glad to hear it," Michael said, knowing he couldn't push for any more answers without causing too much suspicion.

"Shall I come take your garments to the laundry, milord?" Tom asked, then ducked his head. "Since ye've not got a valet."

"Thank you. I would appreciate it."

They left him alone to his now-tepid bath, where he sank in and gave thought to how he could use Tom and Will. He couldn't keep an eye on Cecilia every moment, but if he knew she had trustworthy servants about her, that would help.

After his bath, he deliberately lingered near Cecilia's study as she worked, so she'd get used to seeing him now and again throughout the house. He wanted her to know she had someone to call upon for help should she need it.

Seeing her before dinner was more arousing than he'd imagined it could be after one virginal kiss. Her face reddened when she first saw him across the drawing room, and for once he was glad Appertan was more interested in the bottom of his brandy glass than anything else. That allowed Michael to stare at her as he wanted, to remember the kiss and let her realize what he was thinking, all without saying a word.

When she walked into the dining room without waiting for his escort, Michael watched the way her swaying hips made her skirt do a lively dance. She was all grace and elegance, her blond hair immaculate, not a lock cascading down her perfect neck. He assisted her into the chair.

Appertan gave a snort. "I'm sure Cecilia never seated herself before you arrived."

Michael eyed his afternoon opponent, who sported a faint bluish purple bruise beneath one eye. "A lady always welcomes assistance."

"Perhaps a lady doesn't wish to feel like a fragile flower," Cecilia said dryly.

"No?" Michael was still behind her, hands on her chair, trying not to openly enjoy the view down the front of her cleavage.

With an exaggerated sigh, Appertan looked away.

"You do not feel appreciated when a man assists you?" Michael asked her.

Appertan grumbled almost inaudibly, "Cecilia, just put all of us out of our misery and tell him to go away."

"Pardon me? I didn't quite hear you," Michael said.

The earl didn't repeat his comment, and Michael walked to his own chair.

As the first entrée of curried fowl and boiled rice was served, Cecilia looked pointedly at her brother. "When your guardian arrives, do you have any recent concerns we should discuss?"

Appertan shrugged. "No. You'll show him your journals and account books, he'll spend a day closeted with them, then he'll pretend he wants to have a meaningful conversation with me. At last he'll be on his way, feeling like he's done his duty."

"What an interesting arrangement," Michael said. "He makes certain all is well but doesn't care how that's accomplished, which suits you both. Luck has gone in your favor."

Appertan frowned. "How's that?"

"Because your sister assists you in overseeing the household." "Assists" was too minor a term to encompass Appertan's utter disregard of his duties, but Michael couldn't risk alienating him just then. And as for Cecilia, she'd put aside her own future for the brother she loved. How would she feel when he no longer needed her? "And Lady Blackthorne was lucky as well because she is permitted to do as she pleases, especially since marriage to me removed the impediment of her own guardian. I imagine there are many guardians who would have insisted on doing much of the work themselves."

"His lordship is a busy man," Cecilia said, after swallowing a taste of rice. "He has recently proposed several bills in the House of Lords, and he's in the midst of restoring his own estates."

Restoring? Michael focused on her. "It sounds as if his estates had deteriorated."

"I believe he spoke of the work as basic maintenance that occasionally needs to be done when one owns property," she explained.

Appertan leaned toward Michael. "But then you wouldn't know much about that."

Michael arched a brow. "And why wouldn't I, as I own a landed country house?"

"Just like I have my guardian and Cecilia to 'assist' me," Appertan said, smirking, "you have your brother. Seems neither of us cares for the work of owning land. At least I didn't run away."

"So you believe a man who feels a calling to serve his country is simply running away?"

"I'm certain he didn't mean that," Cecilia said, her lovely brow furrowed as she sent a pointed glance at her brother. "Can we not have one peaceful evening? After dinner, we can relax together as our family used to, instead of you rushing off, Oliver. I'll play the pianoforte, and you can sing."

Michael tried to imagine that domestic scene and failed. Appertan met his gaze, and in that moment, they both sobered, as if they shared a realization that

Cecilia perhaps should not be left alone. Or was Appertan simply acting?

"I'll stay for a while," Appertan said at last. "But remember, you haven't named him as family yet."

A faint blush swept her cheeks, and she was so lovely that Michael didn't take any offense. Not that he would have anyway; he'd known from the beginning that she would not be easily won over. She was a challenge, and the triumph of winning such a strong woman would be sweet.

He thought of the evening ahead—and the night, which he could no longer risk letting her spend alone.

Chapter 12

Cecilia followed the men to the main drawing room, where the pianoforte took up one corner, and several chairs and sofas were grouped nearby as if awaiting a performance. She wished Penelope had come to dinner that night, for she suddenly felt self-conscious and ridiculous. Oliver didn't want to be there—perhaps he now only had one use for Cecilia, and that was as his business steward. And Lord Blackthorne? He said he would remain her husband, and he was doing everything possible to make her agree. She should feel . . . crowded, smothered, irritated, but, instead, she could barely keep her gaze off him, wished desperately that she could kiss him again.

Marriage to him would be the end of her perfect life, where she controlled her own destiny and answered to no one.

Except Lord Doddridge, she thought, feeling bemused. But he'd never bothered her, and certainly Oliver didn't, at least as far as her management of the vast Appertan estates. But now there was Lord Black-thorne, and to honor her father, he was trying to remake Oliver into a dependable man. A very good goal, and she definitely—someday—wished that Oliver would be able to do the work she did.

Unless she was more selfish than she'd imagined, wanting the reins of the earldom without the title, and *that* was why she resisted Lord Blackthorne's efforts with Oliver.

She watched Oliver pour himself a brandy, then begrudgingly offer one to Lord Blackthorne, who declined.

"I need all my faculties to decipher this book," he said, picking up Jane Austen's *Pride and Prejudice.*

She turned away, struggling to hide a smile. Who would have guessed such a sober man hid a sense of humor? She didn't want to know these things about him. She went to the pianoforte. "I know I volunteered to play, my lord, but do not assume I am supremely talented. Every young lady learns to play. Whereas my brother—"

"Isn't going to sing," Oliver interrupted. "But I'll turn the pages for you."

She hid her disappointment, hoping he'd change his mind. At the keyboard, she tried to clear her head, to recapture what it had once been like to be a family, to spend an evening together. In her mind, she returned to their bungalow in Bombay, imagining her brother

Gabriel still alive, teasing Oliver, making their mother smile and distracting her from the anxious looks she usually bestowed on their father.

"What are you thinking?" Lord Blackthorne asked, from his place on a nearby sofa.

She gave him a wry smile. "I am remembering evenings from my childhood, when our father used to have us perform."

"He was very proud of you both," Lord Blackthorne said. "There were nights when we were not permitted to sleep, waiting to move into position for a dawn engagement. We all took turns talking about our families, and your father participated just as freely."

"What did he say?" she asked, feeling wistful, even as her fingers began to play a melody she knew by heart.

Oliver pretended to ignore them, leafing through sheet music with great concentration.

"He spoke often of stories of Lord Appertan at Eton," her husband said. "I heard about a particular archery incident."

Oliver remained hunched over the table full of music, but he was no longer searching through them, his fingers still, his head tilted. Cecilia felt sad even as the amusement of that famous family incident returned.

Lord Blackthorne looked at her brother. "Did you really try to prove you could shoot your arrow through the skirt of your tutor's academic gown without hitting the man himself?"

For the first time in a long while, Oliver wore a smile that wasn't tinged with arrogance or sarcasm. Cecilia started to laugh. All her concerns slipped away, and she pretended she had back her brother of old.

Oliver sipped his brandy and eyed Lord Blackthorne. "I pinned him to a tree. I was quite the hero, even when I was flogged afterward."

Lord Blackthorne just shook his head. "You were lucky you didn't pierce his leg—or anything else." He glanced at Cecilia. "He spoke of you, too. For a woman who claims she doesn't like the adventure of the Indian countryside, it seems you could be quite daring."

"Tell me something he said about me," Cecilia said with an eagerness she didn't try to hide.

Lord Blackthorne gave her his faint smile. "I heard you used to go on long walks even as a child—and without permission. There's an ancient castle ruin nearby, isn't there?"

She threw back her head and laughed in a most unladylike way. Her husband's eyes sparkled as he watched her, and to hide the warmth of her response, she glanced at her fingers moving on the keys.

"I was convinced there was a hidden dungeon there, no matter how many people told me otherwise," she said. "I had to go explore."

"I like that spirit of adventure," Lord Blackthorne said softly.

She couldn't meet his eyes. "Yes, well, I could have been seriously hurt."

"But you weren't," he countered. "I hear you found the undercroft and were convinced that instead of storage, it housed evil knights."

"It was my special hiding place," she mused, far-off memories moving slowly through her mind. "I did my studies there by candlelight when I was older. It's been a long time since I went back. It really is too dangerous."

"I'd like to see it," he answered.

They looked at each other for long moments, and she imagined taking him there, showing him the places she'd hidden unafraid, knowing he'd take that as proof that she could be the kind of wife he wanted, one who'd follow the drum into any adventure. She looked away.

"I take it you weren't very daring at school, Blackthorne," Oliver interrupted.

"I didn't go to school."

Oliver boldly asked the question she wanted answered. "Why not?"

"Because my father refused to send me. He preferred to have us tutored at home."

She looked back down at her fingers moving over the keys. Tutored at home? How very strange for a viscount's heir.

Oliver grunted. "There were days I wished I'd been allowed to stay home." Then he glanced speculatively at Lord Blackthorne. "Did you wish you could have gone?"

"Yes. From what I understand, you often meet your lifelong friends there. Luckily, I met mine in my regiment."

"Do you miss them?" Cecilia asked, feeling a pang of sorrow for Hannah.

A darkness seemed to briefly cross his face and was gone so quickly she thought she imagined it.

"Actually, my two closest friends and I returned to England together."

"Do I know them?" Oliver asked.

"Rothford and Knightsbridge," Lord Blackthorne answered.

The Duke of Rothford and the Earl of Knightsbridge, she thought in surprise. No lowly soldiers, those men. They'd purchased commissions in their youth, and would have been Lord Blackthorne's superiors. It seemed he got on well with authority, unlike her brother.

"They have both sold their commissions and officially retired from the army," Lord Blackthorne continued. "So when I return to India, it will be without them."

Return to India. That phrase sent a surprising shiver of sadness through her. She wanted him gone—why did the thought so disquiet her?

The silence grew tense, and Cecilia felt a need to change the subject. To Lord Blackthorne, she said, "So what childhood memory did you discuss with your fellow soldiers on those long lonely nights?"

"I had little to say," he answered, smoothing his hand over the cover of the book almost absently.

"You were so very perfect as a child?" Oliver taunted.

"'Boring' is the better word," Lord Blackthorne said wryly. "Every chance I got, I played with my toy soldiers and staged elaborate battles in the library. My mother permitted me to keep them set up for days, so that I could conduct entire wars. And when I outgrew that, I buried myself in war history and battlefield memoirs."

"You really were boring," Oliver said, setting a song sheet on the piano, then leaning against a sideboard to contemplate his ever-receding brandy.

Lord Blackthorne's childhood sounded lonely to Cecilia. "What did your brother do while you prepared yourself to be a soldier?"

He shook his head with bemusement. "He released frogs onto my battlefields, dragged me fishing, and occasionally agreed to a sword battle with sticks."

"We could still fence," Oliver interjected.

"No sharp weapons," Cecilia reminded them, but inside, she felt glad that Lord Blackthorne's brother had played with him. He had those memories—she had memories, too. And they never discussed them, as if Gabriel hadn't existed. Obviously, even her father kept quiet about his son, for Lord Blackthorne had never heard of him.

"Our brother Gabriel was a daring prankster," she said, glancing at Oliver. "Do you remember when Gabriel confronted that pack of wild dogs in Bombay?"

Oliver tensed, and she worried she'd made a mistake.

"Your brother had to be quite young," Lord Blackthorne said.

"He was eight." Oliver took a sip of brandy. "Cecilia told him to stay in the carriage, but he wouldn't. I egged him on."

"Our family used to take carriage rides in the evening along the Esplanade," Cecilia explained. "It was near the seashore, and there were rotting carcasses and . . . other things thrown there by the fishermen. The smell—" She gave a shudder, and said to Oliver, "Do you remember?"

"How could I forget?" he murmured.

Cecilia turned back to Lord Blackthorne. "There was a pack of wild dogs that fed there, and if you were foolish enough to leave your carriage to walk the sand, they would attack. Gabriel was determined to see how far from the carriage he could go before spotting them."

"I assume your parents didn't approve," Lord Blackthorne said.

"Of course not." Cecilia smiled. "But Gabriel had it all planned, and darted out of the carriage before Mother could stop him. He chose a night Papa wasn't with us. While she shrieked, and the coachman hesitated to risk his own life, Oliver and I crowded the single window to watch. Gabriel went twenty paces before the dogs appeared over the nearest mound. We screamed his name, and he ran back, vaulting into the carriage, falling onto the floor laughing, while Mother slammed the door shut and pounded on the roof for the coachman to drive off. We were all flung back by the speed of those panicked horses." Her smile faded. "He was very daring."

"And it killed him," Oliver said, turning to look out the window as if he could see anything in the night.

"How did he die?" Lord Blackthorne asked.

She winced, but Oliver didn't respond. It had been ten years, after all. She found she didn't want to tell the story either.

"Go ahead, say it," Oliver prodded, looking down at her where she sat hunched on the piano bench. "You brought it up."

Something in her eased when he didn't openly blame her for Gabriel's death. But she had enough guilt of her own.

Lord Blackthorne was studying them closely. "It is obviously a painful memory. You don't need to speak of it."

But she was watching Oliver, and thought of the pain of never speaking of his beloved twin. "He was killed by a crocodile," she whispered.

Lord Blackthorne frowned.

"You probably expected a fever to have taken him,"

she said, her voice hoarse now. "He pushed me out of the way—saved my life." She was supposed to be watching over him—his death was all her fault. It should have been her whose body was never found, not her sweet little brother.

She waited for Oliver to condemn her as she condemned herself. Sometimes, she felt like she was always waiting for that.

"He would have been the earl," Oliver said. "A better one than I." He drained his brandy and poured another.

"That's not true," she insisted.

When Oliver didn't answer, she began to play the piece he'd picked out, but he didn't join in, as if he didn't want to be that sort of brother anymore.

"I have to leave," Oliver said, when she'd finished.

Michael watched Cecilia's face, saw the disappointment and sadness that she so quickly hid. Now that he'd heard the tragic story of her brother, it was obvious she had much practice at concealing her emotions—and her guilt. She must never have gotten over being the one who lived instead of dying. Her worried gaze followed her brother to the door, even as her fingers touched her locket.

"You are very talented," Michael said into the silence that followed.

She glanced at him, then looked back down at the keyboard. "Thank you," she murmured.

"Appertan will be all right." He wanted to lift the

concern from her eyes, make her happy, but she didn't want him to do that.

She gave a faint smile. "I hope so."

"That locket you wear—does it have something to do with Gabriel?"

She looked down at it, then glanced at him, wearing a sad smile. "Each side is a miniature of my brothers just before Gabriel's death. Although they were identical, I could always tell them apart."

She opened the locket and held it up to him, displaying the small faces of two laughing boys, both with tousled, lighter blond hair than Appertan had now.

"The artist tried to persuade them to be serious," she continued, "as the subject of such paintings usually are, but they just . . . couldn't."

When she closed the locket, he said, "Does Lord Appertan look at the miniatures?"

"No."

"I imagine becoming the earl made him relive the death of the brother he's now replaced. That is only natural."

"Do you think so?" She sounded hopeful.

"I do. We'll continue what we've been doing. It will help. Will you play another song for me?"

She nodded, and to his surprise, she began to hum and eventually sing, her voice simple and pure, her beauty angelic in the candlelight. Michael let peace wash over him, as if the world's cares could remain beyond the closed doors. He knew desire could forge a bond between two people, but he'd never imagined that contentment and happiness could be just as seductive. She made him happy, just being with her. But they would be separated soon.

The last notes of the song trailed off, and Cecilia rose to her feet. "I believe I'll retire for the evening. Don't let me inconvenience—"

But he'd already arisen. "I'll escort you."

She bit her lip but didn't protest. Will waited in the shadows of the entrance hall with a candleholder, and Michael accepted it. Side by side, they walk up the main staircase, and he wondered if she remembered the terror of beginning to fall just a few days before. Her expression was impassive, showing him nothing.

"I understand you've recently hired a watchman," he said.

"I have. He joins two others. The grounds are extensive, and I don't want miscreants to assume we are ripe for their mischief."

"Do they patrol indoors?"

"Patrol? My lord, we are not a regiment stationed near the enemy."

"Forgive my wording, but you know what I mean."

She sighed. "Talbot is responsible for locking all the entrances, and he's spent his life doing exemplary work. The servants know they are not to leave the house during the night. We are secure, Sergeant."

Though he wanted to chuckle at her use of his rank, he was too concerned about the hours they would spend apart—when she would be alone. Any servant could grant access to the house in the middle of the night, circumventing outdoor watchmen.

At her door, she opened it before he could, murmured a quick "Good night," and ducked inside, closing it behind her. He heard the key turn in the lock.

He sighed, not expecting anything else, no long kiss or invitation to join her. But he was glad she was safely locked inside and made sure the dressing-room door was locked as well. In his own room, the bed was turned down invitingly, but he wouldn't be using it although he did disturb it so that the servants wouldn't realize what was going on. His wife might be in danger. Silently, he entered the dressing room she'd abandoned as some sort of no-man's-land since his arrival. By leaning his head near the door, he could hear her speak with her maid, and relaxed at their soft laughter.

Then he limped as quickly as he could back downstairs, using only the faint moonlight through the windows to guide him. He checked every exterior door although it took him almost an hour to do so. Talbot was doing his duty, at least.

When he returned to the dressing room, he could no longer hear anyone speaking in Cecilia's room. He closed his eyes and put his hand on the doorknob, remembering how she'd looked when she slept. After removing his coat and boots without a sound, he lay down on the cot kept there in case the maid needed to remain nearby.

He fell asleep, but in the way of sleeping lightly, he was restless, with dreams invading his mind. His dead friends returned to him again, as they'd begun to do every night. In some ways, seeing their deaths over and over again would be easier than imagining their lives if they'd lived, but tonight his dreams gave him the future that might have been. He saw the late earl in command of his estates, guiding his son, allowing Cecilia peace of mind. His two dead friends returned to England, one to a wife and child, the other to see his sister settled before embarking on his own search for a wife.

Michael forced himself to awaken. They were dead—many men had died in the empire's endless quest to remain strong. And he was alive. He didn't feel guilty about things that couldn't be changed, so what were his dreams trying to make him see?

It was still several hours before dawn, but after listening at Cecilia's door again, Michael did another slow patrol through the castle. The doors were still locked, but that didn't mean he could relax.

Cecilia awoke just before dawn, when the world was gray with the promise of a new day. But she felt sluggish rather than energized. She'd heard footsteps several times outside her door and had tensed with fear, but no one had tried the knob. Surely it was a servant passing by in the night, seeing to Oliver.

Or a restless Lord Blackthorne. She was surprised he hadn't insisted on escorting her directly into her room. Since their kiss, she felt like he hadn't left her alone, and that was making her even more nervous because of the way he drew her to him.

She was already dressed by the time Nell arrived and had even pulled her own hair back. The maid tsked at her.

"I have so much to do today," Cecilia insisted. "Do I look presentable?" She took a piece of toast from the tray, slurped her hot chocolate, and started for the door, determined that she was not going to alter her life because of fear.

"Ye didn't even let me reply!" Nell cried, hands on her hips.

"Sorry!" She opened up her door—and found Lord Blackthorne seated on a bench beneath a wide landscape painting.

"I thought I'd accompany you on your walk," he said, standing up.

He was so overpowering, even in the high-ceilinged ornate corridor. She glanced behind to see Nell looking past her, full of interest and approval. Since when had Lord Blackthorne begun to win over her servants, even her own lady's maid? She frowned at Nell, who quickly busied herself in the wardrobe.

Cecilia wanted to refuse him but knew that would make him suspicious, and even more insistent about accompanying her. So she smiled tightly, tossed her piece of toast back on its plate, and allowed him to fall in beside her. He was carrying a basket that bumped rhythmically against his good leg.

"What is that?" she asked with suspicion.

"Breakfast. It seems your cook has heard you are not eating enough. I believe I saw a simple piece of toast in your hand—and you didn't finish it."

"Are you spying on me?" she demanded, coming to a stop.

He pivoted about the cane and looked down at her. "Your cook came to *me,* the man you've proclaimed as your husband—although you've not convinced yourself."

She flushed. "We've discussed this. It's only been a few days. I haven't decided."

"And now that I've kissed you, you seem even more against the idea of spending time with me."

She swept past him. "Just because you wish to remain married doesn't mean I do."

"The longer you take, the more scandal it will be."

He was right—she hadn't been thinking deeply about it, weighing her options. She was too concerned with her brother's future—and with the "accidents" that had plagued her.

"Lord Blackthorne, I don't even know how to *begin*

to trust you!" They were near the balustrade that wound about the entrance hall, and her voice echoed. She winced and looked about but didn't see any servants nearby. "Yet denying this marriage means becoming a ward again, and I don't want that."

"When I meet Lord Hanbury, perhaps I'll see your problem."

"Lord Hanbury was my guardian. Lord Doddridge is Oliver's. Oliver . . . chose him when he inherited the earldom."

Lord Blackthorne went still. "Excuse me?"

"Lord Doddridge was a friend of my father's, but a man more prominent in London. Oliver chose him as someone who would understand what a new earl was going through. Regardless, this doesn't matter to me right now."

"Of course it does. Appertan will turn twenty-one within the year, and no longer need a guardian at all. But if you're under guardianship, you will not be able to so easily control him or the estate—your reasoning for our marriage, I believe. That—and access to your funds. You may do as you please financially, yet I will keep you from scandal, keep you safe."

"Safe from what?" she whispered, looking up into his eyes.

"I don't know," he answered back, just as softly.

Then he touched her arm, and she flinched.

"What do you need protection from, Cecilia?"

She pulled away from him. "You're being ridiculous. I am perfectly safe. Now let's walk if we're going to do this."

To her relief, he remained silent, both of them inhaling the autumn scents of harvested grains and the richness of the earth being plowed for the spring wheat crop. He didn't try to come up with awkward conversations, for which she was grateful. Gradually she relaxed, letting the peace of the countryside soothe her as it always did. Her tenants were growing used to them both and no longer sent him suspicious glances—although they should, she reminded herself.

When they crested a low hill, they could see the New River winding its way toward London, and the windows of Appertan Hall glittering in the rising sun, as they'd done for hundreds of years. Cecilia looked upon it all and knew that her family had taken good care of it, encouraged growth, and protected its people. And within the year, Oliver could change all that if he didn't mend his ways.

Lord Blackthorne said, "Let us have our picnic here."

From within the basket, he removed a blanket and awkwardly tried to spread it out himself.

"I might have overdone it boxing yesterday," he said ruefully.

She straightened out the blanket, surprised he would admit any kind of weakness to her. "Shall I help you to sit?"

He arched a brow. "I am not in my dotage yet, Cecilia."

She raised both hands in surrender even as she knelt. "You're the one who said you were feeling stiff today."

He smoothly lowered himself to the ground with the aid of the cane. "Shall we see what Cook prepared?"

It was a feast of sliced ham, bread with butter and jam, several apples, and cider in a corked bottle. Cecilia was glad to have something with which to busy her hands. Lord Blackthorne watched as she unbuttoned and removed her gloves, as if even such innocent skin fascinated him. The wind caught her hair, loosening the occasional curl, and she kept impatiently tucking each behind her ear. Then, to her surprise, Lord Blackthorne caught her hand, and with the other, he slowly slid the hair behind her ear, letting his bare fingers linger. She shivered, and had no choice but to meet his eyes.

"Don't," she whispered, imploring him.

"Don't what?" he answered in a husky voice. "Touch my wife? We are in public, in the middle of the façade you created."

She stiffened. "That is unfair."

"I know, but it's the truth. Now you say we are to hold a dinner party tomorrow. Like the ladies from Enfield—"

"Who will be there," she interrupted glumly.

"—will others believe you were enraptured by my way with the written word?"

She looked down at her knees almost touching his thigh. He leaned back, bracing himself on one hand, the better to see into her face, she knew.

"Yes," she whispered.

"How shall I behave? What would you like me to do? And don't say 'disappear,' because that will not happen."

She tried not to smile but couldn't help it. She saw his expression relax, those dark brown eyes softening. She felt trapped there, trying to see into his soul.

"Behave as you wish," she said simply. "I cannot tell a grown man what to do. I only ask that you not . . . ingratiate yourself with everyone."

"You fear I am so quick with conversation and friendship?" he said dryly.

"I have put you in a terrible position, I know." She covered her face and sighed before looking at him again. "It isn't fair, this marriage I asked of you. You should go now, before my demands get worse. When I decide, I'll . . . send word. Surely your family misses you."

"Go now, so you can deny that I'm your husband?" he said gently.

"I haven't let you be my husband. I probably won't."

"In the eyes of the law—"

"We don't know what the law truly says!"

"In the eyes of Society—"

"Stop!"

She put her hand over his mouth, a childish move, but it suddenly felt very adult. He caught her hand and briefly held it there, and when she felt the touch of his tongue tasting her bare palm, she gave a shudder as the sensation burned a path clear into the depths of her stomach. She caught her breath.

He let her go, and when she clasped her hand back against her chest, he leaned toward her. "Has any man made a simple kiss on your hand feel like that?"

"That wasn't a kiss! It was—it was—" What was it? She couldn't even describe it.

"I want to taste even more of you," he said hoarsely, cupping her face with one hand.

Her mouth fell open as she imagined his lips on hers again, parting, and the taste of his tongue. She'd been imagining that taste ever since their first kiss. His palm was hot on her cheek, his face so close she thought he might kiss her again, right there in the open, where anyone could see.

"I won't be a—a *thing* you owe my father," she whispered.

"Though I never saw it coming, what's between us is so much more than that—can't you tell?"

"No, I can't!" She broke away. "Now stand up so I can fold the blanket. I must get back."

He remained silent on the walk back to the house, and she kept in front of him, not wanting to look at his face, to remember the burning intensity he'd shown her.

Talbot met them in the entrance hall. "Lady Black-thorne, Lord Doddridge has arrived and is already in your study."

Relief swept over her like cool water over a burn. "Thank you, Talbot, I will go to him." She glanced over her shoulder at Lord Blackthorne, not meeting his eyes. "Have a good morning, my lord."

He bowed, the picnic basket in one hand, the cane in the other, studying her with too knowing a gaze. She hurried off to meet with Lord Doddridge, feeling herself again, calm and in control in her study, not like that windswept girl on a hill who didn't know what she wanted.

Chapter 13

Michael watched her flee, noticed that even Talbot almost arched a brow at the last twitch of her skirts.

"May I take the basket from you, my lord?" Talbot asked smoothly.

"I'll accompany you to the servants' wing," Michael said, handing over the basket.

If that made Talbot curious, he would never reveal it. Together, they walked through the older section of the castle, into the servants' wing that had been built in the eighteenth century for more modern times. They passed a wine storage room, beer cellar, and the plate scullery.

"What can you tell me about Lord Doddridge?" Michael asked.

Talbot answered promptly. "He has been a gracious guardian to Lord Appertan."

"But a recent one, according to my wife."

"I do believe that is so, my lord."

Michael felt a pinch of frustration, but he'd known it would be difficult to discover things from such a loyal employee. "And the first guardian?" he asked.

Talbot waited for a maid to pass, her eyes downcast, then he gestured for Michael to enter a small room, obviously his office, with a desk, sideboard, and several chairs. A small window looked out on the garden, surely a sign of his respected position in the household to have such a view.

"My lord, I am not certain what you require of me—"

"Some help, Talbot. Your mistress asked for my assistance with Lord Appertan and his behavior. But if I don't know everything that is going on, how can I help her? It's obvious she is worried about her brother, and if I can do anything to ease her mind, I want to do it."

Talbot hesitated, and in that moment, Michael realized that if Talbot knew the strained status of the marriage, he would never help Michael at all. But at last he gestured to a chair, and instead of walking behind his desk, pulled up another chair next to Michael.

"My lord, I am only the butler," he said quietly. "But I have been with this household my entire adult life, as has Mrs. Ellison. We both want his lordship and Lady Blackthorne to be content with their lives. But do I know things of a personal nature? Perhaps some, most of which I would not dream of sharing with anyone, even my lady's husband. I would not long be trusted as a butler if I betrayed confidences that I overheard in the course of my duties. But as to their guardians, I might be able to briefly converse although I don't believe what I know is of much benefit."

"That's a fair answer," Michael said, crossing his arms over his chest as he studied the other man. "So tell me about the first guardian, the one they both shared."

"The guardianship was arranged long ago with a cousin of their mother's, someone who would not be in line to inherit any part of the earldom. But he was a country cousin who seldom went to London. Young Lord Appertan chafed almost immediately, for their guardian never went to Town, and only made rare appearances at Appertan Hall. I do believe that Lady Blackthorne concluded they felt it difficult to properly chaperone an heiress, and did not wish to deal with Lord Appertan's . . . high spirits."

"So once Appertan became the earl, he had a right to choose his own guardian, and Lord Doddridge suited him, according to my wife."

"I imagine all young men wish to do whatever they please," Talbot said in a faintly amused voice. "Lord Doddridge permitted this, as long as he could be certain the estates were being properly cared for. When Lady Blackthorne proved she could function in that capacity, he stipulated that he would visit once a month to be apprised. But surely you know most of this, my lord."

"Did you ever hear that Lord Doddridge might have deliberately sought the position of Lord Appertan's guardian?"

"Sought?" Talbot echoed, frowning. "As in, for a motive all his own?"

Michael nodded.

"I'm sorry, my lord, but that I don't know."

"And he doesn't benefit in any way?"

"I believe not."

This was pointless. How could he ask the butler if Lord Doddridge would benefit if Cecilia were dead? It would sound . . . ominous.

"Thank you for your information, Talbot," Michael said. "I'll be having dinner with the man tonight and no chance to discuss him with my wife beforehand. You've been helpful. Do you mind if I ask about the new servants most recently hired?"

Talbot frowned. "There have only been three, my lord, only one of whom is under my direct control. Susan, the new maid, works for Mrs. Ellison, and Parsons, the watchman, is overseen by the gamekeeper. The page, Francis, runs errands and does the occasional task about the house when the footmen are too busy."

"How old is he?"

"Seventeen. He, of course, aspires to be a footman. But we are his first employer."

The boy was certainly old enough to be up to mischief if he wanted to. And Susan also had the run of the house, but Michael remembered the horrified expression on her face when the bust fell toward Cecilia.

"My lord, have we given you some reason to question our hiring decisions?"

Michael would have liked to confide in Talbot but worried that his suspicions might become common knowledge. "I know Susan the maid is also relatively new, and that accident involving the falling bust concerns me. My wife almost died."

Talbot studied him gravely. "And you fear for her. I understand."

"Due to my military career, we will most likely be separated for long periods of time." How strange that he would have settled for this so easily once upon a time, but now that he was so against it, he didn't have the first idea how to solve it. "I need to know that my wife is safe, Talbot. Can you do me a favor and recheck the references and the backgrounds of the new people hired?"

"Of course, my lord. I will confer with the steward and see it done."

Michael stood up with the aid of his cane. "Thank you. I know I have no true standing within this household, but I appreciate your taking my concerns seriously."

"Lady Blackthorne often remarked on the late earl's high praise of you, my lord. I am grateful to see your concern for her, considering . . ." He trailed off.

"Considering I agreed to marry her sight unseen?" Michael answered dryly.

Talbot gave a brief nod.

"I am more than content with my decision." He only hoped that someday Cecilia would say the same.

Before dawn the next morning, Cecilia congratulated herself for getting out of the Hall before the sun was even up. Surely she was safe in broad daylight, out among her people. She needed a walk to help her think, and she couldn't do that with Lord Blackthorne dogging her heels. It would be a long day, much of it spent answering more of Lord Doddridge's questions before welcoming a large party of guests for dinner.

The old man was as genial as always, and she received the usual pats on the head for a job well-done, as if she were his favorite pet who performed all the right tricks. He did appreciate her work because, of course, it left less for him to do, but he was so very patronizing.

Her thoughts wandered as always to Lord Blackthorne, who'd attempted to seduce a decision from her on their marriage. He wanted her to trust him, and often she felt like she couldn't trust anyone but herself. She remembered her panicked suggestion that perhaps he should visit his family. He wasn't going to do that. So last night, she'd realized she could bring his family to him and had written a letter to his mother, sending it the half day's journey this morning with a footman. She was still congratulating herself.

As the gray light gave way to the first rays of the sun, she waved to gardeners and grooms, dairymaids and plowboys. Farther from the hall, she followed her usual path along a creek and into a dense copse of woodland. She could smell the falling leaves of oak and sycamore, see the muted colors of autumn mixed in with the green. Leaves already formed a dense carpet across the path, and she kicked at them, trying to summon up her usual optimistic start to the day.

Suddenly, the ground seemed to give way before her. She'd been moving so quickly, all she could do was flail her arms as she fell forward, where leaves now trickled between branches that had been laid as a distraction. She crashed through them and down into a hole, landing hard on her side, her breath knocked from her to leave her gasping. Dazed and shocked, she tried to roll onto her back, and it was as if every bone in her body had been realigned in the fall, and now protested painfully. For what seemed like endless moments, she gaped up at the overcast sky glimpsed between treetops. Crisp leaves continued to fall gently on top of her, along with the faintest drops of a light mist.

The cool wetness seemed to make her brain function again, and she slowly pushed herself into a sitting position. The ground oozed with mud, her filthy skirts were twisted around her. And although it hurt to take a deep breath, she hadn't hit her head. Her limbs seemed to work, and there was no blood. She'd been so lucky, she thought, hugging herself.

And then she realized she'd walked this same path yesterday, and the hole hadn't been there. Why would someone dig in the middle of a little woodland? It wouldn't be for a well—there was no cottage nearby, and the creek was so close that moisture continued to ooze slowly into the hole.

Holding on to a root protruding from the earthen wall, she got to her feet—and realized that she couldn't reach the top of the hole. Standing on her tiptoes, she tried over and over, but only managed to dislodge dirt that fell into her eyes and mouth, making her cough and gag, even as her eyes ran.

She was trapped.

Fear shot through her, and she crouched against the edge of the hole, as if someone would start shooting down at her, as if she were a deer with a broken leg—or something equally expendable.

Had—had someone done this deliberately?

No, she told herself. It had to be an accident. If deliberate, the person would know she walked this way nearly every day, had done so only yesterday. Everyone would be able to find her, especially Lord Blackthorne, who surely knew her customary paths by now.

There might be people who would think he had motive not to find her, but she refused to believe it. Whoever put her there knew she might be found soon, which meant they only wanted to harm her—or did they think the fall would kill her?

She hugged herself, feeling the cold mud surrounding her bare stocking. Somehow she'd lost a shoe, she thought a bit wildly.

And then she started to scream for help.

She walked these paths every day, knew how desolate they could be—especially in bad weather, she realized bleakly, as rain began to fall in earnest. So she screamed louder, reminding herself that *someone* in her household would miss her and come looking.

Michael stood in the breakfast-parlor window, staring out at the bleak landscape through the rain that ran in rivulets down the diamond-shaped panes of glass. His jaw ached from all the clenching he'd done since the moment he realized Cecilia had left on her walk without him. He'd known in his gut he had to accompany her everywhere, and now something was wrong. She hadn't returned in her normal time.

He pivoted about his cane and saw Lord Doddridge calmly eating his bacon and mushrooms, buttering a muffin, his lined face unconcerned as he squinted at the *Times*. He was a short man, but his posture was unbowed, as if he met the world squarely and was confident in his ability to handle anything. Did he think that everyone was just as capable as he was, leaving him unconcerned about Cecilia?

Or was he unconcerned because he was in on some sort of plot?

Appertan lounged almost regally in his chair, watching Michael, then rolled eyes. "She got caught in the rain and is waiting it out somewhere. You don't need to be so worried."

And then he looked away, because he damn well knew why Michael was worried. Did he look away out of guilt?

The uncertainty was the worst part—whether or not someone was trying to kill her, and if so, who it was. But that didn't matter right now, so much as finding her and making sure she was all right.

"I can't wait here any longer," he said, limping swiftly toward the door.

Doddridge glanced up at him with curiosity. The old man hadn't said much when they met this morning, only arched a brow when Appertan had introduced Michael as Cecilia's husband, looking him up and down without stating his conclusions. He shook his head and went back at his newspaper.

"You're going out in this?" Appertan demanded. "She'll laugh at you when you find her—or she'll be angry that you didn't trust her to handle herself."

"I'll accept any of that as long as I know she's well." He glanced at Talbot, who was looking relieved. "Can you send someone to the stables to prepare my mount while I retrieve my cloak?"

A half hour later, Michael was riding across the grassy park, feeling like himself again on his horse. He followed Cecilia's usual path, asking the occasional tenant or servant if she'd been seen. She had, but then most pointed to the dripping sky and said they had gone indoors and hadn't seen her return. After an hour, the sick feeling in his stomach seemed to be spreading, clenching his heart, bringing an ache that battered the inside of his skull. She meant so much to him already. Her sunny letters to India had never failed to cheer him even though he knew they'd masked pain. He'd been a stranger to her, someone she didn't have to care about, but she'd taken the time for him. But then, she took care of everyone residing on their estates, believed she could make the world right for her younger brother though he was a grown man and should have been taking care of *her*. She thought the best of everyone—yet someone might be trying to kill her, and she knew that, and was trying to deal with it on her own.

Michael slowed his mount when he reached the woodland. She could be lost within the trees, her ankle twisted, looking for shelter. "Cecilia?" he shouted, as the rain trickled beneath his collar like a cold brush of reality. He slowed his horse to a walk, feeling that old stiffening in his neck that he'd always trusted. Some men felt it in their gut, but he trusted his neck. "Cecilia?"

And then he thought he heard the faintest cry. He froze, and his horse did the same, its ears twitching. Slowly, he went forward, and the cry became louder, though hoarse.

"I'm here! But beware the hole!"

He came up short when he understood her and dismounted. He could see the hole now, a gaping blackness in the center of the narrow path. Cursing under his breath, he pulled the cane out of the strap behind the saddle, and limped forward. He saw the top of her blond head before he reached the edge, and went down on his knees to peer in.

"You came," she cried, sagging back against the dirt wall that was etched with rivulets of water and mud.

The color of her gown was indiscernible, her hair and face matted with mud. But she was alive and on her feet and staring up at him with hope.

"Are you injured?" he demanded.

She shook her head. "But I can't get out. If you hadn't come . . ."

She trailed off, swallowing, and he knew she'd feared that she'd been abandoned.

"I'll always come for you, Cecilia," he said. Then he saw a stone as she dropped it, the gouges in the wall one above the other near a tree root. "Were you trying to dig stairs?"

Her blue eyes lightened with satisfaction. "Yes, I was. But it's very muddy, and I wasn't sure they could hold my weight, even if I supported myself with the root."

"You're a resourceful woman," he said with admiration, watching her blush beneath the layer of dirt on her skin. "And you never lost your head. Take my hands, and I'll pull you to safety."

Her hands were slick with mud, and he could feel her trembling. As he pulled, she used her feet to climb up the rough walls of the hole. When she emerged, she collapsed against him. He held her tight, kissing the top of her head over and over, feeling more relieved and full of fear than he'd ever felt on a battlefield.

She clutched at him for a moment, her heart pounding against his chest, her body quaking. And then he realized how cold she was, for her hands were like ice. He held her back a bit although she was still in his lap.

Chafing her dirty hands between his, he stared into her face. "What happened?"

"I don't know," she said between chattering teeth. "One moment, I was striding along; the next, I was falling forward. I'm so lucky—I could have broken my neck!" She stared up at him almost wildly.

He took her cold face between his hands. "Thank God you're all right. I knew something was wrong even though everyone else thought you'd sought shelter from the rain."

"Thank you," she whispered, then dropped her gaze.

"Let me get you home. We'll talk then."

He saw her chin lift, the mutinous curve of her mouth, as if she planned to keep everything in. Well, he'd just see about that. He stood up first, and when he pulled her up after him, she swayed.

"Goodness, my skirts are heavy when they're full of mud," she said, her lightheartedness obviously forced.

"The horse won't care."

She pulled back and stared up at him. "We are not riding together."

He rolled his eyes even as the rain streaked down, washing more of the mud from her stubborn face. "Do you hear yourself? Do you plan to walk back in this weather? I'll mount first, then pull you up."

She opened her mouth as if to protest, but he ignored her, mounting and securing his cane, before reaching down a hand. With an exaggerated sigh of surrender, she put her foot on top of his in the stirrup, and he had an intriguing glimpse of her damp stockings. Then he pulled, and he managed to toss her across his lap although she obviously meant to ride behind.

"This is . . . uncomfortable," she fumed.

He slid back in the saddle so that her hip wasn't jammed against the pommel. "For me, too. But I'll suffer quietly."

Of course, he was suffering in ways she couldn't imagine, with her body so intimately close to his. He opened his cloak and pulled it around her, sharing his heat. He felt her stiffen, thought she'd protest, but then, with a sigh, she sank back against him. They rode home in silence, and he wasn't surprised to see Talbot, Mrs. Ellison, and Nell waiting beneath the portico, wearing relieved expressions. But her brother wasn't there.

Mrs. Ellison and Nell took charge, hustling Cecilia away. Talbot called for Tom and Will to see to bathing tubs for both rooms. Michael had a brief flash of sharing a brimming tub with his wife, but he put it from his mind—for now.

Talbot was staring at him. "My lord, do tell me what happened. Lady Blackthorne looks a fright."

Michael saw Appertan leaning in the doorway of the drawing room, and Doddridge hovering just behind, wringing his hands together.

"Do you want to know, too?" Michael asked his brother-in-law.

Appertan frowned. "What kind of question is that?"

Michael glared at him. "It's a good thing I didn't listen to you. She'd fallen into a hole."

"Why wasn't she walking her normal route?" Appertan asked irritably.

"She was. That hole wasn't there yesterday."

He saw Talbot inhale and Appertan's eyes widen, even as Doddridge gaped.

"A hole?" Appertan echoed. "She wasn't limping."

"The hole was deep enough that she couldn't escape. I heard her screaming for help."

Appertan grimaced and ran a hand through his hair before eyeing Michael once again. "My thanks for your gallant rescue. Go take care of yourself before you catch a fever."

"Shall I escort you, Lord Blackthorne?" Talbot asked.

"I'm fine." He glanced back at Appertan. "I'll speak with you soon."

"I assume you'll be speaking with my sister first. We can cancel the dinner this evening if she likes."

Michael was tempted to decide in her stead, saying of course they should cancel it. But there would be so many people who knew her—possible suspects. Yet it wasn't up to him. "I'll let you know."

He went up to his bedroom to change, and then confront his wife.

Chapter 14

Cecilia couldn't stop shaking, even after submerging herself in a steaming bath. Nell wanted to bundle her into bed for the day with hot compresses, but Cecilia was too impatient for that, dressing in a plain, loose gown, then pacing after Nell brought her a tray of carrot soup, bread, and hot tea.

When she was alone, Cecilia looked crossly at the tray. "I'm not sick."

But inside, she was sick at heart. She was so used to being in control of every situation, and these—these accidents made her feel like cowering under her covers and never leaving her room. She couldn't live like that. Uncertainty and fear were making her question everything.

Except . . . Lord Blackthorne. He'd rescued her from the hole, confirming her belief in his innocence. Nell confided that he'd been worried through breakfast, whereas Oliver said that surely the storm had delayed her.

As if her own brother didn't want her found.

Cecilia felt the prick of tears again, put her palms over her eyes, and willed them away. Crying wouldn't help.

A knock on her door made her straighten, and she tried to compose herself as she called for the person to enter. She wasn't surprised to see her husband, his gaze focused darkly on her, taking everything in. With her old garments on, and her hair pulled back with a simple bow, she felt unmade, unkempt, which was the most ridiculous thing to think at such a time. But Lord Blackthorne seemed to do that to her.

He closed the door and leaned both hands on his cane as he studied her.

"Do I pass inspection?" she asked wryly.

"You clean up well."

She almost laughed at that even though she wasn't amused.

"How do you feel?"

She hesitated. "It hurts to take a deep breath."

"Your ribs."

"So the doctor informs me. I have some aches, but he says I was very lucky, and there's nothing he can do for me except prescribe rest and warm baths for my pain."

In her mind, she was in the cold mud again, feeling the rain start, wondering with terror what it would be like to waste away like a trapped animal.

"Try not to think about it," he said, his voice gentler.

She blinked at him. "We've been acquainted just over a week, and already you read me too well."

"Too well? Do you not think I've spent the last several hours imagining what might have happened if I hadn't found you? From the looks of you, you've done the same."

She gave him a weak smile.

"So tell me what happened," he continued, his voice businesslike again. "And then we notify the constable."

Her head came up. "No. Surely some poacher dug a hole to—"

"Enough with these games where you pretend to ignore the truth," he interrupted.

He limped toward her until she had to arch her neck to look up at him.

"You don't believe any of this was an accident, and I'm done going along with your games of fancy, where you wish things were different."

"What are you saying?"

"We're all concerned about you, and we've shared information. Miss Webster confided your concerns to Appertan, who confided in me. You think someone might be trying to harm you—or even kill you."

She'd said that to Penelope, but hearing the cold, hard words from her husband's mouth felt . . . different, and very real. "I . . . I imagine I shall keep my secrets from now on."

He groaned and ran a hand through his dark hair. *"That's* your response? That you wish you'd said nothing? Would you prefer I think you had some bad luck, so that when this villain succeeded, we could have only complained about how we wish we'd known?"

She looked away from his focused gaze, hearing the frustration in his voice even though he didn't raise it. He was not a man to lose control, to react without thinking. "Lord Blackthorne—"

"My name is Michael. I've been 'Sergeant' or 'Blackthorne' for so long that I forget what my Christian name sounds like. I would like you to use it."

"Michael," she said in a soft voice.

Some part of him must have relaxed, for he spoke in a more normal tone. "When you fell into the hole, you saw and heard no one?"

"Not until you arrived." She folded her hands at her waist.

"And since this all started at the time of my arrival, do you think I'm capable of this?"

"No."

"What can I say to convince you that—" He broke off in sudden realization of her denial. "My rescue today must have convinced you of my innocence."

"Not really. I simply . . . never believed you capable of it even when I wondered if I was being naïve." Her father had known Michael for years under the worst sort of conditions and only had high praise for him.

Ever since his arrival, although they disagreed about their marriage, he'd abided by her wishes and even tried to help her brother.

"Thank you," he said softly, his eyes momentarily tender.

The answering sweet ache deep inside her was unsettling.

He cleared his throat. "Then call the constable," he said again.

She briefly closed her eyes. "And what would I say, Michael? That I tripped down the stairs? That a maid admitted she thought she'd accidentally bumped the bust that fell on me? And now—a hole? The constable sees poacher traps every day!" And the most damning reason: the person with the best motive to harm her was her brother, whose life she controlled. But since he could take all of that control away from her—and she so loved him—she refused to believe he might be guilty and didn't want anyone else tarnishing his reputation by suggesting it aloud. "Michael, I have no *proof.*"

"But if we talk to the constable," Michael continued, "then he'll be on the alert."

"Any more than you already are? You *live* here."

"Are you saying you *trust* me to take care of you?"

"I don't know what I believe." To her dismay, her voice cracked, and she cleared her throat to cover the weakness. Was she really like her mother? Cecilia had tried so hard to be confident in her own worth, but her mother could never trust in that, could never trust the men in her life. Maybe Cecilia was the same way, and she'd never realized it. She didn't trust Oliver to manage the estate; she didn't trust Michael to be a husband to her. Those fears had made her mother a miserable, clinging woman who'd destroyed every small happiness that came her way.

It all came down to trust, and Cecilia didn't know how to trust anyone but herself. How could that be, when she'd had such a wonderful father? Perhaps she thought no man could ever compare. Was a lack of trust the reason she never wanted to marry, why she was so content to take over the estates herself? Putting herself in someone else's hands seemed like the worst mistake imaginable. It was better to be alone.

"We need to cancel this dinner," he suddenly said.

He was standing near the window, looking out on the park, his expression cool and composed. Appertan Hall was just a place to him, but to her, it was an integral part of her life, as necessary as her blood. And somewhere out there was a person who wanted her dead.

"This dinner might have suspects," she said. "You're a soldier—isn't it your duty to investigate?"

"I've already begun." He glanced at her pointedly.

"You have? What have you learned?"

"I don't have time to lay it out for you today—unless you're canceling the dinner."

She lifted her chin. "No."

Then he came to her, so swiftly she almost fell back a step. He caught her as she began to sway, his hands cupping her waist, his face leaning toward her.

"I will keep you safe, Cecilia," he whispered with urgency.

How could he? If someone who knew and loved her wanted her dead . . .

But no, that was a fatalistic attitude. The villain didn't have to be Oliver. Perhaps there was someone else.

She stepped back, and Michael's warm hands fell away from her waist. "Then I'll see you for dinner," she said.

He looked as if he wanted to say something else, then he pressed his lips in a straight line, nodded, and limped toward the dressing-room door.

He suddenly stopped, and said over his shoulder. "Don't mistake a simple limp for weakness, Cecilia. I will ensure your safety, whatever I have to do."

And then he left, and all she could do was hug herself. Sometimes she wished she were the type of woman who would fling herself into a man's arms and beg to be rescued.

But she would never let that happen.

Cecilia spent much of the day in her bedroom, where Mrs. Ellison came to consult her about the seating for the dinner party and a problem with the menu. Cecilia was glad to think about something other than the suspicions buzzing endlessly around in her brain. When Mrs. Ellison hinted that they could still cancel because of the unfortunate accident, Cecilia firmly refused.

Late in the afternoon, Talbot informed her that Penelope and Oliver were awaiting her in the library. She would have preferred to talk to them at dinner, where she wouldn't have to relive the accident again. But she had no choice. She went downstairs, glad for Talbot's escort, and entered the book-lined room, with its leather furniture. She saw the way that Penelope glanced worriedly at the plain gown Cecilia was wearing, and Oliver stared at her over his brandy glass.

As Talbot pulled the door shut behind him, Cecilia looked down at herself, and said lightly, "You caught me before I could prepare for dinner."

Penelope rushed to hug her, then gripped her upper arms and stared into her eyes. "You look as if nothing has happened!"

Cecilia felt as ancient and tired as a god who'd lost his powers. "Believe me, my aches and pains tell me otherwise."

"There's a bruise on your cheek," Oliver said.

Cecilia touched it with her fingers. "I thought Nell did an admirable job hiding it."

"But I know you too well," he said, turning to refill his glass.

The tightness in her throat threatened to choke her, to cause a terrible waterfall of tears.

"Do you know who dug the hole?" Penelope asked.

She shook her head.

"Do you think someone meant to take down a deer?" Oliver tilted his head as he studied her.

Cecilia hesitated, wondering if he was implying that he didn't believe her. "I hope so. But I understand that both of you repeated my concerns, and now Lord Blackthorne knows I believe these are more than accidents."

Penelope winced. "Oh, dear. I thought your brother deserved to know. Was that wrong of me?"

Cecilia took her hand and gave a tired smile. "No, I understand your concern." Then she glanced at Oliver. "I imagine you thought my husband should know."

Oliver shrugged. "Seems you didn't bother to tell him. Was that because you think he's trying to kill you?"

Penelope gasped aloud, and Cecilia stiffened, surprised to feel herself defensive on Michael's behalf.

"No," Cecilia said. "There's no motive for him to do so. He will inherit none of my money. And he was Papa's good friend for many years."

Oliver shrugged. "He and I discussed many different suspects."

"He offered to tell me everything."

"As *you* should have done with me," Oliver countered. He looked mutinous and angry, as if he realized she didn't trust him. But how could he know the depths of her suspicions? Even she didn't want to consider the worst.

Penelope glanced at each of them with concern. "You have had a terrible day, Cecilia. If I'd known, I would have come earlier to help you deal with this dinner party."

"Mrs. Ellison has it so well in hand that even I have had little to do today, but it is very sweet of you to offer."

"You could sit and relax, and I would be happy to read to you."

Cecilia opened her mouth to decline, but Penelope seemed so anxious to help in any small way. She finally smiled. "That would be lovely."

Penelope glanced at Oliver. "Do you mind, Oliver?"

He gestured with his glass. "Good of you to help. I'll be in the billiard room."

Anything to escape, Cecilia thought, faintly smiling as she watched him leave the room. But her smile faded, and her chest hurt, but it wasn't because of her fall that morn.

Was she losing her last brother?

Michael went down to the drawing room before the dinner guests were due to arrive. Dozens of lamps had been lit to emphasize the ancient weapons displayed high on the stone walls. Fresh flowers festooned each table, and the smell was almost overpoweringly sweet.

It was difficult to think about entertaining guests after what had happened that morning. And it was a mark of Cecilia's bravery—or stubbornness—that she was going through with it. He stalked to the French doors and looked out through the windows at the gardens, where dusk had fallen. Long shadows crept across the ground like fingers pointing at the castle.

Logically, he understood that since the "accidents" had begun right after he arrived, she might suspect him. But she didn't, as if she'd grown to trust him. He felt elated and hopeful, until he remembered the bust shattering on the marble, and looking over the balustrade to see Cecilia gaping up at him from where she'd tumbled to the floor. She'd almost fallen down the stairs the first night he arrived. Yet she'd gone on denying what had happened, pretending everything was all right.

He'd thought the way she kept her distance from him was about their marriage, his insistence on remaining in the union and her resistance to the whole idea. And then there was her brother and his many problems, and the future certainty that she'd have to give up running the empire she'd nurtured. There were so many reasons for her to be upset—he'd just never considered that she was frightened for her life.

After leaving her earlier, he'd gone to meet with Talbot, who'd already looked into the new servants again. The page, Francis, was the only one hired without references, but he was a parish boy, whom everyone knew. Talbot had heard a story or two about the boy brawling with friends, or fishing when he should be working, but nothing that would implicate him as a murderer. But then again, a page had tasks all over the house, errands for this person or that. He'd least be missed. But dig a hole to kill his mistress? That would achieve nothing but her death, and how could Francis possibly want revenge against a mistress beloved by the entire staff?

The new watchman, Parsons, had grown up in Enfield, moved to London as a young man, then recently returned to support his wife and two babies. His London references were impeccable. And as for timing, the watchmen had a nightly schedule where they checked in with each other routinely as they patrolled the grounds. A watchman would have been noticed if he was lurking in the Hall the day the bust fell. And Susan, the maid? He'd seen her face during the incident, believed down to his soul she'd been shocked and horrified. And again, her brothers Tom and Will lived in the Hall, too. What motive could she have? Servants as suspects just seemed so implausible.

Voices disturbed Michael's rumination, and he turned, realizing he stood in the shadows by the French doors, for Miss Webster and Appertan had not seen him. She was obviously besotted with the young lord, worshipping him with her eyes when he wasn't looking, smiling and tossing her head when he might be admiring her figure. Michael felt so much older than either of them. It seemed long ago that a young girl wanted to impress him. And even then, it had only been because of the lies his father told about the status of their family.

Though Appertan seemed to expect such feminine attention, there was a distant focus to his eyes if Miss Webster wasn't speaking. Michael wondered if he worried for his sister—or worried he might get caught. How was Michael supposed to make sure Cecilia was never alone with him again? He was her brother! Michael had put together a contingent of servants, led by Talbot and Mrs. Ellison, to make certain that Cecilia never went anywhere alone, though his proud wife would certainly protest.

It was Mrs. Ellison who escorted her into the drawing room. Michael gritted his teeth, remembering the way the housekeeper had reddened when she'd told him Cecilia's wish to make her entrance without him.

"She's beside herself right now, my lord," Mrs. Ellison had whispered. "Give her time. She's used to being on her own, poor thing."

He'd acquiesced reluctantly, and now, as Cecilia arrived, he felt himself relax at last. For just a moment, she paused on the threshold, and he saw her gaze take in Appertan and Miss Webster, who stood talking quietly together, not noticing her. Her blue eyes, usually so lively, looked momentarily bruised and sad. Michael couldn't imagine what it would be like to wonder if the brother she'd helped raise was a villain.

When Appertan glanced up at her, Cecilia blossomed with a smile. It was all an act, but in that moment, she shone with a radiance that made Michael ache both in sympathy for her and in painful desire. Her blond hair was upswept, and several tiny ringlets danced about her ears and brushed her shoulders. Her gown matched the deep blue of her eyes and sparkled with beading across her square-cut bodice. Her bare shoulders looked vulnerable and tempting at the same time, and her cleavage was close enough to the edge of propriety as a married woman was allowed, enough to make her husband practically drool. Her waist was tiny, and her hips flared out, emphasized by the sweep of her skirts and the graceful way she moved.

When their gazes met, everything else seemed to stop. If he had seen her across a London ballroom, he'd have known she was out of his reach, a goddess among mere mortals. He noticed only distantly the pleased smile Miss Webster granted Appertan, as if to tell him she approved of Cecilia's marriage. Appertan didn't smile back.

But Cecilia was Michael's wife, and he meant to keep it that way, whatever her brother thought. He limped toward her now, surprised when she swept into a curtsy that allowed him to see even more of the valley between her breasts. Other men would see that sight tonight, and he didn't like the ugly jealousy that stirred in him. How would it be, night after night, imagining her half a world away from him, meeting the rakes of Society?

"You look handsome tonight, my lord," she murmured.

"My trunk of clothing finally arrived from the steamship," he said. "Even in Bombay, we had need of evening garments, but of course, you must remember that."

"We did try to copy English society as much as possible," she admitted.

Now that he was closer, he could see the bruise marring her cheek beneath the powder. He cupped her cheek, lightly touching it with his thumb. He felt her shiver.

"Does that hurt?" he asked quietly.

She shook her head. "Only if one presses hard."

He allowed himself one last brush of her skin, then let his hand fall away.

"Be careful," he murmured. "You realize, of course, that you can never leave this room unattended."

"I know."

She seemed almost relieved when Talbot announced the first guests. Mrs. Webster arrived with her son and his wife, Miss Webster's parents, and Michael saw the way they doted on Appertan as if he'd long been a part of their family. What was it about the young man that made everyone treat him that way? Michael wondered irritably.

And then Cecilia turned toward him expectantly, her smile pleasant and proud. For the next half hour, he was introduced to two dozen neighbors and friends. He knew many had been eager to meet him and felt uncomfortable as their avid gazes looked him over. His family had never socialized much once the estate had gobbled up his mother's dowry. But he was surprised how much his military experiences assisted him on such an evening since he'd often attended events in Bombay with Lord Appertan. He answered questions and appeared interested; little more was required of him as the center attraction that evening.

To his surprise, several of Appertan's friends arrived, including Rowlandson. Cecilia did not make much of this though she quietly spoke to Talbot about the dinner seating when she had the chance. Michael didn't glare at Rowlandson but kept his gaze cool and narrowed, and was surprised by the man's confusion.

Eventually, he and Cecilia were separated, and he made it a point to thread his way through the chattering crowd right for Rowlandson.

The other man eyed him nervously. "My lord?"

"I'm surprised you attended, sir," Michael said in a low, barely restrained voice.

"I was sure the absence of my invitation had been

accidental." Rowlandson's gaze searched the crowd, then landed on Appertan with confusion.

Michael frowned. "Do you not remember what happened at the taproom a few days ago?"

"I was deep in my cups," Rowlandson said with a wince. "I remember your being there, but little else. I hope I did not . . . offend you."

"Offend me? You terrorized a maid, and we had words about the subject. I threatened you."

Rowlandson blanched. "Truly? Forgive me for not remembering." He looked down at his hands as if desperate for alcohol.

"Perhaps you need to drink less," Michael said sarcastically.

Or perhaps Rowlandson remembered it all and was pretending not to. Could he and his cronies still hold a grudge against Cecilia because she'd practically banished them from Appertan Hall? Inebriation could make some men lose the last of their inhibitions. Perhaps Rowlandson's fondling a maid wasn't that far removed from trying to incapacitate Cecilia, if not kill her.

"You are correct, my lord." Rowlandson shrugged. "I allow drink to consume me when I shouldn't."

He seemed pliable, so Michael decided to use that to his advantage. "I imagine it's difficult to avoid alcohol when Lord Appertan and all your other friends are imbibing at great speeds."

Rowlandson nodded ruefully. "It is true. I can't seem to deny myself when others aren't."

"Does that include gambling? There was a bit of that going on the other night, but I wasn't certain if Lord Appertan approved."

"Approved?" Rowlandson echoed, then laughed. "He indulges his betting instincts like the rest of us."

"So it's common among your set?"

"As common as among any group of men."

"I imagine you all must go through your allowances quickly."

Rowlandson reddened and couldn't meet Michael's gaze. "Occasionally, yes, but Appertan is always the one with the cool head about such things."

Cool head? Not a term Michael would have used to describe his brother-in-law. "Appertan doesn't gamble?"

"Not to excess, unlike . . . some of us."

Michael didn't think Rowlandson's face could get any redder. He lowered his voice as if in confidence. "There were ladies expected the night your crowd played billiards here, a different kind of excess for someone like Appertan."

Rowlandson showed the first signs of confused unease. "The women were for others, not Appertan. He's surprisingly dull where the fair sex are concerned. Loyalty to his fiancée and all that. Seems *before* marriage should be the time for a last fling, eh?"

First coolheaded, and now twenty years of age and not chasing wild young women? Why did this not seem like the Appertan Michael had known these last few days?

Michael looked around the room. "I don't see many of your other friends here. Are they back in London?"

"Some, but most live within an hour's ride or so. We used to stay at Appertan Hall, but recently . . ." He let his words trail off, then shrugged, as if he didn't want to disparage Cecilia to her husband's face. "I mean no disrespect to Lady Blackthorne," he quickly added, his expression striving for sincerity. "A few even considered courting her, and I heard one had even gone so far as to make his intentions known, but Appertan wouldn't tell me who it was." He slowly smiled and gestured with his chin. "Could be any one of those fools flocking around her, yes?"

Michael turned his head sharply, and there was Cecilia, bathed in golden light from the chandelier overhead, several "fools" too close. They gazed with varying degrees of admiration and regret, but how to know what they were truly thinking?

She smiled at them all with a soft, pretty sweetness, as if she had forgotten what such attention was like. Suddenly, from somewhere deep inside Michael's brain, he found himself thinking, *Not again.*

Whoa, he told himself, as if he were a racehorse off on the wrong course. Cecilia was not like his mother, except for beauty and wealth. His mother might have been an heiress, but she'd been known to have loose standards of fidelity, and his fortune-hunting father had taken her off her family's hands.

It was an ugly story, and Michael's father had only let it slip once, when he'd had too much to drink. He'd even implied that perhaps Michael's brother Allen wasn't truly his son. Michael had always believed his mother made the best of their situation. Never had she complained, as their status was lowered, along with their money, and her family would have nothing to do with her. She'd been a caring, loving mother.

Michael had successfully pushed those old, ugly accusations from his mind until he saw Cecilia surrounded by adoring young men. He now realized why he'd been relieved when he'd thought her plain, and the sight of her true beauty had surprised him—he'd felt the shock and recognition of possibly repeating his father's life.

Though he'd vowed to marry on his own terms, instead he'd married a ravishing heiress. It didn't matter that he hadn't accepted her money. He knew what it looked like—as if he'd tricked her into marrying him from halfway around the world.

The guests' gazes he'd thought simply intrigued now seemed to have a dark edge, and it took him a moment to call himself away from such foolishness. He knew who he was, and it wasn't an imitation of his father. What Cecilia thought was all that mattered.

"Lady Cecilia!" called a young man's voice from near the doorway.

Michael couldn't see who it was, but he heard several gasps, saw people whispering together. The crowd parted before the quick strides of a young man, with longish blond hair disarrayed, as if he'd traveled there in haste. His face practically beamed with happiness.

"Lady Cecilia!" he said again, taking both her gloved hands in his. "I just returned from the Continent yesterday, and traveled to Enfield just to see you. I haven't even had a chance to speak with my parents—"

"Roger," began an older woman nervously, touching his arm, the feather in her gray hair bobbing forward. "I didn't even know the date of your arrival."

"I know, Mother," he said, his gaze obviously entranced by Cecilia. "The housekeeper told me where you were. How fortunate!"

"We really must talk," his mother said, looking around as if for support, but if her husband was in the room, he didn't step forward.

"Lady Cecilia, you look lovely," Roger continued, never taking his eyes from her, "no longer in mourning, I see."

Michael limped toward them, taking his time, wondering how the tableau would play out. Cecilia glanced at him with bewildered blue eyes, and in that moment, he realized she didn't quite understand Roger's enthusiasm.

She began to say, "Mr. Nash—"

"Surely you'll allow me to call upon you again," Roger Nash interrupted. "I could take you driving, and oh, the picnics we used to have." He smiled at his wide-eyed mother. "Of course, you can chaperone us, Mother. I'd never subject Lady Cecilia to improprieties."

Michael gave a bow as he reached them, twining his arm with his wife's, surprised to feel possessive. "Cecilia, may I be introduced to your friend?"

Nash looked at him at last, and his brilliant smile faded at the edges, as if Michael's familiar use of her Christian name had at last penetrated.

"Mr. Nash, allow me to present my husband, Lord Blackthorne."

Chapter 15

Cecilia felt almost nauseous with fatigue and sadness as she watched Mr. Nash's happy expression fade into confusion and disbelief. He hadn't known she was married, that much was evident. He'd been an ardent suitor, but had dutifully gone to travel the Continent because his parents thought him too young to pursue a wife.

He must have heard she'd gone into mourning and just assumed he had plenty of time to return and pick up where he had left off courting her.

And there was Michael, one hand on his cane, the other tucked behind his back, his posture proud with military bearing, his expression cool and sober, his very maturity making Mr. Nash look like an exuberant boy. If Michael cracked a smile, maybe this would be easier on the young man—or maybe worse, she suddenly realized. Michael's very look seemed challenging, as if Mr. Nash could compete for Cecilia's hand, and Michael would have to accept the challenge.

None of that was true. Mr. Nash was a distant memory of her youth, when young men pursued her, and she was half-flattered, half-exasperated. Michael now seemed all that was dangerous and threatening, not to her person but to her ability to remain aloof, to be herself. He was drawing her in, luring her to risk everything for the chance to be . . . intimate with him.

"Forgive me, my lady," Mr. Nash now said stiffly. He gave a cool nod to Michael. "I ask the same if I have offended you, Lord Blackthorne. I did not know that Lady Blackthorne had married."

"Understandable," Michael said. "I was in India when the marriage was performed there."

Cecilia wanted to wince at the confused look on Mr. Nash's face, as if he couldn't understand why she'd marry that way when there were so many local young men to choose from. Several of her former suitors were in attendance. They'd all been neighbors—she could hardly invite their parents and not them.

Mr. Nash gave a clipped bow to Cecilia. "My felicitations, Lady Blackthorne." And then he escorted his mortified mother away.

"Are you well?" Michael murmured.

"I am." Cecilia stifled a sigh.

He leaned over her almost protectively—or possessively. It might look many ways to her guests. But she heard the concern, felt the steadiness of his solid arm within hers. She remembered with a flash looking up from that muddy pit just that morning, and seeing his wet face staring down at hers with determination. She'd never been so happy and grateful to see anyone in her life.

"There are several men here who seem to regret our marriage," he said, frowning.

She attempted a smile for the benefit of their curious guests. "Perhaps. But there are also many women here, who upon meeting you, now think our marriage makes sense."

He looked truly baffled, and she found herself shaking her head ruefully.

"My lord, you are a handsome man—and a viscount. I am the daughter of an earl, an heiress. Both of us could have married far more conventionally than we did."

"I am handsome?" His brow wrinkled.

"Are you looking for a compliment?" she asked. "It is simply that now that they've seen you, my neighbors think I am not so . . . eccentric."

Again, he offered the faint smile that hinted at more. "It was eccentricity that brought us together?"

"No, it was about control," she whispered, looking away and blinking at the sudden moisture in her eyes. "I thought I could control a husband from halfway around the world, just like I guess I control Oliver, even though I never meant that to happen."

He said nothing, only watched her with intensity, as if she were a laboratory experiment.

"But I'm not in control of anything, am I?" she asked, pasting a bright, practiced smile on her face.

"That's not true," he answered solemnly. "You are the master of an entire earldom. I wonder how many men here realize that."

She shrugged, but something inside her felt a touch of pride.

"But as for this mystery that has upset the household, we will solve it, so that you'll no longer feel so unsettled."

"'Unsettled,'" she echoed. "What an understatement." Then she stiffened as she saw someone approach. She held Michael's arm even closer as she murmured, "Now here is a suitor who often wouldn't accept no. Perhaps you will be handy to have around tonight."

Michael's dark eyes glinted. "I don't mind being used by a beautiful woman."

She arched a brow. "'Used'? What a wicked word."

"And it has very many meanings of which I will be pleased to show you."

She didn't quite understand what he meant, but it felt decidedly wicked, and to her surprise, that felt decidedly . . . good. Heavens, she didn't even understand her own thoughts on that crazy day.

For the half hour before dinner, she treated Michael's

arm as if she needed it to stand, drawing Oliver's tipsy, amused regard and Penelope's curious smile. Michael was large and threatening, but under a very civilized veneer that seemed a touch thin. She felt glad of his dangerous air, surrounded by all these people she no longer knew if she could trust.

These were her neighbors—was one of them trying to kill her? Perhaps she should hope they were, so it wouldn't be her brother. *Oh please, God, not my brother.*

Oliver was standing near his guardian, Lord Doddridge, who still had the same bewildered, concerned look on his face he'd worn from the moment he'd heard about her rescue. He was speaking in low tones to her brother, who kept nodding absently, while staring down into his drink. Was Lord Doddridge concerned about what would happen if she no longer had control of the estate? Surely, that would make things *worse* for him if he had to oversee Oliver closely.

Unless he and Oliver already had some sort of furtive agreement. Oh, she wished she could just shut off her mind.

At last, Talbot announced that dinner was served. She tried to concentrate on her food and not look at Michael, who, although seated with Penelope on one side, seemed to be talking intently across her to Lord Carrington, another man who'd once fancied himself Cecilia's suitor.

Last year, she would have seated Hannah at Michael's side, the better to ease his transition into their small society. She'd never imagined how easily Penelope would fill her sister's role in their parish, in Cecilia's heart. Sometimes, she could almost pretend the worst hadn't happened.

But Cecilia couldn't hear their conversation. Instead, she listened to two of her father's old friends, who might have thought they were speaking in controlled tones but who were really talking loudly about the letters her father used to send.

"He's not what I imagined," Sir Eustace Venn was saying, his voice tremulous with age, along with his jowls.

Then Cecilia realized that he glanced at Michael, and she tried to pretend she was studying the menu as the footmen began to ladle soup into a bowl before each guest.

"He seems so young," answered Mr. Garnett, his muttonchop sideburns emphasizing the lean boniness of his face. "Not at all the seasoned, talented soldier Appertan proclaimed him."

More than one nearby guest glanced at her, but no one stopped the old men from conversing, and she wasn't about to embarrass them. Frankly, she wanted to hear what they had to say.

Sir Eustace slurped a spoonful of soup, then thankfully used a napkin. "Ruthless, that's what Appertan called him. Said he always went beyond anything asked of him. Deadly with a gun and sword."

"Not afraid to use them," Mr. Garnett answered. "Once, when his gun had been discharged, he used his bayonet on one man, his sword on another almost simultaneously. Not a scratch on him, eh? Wonder how he got the limp."

She winced at their vivid descriptions, then stared again at her husband, who although dressed in elegant evening clothes, seemed as sober as a magistrate. There might be some who did not want to hear of their husbands' having to kill—but part of her was satisfied that he would never give up until he knew who was trying to harm her.

Then he glanced at her with eyes that seemed briefly warm with understanding.

For just a moment, she felt almost . . . safe.

But she wasn't safe, she reminded herself, gazing again at all her dearest neighbors and wondering if one of them was a killer.

All through dinner, Michael did his best to get an understanding about Lord Carrington, seated on the other side of Miss Webster. She eagerly attempted to facilitate a conversation between both men, but he could hardly tell her to be quiet so that he could get a measure of the man who'd once courted Cecilia. After dinner, he made sure to play cards at the same table as the man, understanding his very arrogance, as if he could have anything within his grasp.

But Carrington hadn't won Cecilia, Michael thought with satisfaction, then almost had to smile at himself. *He* hadn't won Cecilia either—she'd come to him in desperation.

But he ruled Carrington out as a suspect when someone else told him his lordship had already proposed to a girl he'd spent a year pursuing.

At one point, he heard Cecilia explaining the rumors neighbors had heard, about her falling into the poaching hole. She made it sound so amusing, as if she were in no danger at all. If the villain were in attendance he would surely believe he was as yet undiscovered.

At last, the guests began to dwindle away as, one by one, Talbot announced the arrival of their carriages. When the last guest had departed, and Oliver had gone off to meet up with friends, Michael watched Cecilia's shoulders slump, as if it had only been sheer will keeping her upright. Several maids moved silently through the drawing room, beginning to collect glasses.

He put his arm around Cecilia's waist. "Do you need help to your room?"

The fact that she didn't even shake him off attested to her exhaustion.

"I could sweep you right off your feet," he added.

That succeeded in coaxing a smile from her. "No,

my limbs are working." But she didn't protest when he took her arm and led her toward the double doors.

At the stairs, they took a candle from Will the footman and ascended to the family wing. In Cecilia's bedroom, Nell was dozing by the fire but came to her feet with a smile. Michael left them and found Tom the footman waiting in his room. He'd begun to take turns with his brother acting as Michael's valet. But Michael only removed his coat, waistcoat, and white cravat before dismissing Tom. He paced his room impatiently, then opened the door at a knock.

"I'm done for the night," Nell told him.

He wished her a good night, then went through the dressing room and knocked on Cecilia's door.

There was a long pause, long enough that he wondered if she would ignore him. His hand was already on the knob when he heard her call, "Come in, Michael."

He closed the door behind him and leaned against it, feeling compelled to take hold of his restraint. Cecilia wore a dressing gown, which only emphasized how small and defenseless she really was. Then he remembered the marks on the side of the dirt hole, where she'd tried to claw her way out. She was stronger than she appeared.

But now that she'd washed away the concealing powder, the bruise on her cheek looked stark and ugly, a reminder of someone's cruelty.

She stood in the center of the room and gracefully

tilted her head. "Did you forget something, Michael?"

"Perhaps you did, if you think I'm going to allow you to be alone tonight."

Cecilia felt a frisson of excitement that didn't bode well for her vaunted mastery of any situation. Michael walked toward her out of the shadows, his shirt gleaming white, the collar open to display his tanned throat. His dark eyes beheld her as if they had the power to coerce her into . . . anything.

"Michael, you sleep right next door. I think—"

"The past two nights I slept on the cot in the dressing room."

Her eyes widened. "I had no idea."

"But that didn't help protect you, did it? From now on, either the most trusted servants or I will be with you at all times."

She wanted to object, feeling as if her life was no longer her own. But it would be foolish to risk death because things were spiraling out of her control.

"I can call Nell back," she began.

"That won't be necessary."

She could not help but glance at the bed.

"You have a chaise longue." He gestured to the long reclining chair she kept near the window for better reading light. "I would never force you to do something you're not ready for."

They stared at each other, a silent battle of wills, one she should not even try to win.

"Very well," she murmured. She went to the bed and removed the counterpane, taking it to the chaise, along with a pillow.

When he tried to lay the bedding out, she wouldn't allow it, doing it herself while he clenched his cane.

"This isn't about your being unable to help yourself, you know," she said, feeling the presence of him behind her even though she wasn't looking. "This is about my obligation."

"'Obligation,'" he said, drawing it out. "What an interesting choice of word."

She winced. "I didn't mean—"

"Cecilia," he said softly, putting a hand on her arm. "You take everything so seriously."

"And you don't?" She regarded him over her shoulder as she straightened the pillow for a second time.

"I can be too serious, which is perhaps why I recognize a fellow sufferer."

"You know," she said, walking away from the chaise with an attempt to appear casual, "two of my father's old friends were talking about you at dinner tonight, and I think they could be counted on to believe you far too serious."

He said nothing.

"You're not curious?"

"You wouldn't have brought it up if you didn't mean to tell me."

She rolled her eyes. "They were actually complimentary about your ruthlessness in battle, mentioning several examples of your determination not to quit."

He nodded but remained silent.

"You expect me to trust you when you don't talk about these things?" she asked with exasperation.

"There is little I can say since I do not intend to discuss my war experiences with you. I won't discuss the things I saw, or what I had to do to keep my men safe."

She studied him in surprise. Her father used to have many anecdotes to tell, even if he'd tamed them for civilian ears. She couldn't be surprised at Michael's modesty, of which he'd shown plenty, but there seemed to be something else going on inside him.

"Do you think I couldn't understand what you've had to do?" she asked softly. "I lived in India, remember, and my father told us things that perhaps he shouldn't have."

He stared at her impassively for a moment, before saying, "It was difficult enough to live through some events, Cecilia. Why would I want to relive them?"

She felt a pang of sympathy for him and knew the sacrifice it took to defend the Crown. If he didn't want to discuss it, who was she to press him for answers or explanations? Unless . . . she wanted him to trust her with the worst of it, to perhaps unburden himself.

Oh God, did that mean she wanted his trust because she wanted to offer hers?

As if reading her mind, he said, "Does this mean

you're ready to discuss your relationship with your brother?"

"We've already done that," she said crisply, beginning to blow out candles around the room.

He stood unmoving, watching her. "Cecilia, you've allowed me to be here tonight. It's obvious you no longer believe I might harm you. It warms me to have your trust."

"Just because I might not think you're a murderer doesn't mean I trust you," she shot back, her hands gripped behind her back.

For the first time, he gave her a real smile, one of indulgence and surprising tenderness. It took her breath away, made her realize that he did not easily show the world this side of himself. But he showed it to her.

"You trusted me enough to keep away all your old suitors tonight."

She couldn't deny that.

He began to walk toward her. "I feel so used," he said softly.

She bit her lip, trying not to smile. But that urge faded into uncertainty and excitement when he didn't stop walking, and she was forced to back up until her knees hit the edge of the chaise longue, and she sat down with a thump. He loomed over her, bracing himself with his hand on the curved backrest.

"I think you owe me something," he continued.

Very gently, he cupped the side of her face, then slid

his hand back into her braided hair. To her surprise, it soon fell down around her shoulders.

"You have the most beautiful hair," he said hoarsely.

His gaze seemed to devour her, and instead of uneasy, she felt a rise of excitement that seemed all out of proportion to his touch. No man had ever made her feel this way—which was perhaps why none of them lured her into marriage at a younger age.

This thrilling sensation must be desire, a need that was taking hold of her, making her want to explore. She'd always been curious about the world, but never had she felt this kind of yearning.

"And what do you think I owe you?" she whispered, tilting her head up to meet his intent gaze as his hand continued to move through her hair.

"At least a kiss."

He leaned lower until their breaths mingled. He didn't wait for her acceptance, and she couldn't even have spoken, with her breath coming so fast. When his mouth touched hers, she expected the gentle kiss he'd given her before, but this one was totally different, urging her lips apart once, twice, then his tongue sought entrance, and she granted it in shock, even as a moan escaped her. He swept her mouth like a conqueror, played with her tongue until, at last, she responded with her own tentative exploration. He nibbled her and tasted her, suckled her or plundered like a pirate taking what he wanted.

And she gave it to him willingly, so caught up in his need of her—and her need for him, she realized in astonishment. She felt desperate enough to reach for him, to run her hands up his arms, to hold him tight.

Still kissing her, he sat down on the edge of the chaise, leaning her onto the long, curving backrest. He began to press kisses along her jaw and down her throat, nuzzling her, licking her. She made little noises, whimpers of need that should have embarrassed her, but didn't. She held his head to her, felt the full softness of his hair between her fingers. And then his mouth moved lower, and lower still, as he parted her dressing gown. She was holding her breath in anticipation, knowing she should stop him, even as a sly voice whispered, *He is your husband.*

He pressed kisses along the neckline of her nightgown, until she squirmed beneath him, desperate for more, though she didn't know what. He skimmed his lips along her breasts, and then through the silk of her gown, he took her nipple into his mouth. She cried out and arched her back, shocked and aroused and joyful all at the same time. She'd never imagined such intense feelings, and it only doubled when he cupped her other breast with his palm and gently kneaded it. With his fingers, he rolled one nipple, with his tongue he licked the other, until she was quivering and desperate. She gripped handfuls of his shirt, sliding it up his back so she could touch his hot skin beneath. To her surprise, he sat up long enough to pull the shirt off over his head, and she stared in surprise at the muscular expanse of his chest, the scars, one near his shoulder, another on his arm, a third along his ribs, like something sharp had deflected across the bones.

"Oh, Michael," she whispered, touching the one on his side. "You've been so hurt."

She sat up, and he stiffened, his hungry expression fading away into impassivity as if he thought he'd lost her. She slid her dressing gown off her shoulders. It pooled on the chaise, and his eyes seemed to smolder.

"Cecilia."

He whispered her name with relief and urgency and the hunger that made her feel like she was the only woman in the world, the center of his universe.

And then he pulled the ribbon of her nightgown, and the neckline parted at her shoulders. His fingers spread it wider, brushing across her sensitive skin, freeing her breasts. Her nudity almost shocked her, but he cupped them and once again worshipped them with his mouth, until she was moaning and moving fitfully in her tangled nightgown. Then he lifted her free of it, and she was naked in his bare arms, feeling every inch of his hot skin against hers. He limped across the room to the bed and spread her out across it, his hands sliding down her torso and thighs as he stood up.

She lay there naked, her hair all around her, and watched him finish disrobing. He bent to remove his trousers and undergarments, and when he straightened, she stared at her first sight of a naked man, his erection prominent in his dark hair. She was distracted by the web of raw-looking scars twisting down his thigh.

"Oh, Michael," she breathed, wincing in pain for him.

She reached to touch his scars, but he caught her hands.

"Not now. They mean nothing to me."

And then she forgot them, too, because he stretched out on top of her, every inch of their bodies touching. He felt so different from her, hard where she was soft. She could feel his penis cradled against her belly, strange and threatening and intriguing all at the same time.

He started kissing her again, deep, drugging kisses over and over, taking her mouth, seducing her thoughts and will until she was nothing but aching need. She held him to her, desperate to be closer. She wanted to wrap herself around him, and parted her legs to do so. But then he settled between her hips, rocking against her.

She cried out at this new, deeper, stronger jolt of desire. Pressing herself against him, she murmured, "Please, oh, please, tell me what I should do."

He chuckled against her neck, and she lifted his head to stare at him, shocked. His mouth was still wide with amusement, his brown eyes soft with warmth.

"I'll show you everything," he whispered, "but not so quickly. I feel I've waited a lifetime for you." He slid off her, resting on his side.

She groaned and reached for him.

"Not yet, my inquisitive one. You aren't in command here."

Then he kissed her again, and his hands took a journey down her body, caressing and teasing her breasts and belly, moving ever closer to the part of her that burned to be touched, even as somewhere inside her she felt hesitant. She ignored the cautious voice that ruled so much of her life. When his hand slid along her thighs, she only briefly considered holding them shut. But they opened as if of their own accord. His fingers brushed her curls and slid deeper, stroking her. Gasping at the shocking pleasure, she buried her face in his shoulder, unable to look at him when he was doing such brazen things to her.

The pleasure suffused her, built inside her until she was panting. He was gentle at first, then bolder, and she couldn't help noticing how wet she was, how easily his fingers slid along the crease of her body. She was straining for something elusive and so powerful, then gaped up at him when he suddenly pressed her onto her back.

"Michael!"

He covered her body with his, and she felt his erection slide along her. She shuddered, her need cresting again, when he suddenly drove home. More shocked than hurt, she was amazed that the two of them fit together at all.

He bent to kiss her mouth. "Are you . . . all right?" he asked, his voice tense, his expression almost angry, although she knew he wasn't, not if he felt anything like she did.

"I'm fine. But please—"

She broke off as he pulled back, then surged in again, shocking her very nerves into a rising explosion that, with just one more thrust, sent her helplessly over an edge into a shuddering oblivion of blinding pleasure. He kept moving, harder and faster, and she didn't know where the first wave of pleasure ended and more began.

She knew when his own climax took him by the way he groaned into her shoulder, then collapsed onto his forearms, bearing much of his weight. They were both breathing hard, gasping, and she could only stare up at him in wonder.

Chapter 16

As Michael gazed into Cecilia's damp, flushed face, he couldn't remember a time when he had felt more at peace. His body was still afire with lust, and he could have kept pumping away until he was ready to do it all over again, but his wife had been a virgin.

At last, she was his wife in truth.

She searched his face with wide eyes, her lips parted. She almost seemed bewildered, as if emerging from a dream. Very carefully, he slid out of her body, already missing her as if he'd found what he'd been searching for his whole life. He rolled onto his back, then gathered her against him so that her cheek rested on his shoulder. But she seemed tense, as though she might flee if he made one wrong move. So he said nothing, just stroked her hair where it tumbled in a tangle across his chest.

Then, to his surprise, her eyes drifted closed, and she fell asleep without a word.

Michael was usually the silent one in any relationship, and her behavior briefly puzzled him. But she'd been fearing for her life for days now, perhaps lying awake, listening for footsteps. He winced, remembering how many times he himself had walked past her door as he patrolled the corridors.

He came up on his elbow to blow out the last candle, then drew the blankets over them both. He kissed her tousled hair, silently promising she would never have to be alone with her worry again.

Cecilia slowly came awake, warm to her core, vaguely surprised that sunlight streamed in the windows. She'd never drawn the curtains, she drowsily thought. And she never slept this long.

And then all the rest of her senses returned in a rush as she realized she was lying on her side, that Michael was snug against her back, their naked bodies spooned together, his very obvious arousal nestled against her backside. His large arm encompassed her waist, his hand loosely cupping her breast.

She went tense with surprise and burgeoning regret, even as she heard him snore softly into her ear. Letting out her breath, she closed her eyes, barely stopping herself from groaning loud enough to wake him.

What had she done?

She'd become his wife in truth, and any chance of invalidating the marriage was gone. Her emotions seemed all jumbled inside her as the memories of their night together overwhelmed her. She'd been like an animal, so desperately in need of him, she'd allowed him to do . . . anything he wanted. It had felt good, no doubt about it, but that didn't make such absolute baseness forgivable.

She moved the tiniest bit and could already feel a tenderness at the juncture of her thighs from his lovemaking. He'd been forceful and overpowering, and she'd wanted all of it. Even now, as she stared down at his hand against her breast, she could have pressed herself into him to feel it all over again.

She couldn't be so close to him; she couldn't want him this much, depend on him. He was leaving her, and she wasn't going with him. She might be married, but it didn't mean she would lose herself in him, or lose herself in sorrow when he left. She would go on as she had before, in control of her life and her emotions. She wouldn't let herself love him or need him—he had to understand that.

But, of course, she needed his help to find whoever wanted to harm her.

But oh God, he felt so good against her, his body sinfully warm and alluring. She could have sunk into him, beneath him, and let all that rough masculinity consume her. Instead, she gritted her teeth and forced herself to slide toward the edge of the bed.

He caught her back against him, and she gasped.

"Good morning, wife," he murmured into her ear.

She shivered at the rumbling of his voice, which seemed to echo through his ribs and into hers. His hand was no longer loose but cupped her breast firmly, playing with it, teasing it into a point that abraded his palm and made a surge of pleasure shoot all the way into the pit of her stomach. And then he slid his hand down her torso and between her thighs to boldly cup her.

She pushed him off her and vaulted from the bed, standing dazed and naked on the carpet. Where were the garments she'd so wantonly relinquished in her frenzy the night before?

Michael pushed himself up on one arm, his eyes full of admiration, the covers falling loosely about his waist. "You look exquisite with the morning sun bathing you in light."

Without thinking about it, she crossed her arms over her breasts and groin. Laughing, he dropped back on the bed, arms wide, body arched as he seemed to stretch every muscle. She gaped at him, shocked at how much she enjoyed the sight of all the masculine beauty dominating her feminine bed.

He grinned at her, as if he knew what she was thinking. She couldn't stop staring at his face either, the way his smile transformed her sober soldier into a lighthearted lover. Once again, she had the strangest feeling that only she had ever been privileged enough to see this satisfied, relaxed side of him. It made her feel all funny and melancholy and sweet inside, and she desperately ran for her dressing gown. Only when it was belted around her did she let out her breath and close her eyes.

She practically jumped a foot when she felt his arms close about her from behind.

"Come back to bed," he urged.

"You're naked!"

She tried to pull away, but he seemed to think it a game and only held her tighter.

"Naked and eager for you," he replied.

"I can't do this!" she cried.

He let her go, and she only briefly saw his happiness fade before she firmly turned her back.

"Please don your trousers. I can't—I can't talk when you're like"—she waved her arm in his direction—"that!"

After a minute of rustling, he quietly said, "Very well, I'm decent. Now you can talk to me."

She turned around to find him leaning on his cane, nude from the waist up. Briefly, she had a flash of memory of the terrible wound in his leg. But she couldn't afford to feel any sympathy right now.

And she couldn't keep looking at his impressive chest, full of muscles she couldn't imagine having, tiny ripples of them leading down his stomach. She forced herself to bravely meet his eyes and not feel sadness at the lack of emotion there. Only moments ago, he'd been so happy, but she couldn't let him think that was how their life would now be.

"I guess you have what you wanted, a legal marriage," she said, trying to sound as impassive as he always could. "I know I initiated all of this." She threw her arms wide. "But I would have ended it, and you pursued me."

"You're my wife. What did you expect me to do? I did not *force* you to make love with me last night."

"I know," she whispered, letting out her breath in a sigh. "I'm not blaming you."

The tension in his shoulders eased, and he took several steps toward her. "Then why are you so upset?" he asked in a quieter voice.

"Because intimacy doesn't change things between us! You need to know that. We can't have a normal marriage. You're going back to India, and I'm staying here."

He inhaled. "After this, I thought you'd see we belong together. When Oliver reaches his maturity, you'll be free of the estate. You could travel."

"First, you imply that my brother might mean me harm, and now you're talking as if he's a functioning earl, ready to assume every responsibility. Which is it, Michael?"

"I don't know," he admitted. "We will find out who wants to harm you, then we'll deal with what comes after."

"I know how I want to deal with what comes after," she said, trying to sound like she had everything figured out. "You have a career in the army, and I'm here. I can't risk the livelihood of everyone on all the Appertan estates by abandoning them."

"And I can't abandon my family without a source of income," he answered, sighing. "I have some small shipping investments just beginning in India. Perhaps sometime in the future . . ."

"And you'd just give up on your career, what you're best at?" she asked pointedly. "Or do you think I'd blithely follow you to India? I won't, Michael. That country was the death of my brother and mother, even my father. It tore apart our family. I won't be second place again."

They stared at each other, and she tried to keep composed, but for some reason, her eyes were stinging, and she knew her nose was getting red.

And then a knock sounded at the door, startling her. "May I answer my own door? I don't imagine a villain would ask permission to enter."

"If it's the easiest, most unexpected way to get to you, he might." He raised his voice. "Who's there?"

"Nell, milord."

"We still have much to discuss about your current situation," Michael said, pulling his shirt over his head and tucking it into his trousers.

His choice of words was almost amusing. She found it easier to breathe without staring at all his flesh, remembering where she'd pressed her lips, how she'd licked the salt from his skin. It was as if she were a different person in the night. "Please allow me to dress first. I'll have Nell send up breakfast, and we can eat here in privacy, where no one will overhear us."

"Very well."

"Come in, Nell," Cecilia called, trying not to sound relieved.

As the maid bustled in, Cecilia knew her own face was bright red. The counterpane was in a pile near the chaise longue, and to her horror, her nightgown was in a discarded heap nearby.

"I've a bath on its way, Lady Blackthorne," Nell said, nodding politely to Michael. "Milord, Tom tells me he's seein' to one for you."

"My thanks, Nell," he said.

Then, to Cecilia's surprise, he took her hand and brought it to his lips. She wanted to pull away, to furiously ask if he'd heard anything she said.

"Until breakfast, Cecilia," he murmured, and in his eyes was a promise that their discussion wasn't over yet.

She couldn't help but stare after him as he started to leave the room.

Suddenly, Nell called, "Wait, milord, I've a message for ye. In the commotion of Lady Blackthorne's scare yesterday, and then dinner, Will forgot to let ye know he returned with a letter from yer family."

"Returned?" Michael said blankly.

Cecilia winced. "Because of yesterday's . . . upheaval, I forgot to tell you that I sent a letter to your family first thing in the morning inviting them for a visit." He frowned at her, and she hurried on. "I felt bad that you'd delayed visiting them, and I didn't want your mother to think that a woman of poor manners had married her son."

When he narrowed his eyes, it was obvious that he didn't believe her explanation for even a moment.

But he turned to Nell. "And where is the message?"

She removed a sealed envelope from a pocket in her apron and handed it to him. Without looking at Cecilia, he left the room.

She stared after him, feeling both guilty she hadn't told him and irritated that he had chosen not to share the letter with her. But, of course, she would hate it if he'd gone behind her back in the same manner. Her actions seemed . . . underhanded.

She heard Nell moving about the room, humming even as she picked up the nightgown. There was nothing normal about this situation, though Nell pretended otherwise. When the maid began to remove the bedsheets, Cecilia groaned and closed her eyes, remembering that there might be evidence of her "wedding night."

"Now there's nothin' to be shy about, milady," Nell said matter-of-factly. "I knew the moment you were left to die in that hole that his lordship would never let

you sleep alone. And such a virile man as hisself? O'
course he would never be able to keep his hands from
his own wife, beauty that ye are. And I say it's about
time. Everyone could see how fascinated ye both were
with the other."

"Everyone but me, apparently," Cecilia said grump-
ily, sitting down at her dressing table and glancing at
the mirror. She stared in horror at her wild hair, her
bare throat, the gaping dressing gown that showed far
too much of her breasts. "Good lord!"

"That's what a man likes to see in the mornin'," Nell
said with satisfaction.

"And how do you know that?" Cecilia demanded.

"I hear things . . ." she said innocently, then went
back to humming.

Cecilia slipped behind the changing screen while
the pages carried in the bathing tub and buckets of hot
water. The bath felt soothing, and she tried not to think
of anything, simply let Nell care for her.

Nell tsked over her bruised cheek. "Ye poor mite,"
she murmured.

"I'm all right," Cecilia said. "And I promise I'll take
things easy today."

"Good, ye deserve to be pampered and petted."

And then she chuckled, even as Cecilia felt her face
heat with embarrassment. Her gaze kept returning to
the dressing-room door, as if she expected Michael
to burst back in, wearing the furious expression she'd

only seen once, when Sir Bevis had attacked her during Oliver's billiards party. She should be relieved, she told herself. She wanted to keep some distance between them, and the letter would certainly help. But Michael didn't arrive, and soon she was dressed, with breakfast on its way. Dismissing the servants, she went through the dressing room, took a deep breath, and knocked on his door.

Chapter 17

When Michael returned to his bedroom, he stared at the envelope, seeing his mother's slightly messy penmanship, and reluctantly smiled. Cecilia hadn't informed him that she wished to contact his family—and he couldn't be surprised. She'd been looking for any kind of buffer to keep between them—hell, even after the previous night, she was *still* desperate to keep him away from her. There was nothing of proper manners about her letter to his mother and the way she'd gone about it.

Cecilia was afraid, and not just because someone wished her ill. She was afraid of their marriage, of the feelings that overwhelmed even him. There was a part of him that would give up anything for her, even what made him the man he was. And that wasn't the way to keep his self-respect, or win hers.

She didn't want to depend on him, but danger forced her to. And now they'd lain together. She must have been thrilled that his mother's letter distracted him.

He wouldn't be distracted for long. Ripping open the letter, he read the brief note, sighed, and rang the bell for one of his apprentice valets. As if they'd been waiting for his signal, the bath procession began. He studied the pages surreptitiously, but they completed their task with deference. What had he expected—that he might catch an evil grin?

When he was dressed, a knock sounded at the dressing-room door.

"Come in," he called.

Cecilia opened the door, and if she felt at all guilty, her graceful movements didn't betray any hesitation. She glided into the room, and although she was fully buttoned up to a high neckline, he could still recall her lush nakedness as she'd lain beneath him. He was hard in an instant, and it was difficult to collect his thoughts, to remember that he was waging a war for his future, and every small battle counted. Somehow, he would make her change her mind about India.

"I came to apologize." She met his gaze forthrightly. "It was wrong of me to send the letter, but at the time, I felt my actions appropriate."

"Because I could have been a suspect."

"I truly knew you weren't." She pressed her lips together in a thin line.

"I accept your apology."

She blinked in surprise, then with a nod, turned away as if to leave.

"And you feel no curiosity at all?" he called in bemusement.

She froze, then said over her shoulder, "Of course I feel curious, but I would never demand that you share a private letter."

He could almost see the war within her, by her tight shoulders and her fisted hands. But her curiosity won out, and she turned back to regard him.

"Is your mother well?" she asked.

He nodded. "And eager to see us both. She and my brother expected to be leaving at dawn. I imagine they'll arrive by luncheon today."

Her eyes went wide. "Oh my! I'll alert the servants, of course, but . . . is their visit all right with you?"

"I love my family, and I'm eager to see them."

She let out her breath, and he couldn't help but be amused how on one hand she wanted to keep her distance, but on the other, she didn't want to offend him. She was trying to be a good girl at all times, perhaps most especially since she'd done something last night that probably seemed wicked to her virginal self.

"But what you did not anticipate," he continued ruefully, "is that I hadn't told my family of our marriage."

She blinked, then smiled faintly. "I cannot be surprised. We hadn't even met, and perhaps you thought we might never be truly married."

"I never thought that even once—unlike you."

"Then why would you keep that from them? They might have heard through common acquaintances."

"As I've mentioned before, they do not socialize in the same circles you do. They never go to London at all." He hesitated. "Frankly, I thought the news best delivered in person, so they could understand why I would enter into such a . . . contract."

"They would expect that I bring a dowry to the family," she answered flatly.

"Not at all. My father and grandfather were fortune hunters, Cecilia. I vowed to finance our family through my own efforts, and if I married at all, it would not be for money. But, of course, now it looks like I did exactly what I swore I never would—married a wealthy heiress, sight unseen."

"You'll explain things to them." She lowered her gaze, her cheeks flushed. "I'm surprised to find that I feel guilty for not granting you the dowry every man should have when he marries."

He strode to her, unable to keep himself from cupping her face and lifting it until their gazes met. "You didn't buy me, Cecilia, and that's important to me. Our marriage arrangement suited us both, and my family will understand."

He couldn't help himself—he leaned down to kiss her. He wasn't surprised when she ducked away.

"The sun is up, Michael," she said primly.

He smiled. "And you think a husband and wife should not touch each other in the light of day?"

"I have so many things to do to prepare the Hall for the arrival of your family. I will be glad to meet them, and I won't embarrass you."

He stared at her. "Embarrass me? You could never do that, my sweet."

She flinched from his endearment, but he wouldn't stop using it. She could try to keep her distance, but he didn't plan to allow that. However long they had together, he would make the most of it. If he could win her over, perhaps they could have some sort of married life.

"I should go talk to Mrs. Ellison," she said.

"No, we have our own plans to make."

"Then come into my room, where breakfast is probably getting cold waiting for us. We'll ring for a servant."

They passed the news of guests to Mrs. Ellison, then sat down at the small table in Cecilia's room to a meal of lobster and ham, eggs, and hot rolls. Michael was ravenous, but he noticed that Cecilia picked at her food.

"I hope this disinterest isn't worry about my mother," he said. "She's going to think you're wonderful."

"I'm glad," she answered softly. "I don't wish to make things more difficult for you than I already have."

"You mean by thinking I'd try to murder you?" He smiled at her.

She didn't smile back. "I saw you interrogating my former suitors last night. Did you learn anything?"

"I don't think our villain is Carrington or Nash. It would be simple to discover if Nash had returned secretly before yesterday. Too many people talk. And Carrington is obsessed with a young lady he's been pursuing for nigh on a year."

"Oh." The worry lines in her forehead eased with relief. "That is good to hear."

"Not that I appreciated how they all flocked around you like gulls," he added darkly.

Her blue eyes sparkled. "According to you, they're harmless."

"Well, revenge because a woman didn't marry you is a poor motive for murder unless you're insane. They don't seem insane. As for other neighbors, unless you've specifically harmed anyone or his reputation . . ." He let that drag out.

Wide-eyed, she insisted, "Of course not! I am fond of all my neighbors, and they always seem fond of me."

"And if it weren't true, your servants would know from other servants. Both Talbot and Mrs. Ellison insist they've heard nothing disquieting. As for Lord Doddridge, he is leaving this morning, so I suggest we examine the account books after he's gone, looking for any irregularities."

She stiffened. "I go over those books every day. I would see any *irregularities*."

"I know, but he is Appertan's guardian for the moment, and we don't know what agreement they might have negotiated that you know nothing about."

She blanched but didn't protest. He realized she'd considered that even though she didn't want to believe the worst of her brother.

"As for Appertan," he began.

"No." She pushed back her chair and threw down her napkin. "Don't you dare say you believe my own brother would try to harm me."

"Drink does terrible things to people," he said quietly. "I have seen it ruin a good man more than once."

"Not Oliver!" she cried.

He could see her eyes swimming in tears, and the hurt cut him unexpectedly deep. "Until we can definitely rule him out, Cecilia, it makes sense to be wary."

"I'm ruling him out! You promised to help him—is this your way of neglecting that promise?"

"Of course not. I was going to suggest that after Doddridge leaves, you invite Appertan to look over the books with us and discuss investment strategies."

"That is a good idea," she said stiffly.

"You can tell him about our guests as well, so he's not surprised."

"You mean surprised when he's expected to remain home this evening and entertain?"

Michael raised both hands. "That is your decision, not mine." He wanted to keep the mood light between them, especially since his family was coming, but he could not sit back while she ignored the danger her brother might be putting her in. "Cecilia, sometimes I think you blame yourself for your brother's selfish behavior, and that's a mistake."

Her eyes flashed at him.

"He's an adult, who must take responsibility for his own behavior."

"His twin brother died!" she cried softly. "That would hurt anyone."

"Ten years ago, Cecilia," he pointed out.

"You don't get over something like that." A tear slid from her eye, and she impatiently brushed it away. "I've never gotten over it."

"But you became successful, regardless."

"But it was my fault, Michael!" she cried. "Gabriel was under my care, and I didn't see the crocodile! I was reading, for God's sake, absorbed in what I wanted to do, not the responsibilities my parents had asked of me."

"If you blame your thirteen-year-old self, then you must really blame Gabriel for saving you."

She bit her lip, and more tears fell.

"You would have saved him in a heartbeat. He simply beat you to it. Deep inside, Appertan knows he's failing his brother's memory. But he doesn't seem to care. You can't blame yourself."

"Even if you say I didn't fail Gabriel," she said slowly, "I still feel that way. And I won't fail Oliver. You're wrong about him."

"Then begin to let go of the reins you've attached to him. I challenge you to spend a day like a normal young lady instead of an earl. Let me walk Appertan through his duties."

Still, she hesitated, and he ached for the torment she inflicted on herself, the guilt she should not be feeling. She'd done nothing wrong—whereas he himself had made terrible decisions in his own life, and men had suffered and died. The pang of sorrow took him by surprise, and he put it away until the night, when the dreams would come to him.

"I don't believe that's a good idea," she said at last. "Your mother will be arriving."

"Not today, then. When they've gone."

"That could be at least a week."

"No, you don't know my mother. She'll want us to be alone with each other."

She rolled her eyes.

"You don't believe in a honeymoon? Technically, we're on ours. Finding a person attempting to murder you is not what one would consider a honeymoon adventure." He lowered his voice. "Let Appertan run his own estates for a day. You want him to be a good man, a good husband to Miss Webster, don't you?"

"Of course I do," she insisted.

"Appertan reminds me of my father and grandfather, who squandered their estates and money. I wish someone would have helped them before it was too late. Let's help your brother."

"I know you're right," she said in a quiet voice. "But it's difficult for me to abandon the lands and people I love. But . . . my father entrusted Oliver to me. I can't let either of them down. Very well, I'll do as you wish and give Oliver a day."

Just a day, Michael thought, watching as she relaxed enough to finally eat breakfast. He was surprised how difficult it was for her to give up even that one day of control. He suddenly realized it would take her a long time to give up overseeing her brother, even once Appertan had taken over his duties. He would spend their marriage trying to persuade her to join him in India, and the time would never be right.

Cecilia walked Lord Doddridge to the portico midmorning to see him on his way. More than once, he'd said how glad he was that she was unscathed, and he seemed sincere enough. But she was finding it difficult to trust anyone lately, and she wondered if she'd ever be able to feel normal again. What if they never found the person responsible for these "accidents"? Would she have to live in fear for the rest of her life?

Michael waited at the door, watching her, she knew. And she was grateful. He escorted her to the study, where Oliver waited, arms folded across his chest as he glowered at them both. Cecilia talked about the account books, and what Lord Doddridge had been looking at. Though Oliver said little, at least he appeared to be listening, even occasionally nodding. Then Cecilia and Michael discussed the earldom's investments, from mines to shipping to railways, and once or twice, Oliver asked a question. He tried to balk when she said he would be assuming her duties for a day, but it was Michael who pointed out that a steward could cheat an ignorant peer, and Oliver had to know what was involved, even if he wasn't the one who oversaw everything every day. At last, he acquiesced.

When Talbot announced the arrival of Michael's family, even Oliver looked intrigued enough to follow them to the entrance hall.

Cecilia stood back as the Dowager Lady Blackthorne and her son entered Appertan Hall. Both had dark brown hair like Michael's, but Lady Blackthorne's was threaded with silver, which, along with the confident way she carried herself, made her look distinguished rather than old. It was very obvious her beauty had once captured the interest of many a man. Her younger son seemed to be a more genial version of Michael, a bit shorter, lighter of frame, with eyes that crinkled when he smiled, and it seemed as if he smiled often.

Michael grinned as Talbot took his mother's bonnet

and shawl and his brother's hat, then swept them both into his big embrace. Cecilia saw Lady Blackthorne wipe away happy tears, and Cecilia felt the sting of her own. She well knew what it was like not to see someone you loved for months if not years at a time. After Gabriel's death, when she and her mother brought Oliver back to attend Eton, there were long stretches where she never saw her father at all. And now, so many of her family were gone. Perhaps that was why she clung so tightly to Oliver.

And now she was the wife of a soldier, she reminded herself bleakly.

Then Michael turned and gestured toward her. She came forward and let him take her hand.

"Mother, this is Lady Blackthorne, my wife, and her brother, Oliver Mallory, the Earl of Appertan."

Oliver bowed as Cecilia curtsied, and when she rose, she was surprised when Lady Blackthorne sank into her own deep curtsy, then smiled up at Cecilia with spry amusement.

"I never imagined this pleasure," Lady Blackthorne said, her voice deep and rich.

Cecilia smiled, surprised to find herself blushing. "Does that mean you never thought your son would marry?"

"We doubted it," her other son said wryly.

Michael sighed. "This is my brother, Mr. Allen Blackthorne."

Mr. Blackthorne bowed over her hand. "The pleasure is mine, Lady Cecilia. If I had known one could marry such beautiful women in India, I would have enlisted myself."

"But I did not meet him in India," Cecilia said without thinking.

Michael only looked amused as his mother's smile faltered with curiosity.

"Lady Cecilia and I had known each other through letters, and the gracious words of her father," Michael explained.

Cecilia led the way toward the drawing room, noticing that although Mr. Blackthorne looked around appreciatively, Lady Blackthorne was focused on her.

"So . . . you decided to marry without having met each other?" Lady Blackthorne said in bewilderment.

"We married by proxy six months ago," Michael explained.

"No wonder you didn't tell us." Mr. Blackthorne grinned and shook his head.

Lady Blackthorne was not smiling, her concern for her son very obvious. She looked from Michael to Cecilia and back again. Cecilia wanted to cause no damage to the Blackthorne family's harmony, so she walked to Michael's side and took his hand.

He glanced at her swiftly, but if he was surprised, he didn't show it, only squeezed her hand and looked down at her with a tender smile, the smile he'd first gifted her with last night, the one that made her realize that only she would ever see a certain side of him.

Whatever showed in her and Michael's expressions, apparently it was enough for Lady Blackthorne, who let out a sigh and gave a tentative smile.

"Well, I have no right to worry," she began, "and never would I judge. You both seem happy. And Lady Blackthorne, thank you for writing, because it looks like my son is a bit too distracted to remember his mother."

Michael squeezed Cecilia's hand, as if bracing her against the teasing, and she looked up with a reassuring smile.

For a few minutes, they discussed Michael's injury, and he played down its severity, but Cecilia had seen the scars, and knew he might have come close to bleeding to death. She shivered. When Talbot announced luncheon, Cecilia led them all to the conservatory, with its trees and ferns and climbing ivy making the glassed-in room seem like a jungle.

"I thought it would be a nice treat to eat under the autumn sun," Cecilia explained, when her brother rolled his eyes at her. There was nothing wrong with trying to impress one's mother-in-law.

A cloth-covered table and wrought-iron chairs had been placed before the fountain, and the gurgling of the water was a soothing background to their conversation.

Lady Blackthorne openly stared at Cecilia as they

began to eat their breast of veal, and finally said, "Please do excuse my curiosity, but I cannot miss the bruise on your cheek. I hope the injury wasn't more severe."

The whole neighborhood knew of the "poaching accident," so Cecilia explained it as such.

"How terrifying!" Lady Blackthorne gasped, her hand to her chest.

"It was, but I truly didn't fear for long. Your son rescued me within an hour."

Oliver continued to eat, not even raising his gaze. She told herself that he might still feel guilty for assuming she'd merely been avoiding the weather.

Lady Blackthorne cleared her throat delicately. "There was a time when I thought Michael would marry a young lady who lived near our home. Now that I've met you, I'm so very glad he waited."

Cecilia straightened and eyed Michael in surprise, even as she thanked his mother for the compliment. She thought he would be embarrassed, but, instead, his jaw worked for a moment as if he clenched it.

"Mother, you know that was never serious," Mr. Blackthorne began, eyeing his brother.

At last, Michael met his mother's confused gaze. "Did you not realize what Father was doing?"

"I don't understand what you're saying or why you're angry with me." She blushed madly and looked at Cecilia with embarrassed regret.

Michael sighed and reached to touch her hand. "I'm not angry with you. I assumed you knew what Father was up to but were helpless to prevent it."

Cecilia stared at each Blackthorne with curiosity, and knew that Oliver did the same.

Michael turned to Cecilia. "My ancestors married for money."

Lady Blackthorne blanched, as if she didn't like the words said aloud.

"My father was manipulating me into the same. He lied about our circumstances to our neighbor, leading him to believe having his daughter marry me would increase their wealth and connections."

Lady Blackthorne gave a soft gasp. "I never heard this," she whispered.

"It's one of the reasons I had to leave," Michael said, a note of apology in his voice. "I couldn't let him do that to another woman. I didn't want her to grow even more attached to me."

Cecilia stared at Michael, wondering if he'd liked the young lady and regretted that they couldn't marry. And what had it cost his pride to marry her, a wealthy woman? No wonder he'd gladly refused her dowry.

Lady Blackthorne's eyes briefly glistened, but she didn't cry. "Your father had his flaws, but in his own misguided way, he was trying to help you."

Cecilia could see that Michael didn't quite believe that, but he didn't contradict his mother. He kept his fingers linked with his mother's, even as he answered Mr. Blackthorne's questions about where his regiment had recently been stationed. Everyone seemed glad for the distraction except Oliver, who rolled his eyes.

At last, Michael sat back to eye his brother. "So what have you been doing this past year? Your letters were filled with neighborhood doings or estate business, but I felt you were conspicuously leaving things out."

Cecilia was surprised when Mr. Blackthorne received an encouraging look from his mother.

Mr. Blackthorne gave a crooked grin. "I just established my own law practice in St. Albans."

Michael stiffened, and even Oliver stopped eating in surprise. It was not every day that a gentleman went into trade. Oliver gave Cecilia a smug "I told you they were poor" look. Cecilia ignored him, for she knew how personally Michael would take this. He was a proud man, working hard to finance his estate on his own.

"You could have told me what you were doing," Michael said without emotion. "Doesn't it take several years of apprenticeship?"

"I recently finished articling with a well-established solicitor." Mr. Blackthorne hesitated. "I wanted to tell you in person. I've been fascinated by the legal work for the estate, and I decided it was something I wished to pursue."

"So you're enjoying it?" Michael asked doubtfully.

Mr. Blackthorne's grin widened. "I'm enjoying the challenge of it and the work involved. It seems I prefer to be busy most of the day." He glanced at Oliver. "You must understand that, my lord, with the breadth of the earldom you've inherited."

"It's important to surround yourself with knowledgeable people," Oliver answered neutrally.

Mr. Blackthorne nodded. "I've found that to be very true."

Cecilia didn't mind that Oliver avoided mention of the duties she performed. She'd never wanted to embarrass him, only to help him until he was prepared. Michael was right—she hadn't been preparing him well enough, only coddling him.

Lady Blackthorne turned to Cecilia, as if she was anxious to change the conversation from her son's legal practice. "Regardless of things that have been said, I want you to truly believe how glad I am that my son has chosen a bride. I will admit that my marriage was not a happy one, and I lived in fear that my experiences soured Michael on the institution itself. He was always such a sensitive child."

Michael rolled his eyes as Mr. Blackthorne guffawed, and even Oliver grinned. Cecilia knew her bright eyes must betray her, but she struggled to stay serious for her husband's sake.

"Sensitive, Lady Blackthorne? I would be so pleased to hear stories of what my husband was like then."

"Oh, he was very sensitive," Mr. Blackthorne said, struggling to keep from smiling. "So sensitive that he thrashed me when we were pretending to fence with long sticks, so sensitive that he swam in the pond or rowed until exhaustion so he could defeat every other boy in the parish."

Michael calmly continued eating as if he was used to being teased and had long since lost that sort of sensitivity. Cecilia was surprised how much she enjoyed this glimpse into his past, and how relaxed she was becoming among his family. Her family now. When Michael returned to India, she would at least have family to visit, his brother's children to spoil, along with Oliver's children.

After luncheon, she suggested a walk in the garden to see the grounds. Lady Blackthorne fussed over Michael's leg. His face reddened with exasperation, and he overruled his mother's concern. Oliver escaped the outing with "a pressing matter," and she gave him a warning look. He should be there that evening for Michael's family.

When Michael opened the conservatory doors that led to the terrace, he paused on the threshold and eyed Cecilia, saying in a voice meant only for her, "Stay by my side at all times."

"Do you think someone would actually shoot at us?" she whispered in disbelief. "Every attack has looked so . . . accidental."

"Do you know how many people 'accidental' hunting mishaps kill?"

Her eyes widened, and she swallowed. "Oh."

He glanced back at the house, even as they led his family outside. "I wish your brother had come with us."

She stiffened, and said coolly, "Nonsense. I have nothing to fear from him, and I wish you'd stop saying so."

She noticed Lady Blackthorne watching them and gave her a pleasant smile, even as she slid her hand into Michael's arm and briefly leaned her head against his solid shoulder.

"I don't wish to argue, not today," she begged quietly.

He patted her hand. "Of course."

But he didn't smile, and it took everything in her to keep a pleasant expression. Luckily, Mr. Blackthorne began to ask her questions about the estate, and she appreciated the distraction. Forgetting herself, she discussed the mill expansion, the state of the stables, and how many tenants their country seat held versus the other properties.

When, at last, they paused at the gazebo overlooking the pond, Lady Blackthorne said, "My lady, you have incredible knowledge of your brother's property."

"It . . . is a fascination of mine," Cecilia said, blushing. "I try to help Lord Appertan whenever he needs it. Now let's continue walking this path, so you can see the Roman temple my ancestor envisioned."

Michael's mouth twitched as he contained his laughter, while Cecilia simply ignored him and began to point out the landscaping. She was relieved he was over his pique with her, but was beginning to imagine the evening ahead, and what he'd expect of her, now that they were permanently married.

Chapter 18

That night, Cecilia relaxed in her bathing tub, trying to think of nothing at all. But that seldom worked for her, and it didn't now. She had to deliberately call to mind farming chores so she wouldn't think about Michael in the next room.

Which fields would lie fallow during the next spring planting?

Michael, naked, leaning over her in bed, inside her, surrounding her.

She groaned aloud, slapped her hands on the surface of the water, and sank beneath. When she came up, she heard the door to the dressing room slam open.

Michael demanded, "What was that sound?"

And then he came up short as he stared at her.

Nell giggled from somewhere behind her. "Shall I leave you for the evenin', milord?"

"It's not his decision," Cecilia said sternly.

"Please do, Nell, and thank you," Michael answered as if she hadn't spoken.

Frowning, Cecilia sank even lower in the water as Nell's laughter could be heard in the corridor as she closed the door.

And then there was silence. She couldn't look at Michael, only at the soap on the surface of the water. The room was dark, lit only with candles. She prayed he couldn't see beneath the surface.

But he'd already seen everything—kissed her breasts, entered her body, for heaven's sake! *Now* she was being shy?

Michael limped slowly toward her, that tender smile softening his face, the one that melted her insides, tempted her to forget all her promises about how she wanted to live her life.

And in that moment, she realized how easy it would be to agree to anything he wanted, to make him happy. And she might be happy, too—at first. And then the regrets would come.

"I like your mother," she said a bit breathlessly.

He blinked at her, and she realized the introduction of his family as a topic was hardly conducive to romance. She decided to jump right in.

"Can you tell me why your parents' marriage was so unhappy?"

With a sigh, he pulled up a chair next to her and sank into it. She felt like she'd temporarily won, but, of course, she'd have to leave the tub sometime, and he'd be waiting.

Michael sighed. "I've already told you much of the truth—or you've guessed. I vowed never to marry for money, and it was because of my father's and grandfather's decisions where their wives were concerned. They foolishly pursued wealth rather than happiness, and when the money was gone, there was no foundation on which to base a marriage. Everyone was miserable, and when I realized that my father was trying to lead me the same way, I decided that I would seek my fortune in the Far East, beginning with the army, and using the meager earnings left after supporting the estate to invest in shipping and exports."

"And you're so proud of that, I imagine it shocked you that your brother became a lawyer."

"It had nothing to do with pride," he insisted, leaning toward her fervently. "I was worried that if he felt the need to supplement the estate's income, then I'd let them down, that I'd taken too long—ten years now— trying to improve our situation. He deserved better. I remember having to make our own bullets as boys, share the same horse. He never complained."

Cecilia suspected that Michael never did either.

"But he seems happy with his choices," he continued, "and who am I, an army ranker, to tell him what he can or can't do? But it will limit his ability to marry well."

"So did enlisting in the army, but it doesn't seem to have hurt you," she said dryly. She tried to decide what part of her body would best be covered by the facecloth.

When he gave a crooked smile, she hastily said, "But back to your mother. Did she know she'd been used for her dowry?"

"Surely you have friends who worried about such things, and perhaps even you. I believe a woman would know if there was no love involved, don't you?"

She nodded, remembering more than one friend who had accepted a marriage arranged by parents. "I never thought that would happen to me, of course," she said wryly. "I knew my father would never force me into such an arrangement—and yet just by praising you, it was as if he deliberately led me right to you." She shook her head even as she smiled.

"Isn't that a good thing?" he asked softly, pulling his chair a bit closer.

She sank deeper into the tub, and the water sloshed near the rim. "You're certain you don't think of that young lady your father chose for you?"

"I don't even remember her name." His expression sly, he murmured, "You have gooseflesh. It must be getting cold in there."

"Oh, no, I am quite content and relaxed," she said, too quickly. "So your mother accepted the marriage, even though she knew your father didn't love her?"

Michael grinned, but his amusement faded. "She was one of the women with no choice. Once, when he was drunk, my father told me even he didn't want to marry her, but for the money."

She stared at him in bewilderment. "But she seems like a wonderful woman, and you obviously were raised well by her."

"She is wonderful, but from what my father accidentally told me, I think she was considered fast."

Cecilia caught her breath.

"I understand that it's shocking. You'd never know it to meet her. Her father wanted to be rid of her, thought she encouraged young men, and there were whispers that she'd done even more than that."

"Oh, Michael, how terrible for you to hear such things. I don't like your father very much for repeating them."

"He'd never been a man who could be satisfied with a decent life. He always wanted more—more excitement, more money, more respect. You don't achieve respect behaving as he did. As for my mother . . . I don't know how immature she was as a young woman. But she became a wonderful mother, and tolerant of my father, at least in front of us."

He seemed as if he might say more but simply thinned his lips and stared unseeing across the room. Cecilia could only be amazed at how serene and uncomplaining his mother was compared to her own, when the lady had obviously come down in the world.

"I know I wanted all my inheritance for my control

of the earldom," she began slowly, "and I understand that you don't want my dowry because of the things your family has been through. But, Michael, what if you used some of the dowry to purchase an officer's commission?" When he frowned, she went on quickly. "You would earn more money for your family, and I'm sure the connections would help the various enterprises you've begun investing in."

"Thank you, but no. I am content with the life I've made for myself."

She nodded, hoping that making the offer would help her feel better about what she owed him and his family. And also, she almost hoped the whole conversation would put him in a bad mood.

But apparently not, for suddenly he braced his weight on the rim of the tub behind her, then dipped the fingers of his other hand in the soap bubbles floating before her.

She inhaled swiftly. "Michael, surely you can have a bathing tub sent to your bedchamber."

"But there's one right here."

She couldn't stop staring at his hand as if mesmerized. He made slow circles in the bubbles, coming ever closer to her breasts.

"I could scrub your back," he whispered.

She tipped her head back and stared up at him, feeling like she couldn't breathe deeply enough the way his eyes gleamed down upon her. Her body seemed to be coming awake, as if the memories of his lovemaking had lain dormant all day and were now fanned hotly to life by the sight of his eagerness to have her.

He suddenly stood up and pulled his shirt over his head. "What the hell; I could just get in with you."

Shocked and panicky, she surged to her feet without thinking, "No, no, I'm done, it's all yours."

As water sluiced down her body, he laughed and wrapped her in a towel, swinging her into her arms and toward the bed.

"I see how eager you are," he whispered even as he nuzzled her neck and kissed her there. "I'll have my bath later, and maybe I can persuade you to join me."

He set her down on the edge of the bed and began to pat her dry. She felt silly and embarrassed and hot with the desire she felt for him, the desire she could no longer deny.

And then he kissed her, tipping her backward and coming down over her body, exploring her mouth deeply, luring her tongue into his own. With a moan, she gave up trying to pretend she could keep him away from her. He was a man, with a man's needs, and she was his wife. She wrapped her arms about him and kissed him back with a fierce urgency. She moaned as he began to lick the water from her skin, trailing down her body. She cried out when his tongue teased her nipples, and she could have gloried in that forever, but he kept moving down her body, exploring her belly, spreading her thighs.

She stiffened as he knelt at the edge of the bed, staring right at her—there. She came up on her elbows. "Michael, what are you—"

"Relax," he interrupted. "I was in such a rush to have you last night, I didn't explore."

"Oh, that's all right. It's not necessary." She heard herself babbling, even as she trembled with expectation and curiosity and desperation. "In fact, it's been a long day. You must be tired."

He chuckled against her belly, then he said nothing as he moved lower and pressed an intimate kiss between her thighs.

Her hips jolted beneath him, and she covered her mouth to stop her cries. She should stop *him,* but she was overwhelmed and stunned, shocked by the fierce pleasure of his tongue licking her, even *inside* her. She existed in a haze of rising pleasure, shuddering, desperate for the joy she knew awaited her. And it came so suddenly, pouring over her, leaving her gasping and languid beneath him.

He straightened up and leaned over her, grinning.

"You look proud of yourself," she whispered.

"Oh, I am. There's nothing to compare to pleasing one's wife."

She couldn't help smiling at his silliness, even as a secret place in her heart thrummed with a hint of sadness.

He removed the rest of his clothing as she scooted

back into the center of the bed. Crawling on all fours above her, he kissed her over and over until she almost begged him to come inside her. He eased between her thighs and gently claimed her. She gasped in awe at how wonderful it felt to have him deep inside her, as if he could be a part of her forever.

"No pain?" he whispered against her mouth.

She shook her head. "None."

"Good," he breathed in obvious relief.

And then he began to move, sometimes sweeping her away in his urgency and power, other times moving so slowly that she lifted her hips off the bed to capture him. Everything made her ache in new and wondrous ways, and she reveled in it all, even as she knew it could only be temporary.

When Michael awoke before dawn, he tensed, waiting for his wife to flee their bed as she had the day before. But she was still asleep, and he was able to prop himself up on his elbow and study her. Her complexion was not as pale as other English beauties because she preferred to walk the land rather than remain indoors. But he liked that. He lifted a strand of golden hair and inhaled, smelling the elusive, floral scent that he would forever associate with her.

She blinked drowsily and opened her eyes, and he relaxed when she didn't seem surprised to see him. In that moment, as he yearned for her to smile at him, he knew he was falling in love with her, and it had nothing to do with a debt to his past. It was all about the woman she was and how he could no longer imagine his life without her. But what should be a joyous feeling was instead brimming with uncertainty, for although she tolerated him, even desired him, all of it was still very reluctant. Even if she had tender feelings for him, she would never admit it, and it would scare her away if he admitted his own.

She wasn't ready to share thoughts and hopes. He found himself wanting to talk about his brother's law practice, and his concern that Allen would have less time for managing the Blackthorne estate. Cecilia would be the perfect one to take over the work—but she wasn't ready to hear that. She was too focused on her brother.

So he smiled and saved the discussion for a later time. "Good morning, my sweet."

He waited for her to object to the endearment, but instead, she gave him a faint frown.

"You dreamed in the night," she murmured, looking troubled.

He silently cursed the dreams of his fallen comrades, over which he had no control. "I am sorry I disturbed you."

"No, please, you didn't call out or toss around—much. I'm . . . simply not used to someone else being in my bed."

She blushed and briefly looked away, pulling the counterpane closer to her chin like one of the shields on the drawing-room wall that used to guard her ancestors.

"What were you dreaming about?" she asked.

He shrugged and sat up as if to stretch out his back. He couldn't look at her as he misled her. "I don't really remember. Battles, I think. Nothing to speak of."

"It must be terrible to risk your life every day."

She laid her palm low on his back, comforting him. For the first time, he realized he didn't want to tell her about his part in her father's death. But . . . if he was so certain he'd made an honest mistake, and didn't feel guilty, why didn't he wish to tell her? He'd never considered that before.

"Skill and training help a man reduce his risk," Michael said almost absently.

"And you seem a very dedicated sort of man."

Now he heard amusement in her voice, and turned back to study her. She was staring at his torso, at the muscles she probably wasn't used to seeing if her smile was any indication. But then that faded, and he knew she was seeing the scars.

He gestured to them impatiently. "These were wounds of the flesh, none deep. More annoyances than anything else."

"You could have died of infection," she chastised him.

"Perhaps, but I didn't."

He was the one who left the bed first.

Cecilia sat up and watched her husband, feeling even more intrigued now that she'd made love to him twice. She felt she knew him so much more . . . personally, intimately.

And she knew he was holding something back, something about the dreams. It might be something as simple as wanting to keep the dangerous details from her innocent ears, she thought with annoyance. But it wasn't just that. What didn't he want her to know about the dreams?

As he drew on his trousers, she changed the subject. "Though you never rebuked me, I did invite your family to my home, where someone is trying to—harm me. I never thought I might be putting them in danger. They didn't seem . . . real to me, when I was trying to discover the truth about you."

He came back to the bed and looped his arm around the bedpost. "I know. And I do not fear for them here."

"Why not?"

"Because I recently had a discussion with your brother about security. Since your fall into the hole, we've increased the patrols of the watchmen. Tom and

Will have been taking turns in the family wing at night in the corridors."

She slowly smiled. "You thought to discuss it with my brother? Thank you."

He shrugged, and she knew he still didn't trust him, but Oliver was the earl.

When Nell knocked on the door, Michael departed after reminding Cecilia that they would go down to breakfast together. Of course, he was dressed before her and waiting patiently in the corridor to escort her downstairs.

"I seem to remember your waiting for me here before," she said.

"You were trying to elude your husband," he replied, shaking his head.

"If it weren't for this mysterious villain, I would be feeling a bit crowded."

His expression briefly clouded, and she knew she had pricked him. But what else was she supposed to do? They'd never have an idyllic marriage. Regardless of what happened between them in bed, by the light of day they would have to separate. It was best to remember that.

Michael's family joined them at breakfast, although Oliver, as usual, did not. His "pressing matter" of the previous evening had probably brought him home in the wee hours before dawn.

Lady Blackthorne had more questions about Cecilia

herself, as if she wanted to learn everything she could about her new daughter-in-law.

"It must have been very exciting to spend much of your childhood in another country," Lady Blackthorne said with awe.

Cecilia shrugged. "Perhaps. When I was much younger, I thought it an adventure, of course."

She saw Michael glance at her sharply, as if with all her denials, he never imagined she might once have appreciated it.

"My mother wanted to be with my father at all times, so we did not await him in Bombay but followed his regiment wherever it went."

Mr. Blackthorne actually whistled as he stared at her and buttered his toast at the same time.

"We traveled jungles and mountains, waited anxiously behind lines at every engagement." She didn't realize her voice was growing softer with each word as her mind flew back to those dreaded hours, when they wondered if her father lived. She gave a start and forced a smile for her mother-in-law. "My father seemed to have luck on his side."

"Not luck," Michael said. "Talent and intuition. He had a gift for practically reading the mind of the enemy. He seemed to know their intentions before they did and concocted the perfect response, never needlessly cruel, never too timid. He had the respect of his men, his superiors, and the enemy."

Cecilia gazed at him with gratitude, touched.

"The two of you did not meet in those days?" Lady Blackthorne asked.

Michael shook his head. "Cecilia and her mother escorted young Lord Appertan home to attend Eton. After that, she was there sporadically, and we never met. I did meet your mother once, though," he told Cecilia.

"I had not realized," she murmured. "My mother was devoted to my father and did not like to be long parted from him." That sounded so . . . innocent, so simplistic, when the truth was more complicated. Instead, she thought about how Michael had tried to make things easier by not mentioning Gabriel. But her brother deserved to be remembered. So she told them about her little brother's bravery in saving her life, and the loss of his own.

By the end of Cecilia's story, Lady Blackthorne was dabbing her eyes with a handkerchief drawn from her sleeve. "Oh, my dear, I cannot imagine how your family coped. You poor little things—and your poor parents. There is nothing worse than outliving a child. But ah, your Gabriel had such heart."

Cecilia nodded. "My mother was never the same," she admitted, thinking back. "Yes, she came back to England with us at first, but it was so obvious she feared for my father, and that she longed to be with him. And from what my father used to write, when she was with him, she lived in fear for Oliver and me. It was as if she couldn't decide where she needed to be." But being with her father had won out because of all her mother's insecurities. She and Oliver had both needed her, but it had not mattered.

"India killed my mother at last," she heard herself say.

There was a pregnant silence, and she looked around in surprise. Lady Blackthorne's soft eyes were full of sympathy, Mr. Blackthorne's with interest. Michael seemed . . . distant.

"It was a fever," Cecilia explained, spreading her hands. "She was always susceptible to the illnesses there, but she wouldn't leave. I was with her." Now that she'd started, it was as if she couldn't stop, and she knew it was all aimed at Michael, so he'd understand. "I nursed her, and she suffered terribly. My father felt that India and even his career killed her in the end. He was never quite the same after that. He wanted me home with Oliver, where I could take care of him, and we'd have each other."

Michael had known she'd suffered in India, but as they stared at each other, he knew in his heart what she was saying—that she had too many terrible memories of India, that she needed him to know she wouldn't change her mind. He saw India as a country of promise, a way for him to know success he'd never had before, and to her, it was about death and loss. Three members of her family had died there—and he'd been the cause of the last. If he told her . . . she'd include him in all that loss, and their marriage might never recover.

Withholding his past hadn't seemed so important, but he'd realized, after she'd mentioned his dreams, that he was almost lying by not telling her. Could he continue to do that if he loved her? He still remembered how tenderly and sweetly she'd watched him as he talked of her father's bravery, but that tenderness wasn't for him.

Chapter 19

It rained most of the day, and Cecilia fully expected to find indoor amusements for Michael's family, but to her surprise, he took the lead, playing billiards with his brother, then the both of them teaching her to play, while their mother laughed and made her own suggestions. Oliver stopped in for this, amused but not sarcastic, and for a brief time, Cecilia forgot her worries and simply enjoyed having family around her again.

Even as Michael made plans to visit his family soon, and she was included, she didn't know if it would work out that way. Perhaps he still thought he could make her fall in love with him, make her lose every dream she had for herself and the estates. That simply wouldn't happen.

And they got through another day without an attack, and she thanked God fervently.

That night, she reminded herself to keep her distance from Michael, that they couldn't ever have the different types of marriage they each wanted. But she still ended up in bed with him, exploring new ways to pleasure each other, turning off her thoughts and just letting herself feel.

He fell asleep first, and she lay wide-awake, aching over the future. She knew when he started to dream, felt him twitch in his sleep, heard mumbling she couldn't decipher. She turned up the light on the lamp. His face was etched with anguish, and she gently shook his shoulder. He came awake so fast, she gasped and gave a little jump.

"Is something wrong?" he demanded, sitting up with a pistol in his hand.

She stared openmouthed. "No . . . no, nothing's wrong with me. W-where did you get that?"

He exhaled, then slowly slid the gun back beneath his pillow. "I was hardly going to leave you unprotected," he said mildly. "I didn't think you needed to see the weapon."

She swallowed and stared at his pillow, reminding herself that he probably spent much of his life with a weapon close at hand. He saw nothing wrong with it—but for her, it was a scary reminder of how dangerous her life had become.

"Cecilia?" he said curiously. "You woke me for something?"

She dragged her gaze from the pillow and met his. "You were dreaming again."

He seemed to search her face, his expression one of hesitancy and sorrow.

"What is it?" she whispered, touching his arm. "You can tell me."

He closed his eyes. "I didn't want to burden you with any of this."

"How could your dreams be a burden?"

He shook his head. "The dreams are only a result. I've told myself over and over that we made the best decision we could, the honorable decision. And I've lived with it, as I've had to live with so many things done in war in the name of England."

Still holding his arm, she felt his tension. He covered her hand with his own.

"But a decision made in battle impacted so many lives, including yours and your brother's. I thought I didn't feel guilty because I helped make the best decision we could at the moment. But we were wrong, Cecilia, and lives were lost—including your father's."

She inhaled even as she felt the pang of loss.

He ran his hand through his hair. "Because of your father's death, you've had to leave behind the life of a woman and take over for your brother. Appertan no longer has his father's guidance to grow into a good man. And when I saw this, I realized that my actions affected so many things. I'm so sorry, Cecilia." He whispered the last in a husky voice full of regret.

She had to swallow the lump that seemed to grow

in her throat. "Tell me, Michael. I want to know, even if it hurts us both. But wait." She slid from the bed, no longer quite so embarrassed at being nude but not wanting to be so while hearing whatever terrible thing Michael blamed himself for. Once she donned her dressing gown, she turned around to find him buttoning his trousers, then limping toward her.

"Do you need your cane?" she asked.

He shook his head as if in irritation, but she knew him well enough to know he simply wanted to tell her the truth immediately, now that he'd made up his mind.

He stared down at her, his expression serious rather than containing his old impassivity. "We were escorting prisoners, Rothford, Knightsbridge, myself, and a small contingent of soldiers. At the time, we were told our prisoners had been thieves, men, women, and even children, and we saw how hungry they were, thought they were trying to save their families as best they could. But others in command believed they knew more information than they were letting on. We were ordered to escort them to a compound, well hidden from most of the world, a place where secrets were . . . extracted."

She crossed her arms over her chest, feeling a chill raise gooseflesh. "That sounds ominous."

"It is, but sometimes one must do unsavory things in pursuit of justice. We didn't feel that this band of several dozen, half-starved villagers posed any threat— and that was our first mistake. They deceived us,

Cecilia. They deceived us, and we made the decision to let them go."

She didn't say anything—what could she say? She saw how he regretted the mistake, knew it had been made to the best of his ability.

"Those 'starving villagers' came back with reinforcements and attacked. Three good men died—including your father."

She bowed her head, and in some ways, it was as if the grief was fresh again. But she knew it was fresh for Michael, too.

"Rothford and Knightsbridge are back in England to make amends to the families of the other two dead soldiers," Michael continued softly. "They felt a debt of guilt, while I told myself it was one of honor."

A debt? Even now, was she simply a debt to him? But she couldn't want more.

"Everything I've ever learned told me that guilt is a wasted emotion on the battlefield, that decisions have to be made without overthinking them, or lives would be lost. I told myself I would never let emotion hold sway over me. Yet I couldn't watch women and children disappear into that compound. Men died because of my decision, Cecilia, and I see the impact on you and your brother. I thought I kept this secret to protect you, but I realized that if I didn't want to speak of it, there must be a reason. And it's guilt and shame. I'm so sorry, Cecilia. Words are inadequate to what I've cost you."

He gripped her upper arms and stared down at her with the naked emotion of regret and sorrow etching lines in his face.

She wondered if she should feel angry or affronted, but nothing could replace her terrible sadness. "You were fighting a war, Michael," she said tiredly. "You made the best choice you could. Could you control everything that happened afterward, every choice other men made during battle? If you think so, you're arrogant as well as proud."

He slowly sank down onto the chaise longue, and she did the same, so that side by side they stared into the gloom and shadows, into the past. She knew that Michael was a man who grew up learning to hide his emotions, and he'd become a master at it. Somehow, being there with her and Oliver had raised his doubts to a new level, giving her the chance to see into his very soul.

She turned on the chaise until their knees touched and she could look into his face. "You can't blame yourself for Oliver's behavior."

He thinned his lips. "And why can't I? He was forced to become the earl at eighteen."

"His behavior started long before my father's death. In some ways, Gabriel's death changed everything. It was hard enough for me to accept, but when a twin dies, half of the whole . . . it made him alone in the world for the first time. I think Oliver was overly determined to have his own way because now he had to do it all himself. And our mother was no use to him."

"Why not?" Michael asked.

"If anything, she drove Oliver into selfishness because she was so very good at it. Everything in her life was about her need to have Papa nearby, whatever the consequences. She seemed to think she would lose him otherwise though he'd never given her reason to believe so—or so I've assumed." She regarded him thoughtfully.

Michael shook his head. "I never saw your father even look at another woman."

Cecilia tried to smile. "I knew that. But my mother could never believe it, and that is an insecurity that Oliver shares, and selfishness is his way to overcome it."

"Could selfishness drive your brother to do things he'd never considered before?"

She shivered, knowing what Michael was asking. "I just don't see why," she whispered at last. "I'd give him control of anything he wanted."

"Does he know that, Cecilia?" Michael asked gravely. "Or would he be justified in thinking you don't trust him."

"Trust him?" She stood up swiftly. "Of course I trust him! I'm the one telling *you* he's innocent."

"But maybe he feels you *don't* trust him, that you'll spend the rest of your life looking over his shoulder."

"That's not true," she said, feeling almost queasy. But was it? "I've told you I'm going to have nothing to do with the estate for a day after your family leaves. But I want him to know he can ask me questions. Is that wrong?"

"Though I wish I could tell you, Cecilia, it's obvious my judgment is as flawed as the next man's. But I think you're doing the right thing beginning to step back."

She shrugged. "Sometimes I wonder if Oliver is . . . hiding something that's affected him more than he could ever tell me."

Michael studied her in surprise. "And you've never asked him?"

"I've only recently had this nagging thought, and I can't shake it. I—I didn't tell you because part of me feared he was hiding his involvement in the attacks on me. But now . . . I don't think so. It's something else. And I'm going to discuss it with him." She lifted her chin resolutely.

Michael frowned. "I'm not certain it's a good idea to antagonize him."

"I won't do that. I will simply ask as a concerned sister. Maybe he'll tell me something that will convince me he's innocent of attempted murder."

"I'd like to be there."

"No."

"Cecilia, I'm not leaving you alone with him."

She closed her eyes, wondering how her life had

become so warped that even her own brother might be a danger. "We'll see. Or maybe you can be nearby on the terrace, as you were that day the ladies from Enfield visited."

He nodded, and they remained quiet for several minutes, both thinking their own thoughts.

"I can't believe you have no harsh words for me," he said at last, lifting both her hands in his.

"You have punished yourself enough," she answered. "My father loved you like a son, and he would be the first to understand."

Gently, he drew her into his arms. "Cecilia—"

He said her name with aching tenderness, then simply stopped.

"Yes?" she whispered.

He turned his head until they were face-to-face, then kissed her softly. "Thank you."

When they returned to bed, he fell into what seemed like a dreamless sleep, while she lay awake, wondering what he'd meant to say, feeling both relieved and mournful that he hadn't said it.

But Michael didn't fall asleep as quickly as he'd wanted. He could not believe how easily Cecilia had taken the news that her father had died because of his poor decision. In some ways, he didn't feel he deserved her understanding, and in others, he was so grateful as to feel ridiculously weak about it. He'd almost shown his gratitude by confessing his love for her, and that would have been a mistake. Their relationship was yet fragile, and its continuation in no way certain. So much depended on the resolution of who was trying to harm her. Michael couldn't hurry that along without going to the constable, and she would have none of it, not if there was a chance her brother—or even his reputation—could be harmed.

That left Michael feeling frustratingly on the defensive, never on attack, forced to ask inadequate questions and simply wait, hoping to intercept the next attack and discover the truth.

In the morning, he saw his family off and was glad they seemed in good spirits at the thought of exchanging visits. He didn't discuss his eventual departure for India since so many things were as yet unresolved. But he wouldn't be having a country squire's marriage of parties and balls and land management. He and Cecilia both knew it.

When they returned to the house, they discovered Oliver about to leave, as if he could escape his agreement to assume his duties for the day. He complained he was invited to a race, and Michael remained silent, watching with relief as Cecilia held firm in her resolve to begin handing over control of the estate.

"Now I have a meeting with Mrs. Ellison in regard to some renovations in the bachelor wing," Cecilia said. "You'll be hosting plenty of house parties when you marry, Oliver. Penelope will want the old castle ready."

And then she left, escorted by Talbot, who'd already promised Michael he would remain near Cecilia at all times.

Michael turned to Appertan. "Your steward would like to meet with you, my lord. Also, a petty session will be held in Enfield this afternoon, and you can see how the local magistrates handle their duties, for you should be assuming that role as well. Would you like me to accompany you?"

"How else will you report to Cecilia?" he asked grimly.

Appertan followed him to the study, where his steward and secretary waited. The morning went well, and Appertan seemed in decent spirits at luncheon. Cecilia didn't ask any estate questions, and neither did Appertan, as if a truce had been declared on business discussions.

Michael studied his wife, knowing how difficult it must be for her to relinquish the work she had such pride in. He prayed that she'd be able to find her own useful life when Appertan no longer needed her. Michael thought of the adventures they could have together in India with a sadness that took on more and more resignation.

It was the afternoon in the magistrate's petty session that turned everything on its head. He and Appertan were observing several cases, and the younger man yawned occasionally to get his point across, though he

seemed interested in spite of himself. But during the
case of a young husband taken to task for failing to support his wife and child, Appertan suddenly said he'd had
enough and left. Gritting his teeth, Michael followed the
earl, seeing the looks from offended townspeople, hearing the whispers. As they rode their horses home, he
tried to engage the young man in conversation, but Appertan appeared deep into his own troubled thoughts.
There could be so many reasons for his behavior.

Back at the Hall, Talbot nodded as they came through
the main door. Miss Webster emerged solemnly from
the drawing room along with Cecilia, who glanced at
Michael with concern. Appertan swore softly under his
breath.

Miss Webster, pale and distraught, dropped into a
stiff curtsy. "My lord, it seems you have once again
forgotten an appointment at my home. My parents were
expecting you."

Appertan smiled briefly at her even as he moved past
her into the drawing room, directly toward the decanter
of brandy on a sideboard. Cecilia opened her mouth as
if to protest, then slowly closed it. Michael hoped she
was starting to realize that by trying to be everything
to him—sister, mother, guardian—she wasn't helping.

Appertan turned to Miss Webster. "Forgive me, Penelope. I was seeing to my estates and attending the
magistrate's petty session in Enfield."

She nodded. "It is your duty, of course."

"Next time I will consult with my secretary first."

Michael felt like rocking back on his heels. That would be an improvement. One afternoon watching a father's irresponsibility had been some kind of last straw? It seemed hard to believe.

Appertan turned to him. "My thanks for your assistance today, Blackthorne. And now, Penelope and I would like to speak alone."

"Of course," Michael said, holding out his arm to Cecilia.

She looked as if she would balk but finally linked her arm with his and left. "We'll leave the door open for Penelope's sake," she said quietly.

And then Appertan closed the door behind them.

Cecilia whirled around, outraged that Oliver would be so thoughtless on Penelope's behalf. She'd just spent an hour consoling the crying girl, and her foolish brother might just make everything worse.

"There's nothing you can do," Michael said softly. "Come to the study, where I can tell you what happened today."

She hesitated, then followed him, gritting her teeth. Once they were alone, she erupted. "You should have seen that poor girl's face when I said Oliver was gone. Her father is threatening to call off the engagement, even though Oliver is an earl! He spends *no* time with her—why did he even become engaged?"

Michael sighed. "He might want what every young

man wants, Cecilia, which with a proper young woman, he can't have without marriage."

She winced. "Surely he's had women before. If he has urges—he could have quietly taken care of that."

"Rowlandson says he doesn't regularly patronize the women of the demimonde, or even the loose women he was going to bring into the house last week."

"So you're saying he might simply want to be with Penelope, and couldn't find a way to do so without making a formal offer?"

Michael shrugged. "Many men have done the same." He glanced in the direction of the drawing room. "I'm glad Talbot is still nearby. I feel better about Penelope's safety."

Cecilia flinched as if he'd struck her. "I hope you don't expect me to . . . *warn* her about something I don't believe is true!"

"We can't go on like this, my sweet. I'm going to need to talk to him honestly, and not just ask if he's having a problem."

"You want to tell him you think he's trying to kill me?" she cried, backing away.

"His behavior is suspicious. He had decent ideas and questions when we were with his steward, but at court this afternoon, he couldn't control himself enough to remain still. We left early. Something is very wrong, and we need to know."

"You really think he's the culprit?" she whispered,

hugging herself, feeling a wave of despondency. "Did you ever think it's not so much about me as it is the money and power of the estate that's tempting someone to do these awful things? Oliver doesn't need me out of the way to have any of it."

"But he might think so."

"You don't have proof! Let's—let's see what happens if I back away completely, let it seem as if you're taking my place in influence with my brother."

He hesitated, then said slowly, "A brilliant idea. And there's a chance it will lessen the danger for you."

"That's not why I'm suggesting it! I don't want you in any danger either. But if I can prove to you it's about the money and power, rather than about me personally, then perhaps we can find a way to prove it's not Oliver. We can find the person trying to control the earldom, and then—and then—" She broke off, staring at Michael and realizing what was different. "You're not using your cane at all anymore."

"No," he said quietly.

She straightened her shoulders. "Things can go back to normal."

"What's 'normal,' my sweet?"

She could have cried at the tenderness in his voice.

"Is it you helping your brother rather than being a wife to me?"

"You married me knowing we'd never have a real marriage, Michael," she said desperately.

He gathered her into his arms. "This is real to me, Cecilia, you're real. My wife, my responsibility."

"You'll return soon to India. Many people only see each other once or twice a year," she insisted. Was she trying to convince herself?

"And that will be good enough for you? What if you're carrying my child?"

She stared up at him, not knowing what to say. She wanted to beg him to stay, even if it meant giving up the career he found the most rewarding. And, eventually, he might begin to resent her for making the choice.

Was *she* supposed to make the choice? Any choice seemed unfair to someone.

He slid his hand to her stomach. "There might be life here, Cecilia, our child. We didn't intend to feel anything for each other, but we do."

"We respect each other," she said at last. "Please respect me enough to know that I can't talk about this while our family is in turmoil."

He sighed and leaned his forehead against hers. "Our family. It sounds good to hear you say that."

They stood holding each other for a long time. She listened to the reassuring beat of his heart, wondered if there was already another heart beating between theirs, nestling inside her body. She felt . . . altered by the thought, by knowing they had responsibilities beyond themselves. That might change everything.

Chapter 20

Cecilia never imagined how difficult it was going to be to abruptly step out of the life of command she'd been living for two years. For two days, Michael dealt with Oliver, who seemed restless and distracted, while she arranged flowers, oversaw menus and the redecorating. She couldn't remember needlework stitches and would have gladly thrown the handkerchief across the room. She felt . . . useless. Of course, she was confined to Appertan Hall and couldn't invite visitors. That made it worse, for she was used to being out among people every day. A servant followed her everywhere she went, making her feel twitchy.

In her obsession with guarding her father's legacy, she'd let her close friends fall away. Now she wrote several letters, hoping to renew old ties. She had no close cousins, and Oliver's precarious place in her life frightened her, and Michael would eventually return to India. She could easily be all alone in the world. Was that what she wanted?

When she first took on Oliver's duties, she'd given no thought to the future, to what she would do when all the responsibility was taken from her. It seemed so foolish now.

As she stood at the French doors overlooking the terrace late in the day, she put a hand on her stomach. Maybe she wouldn't be alone. She hadn't thought about children before Michael, never considered she'd have the time. She'd never felt drawn to be a mother, the way some women did. But now . . . just the thought gave her hope, another person to love and cherish, a connection to Michael.

She could see Oliver and him riding in the distance, coming toward the stables. Their heads were turned as they talked to each other, and she found herself praying that Michael would have words of wisdom for Oliver, something that would help him on his path to maturity.

Then, suddenly, Michael pitched sideways and fell from the horse, the whole saddle sliding off with him. She cried out and flung open the door.

Talbot was beside her in an instant. "Lady Blackthorne, you cannot go outside."

"My husband just fell," she insisted, flinging an arm toward the park. "He might be injured."

Talbot squinted into the distance where she pointed, then sighed. "Very well, I shall accompany you."

They set off across the terrace, practically running down the marble steps that widened out onto the expanse of lawn. Cecilia hastened through the gravel paths of the garden, no longer able to see Michael and Oliver through the shrubbery.

When they emerged once more onto the lawn, her husband was on his feet, bracing himself with an arm around Oliver's shoulders. The rush of relief over-whelmed Cecilia with a sting of tears.

"Michael!" she cried.

His head swung around toward her, and even with some distance between them, she could see his frown. She didn't care. The closer they got, the more she had to tell herself not to fling her arms around him like a foolish girl.

Oh, God, am I falling in love with him?

She could see a bruise on his jaw as she stopped before him but no other damage.

Oliver spoke before she could. "Cecilia, you should have remained inside," he said with exasperation. "You're the one who's a target."

"Apparently not just me," she said between gritted teeth. "Michael, I imagine it's been a long time since you fell from a horse."

He sighed. "Someone cut the girth almost all the way through. My weight eventually completed the deed."

"And you're not hurt?" she asked, her voice embar-rassingly weak.

Michael took her hand. "Reinjured my leg," he said grimly. "Just when I'd stopped using the cane, too."

"Oh, I'm so sorry," she said—and meant it deeply. It had been her idea to turn the focus off herself, just to prove it wasn't about her.

He gave her a tight smile. "Let's get you out of the open."

Talbot took the horses back to the stables, so Oliver could help Michael back to the castle. Once Michael was settled on a sofa, his leg propped up, Oliver brought him a brandy, clinked it with his own, and downed his. Cecilia stared from one man to the other in confusion.

"Are we done for today?" her brother asked impassively.

Michael grimaced. "We are."

Oliver glanced at Cecilia. "Then I'm off to Enfield for the evening."

Michael watched Cecilia's crestfallen expression as her brother left, then the way her wide eyes came back to him. He hastened to reassure her, patting the sofa beside him.

"Truly, I'm all right, Cecilia."

She sank down beside him, then leaned against his shoulder as if in defeat. "I didn't mean for you to get hurt," she whispered. "I wanted to prove this villain was after money and power, not just me."

"And you've been proven brilliant," he said, chucking her under the chin.

She touched his thigh. "Should we call the doctor?"

"I didn't break it, only aggravated it. I know how to

take a fall. It only means a few more weeks with the cane." *A few more weeks in her company,* he thought, grateful.

She straightened up, as if it were weak to lean against one's own husband. "We must talk to the head groom and the stableboys."

"I'm sure Talbot already is. But I imagine whoever did this took care not to be seen."

"I know what you're going to say," she said, her chin jutting forward defensively. "And yes, Oliver could have done this, or had someone do it. But why? He certainly knows you don't stand between him and control of his money, whereas someone else might believe you're starting to influence Oliver too much."

"True, but perhaps this person thinks I'm beginning to control *you*." He held up both hands before she could speak. "But you could be right. Perhaps."

The hope on her face was almost painful to him. He could only imagine how it would feel if people assumed something terrible about his own brother, Allen.

Michael certainly didn't want Appertan to be a villain. Or was that his own guilt talking? Regardless of Cecilia's forgiveness, Michael still felt responsible in some ways for Appertan's plight. Consequently, was he trying to help the young man too much, just like Cecilia was?

"I know you've spoken to some of Oliver's friends," she was saying with animation. "There are so many others who might want to keep a hold on Oliver's old free-spending ways."

"I think you were right last night. We need to talk to your brother. And though you may wish otherwise, I plan to be with you. He's intelligent, and certainly not a fool. If there's manipulation involved, let's see him try it on the two of us."

Cecilia took a deep breath, then let it go. "Very well."

"Good," Michael said, leaning back on the sofa. "Shall we try to catch him before he leaves?"

She nodded, beginning to stand, but Michael didn't release her hand.

"Send one of the footmen, my sweet."

"I feel like such a prisoner," she said in disgust. "I know it's only been days, but I can't remember what it feels like to walk my own home in freedom."

"And now I have to be just as cautious," he said. "Are you glad to have company?"

She frowned at him over her shoulder as she went to the drawing-room door. When she returned, he drew her into his arms and simply held her. Soon, he wouldn't have this, only his memories. He understood everything about her now, the doubts she'd overcome because of her mother's neglect, the trauma of her brother's death, and her self-blame. Yet she'd risen above it all, becoming a wise, good woman who loved her brother regardless of what he'd done.

Michael wanted her to come with him to India, but

was that fair? *He* could be the one to make the choice, to give up the career that gave him the most fulfillment and the pride of being an independent man. He could stay here as Cecilia's husband, with little to do for his small family manor and no way to provide for his wife in the life she was used to except through her own dowry, however much supporting the estate had left of that.

Michael would be . . . a shell of a man, dishonorable. He knew the truth of guilt now. He was not used to feeling like a failure, but he could no longer deny the mistakes he'd made. He had to support his wife and family, and the best way was in India. His estate simply did not yield enough revenue on its own.

He would never force her to follow the drum, after what she'd experienced as a child. So they'd live separately, except for a brief month or two each year.

And his own child, if she conceived? Michael would barely know him or her.

Cecilia spent an hour in the drawing room with her husband, awaiting Oliver. Her brother had been taking a bath in preparation for the evening and agreed to give them a half hour of his time with great reluctance, if the footman Tom's hesitant explanation could be understood.

Cecilia had wanted to pace her frustrations away, still full of nervous energy that her plan had caused

Michael injury. But he had drawn her into his arms until her head settled on his chest. They rested together for long minutes. She should not feel peaceful, but in that moment, she did, and looked up at him in wonder. He kissed her gently, over and over again, soothing her until she thought she could do this forever.

"You don't look like you need to talk to me."

Cecilia jumped and turned to see her brother standing in the doorway, hands on his hips, glowering at them.

"You made us wait," Michael said simply. "We're newly wed—what else should we do?"

Oliver grimaced and turned as if to go.

"No, Oliver, please come talk to us," Cecilia called. "This is so very important."

He trudged toward them like a martyr, taking the seat opposite their sofa, with a low table between them. He couldn't seem to sit still, crossing his lower leg over his knee, then changing his mind, restlessly lacing his hands together over his stomach, then playing with the fringe that decorated the armrest. And through it all, he wouldn't meet her gaze.

She studied him, feeling a sudden calm come over her. He was in trouble, and only she could help him. Something had changed for him these last few days, and this restless nervousness of his was only a symptom. "Oliver, you know someone has been trying to harm me."

He sighed. "I didn't want to believe you at first, but now . . . the evidence is convincing."

"Do you have any idea who it might be?"

He glanced at Michael. "I'm sure you've given this much thought, being a soldier. But even you haven't come up with an answer. And I did think you had the best motivation to harm Cecilia when you first arrived."

"But now this person is targeting me," Michael said softly.

"You can take care of yourself." Oliver's tone was dismissive.

She stiffened but felt the pressure of Michael's hand on hers as if to calm her. She tried to relax.

"But Cecilia," Oliver said, turning back to her, "you don't know how to protect yourself. Perhaps I didn't want to believe the attacks were real because there's still a part of me that thinks all this"—he gestured at the room, but seemed to mean the castle—"has some kind of power to protect us. But I guess that was only true when Father was alive. He would have protected you. I've failed you, just as I failed—"

And then he broke off, staring almost bleakly into the distance. He couldn't mean Gabriel; he wasn't even with them when their brother died.

"You haven't failed me," she said quietly. "Neither Michael nor I has been able to stop these attacks."

"I should have," he said in a hoarse voice. "But I didn't want to see it. I thought . . . if I focused on myself enough, I could forget anything unpleasant. It didn't work."

"What are you trying to forget, Oliver?"

He opened his mouth, but at first nothing came out. Cecilia kept herself from leaning forward, unwilling to break the moment. Then his face wrenched into an awful grimace, and to her shock, a tear slid down his cheek.

"I did something terrible," he whispered, then rubbed the heels of his palms hard into his eyes.

Feeling ill, she told herself to be patient. She thought she might have to restrain Michael, but he was so calm as to be a statue. He radiated acceptance and ease, as if he were leaving the connection between her and Oliver alone.

"Can you tell me what you think you did?" she asked her brother.

"Do you remember the upstairs maid, Jennette, who used to work for us a few years ago?"

Baffled, Cecilia stared at him. This wasn't about the attacks? "Of course. She left our employ and moved away, rather unexpectedly."

"Not unexpectedly," he said, his voice breaking. "I paid her to go away. I'd—I'd seduced her, and she got with child."

A wrenching pain clutched Cecilia's chest as she took a swift breath, and she wanted to press her hand to her heart. "Oh, Oliver," she whispered. "Why didn't you tell me?"

"Tell you?" He gave a harsh laugh that held no amusement. "What was I supposed to say? I was seventeen and stupid. Though I knew several other men who'd done the same thing, I-I panicked, thinking of what Father would say. She didn't want me from the beginning. I made certain she felt . . . she had no choice."

Cecilia covered her mouth, trying not to show her horror that the brother she loved had done something so despicable.

He wiped a hand down his face. "By the devil, I treated her as if she weren't even a person. And when she said there was a baby . . ."

She flinched, as if with another blow.

"I was so angry." His voice trailed off, and he looked dispiritedly at the floor. "After I gave her money and sent her away, I never saw or heard from her again. I thought that would be the end of it." He lifted his head and stared hard into her face. "But I can't forget her, Cecilia. I can't forget what I did to her, or how she looked so lost when I sent her away. When I look in a mirror, I see Jennette, not me anymore."

"And you drink to forget." Her brother's past behavior began to fall into place.

"It doesn't help," he said bitterly. "When you told me what Rowlandson had done to the tavern maid—I'd done so much worse. I let you have my responsibilities so I wouldn't have to think. When Father died . . . oh God, there was a part of me that was glad he would never have to know what I'd done, how I'd betrayed our family name." He covered his face with hands that trembled.

At last, Cecilia looked at her husband. Michael's expression was grim, but he said nothing, only nodded toward her brother. Trusting her.

Oliver gave another shudder and looked up. His eyes were dry, his face haunted by a grief that suddenly made him look ten years older. "I can't go on like this. I know I've relied on you too much, Cecilia, but . . . tell me what to do to make this right again, to find some way to live with myself."

"I think we need to find Jennette," she said in a firm voice. "She's out there alone with your child. Illegitimate or not, this child needs you to provide more than whatever money you gave her. You need to support them both."

He nodded. "Yes, you're right, I know, but . . . how?"

"Let me talk with Mrs. Ellison and see if she knows where the girl went. Servants often leave forwarding addresses to have things sent."

Oliver nodded. "I can talk to her if you'd like."

"No, I—" But she stopped herself. "You're right; you should talk to her."

Oliver slapped his thighs as he stood up. "I'll do it before dinner."

He marched toward the door, and she stared after him, feeling bewildered and heartsick.

At the last moment, he turned back. "Cecilia"—he reluctantly turned his gaze upon Michael—"Blackthorne, thank you for listening, and not judging me too harshly."

"I think you've judged yourself," Michael said impassively. "Now follow through."

The words took on the tone of mild command, but Oliver only nodded and left, closing the door behind him.

Cecilia stared at the door for a long moment, then everything she'd been repressing seemed to choke up her throat. She turned into Michael's arms and buried her face in his chest, weeping. He held her for a long moment, rocking her gently.

When the storm of her emotions had calmed at last, she stared up at him with wet eyes. "I—I don't know what to say. He—he *raped* a girl when he was, what, seventeen?"

"Do you realize how often such things happen among the nobility, Cecilia? At least he's found his conscience at last. So many powerful men believe they can do whatever they want."

"Obviously, he believed it," she said bitterly. "To think he . . . he . . ." She couldn't even find the words, only stared at her husband in confusion.

"He wants to make things right." Michael gripped both her hands in his. "That's a good sign."

"Do you think with all the guilt he's been feeling,

he was the one behind what's been happening to me?" She'd thought her brother incapable of harming her, but he'd had no problem hurting Jennette.

"I don't think so," Michael said at last. "I think his treatment of the maid has been tearing him up inside, not something he might have done to you. Going to court, hearing about the man who'd abandoned his wife and babe, it must have been too much for him at last."

"I don't know what to think of him anymore," she whispered bleakly.

"We can be appalled at his lack of forethought and morals, but certainly, I am not one to judge him, after all the mistakes I made."

"Those were honest mistakes, Michael," she said earnestly. "But what Oliver did . . ." She trailed off, shaking her head. "Yet he's my brother, and I can only hope, by making amends, he becomes a better man."

And then a new thought occurred to her, and she felt a rush of cold clarity. "I remember Jennette, but not well. She was only here for a year, so I don't know the kind of woman she is. But bitterness and hatred can do terrible things to a person. Could she want revenge?"

Michael nodded slowly. "It seems plausible. She might believe you didn't try to help her—or she might think she could ruin Appertan's life by making him look guilty of your murder."

Cecilia sank back against the sofa and closed her eyes. "Oh, but she has a child, Michael, my niece or nephew. I would hate to think she was that kind of woman, for then she might not be a very good mother."

"We can't make judgments until we talk to her."

"You don't think we should let Oliver handle this alone?" she asked in surprise.

"This woman has a reason to hate our family. If Appertan confronts her poorly, it might make everything worse. It seems to me that he would welcome our support."

She sighed with relief. "Thank you. I don't think I could wait around to find out what happens. But then again, we don't even know how long it might take to find her."

"We'll hire an investigator if we have to, my sweet."

As they waited for Talbot's announcement of dinner, Cecilia studied Michael, imagining that as a soldier, he must have had to investigate any intelligence that reached his regiment. He immersed himself daily in a world where good tried to defeat evil, and evil fought back with guile. She saw the nobility and honor of such a life and felt a pang of sorrow, knowing she could never ask him to give it up.

She thought again about Jennette's situation, and the fact that she, too, could be pregnant. "Michael . . . I feel so sorry for Jennette. I can only imagine how alone she felt, how vulnerable. And then to discover that she was with child. She must have desperately wanted to protect that baby, to give it a home. If I'm pregnant . . ."

She trailed off, seeing him watch her intently. "Will our child be pulled between two worlds, just as I was?"

"Your mother made you feel like that, Cecilia," he said with quiet resolve. "And you're not your mother. Our child will know how much he's loved by both of us, regardless of our unorthodox marriage."

Unorthodox marriage, she thought sadly. She wasn't even certain what that meant.

And then Talbot announced dinner, and they followed him down the corridor to the private family dining room. Cecilia kept glancing at Michael, limping at her side, and she knew that "unorthodox marriage" meant that he would leave her. She might not be as fearful and obsessive as her mother, but, for the first time, she had an inkling of her mother's desperation not to be separated from the husband she loved. With Michael gone, her life would become as if black and white. She wouldn't have his wit, his calm strength, or the way he made her feel like the only woman in the world.

She loved him, the honor that made him regret honest mistakes, the loyalty he showed to her father and to his men. But she would never use her love to bind him to her.

The door opened, and Oliver entered the dining room, wearing a puzzled frown. He shut the door behind him and leaned back against it.

"What is it?" she asked as she rose to her feet.

She turned to help Michael, but he'd already followed her, and put a hand on the table to steady himself.

"Mrs. Ellison knows where Jennette is," Oliver said slowly, wiping his hand down his mouth.

"That's good, isn't it?" she asked.

"Penelope's family hired her."

Cecilia blinked in confusion, feeling a distant sense of unreality, a prickling of unease. "Excuse me? How could we have heard nothing of this, not seen her in Enfield?"

Oliver shrugged. "Could she have been hiding, for fear I'd send her away from the only people she knows? I might have, too," he added grimly. "I was certainly frightened enough. Mrs. Ellison says she thought nothing of Jennette's being hired by the Websters because the girl said she felt overwhelmed here and needed to work in a smaller household."

"This would have been three years ago, am I correct?" Michael asked Oliver. "And both of you have visited?"

"Numerous times," Cecilia insisted.

"And never saw Jennette or heard about a baby in the servants' hall?"

"Three years ago . . ." Cecilia suddenly murmured. "Hannah was still alive! She would have told me if she'd known anything about it."

"Why would she have told you about hiring your servant?" Michael asked. "Perhaps she was even embarrassed, as if they'd lured the girl away."

"But . . . none of this makes sense," she insisted.

"It seems we have a mystery," Michael said in his most impassive voice.

Her unease wouldn't go away. "Do you think Jennette stayed nearby to wait for the right time for revenge?"

"What?" Oliver demanded, stepping closer. "You think Jennette—" He broke off as the color drained from his face. "You think she came after you because of me?"

"Perhaps to implicate you," Michael said. "There are not many ways to punish an earl after all, unless the crime is murder."

Chapter 21

First thing in the morning, the three of them set off on horseback for the Websters' manor, barely a mile away. Michael still felt angry that Cecilia refused to remain at home, but he trusted himself to defend her more than any of the servants, so he'd relented at last. She'd been determined to reunite with Jennette, needing to look into her face for herself and see the truth. And perhaps Jennette would speak more freely to another woman.

Michael didn't bother telling her that sometimes evil could mask itself as good and get away with it. Either way, they were probably going to have to involve the constable eventually.

The sky was overcast, and a breeze chilled them. He watched his wife, who, although wearing a cloak, seemed unaffected by the weather, her expression set with determination, ready to fight the world in defense of her brother, as she'd been doing her whole life. Appertan alternated between looking pale with mortification and grim with the knowledge that his behavior could have cost Cecilia her life. Revelation of his deeds would either improve him or ruin him. Michael vowed to make sure it was the former, for the sake of both Mallory descendants—and for their father.

The manor itself was a two-story stone building, surrounded by a white fence with climbing vines that had begun to brown with the encroaching autumn. Trees swayed in the wind near the house, and a gardener could be seen working in the side garden.

After they'd been admitted to a small entrance hall, a maid went to fetch Mrs. Webster, since Mr. Webster wasn't at home. Michael surreptitiously glanced past three doors that opened off the small hall, seeing a library, a sitting room of some sort, and a corridor to the back of the house. He tried to imagine the layout in his mind, wondering where the maid Jennette would be working at the moment—and where she kept her child.

Mrs. Webster hurried from the back of the house, flustered in her plain brown day dress and crooked lace cap. She peered at them above the spectacles perched on her nose. "Oh, dear, my lord Appertan, Lady Blackthorne, Lord Blackthorne, I cannot believe you weren't shown to the parlor! Please, please, make yourself comfortable."

Michael followed his wife and her brother into a small parlor, decorated with family stitchery and amateur watercolors between traditional paintings. He re-

membered meeting Mrs. Webster at the dinner party,
but the woman had left little impression on him except
for her obvious devotion to Miss Webster, and the
glowing pride she'd evidenced at how well married her
daughter would soon be. But, of course, Miss Webster
was the only child they had left. He couldn't imagine
how it must have felt to lose their oldest daughter in
such a tragic drowning.

When they were all seated in the cozy room, Mrs.
Webster smiled overly brightly at Appertan. "My lord,
it is good of you to call upon Penelope. Luckily, she is
at home."

The young earl cleared his throat. "Mrs. Webster,
although I would be pleased to see your daughter, we
have come on another matter. I understand that you
have a maid working for you who once worked at Appertan Hall."

"Why, yes, we do," she said without embarrassment.
"Jennette. A quiet girl, who has suffered terribly. We
felt it right to hire her, when she was too embarrassed
to remain at Appertan Hall."

Mrs. Webster didn't seem to suspect that Appertan
was involved in the maid's abrupt departure.

Appertan swallowed, then straightened his shoulders. "We need to speak to Jennette, Mrs. Webster.
Would you bring her to us?"

Mrs. Webster pulled a bell cord that summoned
a plump, older woman, obviously the housekeeper,

then sent her off with the request. Michael could only imagine the maid's reaction after how Appertan had treated her. If she was innocent of the plot against Cecilia, she'd be frightened that Appertan might send her away permanently—or take her child. If Jennette was guilty . . .

Casually, while Mrs. Webster poured tea, Michael stood, ignoring the shot of pain in his leg as he leaned on his cane and limped to the window. He'd noticed the rear exit was on that side of the house, and he kept watch as if admiring the grounds. No one ran out. Mrs. Webster saw his interest and began to talk about the roses she tended all summer.

Cecilia could barely swallow, she was so nervous. Her spoon rattled against the fragile china cup as she stirred her tea. She'd almost jumped when her husband had stood up, but seeing him at the window, she understood his purpose. Her brother's knee jiggled with nervousness, and she longed to grip it, if only to stop him.

They heard two sets of footsteps in the corridor, and a shot of tension like lightning moved among the three of them. Oliver stood up so fast, he almost tipped over the cup Mrs. Webster was offering him. Baffled, she leaned back to look up, then saw visitors blocking the doorway.

Cecilia held her breath as Jennette stood beside the housekeeper. It was obvious the girl had been crying, for her face was stained with tears, and the housekeeper's blouse was covered in wet spots at the shoulder. Jennette took one look at Oliver and shuddered, averting her eyes. But that shudder wasn't one of anger, but fear.

Cecilia glanced at Mrs. Webster, wondering how she could ask the woman to leave her own parlor.

"I'm not going to hurt you," Oliver told Jennette urgently, as if he didn't care who overheard him.

Jennette trembled and held a handkerchief to her eyes and wouldn't look at him.

"Lord Appertan," Mrs. Webster began, coming awkwardly to her feet, "I don't understand what is going on. Jennette has been an exemplary servant. If you wish to hire her back, the proper etiquette suggests . . ." Her words died away as she looked from person to person. "I don't understand."

"Jennette," Oliver began, stepping forward.

The maid shrank back against the housekeeper, who put a bracing arm around the girl and glared at Oliver, all rigid disdain and disapproval. Cecilia had thought the woman simply overweight, but now she guessed she had the physique of one who'd worked hard all her life, and now she meant to protect the maid under her authority.

"Jennette, please," Cecilia began, "we don't mean to hurt you. We simply need answers."

As if she'd somehow gathered her strength, Jennette gazed at Oliver tearfully. "I knew you'd find me, but I couldn't leave. I had nowhere else to go. You must want the baby, but you can't have her!"

Mrs. Webster's mouth fell open in growing understanding, and it was hard to look at her, knowing what she now thought of Oliver—knowing what everyone would soon think. When Michael came to Cecilia's side and put an arm around her waist, she was grateful for the support.

"I haven't come to take the baby from you," Oliver insisted. "This is about my sister."

"This isn't about Lady Cecilia," Jennette said, her voice rising with hysteria. "She was good to me—but not you!"

Cecilia exchanged a glance with Michael. That didn't sound like someone who wanted to harm her.

Jennette hiccoughed on a sob, then whispered, "I should have gone farther away. But I was tired and sick, and Miss Hannah saw me on the road and insisted I come with her."

"Hannah," Cecilia breathed, feeling an ache of loss, even as she remembered her friend's compassion. Michael gently squeezed her waist.

At the mention of her daughter, Mrs. Webster put her trembling fingers against her lips and bowed her head.

"Miss Hannah said I should stay." Tears fell down Jennette's cheeks. "I—I told her about the babe, but she didn't care, God bless her. When she died, I d-didn't know if I could trust that strange Miss Penelope, but

Miss Hannah had told her everything. What choice did I have?"

Cecilia stiffened, even as she saw Oliver's look of shock. Penelope knew about his bastard? Cecilia felt a tingling down her back, an awareness of something crucial and important. Penelope had known the truth, and she'd still agreed to marry Oliver. That wasn't surprising—she would become a countess, and there were many girls who would wish for that. It wasn't just power and wealth—Penelope loved Oliver.

But . . . wouldn't she have given Jennette money to go away once she was engaged? Instead, Penelope had kept her nearby, under her control. Cecilia almost swayed, knowing how much her own need to be in control had gotten her into trouble. One couldn't control life easily; one had to learn the grace to go along with whatever happened—to trust in God, oneself, and those one loves.

But Penelope . . . Penelope must have thought she might need to use the baby to control Oliver someday.

"Where is your child?" Michael suddenly boomed out.

Jennette shot him a startled look, as if she'd only just realized he was in the room. "Who are you? You're not taking Darlene!"

"I am Blackthorne, Lady Cecilia's husband," Michael said shortly, using Cecilia's previous title as if to make Jennette understand. "Is the child with Miss Webster?"

Cecilia gasped in horror. "You don't think—"

Oliver was gaping like a fish. "No. I don't believe it."

Jennette's blotchy face paled to the color of dough. "What's wrong? Why do you all look like that?" She pushed herself away from the housekeeper and ran out into the entrance hall.

In the sudden commotion of people trying to flee the room, Mrs. Webster fell back in a chair. "What is happening?" she screamed.

"Stay with her!" Cecilia told the housekeeper, who nodded, eyes wide with fear.

Cecilia followed Jennette, Oliver, and Michael up the stairs, running as fast as she could to keep up with them. She remembered the house well, and knew they were headed for the small rooms at the back that constituted the servants' quarters.

"Penelope!" Oliver shouted.

Cecilia shuddered at the fear in his voice, even as a child screamed. Oliver must already be inside the room, while Michael held back a sobbing Jennette. Cecilia ducked beneath Michael's arm before he could stop her.

Penelope stood in the far corner of the bedroom, a chubby blond toddler pressed to her chest. The little girl cried pitiful tears and reached toward her mother.

Penelope ignored her. "Oliver, you need to go home. This doesn't concern you."

She spoke in so calm and rational a tone that Cecilia

felt gooseflesh rise along her arms. But her eyes looked wide and wild.

"She is my daughter, Penelope," Oliver said, a tremor in his voice. "And you knew. Why didn't you talk to me about it?"

"There's nothing to talk about. I'll take her away from here. She doesn't need to disturb us. Jennette was a fool to get with child—I won't be anything like her."

"Of course not," Oliver said reasonably. "You'll be my countess."

"I deserve to be a countess." Penelope nodded. "I've proven I can control you, after all. I know everything that's been happening because I'm very good with servants."

Her eyes slanted toward Cecilia, and the momentary glimmer of hate made Cecilia feel nauseous. She'd trusted Penelope—how had she not seen the truth?

"It was so easy to know everything going on at Appertan Hall," Penelope said conversationally. "Cecilia, you thought you were in charge, but it was really me, as it will always be, once I'm Lady Appertan. Oliver was so easy to handle when he wanted to kiss me. I played Francis, the page, the same way, and he did whatever I wanted, told me all your secrets, until I knew so many bad things about him he couldn't stop doing what I wanted. He's very good at digging—did you notice that? But the bust falling, that was all me. So easy to hide behind those potted ferns you keep everywhere.

After you screamed and everyone looked over the balustrade, off I went."

The child cried out again, and Penelope gave her the sweetest smile. "Don't worry, little Darlene. I'll take care of everything. I know just how to do it." She shot Oliver a sudden look of triumph. "I persuaded you to propose, didn't I?"

"You did."

"You didn't love me, but what does love matter in a marriage? A marriage is about power, and *you* were keeping it from me!" She suddenly pointed her finger at Cecilia.

"I didn't know," Cecilia said, spreading her hands wide to show she meant no harm. She felt Michael holding a fistful of her skirt, as if to keep her near him. She had no intention of rushing forward and risking her niece, not when Penelope was so near the open window.

"You were the reason he wouldn't set a date and make me a countess." Penelope's voice rose slowly with each word. "I love him—I'll make him a good wife and a better man. But not with *you* there." Her green eyes narrowed in rage. "You kept interfering, doing everything for him. I was supposed to be his inspiration, his guide. Why didn't you just leave with your *husband*?" She pointed at Michael, and her whole arm vibrated with her passion. "But no, you had to interfere. Hannah tried to interfere, too. She wanted to tell you about the baby, but I couldn't let her."

Cecilia covered her mouth, afraid she'd scream at the images that now flashed through her mind. Had Penelope killed her own sister?

"What did you do?" Oliver cried, advancing toward her.

Michael pushed Jennette into Cecilia's arms, and Cecilia staggered into the wall to keep the crying maid from rushing toward her daughter. Michael caught up with Oliver.

"Stay away!" Penelope screamed, leaning her hip on the window ledge, Darlene dangling outside, shrieking. "I'll come find you, Oliver, don't worry. We'll be together!"

And then she swept her arm across the nearby table, upsetting a dimmed lamp. The oil spilled across the floor, and a fire started with a "whoosh" of sudden sound.

Cecilia and Jennette screamed; Oliver and Michael launched themselves forward, Michael diving for the nearest carpet to use against the flames. Flinging her leg over the sill, Penelope reached for a branch in the tree that the sisters used to play in as children. But the little girl gave a wild kick, which caught Penelope in the stomach, throwing her off balance. She teetered on the ledge, Darlene squalling and squirming. Oliver caught his daughter just as Penelope lost her grip. She started to fall backward out the window, her expression one of shocked disbelief.

"Penelope!" Oliver shouted.

With a wild grab, he caught her skirt, but as a sharp rip sounded, Penelope screamed and fell. Her voice abruptly went silent.

Cecilia only spared the shaking Oliver a brief glance as she searched for a pitcher of water on the nearby washstand. She flung it at the fire just as Michael ripped the curtains from the wall and tossed them out the window. Still clutching Darlene, Oliver flinched, as if he thought Michael had aimed them at Penelope.

Jennette gave a wild cry and raced forward, and Oliver didn't resist as she reached for the little girl and hugged her to her breast.

"Take them out of here!" Michael shouted.

Oliver pushed Jennette into the corridor and followed her.

Though Michael had the fire almost completely eradicated, Cecilia ran across the hall, found another brimming pitcher, and put out the last of the flames. Then she and Michael stared at each other, coughing with the drifting smoke.

Dazed, she tried to move by him toward the window, but he caught her shoulders, even as they heard the first screams from down below.

"Don't look," he said.

She flung herself into his arms and held on. "She— she killed Hannah," she choked out, sobs overcoming her.

"I know," he soothed, running his hands down her head, across her back.

"She tried to kill me—all the time she was listening to my fears, she was—she was plotting to—to—" She couldn't finish her sentence, could only shudder with grief and confusion. At last, she tipped her head back and gazed helplessly into his tender eyes. "What did I do wrong, Michael?"

"Nothing. She was like this long before your father died, before you took over the earldom. You were just one more obstacle in her way. But it's finished now."

"For you and me, maybe, but the Websters— Oliver—" She sagged against him wearily. "I have to go to him. He'll need me."

"Of course he does."

"But not the way you think," she said, forcing her shaky limbs to hold her upright. "I—I was proud of him today, Michael. Even with the terrible things he's done, today I was proud of him."

During the rest of the traumatic day, Cecilia watched her brother begin to take command. When Michael volunteered to ride for the constable, the sobbing Mrs. Webster begged Oliver to let their family shame remain hidden, so she could mourn her children in peace. Oliver looked at Cecilia, and she stared at the broken woman, who would have to live with the knowledge that one daughter had murdered the other.

And Mrs. Webster didn't even know what Penelope had done to Cecilia.

Cecilia leaned against Michael and gave her agreement for the day's events to be shrouded in secrecy. Penelope fell from the window accidentally, and that's all people would need to know. Even Jennette had calmed down enough to agree, tearfully saying she owed the Websters too much to betray them. Mr. Webster returned home at last, and his wife swooned into his arms. There was still Francis, the page, to deal with, but by the time they'd returned to the Hall, he'd taken his things and fled.

That night, Cecilia stood in her bedroom window, looking out across the darkly shrouded grounds in the direction of the Websters' manor. She'd had time to compose herself, to remember that she was at last free of fear. Slowly, she closed the curtains against the night and turned around.

Michael watched her, leaning on his cane. He'd washed the soot from his face and hands, but a few spots still stained his shirt. It was the first moment they'd had to themselves after dealing with Oliver, Jennette, and their little girl. Jennette had been frightened of what Oliver might do, but he'd offered her a manor at the edge of Appertan Hall's property. He would deed it to his daughter and her mother, as long as he could visit Darlene whenever he wanted, see that she was properly schooled, and someday married well, with a sizable dowry. Jennette had gaped at him, then at Cecilia, who'd smiled, before Jennette buried her face in her daughter's hair and nodded her acceptance.

Now Cecilia looked at Michael, and asked tiredly, "What did you think of Oliver today?"

"He handled himself like a man," Michael said, "but I don't want to talk about him anymore. I want to talk about us."

She'd known this was coming but couldn't think what to say except, "You're still hurt, Michael. We have time to decide—"

"No, I don't need more time," he said urgently, advancing toward her until they were face-to-face. "I love you, Cecilia."

She felt both stunned and humbled by those words, but could she believe them? "Michael, I'm not a debt you owe my father."

"You aren't anyone's debt—you're my wife, and I can't bear the thought of losing you." He dropped his cane and took hold of her upper arms. "Nothing is as important to me as you are, certainly not a career. I'll give it up, Cecilia. I'll stay here with you, or wherever you'd like."

Tears burned her eyes, but they weren't of sorrow. "Oh, Michael, that means so much to me, but listen to what I have to say first. I've always felt so safe here, after all the deaths my family suffered abroad. And being in charge only made me more powerful, as if by controlling everything, I could make sure nothing bad happened. But that wasn't true, was it?" she asked, giving him a sad smile.

He drew her against him. "Cecilia—"

"Let me finish, please. By controlling everything, I held at bay my fears. I think . . . I think I slowly grew frightened of the wide world beyond this estate. I barely went to London. Deep inside, I harbored bitterness toward my father that I kept denying to myself. I—I couldn't forget that the army seemed more important to him than his own family, and I swore to myself that I wouldn't let that happen to me. If I could control everything, I would be safe. I wouldn't marry, wouldn't have children, wouldn't risk losing anyone else. But what kind of life is that? Maybe Oliver and I each panicked in our own way. But I don't need his life anymore. I want my own. I want our children—I want you. *I love you.*"

Smiling, he kissed her cheeks and her forehead. "To hear those words on your lips is the greatest treasure I could ever have," he murmured huskily.

"I don't need Appertan Hall and all the estates, and they don't need me. You may not believe me, but you'll see—I'll give up all my money to the estate."

"I don't need you to be powerless, Cecilia," he told her. "You are an intelligent woman who needs a challenge. That money is yours to invest or do whatever with. You deserve to have the kind of life you've always wanted because you've let yourself suffer under too much guilt. And I haven't felt it enough, never saw the scope of how many lives my actions affected. My insistence on living as an enlisted man has been my pride talking. I've let that rule my life for too long. I'll purchase a commission with some of the dowry, as you wanted me to. You deserve to be an officer's wife."

"Then I'll see what life is like as an officer's wife in India."

His expression grew hopeful as he searched her face, and her smile wobbled with happiness.

"No, Cecilia, I won't ask that of you."

"You aren't asking, I'm telling you. Didn't you hear what I said? I won't be afraid of the world anymore, and as you reminded me, I'm not my mother. I'll come with you to India, and I hope we'll spend several months of each year here in England. The best of both worlds. We can make that happen, Michael."

He kissed her then, drawing her up onto her toes until she had to hold him hard to keep herself from falling. They kissed and laughed and tried to talk over each other.

"I'll need your help, you know," he insisted. "Allen's law practice is growing, and I'll have to take over more of the Blackthorne estate. Who better to run it and see it thrive than you with all your experience?"

"What a challenge!" she cried, flinging her arms wide, knowing he'd catch her. When he drew her back against him, her smile faded, and she cupped his face in her hands. "You make me feel beloved, Michael. You married me when I needed your help, asking nothing in return. I'm asking for your help again. I want to start fresh, to see India through *your* eyes. I want to make sure our children are never afraid of anything."

They slowly kissed, knowing the whole world awaited them.

2112

*G*ive in to your Impulses!

These unforgettable stories only take a second to buy and give you hours of reading pleasure!

Go to *www.AvonImpulse.com* and see what we have to offer.

Available wherever e-books are sold.

AVONIMPULSE